CLASSIC ANIMAL STORIES

CLASSIC ANIMAL STORIES

Compiled by Tig Thomas

Sandy Creek
NEW YORK

An Imprint of Sterling Publishing
387 Park Avenue South
New York, NY 10016

SANDY CREEK and the distinctive Sandy Creek logo are registered
trademarks of Barnes & Noble, Inc.

© 2008 by Miles Kelly Publishing Ltd.

This 2013 edition published by Sandy Creek.

ISBN 978-1-4351-3624-3

Publishing Director Belinda Gallagher
Creative Director Jo Cowan
Senior Editor Rosie McGuire
Senior Designer Simon Lee
Cover Designer Joe Jones
Design Assistant Carmen Johnson
Production Manager Elizabeth Brunwin
Reprographics Stephan Davis
Assets Lorraine King

Made with paper from a sustainable forest

Manufactured in China
Lot #:
2 4 6 8 10 9 7 5 3

12/13

Contents
Friends and Companions

Contents
Myths and Wonders

Contents
Tricks, Traps, and Mischief

Contents
The Hunters

Contents
Tall Tales

Friends and Companions

The Cat that Walked by Himself

From *Just So Stories*

By Rudyard Kipling

HEAR and attend and listen; for this befell and behappened and became and was, O my Best Beloved, when the Tame animals were wild. The Dog was wild, and the Horse was wild, and the Cow was wild, and the Sheep was wild, and the Pig was wild—as wild as wild could be— and they walked in the Wet Wild Woods by their wild lones. But the wildest of all the wild animals was the Cat. He walked by himself, and all places were alike to him.

Of course the Man was wild too. He was dreadfully wild.

He didn't even begin to be tame till he met the Woman, and she told him that she did not like living in his wild ways. She picked out a nice dry Cave, instead of a heap of wet leaves, to lie down in; and she strewed clean sand on the floor; and she lit a nice fire of wood at the back of the Cave; and she hung a dried wild-horse skin, tail-down, across the opening of the Cave; and she said, "Wipe you feet, dear, when you come in, and now we'll keep house."

That night, Best Beloved, they ate wild sheep roasted on the hot stones, and flavoured with wild garlic and wild pepper; and wild duck stuffed with wild rice and wild fenugreek and wild coriander; and marrow-bones of wild oxen; and wild cherries, and wild grenadillas. Then the Man went to sleep in front of the fire ever so happy; but the Woman sat up, combing her hair. She took the bone of the shoulder of mutton—the big, fat, blade-bone—and she looked at the wonderful marks on it, and she threw more wood on the fire, and she made a Magic. She made the First Singing Magic in the world.

Out in the Wet Wild Woods all the wild animals gathered together where they could see the light of the fire a long way off, and they wondered what it meant.

Then Wild Horse stamped with his wild foot and said, "O my Friends and O my Enemies, why have the Man and the Woman made that great light in that great Cave, and what harm will it do us?"

Wild Dog lifted up his wild nose and smelled the smell of roast mutton, and said, "I will go up and see and look, and say; for I think it is good. Cat, come with me."

"Nenni!" said the Cat. "I am the Cat who walks by himself, and all places are alike to me. I will not come."

"Then we can never be friends again," said Wild Dog, and he trotted off to the Cave. But when he had gone a little way the Cat said to himself, "All places are alike to me. Why should I not go too and see and look and come away at my own liking?"

So he slipped after Wild Dog softly, very softly, and hid himself where he could hear everything. When Wild Dog reached the mouth of the Cave he lifted up the dried horse-skin with his nose and sniffed the beautiful smell of the roast mutton, and the Woman, looking at the blade-bone, heard him, and laughed, and said, "Here comes the first. Wild Thing out of the Wild Woods, what do you want?"

Wild Dog said, "O my Enemy and Wife of my Enemy, what is this that smells so good in the Wild Woods?"

Then the Woman picked up a roasted mutton-bone and threw it to Wild Dog, and said, "Wild Thing out of the Wild Woods, taste and try."

Wild Dog gnawed the bone, and it was more delicious than anything he had ever tasted, and he said, "O my Enemy and Wife of my Enemy, give me another."

The Woman said, "Wild Thing out of the Wild Woods, help my Man to hunt through the day and guard this Cave at night, and I will give you as many roast bones as you need."

"Ah!" said the Cat, listening. "This is a very wise Woman, but she is not so wise as I am."

Wild Dog crawled into the Cave and laid his head on the Woman's lap, and said, "O my Friend and Wife of my Friend, I will help Your Man to hunt through the day, and at night I will guard your Cave."

"Ah!" said the Cat, listening. "That is a very foolish Dog." And he went back through the Wet Wild Woods waving his wild tail, and walking by his wild lone. But he never told anybody.

When the Man waked up he said, "What is Wild Dog doing here?" And the Woman said, "His name is not Wild Dog any more, but the First Friend, because he will be our friend for always and always and always. Take him with you when you go hunting."

Next night the Woman cut great green armfuls of fresh grass from the water-meadows, and dried it before the fire, so that it smelt like new-mown hay, and she sat at the mouth of the Cave and plaited a halter out of horse-hide, and she looked at the shoulder of mutton-bone—at the big, broad, blade-bone—and she made a Magic. She made the Second Singing Magic in the world.

Out in the Wild Woods all the wild animals wondered what had happened to Wild Dog, and at last Wild Horse stamped with his foot and said, "I will go and see and say why Wild Dog has not returned. Cat, come with me."

"Nenni!" said the Cat. "I am the Cat who walks by himself, and all places are alike to me. I will not come."

But all the same he followed Wild Horse softly, very softly, and hid himself where he could hear everything.

When the Woman heard Wild Horse tripping and

stumbling on his long mane, she laughed and said, "Here comes the second. Wild Thing out of the Wild Woods, what do you want?"

Wild Horse said, "O my Enemy and Wife of my Enemy, where is Wild Dog?"

The Woman laughed, and picked up the blade-bone and looked at it, and said, "Wild Thing out of the Wild Woods, you did not come here for Wild Dog, but for the sake of this good grass."

And Wild Horse, tripping and stumbling on his long mane, said, "That is true; give it me to eat."

The Woman said, "Wild Thing out of the Wild Woods, bend your wild head and wear what I give you, and you shall eat the wonderful grass three times a day."

"Ah," said the Cat, listening, "this is a clever Woman, but she is not so clever as I am."

Wild Horse bent his wild head, and the Woman slipped the plaited hide halter over it, and Wild Horse breathed on the Woman's feet and said,

"O my Mistress, and Wife of my Master, I will be your servant for the sake of the wonderful grass."

"Ah," said the Cat, listening, "that is a very foolish Horse."

And he went back through the Wet Wild Woods, waving his wild tail and walking by his wild lone. But he never told anybody.

When the Man and the Dog came back from hunting, the Man said, "What is Wild Horse doing here?" And the Woman said, "His name is not Wild Horse any more, but the First Servant, because he will carry us from place to place for always and always and always. Ride on his back when you go hunting."

Next day, holding her wild head high that her wild horns should not catch in the wild trees, Wild Cow came up to the Cave, and the Cat followed, and hid himself just the same as before; and everything happened just the same as before; and the Cat said the same things as before, and when Wild Cow had promised to give her milk to the Woman every day in exchange for the wonderful grass, the Cat went back through the Wet Wild Woods waving his wild tail and walking by his wild lone, just the same as before. But he never told anybody. And when the Man and the Horse and the Dog came home from hunting and asked the same questions same as before, the Woman said,

"Her name is not Wild Cow any more, but the Giver of Good Food. She will give us the warm white milk for always and always and always, and I will take care of her while you and the First Friend and the First Servant go hunting."

Next day the Cat waited to see if any other Wild thing would go up to the Cave, but no one moved in the Wet Wild Woods, so the Cat walked there by himself; and he saw the Woman milking the Cow, and he saw the light of the fire in the Cave, and he smelt the smell of the warm white milk. Cat said, "O my Enemy and Wife of my Enemy, where did Wild Cow go?"

The Woman laughed and said, "Wild Thing out of the Wild Woods, go back to the Woods again, for I have braided up my hair, and I have put away the magic blade-bone, and we have no more need of either friends or servants in our Cave."

Cat said, "I am not a friend, and I am not a servant. I am the Cat who walks by himself, and I wish to come into your cave."

Woman said, "Then why did you not come with First Friend on the first night?"

Cat grew very angry and said, "Has Wild Dog told tales of me?"

Then the Woman laughed and said, "You are the Cat who walks by himself, and all places are alike to you. You are neither a friend nor a servant. You have said it yourself. Go away and walk by yourself in all places alike."

Then Cat pretended to be sorry and said, "Must I never come into the Cave? Must I never sit by the warm fire? Must I never drink the warm white milk? You are very wise and very beautiful. You should not be cruel even to a Cat."

Woman said, "I knew I was wise, but I did not know I was beautiful. So I will make a bargain with you. If ever I say one word in your praise you may come into the Cave."

"And if you say two words in my praise?" said the Cat.

"I never shall," said the Woman, "but if I say two words in your praise, you may sit by the fire in the Cave."

"And if you say three words?" said the Cat.

"I never shall," said the Woman, "but if I say three words in your praise, you may drink the warm white milk three times a day for always and always and always."

Then the Cat arched his back and said, "Now let the Curtain at the mouth of the Cave, and the Fire at the back of the Cave, and the Milk-pots that stand beside the Fire, remember what my Enemy and the Wife of my Enemy has said."

And he went away through the Wet Wild Woods waving his wild tail and walking by his wild lone.

That night when the Man and the Horse and the Dog came home from hunting, the Woman did not tell them of the bargain that she had made with the Cat, because she was afraid that they might not like it.

Cat went far and far away and hid himself in the Wet Wild Woods by his wild lone for a long time till the Woman forgot all about him. Only the Bat—the little upside-down Bat—that hung inside the Cave, knew where Cat hid; and every evening Bat would fly to Cat with news of what was happening.

One evening Bat said, "There is a Baby in the Cave. He is new and pink and fat and small, and the Woman is very fond of him."

"Ah," said the Cat, listening, "but what is the Baby fond of?"

"He is fond of things that are soft and tickle," said the Bat. "He is fond of warm things to hold in his arms when he goes to sleep. He is fond of being played with. He is fond of all those things."

"Ah," said the Cat, listening, "then my time has come."

Next night Cat walked through the Wet Wild Woods

and hid very near the Cave till morning-time, and Man and Dog and Horse went hunting. The Woman was busy cooking that morning, and the Baby cried and interrupted. So she carried him outside the Cave and gave him a handful of pebbles to play with. But still the Baby cried.

Then the Cat put out his paddy paw and patted the Baby on the cheek, and it cooed; and the Cat rubbed against its fat knees and tickled it under its fat chin with his tail. And the Baby laughed; and the Woman heard him and smiled.

Then the Bat—the little upside-down bat—that hung in the mouth of the Cave said, "O my Hostess and Wife of my Host and Mother of my Host's Son, a Wild Thing from the Wild Woods is most beautifully playing with your Baby."

"A blessing on that Wild Thing whoever he may be," said the Woman, straightening her back, "for I was a busy woman this morning and he has done me a service."

That very minute and second, Best Beloved, the dried horse-skin Curtain that was stretched tail-down at the mouth of the Cave fell down—*whoosh!*—because it remembered the bargain she had made with the Cat, and when the Woman went to pick it up—lo and behold!—the Cat was sitting quite comfy inside the Cave.

"O my Enemy and Wife of my Enemy and Mother of my Enemy," said the Cat, "it is I: for you have spoken a word in my praise, and now I can sit within the Cave for always and always and always. But still I am the Cat who walks by himself, and all places are alike to me."

The Woman was very angry, and shut her lips tight and took up her spinning-wheel and began to spin. But the Baby cried because the Cat had gone away, and the Woman could not hush it, for it struggled and kicked and grew black in the face.

"O my Enemy and Wife of my Enemy and Mother of my Enemy," said the Cat, "take a strand of the wire that you are spinning and tie it to your spinning-whorl and drag it along the floor, and I will show you a magic that shall make your Baby laugh as loudly as he is now crying."

"I will do so," said the Woman, "because I am at my wits' end; but I will not thank you for it."

She tied the thread to the little clay spindle whorl and drew it across the floor, and the Cat ran after it and patted it with his paws and rolled head over heels, and tossed it backward over his shoulder and chased it between his hind-legs and pretended to lose it, and pounced down upon it again, till the Baby laughed as loudly as it had been crying, and scrambled after the Cat and frolicked all over the Cave till it grew tired and settled down to sleep with the Cat in its arms.

"Now," said the Cat, "I will sing the Baby a song that shall keep him asleep for an hour."

And he began to purr, loud and low, low and loud, till the Baby fell fast asleep. The Woman smiled as she looked down upon the two of them and said, "That was wonderfully done. No question but you are very clever, O Cat."

That very minute and second, Best Beloved, the smoke of the fire at the back of the Cave came down in clouds from the roof—*puff!*—because it remembered the bargain she had made with the Cat, and when it had cleared away—lo and behold!—the Cat was sitting quite comfy close to the fire.

"O my Enemy and Wife of my Enemy and Mother of My Enemy," said the Cat, "it is I, for you have spoken a second word in my praise, and now I can sit by the warm fire at the back of the Cave for always and always and always. But still I am the Cat who walks by himself, and all places are alike to me."

Then the Woman was very very angry, and let down her hair and put more wood on the fire and brought out the broad blade-bone of the shoulder of mutton and began to make a Magic that should prevent her from saying a third word in praise of the Cat. It was not a Singing Magic, Best Beloved, it was a Still Magic; and by and by the Cave grew so still that a little wee-wee mouse crept out of a corner and ran across the floor.

"O my Enemy and Wife of my Enemy and Mother of my Enemy," said the Cat, "is that little mouse part of your magic?"

"Ouh! Chee! No indeed!" said the Woman, and she dropped the blade-bone and jumped upon the footstool in front of the fire and braided up her hair very quick for fear that the mouse should run up it.

"Ah," said the Cat, watching, "then the mouse will do me no harm if I eat it?"

"No," said the Woman, braiding up her hair, "eat it

quickly and I will ever be grateful to you."

Cat made one jump and caught the little mouse, and the Woman said, "A hundred thanks. Even the First Friend is not quick enough to catch little mice as you have done. You must be very wise."

That very moment and second, O Best Beloved, the Milk-pot that stood by the fire cracked in two pieces—*ffft*—because it remembered the bargain she had made with the Cat, and when the Woman jumped down from the footstool—lo and behold!—the Cat was lapping up the warm white milk that lay in one of the broken pieces.

"O my Enemy and Wife of my Enemy and Mother of my Enemy," said the Cat, "it is I; for you have spoken three words in my praise, and now I can drink the warm white milk three times a day for always and always and always. But still I am the Cat who walks by himself, and all places are alike to me."

Then the Woman laughed and set the Cat a bowl of the warm white milk and said, "O Cat, you are as clever as a man, but remember that your bargain was not made with the Man or the Dog, and I do not know what they will do when they come home."

"What is that to me?" said the Cat. "If I have my place in the Cave by the fire and my warm white milk three times a day I do not care what the Man or the Dog can do."

That evening when the Man and the Dog came into the Cave, the Woman told them all the story of the bargain while the Cat sat by the fire and smiled. Then the Man said, "Yes, but he has not made a bargain with me or with all proper Men after me."

Then he took off his two leather boots and he took up his little stone axe (that makes three) and he fetched a piece of wood and a hatchet (that is five altogether), and he set them out in a row and he said, "Now we will make our bargain. If you do not catch mice when you are in the Cave for always and always and always, I will throw these five things at you whenever I see you, and so shall all proper Men do after me."

"Ah," said the Woman, listening, "this is a very clever Cat, but he is not so clever as my Man."

The Cat counted the five things (and they looked very knobby) and he said, "I will catch mice when I am in the Cave for always and always and always; but still I am the Cat who walks by himself, and all places are alike to me."

"Not when I am near," said the Man. "If you had not said that last I would have put all these things away for always and always and always; but I am now going to throw my two boots and my little stone axe (that makes three) at you whenever I meet you. And so shall all proper Men do after me!"

Then the Dog said, "Wait a minute. He has not made a bargain with me or with all proper Dogs after me." And he showed his teeth and said, "If you are not kind to the Baby while I am in the Cave for always and always and always, I will hunt you till I catch you, and when I catch you I will bite you. And so shall all proper Dogs do after me."

"Ah," said the Woman, listening, "this is a very clever Cat, but he is not so clever as the Dog."

Cat counted the Dog's teeth (and they looked very pointed) and he said, "I will be kind to the Baby while I am in the Cave, as long as he does not pull my tail too hard, for always and always and always. But still I am the Cat that walks by himself, and all places are alike to me."

"Not when I am near," said the Dog. "If you had not said that last I would have shut my mouth for always and always and always; but now I am going to hunt you up a tree whenever I meet you. And so shall all proper Dogs do after me."

Then the Man threw his two boots and his little stone axe (that makes three) at the Cat, and the Cat ran out of the Cave and the Dog chased him up a tree; and from that day to this, Best Beloved, three proper Men out of five will always throw things at a Cat whenever they meet him, and all proper Dogs will chase him up a tree. But the Cat keeps his side of the bargain too. He will kill mice and he will be

kind to Babies
when he is in
the house, just
as long as they
do not pull his
tail too hard.
But when he has
done that, and
between times, and
when the moon gets up
and night comes, he is the Cat
that walks by himself, and all places
are alike to him. Then he goes out to
the Wet Wild Woods or up the Wet
Wild Trees or on the Wet Wild
Roofs, waving his wild tail and
walking by his wild lone.

*One day, bored by his spring cleaning, the Mole
clambered out of his hole and took a walk instead.
He met the Water Rat, who introduced him to the
pleasures of the outdoor, riverside life. The Mole
moved in with Ratty and has never gone back
to his old house.*

Dulce Domum

From *The Wind in the Willows*
By Kenneth Grahame

THE sheep ran huddling together against the hurdles, blowing out thin nostrils and stamping with delicate forefeet, their heads thrown back, and a light steam rising from the crowded sheep-pen into the frosty air, as the two animals hastened by in high spirits, with much chatter and laughter.

They were returning across country after a long day's outing with Otter, hunting and exploring on the wide uplands where certain streams tributary to their own River had their first small beginnings; and the shades of the short winter day were closing in on them, and they had still some distance to go. Plodding at random across the plow, they had heard the sheep and had made for them; and now, leading from the sheep-pen, they found a beaten track that made walking a lighter business, and responded, moreover, to that small inquiring something which all animals carry inside them, saying unmistakably, "Yes, quite right; *this* leads home!"

"It looks as if we were coming to a village," said the Mole somewhat dubiously, slackening his pace, as the track, that had in time become a path and then had developed into a lane, now handed them over to the charge of a well-metaled road.

The animals did not hold with villages, and their own highways, thickly frequented as they were, took an independent course, regardless of church, post office, or tavern.

"Oh, never mind!" said the Rat. "At this season of the year they're all safe indoors by this time, sitting around the fire; men, women, and children, dogs and cats and all. We shall slip through alright, without any bother or unpleasantness, and we can have a look at them through their windows if you like, and see what they're doing."

The rapid nightfall of mid-December had quite beset the little village as they approached it on soft feet over a first thin fall of powdery snow. Little was visible but squares of a dusky orange-red on either side of the street, where the firelight or lamplight of each cottage overflowed through the casements into the dark world without.

Most of the low latticed windows were innocent of blinds, and to the lookers-in from outside, the inmates, gathered around the tea table, absorbed in handiwork, or talking with laughter and gesture, had each that happy grace which is the last thing the skilled actor shall capture—the natural grace which goes with perfect unconsciousness of observation.

Moving at will from one theater to another, the two spectators, so far from home themselves, had something of wistfulness in their eyes as they watched a cat being stroked, a sleepy child picked up and huddled off to bed, or a tired man stretch and knock out his pipe on the end of a smouldering log. But it was from one little window, with its blind drawn down, a mere blank transparency on the night, that the sense of home and the little curtained world within walls—the larger stressful world of outside Nature shut out and forgotten—most pulsated. Close against the white blind hung a birdcage, clearly silhouetted, every wire, perch, and appurtenance distinct and recognizable, even to yesterday's dull-edged lump of sugar. On the middle perch the fluffy occupant, head tucked well into feathers, seemed so near to them as to be easily stroked, had they tried; even the delicate tips of his plumped-out plumage penciled

plainly on the illuminated screen.

As they looked, the sleepy little fellow stirred uneasily, woke, shook himself, and raised his head. They could see the gape of his tiny beak as he yawned in a bored sort of way, looked around, and then settled his head into his back again, while the ruffled feathers gradually subsided into perfect stillness.

Then a gust of bitter wind took them in the back of the neck, a small sting of frozen sleet on the skin woke them as from a dream, and they knew their toes to be cold and their legs tired, and their own home distant a weary way. Once beyond the village, where the cottages ceased abruptly, on either side of the road they could smell through the darkness the friendly fields again; and they braced themselves for the last long stretch, the home stretch, the stretch that we know is bound to end, some time, in the rattle of the door latch, the sudden firelight, and the sight of familiar things greeting us as long-absent travelers from far over sea.

They plodded along steadily and silently, each of them thinking his own thoughts. The Mole's ran a good deal on supper, as it was pitch dark, and it was all a strange country for him as far as he knew, and he was following obediently in the wake of the Rat, leaving the guidance entirely to him.

As for the Rat, he was walking a little way ahead, as his habit was, his shoulders humped, his eyes fixed on the straight gray road in front of him; so he did not notice poor Mole when suddenly the summons reached him, and took him like an electric shock. We others, who have long lost the more subtle of the physical senses, have not even proper terms to express an animal's inter-communications with his surroundings, living, or otherwise, and have only the word "smell," for instance, to include the whole range of delicate thrills which murmur in the nose of the animal night and day, summoning, warning, inciting, repelling.

It was one of these mysterious fairycalls from out the void that suddenly reached Mole in the darkness, making him tingle through and through with its very familiar appeal, even while yet he could not clearly remember what it was. He stopped dead in his tracks, his nose searching hither and thither in its efforts to recapture the fine filament, the telegraphic current, that had so strongly moved him.

A moment, and he had caught it again; and with it this time came recollection in fullest flood—*home!* That was what they meant, those caressing appeals, those soft touches wafted through the air, those invisible little hands pulling and tugging, all one way! Why, it must be quite close by him at that moment, his old home that he had hurriedly forsaken and never sought again, that day when he first found the river! And now it was sending out its scouts and its messengers to capture him and bring him in.

Since his escape on that bright morning he had hardly given it a thought, so absorbed had he been in his new life, in all its pleasures, its surprises, its fresh and captivating experiences. Now, with a rush of old memories, how clearly it stood up before him, in the darkness! Shabby indeed, and small and poorly furnished, and yet his, the home he had made for himself, the home he had been so happy to get back to after his day's work. And the home had been happy with him, too, evidently, and was missing him, and wanted him back, and was telling him so, through his nose, sorrowfully, reproachfully, but with no bitterness or anger; only with plaintive reminder that it was there, and wanted him. The call was clear, the summons was plain. He must obey it instantly, and go.

"Ratty!" he called, full of joyful excitement, "Hold on! Come back! I want you, quick!"

"Oh, *come* along, Mole, do!" replied the Rat cheerfully, still plodding along.

"*Please* stop, Ratty!" pleaded the poor Mole, in anguish of heart. "You don't understand! It's my home, my old home! I've just come across the smell of it, and it's close by here, really quite close. And I *must* go to it, I must, I must! Oh, come back, Ratty! Please, please come back!"

The Rat was by this time very far ahead, too far to hear clearly what the Mole was calling, too far to catch the sharp note of painful appeal in his voice. And he was much taken up with the weather, for he too could smell something—something suspiciously like approaching snow.

"Mole, we mustn't stop now, really!" he called back. "We'll come for it tomorrow, whatever it is you've found. But I daren't stop now—it's late, and the snow's coming on again, and I'm not sure of the way! And I want your nose, Mole, so come on quick, there's a good fellow!" And the Rat pressed forward on his way without waiting for an answer.

Poor Mole stood alone in the road, his heart torn asunder, and a big sob gathering, gathering, somewhere low down inside him, to leap up to the surface presently, he knew, in passionate escape. But even under such a test as this his loyalty to his friend stood firm. Never for a moment did he dream of abandoning him. Meanwhile, the wafts from his old home pleaded, whispered, conjured, and finally claimed him imperiously. He dared not tarry longer within their magic circle. With a wrench that tore his very heartstrings he set his face down the road and followed submissively in the track of the Rat, while faint, thin little smells, still dogging his retreating nose, reproached him for his new friendship and his callous forgetfulness.

With an effort he caught up to the unsuspecting Rat, who began chattering cheerfully about what they would do when they got back, and how jolly a fire of logs in the parlor would be, and what a supper he meant to eat; never noticing his companion's silence and distressful state of mind. At last, however, when they had gone some considerable way further, and were passing some tree-stumps at the edge of a copse that bordered the road, he stopped and said kindly, "Look here, Mole old chap, you seem dead tired. No talk left in you, and your feet dragging like lead. We'll sit down here for a minute and rest. The snow has held off so far, and the best part of our journey is over."

The Mole subsided forlornly on a tree-stump and tried to control himself, for he felt it surely coming. The sob he had fought with so long refused to be beaten. Up and up, it forced its way to the air, and then another, and another, and others thick and fast; till poor Mole at last gave up the struggle, and cried freely and helplessly and openly, now that he knew it was all over and he had lost what he could hardly be said to have found.

The Rat, astonished and dismayed at the violence of Mole's paroxysm of grief, did not dare to speak for a while. At last he said, very quietly and sympathetically, "What is it, old fellow? Whatever can be the matter? Tell us your trouble, and let me see what I can do."

Poor Mole found it difficult to get any words out between the upheavals of his chest that followed one upon another so quickly and held back speech and choked it as it came.

"I know it's a—shabby, dingy little place," he sobbed forth at last, brokenly: "Not like—your cozy quarters—or Toad's beautiful hall—or Badger's great house—but it was my own little home—and I was fond of it— and I went away and forgot all about it—and then I smelt it suddenly—on the road, when I called and you wouldn't listen, Rat—and everything came back to me with a rush— and I *wanted* it! Oh dear, Oh dear! And when you *wouldn't* turn back, Ratty—and I had to leave it, though I was smelling it all the time—I thought my heart would break. We might have just gone and had one look at it, Ratty— only one look—it was close by—but you wouldn't turn

back, Ratty, you wouldn't turn back! Oh dear, Oh dear!"

Recollection brought fresh waves of sorrow, and sobs again took full charge of him, preventing further speech. The Rat stared straight in front of him, saying nothing, only patting Mole gently on the shoulder.

After a time he muttered gloomily,

"I see it all now! What a *pig* I have been! A pig—that's me! Just a pig—a plain pig!"

He waited till Mole's sobs became gradually less stormy and more rhythmical; he waited till at last sniffs were frequent and sobs only intermittent. Then he rose from his seat, and, remarking carelessly, "Well, now we'd really better be getting on, old chap," set off up the road again, over the toilsome way they had come.

"Wherever are you, *hic*, going to, *hic*, Ratty?' cried the tearful Mole, looking up in alarm.

"We're going to find that home of yours, old fellow," replied the Rat pleasantly; "so you had better come along, for it will take some finding, and we shall want your nose."

"Oh, come back, Ratty, do!' cried the Mole, getting up and hurrying after him. "It's no good, I tell you! It's too late, and too dark, and the place is too far off, and the snow's coming! And—and I never meant to let you know I was feeling that way about it—it was all an accident and a mistake! And think of River Bank, and your supper!"

"Hang River Bank, and supper too!" said the Rat heartily. "I tell you, I'm going to find this place now, if I stay out all night. So cheer up, old chap, and take my arm, and we'll very soon be back there again."

Still snuffling, pleading, and reluctant, Mole suffered himself to be dragged back along the road by his imperious companion, who by a flow of cheerful talk and anecdote endeavored to beguile his spirits back and make the weary way seem shorter. When at last it seemed to the Rat that they must be nearing that part of the road where the Mole had been, "Hold up," he said, "Now, no more talking. Business! Use your nose, and give your mind to it."

They moved on in silence for some little way, when suddenly the Rat was conscious, through his arm that was linked in Mole's, of a faint sort of electric thrill that was passing down that animal's body. Instantly he disengaged himself, fell back a pace, and waited, all attention. The signals were coming through! Mole stood a moment rigid, while his uplifted nose, quivering slightly, felt the air. Then a short, quick run forward—a fault—a check—a try back; and then a slow, steady, confident advance.

The Rat, much excited, kept close to his heels as the Mole, with something of the air of a sleep-walker, crossed a dry ditch, scrambled through a hedge, and nosed his way over a field open and trackless and bare in the faint starlight. Suddenly, without giving warning, he dived; but the Rat was on the alert, and promptly followed him down the tunnel to which his unerring nose had faithfully led him. It was close and airless, and the earthy smell was strong, and it seemed a long time to Rat before the passage ended and he could stand erect and stretch and shake himself.

The Mole struck a match, and by its light the Rat saw that they were standing in an open space, neatly swept and sanded underfoot, and directly facing them was Mole's little front door, with "Mole End" painted, in Gothic lettering, over the bell-pull at the side.

Mole reached down a lantern from a nail on the wall and lit it, and the Rat, looking around him, saw that they were in a sort of forecourt. A garden seat stood on one side of the door, and on the other a roller; for the Mole, who was a tidy animal when at home, could not stand having his ground kicked up by other animals into little runs that ended in earth-heaps. On the walls hung wire baskets with ferns in them, alternating with brackets carrying plaster statuary— Garibaldi, and the infant Samuel, and Queen Victoria, and other heroes of modern Italy.

Down on one side of the forecourt ran a skittle alley, with benches along it and little wooden tables marked with rings that hinted at beer mugs. In the middle was a small round pond containing goldfish and surrounded by a cockleshell border. Out of the center of the pond rose a fanciful erection clothed in more cockleshells and topped by a large silvered glass ball that reflected everything all wrong and had a very pleasing effect.

Mole's face beamed at the sight of all these objects so dear to him, and he hurried Rat through the door, lit a lamp in the hall, and took one glance around his old home. He saw the dust lying thick on everything, saw the cheerless, deserted look of the long-neglected house, and its narrow, meager dimensions, its worn and shabby contents—and collapsed again on a hall chair, his nose to his paws.

"Oh Ratty!" he cried dismally, "why ever did I do it? Why did I bring you to this poor, cold little place, on a night like this, when you might have been at River Bank by this time, toasting your toes before a blazing fire, with all your own nice things about you!"

The Rat paid no heed to his doleful self-reproaches. He was running here and there, opening doors, inspecting rooms and cupboards, and lighting lamps and candles and sticking them up everywhere.

"What a capital little house this is!" he called out cheerily. "So compact! So well planned! Everything here and everything in its place! We'll make a jolly night of it. The first thing we want is a good fire; I'll see to that—I always know where to find things. So this is the parlor? Splendid! Your own idea, those little sleeping-bunks in the wall? Capital! Now, I'll fetch the wood and the coals, and you get a duster, Mole—you'll find one in the drawer of the kitchen table—and try and smarten things up a bit. Bustle about, old chap!"

Encouraged by his inspiriting companion, the Mole roused himself and dusted and polished with energy and heartiness, while the Rat, running to and fro with armfuls of fuel, soon had a cheerful blaze roaring up the chimney. He hailed the Mole to come and warm himself; but Mole promptly had another fit of the blues, dropping down on a couch in dark despair and burying his face in his duster.

"Rat," he moaned, "How about your supper, you poor, cold, hungry, weary animal? I've nothing to give you—nothing—not a crumb!"

"What a fellow you are for giving in!' said the Rat reproachfully. "Why, only just now I saw a sardine-opener on the kitchen dresser, quite distinctly; and everybody knows that means there are sardines about somewhere in the neighborhood. Rouse yourself! Pull yourself together, and come with me and forage."

They went and foraged accordingly, hunting through every cupboard and turning out every drawer. The result was not so very depressing after all, though of course it might have been better; a tin of sardines, a box of captain's biscuits—nearly full—and a German sausage encased in silver paper.

"There's a banquet for you!" observed the Rat, as he arranged the table. "I know some animals who would give their ears to be sitting down to supper with us tonight!"

"No bread!" groaned the Mole dolorously; "no butter, no—"

"No pate de foie gras, no champagne!" continued the

Rat, grinning. "And that reminds me—what's that little door at the end of the passage? Your basement, of course! Every luxury in this house! Just you wait a minute."

He made for the basement door, and presently reappeared, somewhat dusty, with a bottle of beer in each paw and another under each arm. "Self-indulgent beggar you seem to be, Mole," he observed. "Deny yourself nothing. This is really the jolliest little place I ever was in. Now, wherever did you pick up those prints? Make the place look so homelike, they do. No wonder you're so fond of it, Mole. Tell us all about it, and how you came to make it what it is."

Then, while the Rat busied himself fetching plates, and knives and forks, and mustard which he mixed in an eggcup, the Mole, his bosom still heaving with the stress of his recent emotion, related—somewhat shyly at first, but with more freedom as he warmed to his subject—how this was planned, and how that was thought out, and how this was got through a windfall from an aunt, and that was a wonderful find and a bargain, and this other thing was bought out of laborious savings and a certain amount of "going without."

His spirits finally quite restored, he must needs go and caress his possessions, and take a lamp and show off their points to his visitor and expatiate on them, quite forgetful of the supper they both so much needed; Rat, who was desperately hungry but strove to conceal it, nodding seriously, examining with a puckered brow, and saying, "wonderful," and "most remarkable," at intervals, when the chance for an observation was given him.

At last the Rat succeeded in decoying him to the table, and had just got seriously to work with the sardine-opener when sounds were heard from the forecourt without—sounds like the scuffling of small feet in the gravel and a confused murmur of tiny voices, while broken sentences reached them: "Now, all in a line—hold the lantern up a bit, Tommy—clear your throats first—no coughing after I say 'one, two, three'. Where's young Bill? Here, come on, do, we're all a-waiting—"

"What's up?" inquired the Rat, pausing in his labors.

"I think it must be the field mice," replied the Mole, with a touch of pride in his manner. "They go around carol-singing regularly at this time of the year. They're quite an institution in these parts. And they never pass me over—they come to Mole End last of all; and I used to give them hot drinks, and supper too sometimes, when I could afford it. It will be like old times to hear them again."

"Let's have a look at them!" cried the Rat, jumping up and running to the door.

It was a pretty sight, and a seasonable one, that met their eyes when they flung the door open. In the forecourt, lit by the dim rays of a horn lantern, some eight or ten little field mice stood in a semicircle, red worsted comforters round their throats, their forepaws thrust deep into their pockets, their feet jigging for warmth. With bright beady eyes they glanced shyly at each other, sniggering a little, sniffing, and applying coat sleeves a good deal. As the door opened, one of the elder ones that carried the lantern was just saying, "Now then, one, two, three!" and forthwith their shrill little voices rose on the air, singing one of the old-time carols that their forefathers composed in fields that were fallow and held by frost, or when snow-bound in chimney corners, and handed down to be sung in the miry street to lamp-lit windows at Yule-time.

Villagers all, this frosty tide,
Let your doors swing open wide,
Though wind may follow, and snow beside,
Yet draw us in by your fire to bide;
Joy shall be yours in the morning!

Here we stand in the cold and the sleet,
Blowing fingers and stamping feet,
Come from far away you to greet—
You by the fire and we in the street
Bidding you joy in the morning!

For ere one half of the night was gone,
Sudden a star has led us on,
Raining bliss and benison—
Bliss tomorrow and more anon,
Joy for every morning!

Good man Joseph toiled through the snow
Saw the star o'er a stablelow;
Mary she might not further go—
Welcome thatch, and litter below!
Joy was hers in the morning!

And then they heard the angels tell
"Who were the first to cry nowell?
Animals all, as it befell,
In the stable where they did dwell!
Joy shall be theirs in the morning!"

The voices ceased, the singers, bashful but smiling, exchanged sidelong glances, and silence succeeded—but for a moment only. Then, from up above and far away, down the tunnel they had so lately traveled was borne to their ears in a faint musical hum the sound of distant bells ringing a joyful and clangorous peal.

"Very well sung, boys!" cried the Rat heartily. "And now come along in, all of you, and warm yourselves by the fire, and have something hot!"

"Yes, come along, field mice," cried the Mole eagerly. "This is quite like old times! Shut the door after you. Pull up that settle to the fire. Now, you just wait a minute, while we—Oh, Ratty!" he cried in despair, plumping down on a seat, with tears impending. "Whatever are we doing? We've nothing to give them!"

"You leave all that to me," said the masterful Rat. "Here, you with the lantern! Come over this way. I want to talk to you. Now, tell me, are there any shops open at this hour of the night?"

"Why, certainly, sir," replied the field mouse respectfully. "At this time of the year our shops keep open to all sorts of hours."

"Then look here!" said the Rat. "You go off at once, you and your lantern, and you get me—" Here much muttered conversation ensued, and the Mole only heard bits of it, such as—"Fresh, mind!—no, a pound of that will do—see you get Buggins', for I won't have any other—no, only the best—if you can't get it there, try somewhere else—yes, of course, home-made, no tinned stuff—well then, do the best you can!"

Finally, there was a chink of coin passing from paw to paw, the field mouse was provided with an ample basket for his purchases, and off he hurried, he and his lantern. The rest of the field mice, perched in a row on the settle, their small legs swinging, gave themselves up to enjoyment of the fire, and toasted their chilblains till they tingled; while the Mole, failing to draw them into easy conversation, plunged into family history and made each of them recite the names of his numerous brothers, who were too young, it appeared, to be allowed to go out a-caroling this year, but looked forward very shortly to winning the parental consent.

The Rat, meanwhile, was busy examining the label on one of the beer-bottles. "I perceive this to be Old Burton," he remarked approvingly. "*Sensible* Mole! The very thing! Now we shall be able to mull some ale! Get the things ready, Mole, while I draw the corks."

It did not take long to prepare the brew and thrust the tin heater well into the red heart of the fire; and soon every field mouse was sipping and coughing and choking (for a little mulled ale goes a long way) and wiping his eyes and

laughing and forgetting he had ever been cold in all his life.

"They act plays too, these fellows," the Mole explained to the Rat. "Make them up all by themselves, and act them afterward. And very well they do it, too! They gave us a capital one last year, about a field mouse who was captured at sea by a Barbary corsair, and made to row in a galley; and when he escaped and got home again, his lady-love had gone into a convent. Here, *you!* You were in it, I remember. Get up and recite a bit."

The field mouse addressed got up on his legs, giggled shyly, looked around the room, and remained absolutely tongue-tied. His comrades cheered him on, Mole coaxed and encouraged him, and the Rat went so far as to take him by the shoulders and shake him; but nothing could overcome his stage fright. They were all busily engaged on him like watermen applying the Royal Humane Society's regulations to a case of long submersion, when the latch clicked, the door opened, and the field mouse with the lantern reappeared, staggering under the weight of his basket.

There was no more talk of play-acting once the very real and solid contents of the basket had been tumbled out on the table. Under the generalship of Rat, everybody was set to do something or to fetch something. In a very few minutes supper was ready, and Mole, as he took the head of the table in a sort of a dream, saw a lately barren board set thick with savory comforts; saw his little friends' faces brighten and beam as they fell to without delay; and then let himself loose—for he was famished indeed—on the provender so magically provided, thinking what a happy home-coming this had turned out, after all.

As they ate, they talked of old times, and the field mice gave him the local gossip up to date, and answered as well as they could the hundred questions he had to ask them. The Rat said little or nothing, only taking care that each guest had what he wanted, and plenty of it, and that Mole had no trouble or anxiety about anything. They clattered off at last, very grateful and showering wishes of the season, with their jacket pockets stuffed with remembrances for the small brothers and sisters at home. When the door had closed on the last of them and the chink of the lanterns had died away, Mole and Rat kicked the fire up, drew their chairs in, brewed themselves a last nightcap of mulled ale, and discussed the events of the long day.

At last the Rat, with a tremendous yawn, said, "Mole, old chap, I'm ready to drop. Sleepy is simply not the word. That your own bunk over on that side? Very well, then, I'll take this. What a ripping little house this is! Everything so handy!"

He clambered into his bunk and rolled himself well up in the blankets, and slumber gathered him forthwith, as a swathe of barley is folded into the arms of the reaping machine. The weary Mole also was glad to turn in without delay, and soon had his head on his pillow, in great joy and contentment. But before he closed his eyes he let them wander around his old room, mellow in the glow of the firelight that played or rested on familiar and friendly things which had long been unconsciously a part of him, and now smilingly received him back, without rancor.

He was now in just the frame of mind that the tactful Rat had quietly worked to bring about in him. He saw clearly how plain and simple—how narrow, even—it all was; but clearly, too, how much it all meant to him, and the special value of some such anchorage in one's existence. He did not at all want to abandon the new life and its splendid spaces, to turn his back on sun and air and all they offered him, and creep home and stay there; the upper world was all too strong, it called to him still, even down there, and he knew he must return to the larger stage. But it was good to think he had this to come back to; this place which was all his own, these things which were so glad to see him again, and could always be counted upon for the same simple welcome.

Bucephalus

By James Baldwin

OLD Philonicus of Thessaly was the most famous horse-raiser of his time. His stables were talked about from the Adriatic Sea to the Persian Gulf, and many of the best war steeds in Greece and Asia Minor had been bred and partially trained by him. He prided himself particularly on his "ox-headed" horses—broad-browed fellows, with large polls and small, sharp ears, set far apart. Proud creatures these were, and strong, and knowing, and high-spirited— just the kind for war steeds; and that was about all that horses were valued for in those days.

Among these "ox-heads" there was one which excelled all others in courage, beauty, and size, but which, nevertheless, was a source of great concern to his master. He seemed to be altogether untamable, and, although he was now fourteen years old, there was not a horseman in Greece who had ever been able to mount him. He was a handsome creature—coal-black, with a white star in his forehead. One eye was gray and the other brown. Everybody admired him, and people came great distances to see him. Had Philonicus been less shrewd, he would have sold him for half the price of a common steed, and been glad that he was rid of him. But, like most men who spend their lives among horses, he knew a thing or two. He kept the horse's untamableness a secret, and was careful that only his good points should be exhibited. Everybody who had any use for such an animal wanted to buy him.

"What is the price?"

"Thirteen thousand dollars."

That answer usually put an end to the talk. For, as an ordinary horse might be bought at that time for about seventy dollars, and a thoroughbred war steed for two hundred, who was going to pay such a fabulous price? Half a dozen fine houses could be built for that money. There were rich men who made Philonicus some very handsome offers—a thousand dollars, five thousand, eight thousand—but he held steadily to his first price, and the longer he held to it the more anxious everybody became to buy.

At last, however, after the horse had reached middle age,

shrewd Philonicus got his price. King Philip of Macedon, who was ambitious to become the first man of Greece, was the purchaser; and Philonicus, after hearing the gold pieces jingle in his strong-box, led the great Bucephalus up to the Macedonian capital and left him safely housed in the king's stalls. He was careful, no doubt, to get back into his own country before Philip had had time to give the steed any kind of examination.

You may imagine what followed. When the horse was brought out upon the parade ground for trial, the most skillful riders in Macedon could not mount him. He reared and plunged, and beat madly around with his sharp hoofs, until everybody was glad to get safely out of his reach. The greatest horse-tamers of the country were called, but they could do nothing.

"Take him away!" cried the king, at last, in great rage. "That man Philonicus has sold me an utterly wild and unbroken beast, under pretense of his being the finest horse in the world; but he shall rue it."

But now Bucephalus would not be led away. The horse-tamers tried to throw ropes over his feet; they beat him with long poles; they pelted him with stones.

"What a shame to spoil so fine a horse! The awkward cowards know nothing about handling him!" cried the king's son, Alexander, who was standing by.

"Are you finding fault with men who are wiser than yourself?" asked the king, growing still more angry. "Do you, a boy twelve years old, pretend to know more about handling horses than these men, whose business it is?"

"I can certainly handle this horse better," said the prince.

"Suppose you try it!"

"I wish that I might."

"How much will you forfeit if you try, and fail?"

"I will forfeit the price which you paid for the horse," answered Alexander.

Everybody laughed, but the king said, "Stand away, and let the lad try his skill."

Alexander ran quickly to the horse and turned his head toward the sun, for he had noticed that the animal was afraid of his own shadow. Then he spoke softly and gently to him, and kindly stroked his neck. The horse seemed to know that he had found a friend, and little by little his uneasiness left him. Soon with a light spring the lad leaped nimbly upon his back, and without pulling the reins too hard, allowed him to start off at his own gait; and then, when he saw that the horse was no longer afraid, but only proud of his speed, he urged him with voice and spur to do his utmost. The king and his attendants were alarmed, and expected every moment to see the boy unseated and dashed to the ground. But when he turned and rode back, proud of his daring feat, everybody cheered and shouted—everybody but his father, who wept for joy and, kissing him, said: "You must look for a kingdom which is worthy of you, my son, for Macedonia is too small for you."

After that, Bucephalus would allow his groom to mount him barebacked; but when he was saddled nobody but Alexander dared touch him. He would even kneel to his young master, in order that he might mount more easily; and for sixteen years thereafter he served him as faithfully as horse ever served man. Of course, he was with Alexander when he conquered Persia, and he carried him into more than one hard-fought battle. At one time (I think it was in Hyrcania) he was stolen; but his master made proclamation that unless he were forthcoming within a certain time, every man, woman, and child in the province should be put to death, and it was not long before he was brought back.

In the great battle that was fought with King Porus, of India, Alexander recklessly rode too far into the enemy's ranks. The horse and his rider became the target for every spear, and for a time it seemed as if neither could escape. But the gallant Bucephalus, pierced by many weapons, and with streams of blood flowing from his neck and sides, turned about and, overriding the foes which beset them, rushed back to a place of safety. When he saw that his master was out of danger and among friends, the horse sank down upon the grass and died. Historians say that this happened in the year 327 BC, and that Bucephalus had reached the good old age—for a horse—of thirty years.

Alexander mourned for him as for his dearest friend, and the next city which he founded he named Bucephalia, in honor of the steed that had served him so well.

*Black Beauty is a horse. He has had many masters,
but has never forgotten his first home, and the kind
stable boy who once made him ill by giving him
cold water to drink when he was overheated. His
owners have sometimes treated him badly and
sometimes kindly, but he has always worked hard.*

Black Beauty's Final Home

From *Black Beauty*

By Anna Sewell

I WAS sold to a corn dealer and baker whom Jerry knew,
and with him he thought I should have good food and
fair work. In the first he was quite right, and if my master
had always been on the premises I do not think I should
have been overloaded, but there was a foreman who was
always hurrying and driving everyone, and frequently when
I had quite a full load he would order something else to be
taken on. My carter, whose name was Jakes, often said it
was more than I ought to take, but the other always
overruled him, saying "Twas no use going twice when once
would do, and he chose to get business forward."

Jakes, like the other carters, always had the check-rein up, which prevented me from drawing easily, and by the time I had been there three or four months I found the work telling very much on my strength.

One day I was loaded more than usual, and part of the road was a steep uphill. I used all my strength, but I could not get on, and was obliged continually to stop. This did not please my driver, and he laid his whip on badly. "Get on, you lazy fellow," he said, "or I'll make you."

Again I started the heavy load, and struggled on a few yards; again the whip came down, and again I struggled forward. The pain of that great cart whip was sharp, but my mind was hurt quite as much as my poor sides. To be punished and abused when I was doing my very best was so hard it took the heart out of me. A third time he was flogging me cruelly, when a lady stepped quickly up to him, and said in a sweet, earnest voice, "Oh! Pray do not whip your good horse any more; I am sure he is doing all he can, and the road is very steep; I am sure he is doing his best."

"If doing his best won't get this load up he must do something more than his best; that's all I know, ma'am," said Jakes.

"But is it not a heavy load?" she said.

"Yes, yes, too heavy," he said; "but that's not my fault; the foreman came just as we were starting, and would have three hundredweight more put on to save him trouble, and

I must get on with it as well as I can."

He was raising the whip again, when the lady said,

"Pray, stop; I think I can help you if you will let me."

The man laughed.

"You see," she said, "you do not give him a fair chance; he cannot use all his power with his head held back as it is with that check-rein; if you would take it off I am sure he would do better—do try it," she said persuasively, "I should be very glad if you would."

"Well, well," said Jakes, with a short laugh, "anything to please a lady, of course. How far would you wish it down, ma'am?"

"Quite down, give him his head altogether."

The rein was taken off, and in a moment I put my head down to my very knees. What a comfort it was! Then I tossed it up and down several times to get the aching stiffness out of my neck.

"Poor fellow! That is what you wanted," said she, patting and stroking me with her gentle hand; "and now if you will speak kindly to him and lead him on I believe he will be able to do better."

Jakes took the rein. "Come on, Blackie." I put down my head, and threw my whole weight against the collar; I spared no strength; the load moved on, and I pulled it steadily up the hill, and then stopped to take breath.

The lady had walked along the footpath, and now came across into the road. She stroked and patted my neck, as I had not been patted for many a long day.

"You see he was quite willing when you gave him the chance; I am sure he is a fine-tempered creature, and I dare say he has known better days. You won't put that rein on again, will you?"—for he was just going to hitch it up on the old plan.

"Well, ma'am, I can't deny that having his head has helped him up the hill, and I'll remember it another time, and thank you, ma'am; but if he went without a check-rein I should be the laughing-stock of all the carters; it is the fashion, you see."

"Is it not better," she said, "to lead a good fashion than to follow a bad one? A great many gentlemen do not use check-reins now; our carriage horses have not worn them for fifteen years, and work with much less fatigue than those who have them; besides," she added in a very serious voice, "we have no right to distress any of God's creatures without a very good reason; we call them dumb animals, and so they are, for they cannot tell us how they feel, but they do not suffer less because they have no words. But I must not detain you now; I thank you for trying my plan with your good horse, and I am sure you will find it far better than the whip. Good-day." And with another soft pat on my neck she stepped lightly across the path, and I saw her no more.

"That was a real lady, I'll be bound for it," said Jakes to himself; "she spoke just as polite as if I was a gentleman, and I'll try her plan, uphill, at any rate;" and I must do him the justice to say that he let my rein out several holes, and going uphill after that, he always gave me my head; but the heavy loads went on. Good feed and fair rest will keep up one's strength under full work, but no horse can stand against overloading; and I was getting so thoroughly pulled down from this cause that a younger horse was bought in my place. I may as well mention here what I suffered at this time from another cause. I had heard horses speak of it, but had never myself had experience of the evil; this was a badly-lighted stable; there was only one very small window at the end, and the consequence was that the stalls were almost dark.

Besides the depressing effect this had on my spirits, it very much weakened my sight, and when I was suddenly brought out of the darkness into the glare of daylight it was very painful to my eyes. Several times I stumbled over the threshold, and could scarcely see where I was going.

I believe, had I stayed there very long, I should have become purblind, and that would have been a great misfortune, for I have heard men say that a stone-blind horse was safer to drive than one which had imperfect sight, as it generally makes them very timid. However, I escaped without any permanent injury to my sight, and was sold to a large cab owner.

Hard Times

My new master I shall never forget; he had black eyes and a hooked nose, his mouth was as full of teeth as a bulldog's, and his voice was as harsh as the grinding of cart wheels over graveled stones. His name was Nicholas Skinner, and I believe he was the man that poor Seedy Sam drove for.

I have heard men say that seeing is believing; but I should say that feeling is believing; for much as I had seen before, I never knew till now the utter misery of a cab-horse's life.

Skinner had a low set of cabs and a low set of drivers; he

was hard on the men, and the men were hard on the horses. In this place we had no Sunday rest, and it was in the heat of summer.

Sometimes on a Sunday morning a party of fast men would hire the cab for the day; four of them inside and another with the driver, and I had to take them ten or fifteen miles out into the country, and back again; never would any of them get down to walk up a hill, let it be ever so steep, or the day ever so hot—unless, indeed, when the driver was afraid I should not manage it, and sometimes I was so fevered and worn that I could hardly touch my food. How I used to long for the nice bran mash with niter in it that Jerry used to give us on Saturday nights in hot weather, that used to cool us down and make us so comfortable. Then we had two nights and a whole day for unbroken rest, and on Monday morning we were as fresh as young horses again; but here there was no rest, and my driver was just as hard as his master. He had a cruel whip with something so sharp at the end that it sometimes drew blood, and he would even whip me under the belly, and flip the lash out at my head. Indignities like these took the heart out of me terribly, but still I did my best and never hung back.

My life was now so utterly wretched that I wished I might drop down dead at my work and be out of my misery, and one day my wish very nearly came to pass.

I went on the stand at eight in the morning, and had done a good share of work, when we had to take a fare to the railway. A long train was just expected in, so my driver pulled up at the back of some of the outside cabs to take the chance of a return fare. It was a very heavy train, and as all the cabs were soon engaged, ours was called for. There was a party of four: a noisy, blustering man with a lady, a little boy and a young girl, and a great deal of luggage. The lady and the boy got into the cab, and while the man ordered about the luggage the young girl came and looked at me.

"Papa," she said, "I am sure this poor horse cannot take us and all our luggage so far, he is so very weak and worn out. Do look at him."

"Oh! He's all right, miss," said my driver, "he's strong enough."

The porter, who was pulling about some heavy boxes, suggested to the gentleman, as there was so much luggage, whether he would not take a second cab.

"Can your horse do it, or can't he?" said the man.

"Oh! He can do it all right, sir; send up the boxes, porter; he could take more than that;" and he helped to haul up a box so heavy that I could feel the springs go down.

"Papa, papa, do take a second cab," said the young girl in a beseeching tone. "I am sure we are wrong, I am sure it is very cruel."

"Nonsense, Grace, get in at once, and don't make all this fuss; a pretty thing it would be if a man of business had to examine every cab-horse before he hired it—the man knows his own business of course; there, get in and hold your tongue!"

My gentle friend had to obey, and box after box was dragged up and lodged on the top of the cab or settled by the side of the driver.

At last all was ready, and with his usual jerk at the rein and slash of the whip he drove out of the station.

The load was very heavy and I had had neither food nor rest since morning; but I did my best, as I always had done, in spite of cruelty and injustice.

I got along fairly till we came to Ludgate Hill; but there the heavy load and my own exhaustion were too much. I was struggling to keep on, goaded by constant chucks of the rein and use of the whip, when in a single moment—I cannot tell how—my feet slipped from under me, and I fell heavily to the ground on my side. The suddenness and the force with which I fell seemed to beat all the breath out of my body. I lay perfectly still, indeed, I had no power to move, and I thought now I was going to die. I heard a sort of confusion around me, loud, angry voices, and the getting down of the luggage, but it was all like a dream. I thought I heard that sweet, pitiful voice saying, "Oh! that poor horse! it is all our fault."

Someone came and loosened the throat strap of my bridle, and undid the traces which kept the collar so tight upon me. Someone said, "He's dead, he'll never get up again."

Then I could hear a policeman giving orders, but I did not even open my eyes; I could only draw a gasping breath now and then. Some cold water was thrown over my head, and some cordial was poured into my mouth, and something was covered over me. I cannot tell how long I lay there, but I found my life coming back, and a kind-voiced man was patting me and encouraging me to rise. After some more cordial had been given me, and after one or two attempts, I staggered to my feet, and was gently led to some stables which were close by. Here I was put into a well-littered stall, and some warm gruel was brought to me, which I drank thankfully.

In the evening I was sufficiently recovered to be led back to Skinner's stables, where I think they did the best for me they could. In the morning Skinner came with a farrier to look at me. He examined me very closely and said: "This is a case of overwork more than disease, and if you could give him a run off for six months he would be able to work again; but now there is not an ounce of strength left in him."

"Then he must just go to the dogs," said Skinner. "I have no meadows to nurse sick horses in—he might get well or he might not; that sort of thing don't suit my business; my plan is to work 'em as long as they'll go, and then sell 'em for what they'll fetch, at the knacker's or elsewhere."

"If he was broken-winded," said the farrier, "you had better have him killed out of hand, but he is not; there is a sale of horses coming off in about ten days. If you rest him and feed him up he may pick up, and you may get more than his skin is worth, at any rate."

Upon this advice Skinner, rather unwillingly, I think, gave orders that I should be well fed and cared for, and the stable man, happily for me, carried out the orders with a much better will than his master had in giving them. Ten days of perfect rest, plenty of good oats, hay, bran mashes with boiled linseed mixed in them, did more to get up my condition than anything else could have done. Those linseed mashes were delicious, and I began to think, after all, it might be better to live than go to the dogs. When the twelfth day after the accident came, I was taken to the sale, a few miles out of London. I felt that any change from my present place must be an improvement, so I held up my head, and hoped for the best.

At this sale, of course I found myself in company with the old broken-down horses—some lame, some broken-winded, some old, and some that I am sure it would have been merciful to shoot.

The buyers and sellers, too, many of them, looked not much better off than the poor beasts they were bargaining about. There were poor old men, trying to get a horse or a pony for a few pounds, that might drag about some little wood or coal cart. There were poor men trying to sell a worn-out beast for two or three pounds, rather than have the greater loss of killing him. Some of them looked as if poverty and hard times had hardened them all over; but there were others that I would have willingly used the last of my strength in serving; poor and shabby, but kind and human, with voices that I could trust. There was one tottering old man who took a great fancy to me, and I to him, but I was not strong enough—it was an anxious time! Coming from the better part of the fair, I noticed a man who looked like a gentleman farmer, with a young boy by his side. He had a broad back and round shoulders, and a kind, ruddy face. When he came up to me and my companions he stood still and gave a pitiful look around upon us. I saw his eye rest on me; I had still a good mane and tail, which did something for my appearance. I pricked my ears and looked at him.

"There's a horse, Willie, that has known better days."

"Poor old fellow!" said the boy, "Do you think, grandpapa, he was ever a carriage horse?"

"Oh, yes! My boy," said the farmer, coming closer, "He might have been anything when he was young; look at his nostrils and his ears, the shape of his neck and shoulder; there's a deal of breeding about that horse." He put out his hand and gave me a kind pat on the neck. I put out my nose in answer to his kindness. The boy stroked my face.

"Poor old fellow! See, grandpapa, how well he understands kindness. Could not you buy him and make him young again as you did with Ladybird?"

"My dear boy, I can't make all old horses young. Besides, Ladybird was not so very old, as she was run down and badly used."

"Well, grandpapa, I don't believe that this one is old; look at his mane and tail. I wish you would look into his mouth, and then you could tell; though he is so very thin, his eyes are not sunk like some old horses'."

The old gentleman laughed. "Bless the boy! He is as horsey as his old grandfather."

"But do look at his mouth, grandpapa, and ask the price. I am sure he would grow young in our meadows."

The man who had brought me for sale now put in his word. "The young gentleman's a real knowing one, sir. Now the fact is, this 'ere hoss is just pulled down with overwork in the cabs. He's not an old one, and I heerd as how the vetenary should say, that a six months' run off would set him right up, being as how his wind was not broken. I've had the tending of him these ten days past, and a gratefuller, pleasanter animal I never met with, and 'twould be worth a gentleman's while to give a five-pound note for him, and let him have a chance. I'll be bound he'd be worth twenty pounds next spring."

The old gentleman laughed, and the little boy looked up eagerly. "Oh, grandpapa, did you not say the colt sold for five pounds more than you expected? You would not be poorer if you did buy this one."

The farmer slowly felt my legs, which were much swelled and strained; then he looked at my mouth. "Thirteen or fourteen, I should say; just trot him out, will you?"

I arched my poor thin neck, raised my tail a little, and threw out my legs as well as I could, for they were very stiff.

"What is the lowest you will take for him?" said the farmer as I came back.

"Five pounds, sir; that was the lowest price my master set."

"'Tis a speculation," said the old gentleman, shaking his head, but at the same time slowly drawing out his purse, "quite a speculation! Have you any more business here?" he said, counting the sovereigns into his hand.

"No, sir, I can take him for you to the inn, if you please."

"Do so, I am now going there."

They walked forward, and I was led behind. The boy could hardly control his delight, and the old gentleman seemed to enjoy his pleasure. I had a good feed at the inn, and was then gently ridden home by a servant of my new master's, and turned into a large meadow with a shed in one corner of it.

Mr Thoroughgood, for that was the name of my benefactor, gave orders that I should have hay and oats every night and morning, and the run of the meadow during the day, and, "You, Willie," said he, "must take the oversight of him; I give him in charge to you."

The boy was proud of his charge, and undertook it in all seriousness. There was not a day when he did not pay me a visit; sometimes picking me out from among the other horses and giving me a bit of carrot, or something good, or sometimes standing by me while I ate my oats. He always came with kind words and caresses, and of course I grew very fond of him. He called me "Old Crony," as I used to come to him in the field and follow him about. Sometimes he brought his grandfather, who always looked closely at my legs.

"This is our point, Willie," he would say; "but he is improving so steadily that I think we shall see a change for the better in the spring."

The perfect rest, the good food, the soft turf, and gentle

exercise soon began to tell on my condition and my spirits. I had a good constitution from my mother, and I was never strained when I was young, so that I had a better chance than many horses who have been worked before they came to their full strength. During the winter my legs improved so much that I began to feel quite young again. The spring came around, and one day in March Mr Thoroughgood determined that he would try me in the phaeton. I was well pleased, and he and Willie drove me a few miles. My legs were not stiff now, and I did the work with perfect ease.

"He's growing young, Willie; we must give him a little gentle work now, and by mid-summer he will be as good as Ladybird. He has a beautiful mouth and good paces; they can't be better."

"Oh, grandpapa, how glad I am you bought him!"

"So am I, my boy; but he has to thank you more than me; we must now be looking out for a quiet, genteel place for him, where he will be valued."

One day during this summer the groom cleaned and dressed me with such extraordinary care that I thought some new change must be at hand. He trimmed my fetlocks and legs, passed the tarbrush over my hoofs, and even parted my forelock. I think the harness had an extra polish. Willie seemed half-anxious, half-merry, as he got into the chaise with his grandfather.

"If the ladies take to him," said the old gentleman, "they'll be suited and he'll be suited. We can but try."

At the distance of a mile or two from the village we came to a pretty, low house, with a lawn and shrubbery at the front and a drive up to the door. Willie rang the bell, and asked if Miss Blomefield or Miss Ellen was at home. Yes, they were. So, while Willie stayed with me, Mr Thoroughgood went into the house. In about ten minutes he returned, followed by three ladies; one tall, pale lady, wrapped in a white shawl, leaned on a younger lady, with dark eyes and a merry face; the other, a very stately-looking person, was Miss Blomefield. They all came and looked at me and asked questions. The younger lady—that was Miss Ellen—took to me very much; she said she was sure she should like me, I had such a good face. The tall, pale lady said that she should always be nervous in riding behind a horse that had once been down, as I might come down again, and if I did she should never get over the fright.

"You see, ladies," said Mr Thoroughgood, "many first-rate horses have had their knees broken through the carelessness of their drivers without any fault of their own, and from what I see of this horse I should say that is his case; but of course I do not wish to influence you. If you incline you can have him on trial, and then your coachman will see what he thinks of him."

"You have always been such a good adviser to us about our horses," said the stately lady, "that your recommendation would go a long way with me, and if my sister Lavinia sees no objection we will accept your offer of a trial, with thanks."

It was then arranged that I should be sent for the next day.

In the morning a smart-looking young man came for me. At first he looked pleased; but when he saw my knees he said in a disappointed voice:

"I didn't think, sir, you would have recommended my ladies a blemished horse like that."

"Handsome is that handsome does," said my master; "you are only taking him on trial, and I am sure you will do fairly by him, young man. If he is not as safe as any horse you ever drove send him back."

I was led to my new home, placed in a comfortable stable, fed, and left to myself. The next day, when the groom was cleaning my face, he said: "That is just like the star that Black Beauty had; he is much the same height, too. I wonder where he is now."

A little further on he came to the place in my neck where I was bled and where a little knot was left in the skin. He almost started, and began to look me over carefully, talking to himself.

"White star in the forehead, one white foot on the off side, this little knot just in that place;" then looking at the middle of my back—"and, as I am alive, there is that little patch of white hair that John used to call 'Beauty's three-penny bit'. It must be Black Beauty! Why, Beauty! Beauty! Do you know me? Little Joe Green, that almost killed you?" And he began patting and patting me as if he was quite overjoyed.

I could not say that I remembered him, for now he was a fine grown young fellow, with black whiskers and a man's voice, but I was sure he knew me, and that he was Joe Green, and I was very glad. I put my nose up to him, and tried to say that we were friends. I never saw a man so pleased.

"Give you a fair trial! I should think so indeed! I wonder who the rascal was that broke your knees, my old Beauty! You must have been badly served out somewhere; well, well, it won't be my fault if you haven't good times of it now. I wish John Manly was here to see you."

In the afternoon I was put into a low park chair and brought to the door. Miss Ellen was going to try me, and Green went with her. I soon found that she was a good driver, and she seemed pleased with my paces. I heard Joe telling her about me, and that he was sure I was Squire Gordon's old "Black Beauty."

When we returned the other sisters came out to hear how I had behaved myself. She told them what she had just heard, and said: "I shall certainly write to Mrs Gordon, and tell her that her favorite horse has come to us. How pleased she will be!"

After this I was driven every day for a week or so, and as I appeared to be quite safe, Miss Lavinia at last ventured out in the small close carriage. After this it was quite decided to keep me and call me by my old name of "Black Beauty."

I have now lived in this happy place a whole year. Joe is the best and kindest of grooms. My work is easy and pleasant, and I feel my strength and spirits all coming back again. Mr Thoroughgood said to Joe the other day: "In your place he will last till he is twenty years old—perhaps more."

Willie always speaks to me when he can, and treats me as his special friend. My ladies have promised that I shall never be sold, and so I have nothing to fear; and here my story ends. My troubles are all over, and I am at home; and often before I am quite awake, I fancy I am still in the orchard at Birtwick, standing with my old friends under the apple trees.

The Death of Gellert

By P. H. Emerson

PRINCE Llewelyn had a favorite greyhound named Gellert that had been given to him by his father-in-law, King John. He was as gentle as a lamb at home, but a lion in the chase. One day Llewelyn went to the chase and blew his horn in front of his castle. All his other dogs came to the call but Gellert never answered it. So he blew a louder blast on his horn and called Gellert by name, but still the greyhound did not come. At last Prince Llewelyn could wait no longer and went off to the hunt without Gellert. He had little sport that day because Gellert—the swiftest and boldest of his hounds—was not there.

He turned back in a rage to his castle, and as he came to the gate, who should he see but Gellert come bounding out to meet him. But when the hound came near him, the Prince was startled to see that his lips and fangs were dripping with blood. Llewelyn started back and the greyhound crouched down at his feet as if surprised or afraid at the way his master greeted him.

Now Prince Llewelyn had a little son a year old with whom Gellert used to play, and a terrible thought crossed the Prince's mind that made him rush toward the child's nursery. And the nearer he came the more blood and disorder he found about the rooms. He rushed into it and found the child's cradle overturned and daubed with blood.

Prince Llewelyn grew more and more terrified, and sought for his little son everywhere. He could find him nowhere but only signs of some terrible conflict in which much blood had been shed.

At last he felt sure the dog had destroyed his child, and shouting at Gellert, "Monster, thou hast devoured my child," he drew out his sword and plunged it in the greyhound's side, who fell with a deep yell, still gazing into his master's eyes.

As Gellert raised his dying howl, a little child's cry answered it from beneath the cradle, and there Llewelyn found his child, unharmed and just awakened from sleep.

But just beside him lay the body of a great gaunt wolf all torn to pieces and covered with blood. Too late, Llewelyn realized what had happened while he was away. Gellert had stayed behind to guard the child and had fought and slain the wolf that had tried to destroy Llewelyn's heir.

In vain was all Llewelyn's grief; he could not bring his faithful dog to life again. So he buried him outside the castle walls within sight of the great mountain of Snowdon, where every passer-by might see his grave, and raised over it a great cairn of stones. And to this day the place is called Beth Gellert, or the Grave of Gellert.

Myths and Wonders

The Labors of Hercules

By Mary E. Burt and Zenaïde A. Ragozin

FAR away in the land of Argos there once lived a beautiful maiden, the daughter of a brave king. She was tall and fair and her name was Alkmene. Her father was rich in the possession of many oxen.

Her husband also owned great herds of oxen. He had so many that he could not tell them from those of the king. So he quarreled with the king and slew him. Then he took Alkmene and fled from his native land. They came to Thebes and made it their home.

Here Hercules was born, the babe who was stronger than the strongest of men. The goddess, Hera, hated Hercules. She was the wife of Zeus, the Lord of Thunder and King of Heaven. Hera was angry because Zeus loved him, and she was jealous because Zeus had foretold that Hercules would become the greatest of men. More than that, Zeus had deceived Hera and sent the infant Hercules to her to be nursed that he might be made strong and godlike by tasting divine milk.

So Hera sent two large snakes to devour the babe when she found out what child it was that she had fed. Hercules lay asleep in the great brazen shield which his father carried in battle, for he had no other cradle. The fearful serpents crept up with open mouths into the shield with the sleeping babe.

As soon as Alkmene saw them she was terribly frightened and called in a loud voice for help. His father, hearing the outcry of Alkmene, ran into the house with his sword drawn and a great many warriors came with weapons in their hands.

Hercules was only eight months old, but before his father could reach him he sat up in his bed and seized the serpents by their necks with his little hands. He squeezed and choked them with such force that they died.

When Alkmene saw that the two snakes were dead and that Hercules was safe, she rejoiced greatly. But Hera's heart was filled with wrath and she began to plan more mischief against the child.

Hercules had his free will as long as he was a boy. His

teachers were celebrated heroes who taught him boxing, wrestling, riding, and all kinds of games. He learned to read and write and to hurl the spear and shoot with bows and arrows. Linos taught him music.

Hercules had a violent temper, and one day as Linos was teaching him to play the lute, the good teacher had reason to punish him. Hercules flew into a rage at this and struck Linos and killed him. Then his father sent him to the hills and left him to the care of herdsmen.

The boy grew to be very large and strong. While he was yet a youth he slew a lion of great size that had killed many of his father's cattle. He went home wearing the lion's skin as a sign of his victory. Because he was so brave, the King of Thebes gave his daughter to him in marriage and he lived happily with her for many years. But a sudden insanity came upon him during which he mistook his wife and children for wild beasts and shot them down with his bow and arrows. When Hercules recovered from his insanity and saw what he had done his grief was boundless.

The wrath of Hera followed Hercules. When Zeus saw that Hera's heart was filled with anger toward Hercules, he mused within his own mind how he might best appease her resentment and protect the young man.

So he called the gods together in council and they advised that Hercules be placed in bondage to his uncle Eurystheus, to serve him as a slave, and they ordained that he should perform twelve hard tasks, after which he would be numbered among the gods.

Eurystheus was a mean fellow, stupid, and cowardly. He was glad enough to have a chance to bully a man wiser and stronger than himself. He was born in Tiryns, a great fortress with many castles, built upon a large rock, but he had been made King of Argos and lived in the capital, Mykense, and he resolved to keep Hercules as far away from the kingdom as possible, for in his heart he was afraid of him.

Hercules was grieved at being compelled to serve a man so much below him in strength and character, so he consulted the oracle at Delphi to see if there was any escape, but he did not murmur, for he was willing to obey the law of the gods.

The oracle of Delphi was a mysterious influence, a divine spirit which expressed itself through a priestess living in a sacred temple. It was supposed to be the voice of the god Apollo using this human agency for making known his will to men. The priestess became inspired to utter Apollo's holy laws by sitting on a golden tripod (or stool with three legs) over a chasm in the rock, from whence arose a sacred, sulfurous vapor which she breathed in as the breath of the god, and which caused her to breathe out his commands in wonderful sayings.

The chasm from which the vapor issued was called The Chasm of the Oracle, and was in a large apartment or room in the temple. This celebrated temple had many columns of marble and splendid rooms made beautiful with thousands of marble statues. It stood on the side of Mount Parnassos, whose snow-covered head reaches into the clouds and looks down into the blue Gulf of Corinth below it to the south.

It was here that Apollo killed the great dragon, Pytho, which had been the scourge of the land for many years, and the grateful people built the temple in his honor. The oracle bade Hercules go forth to be the slave of Eurystheus and so atone for all his sins, but it gave him as a compensation a dear friend, Lolaos, who was also his young nephew. Wherever Hercules went Lolaos went with him and helped him.

The First Labor: The Nemean Lion

It happened that a fearful lion lived in Nemea, a wild district in upper Argolis, and it devastated all the land and was the terror of the inhabitants. Eurystheus ordered Hercules to bring him the skin of this lion. So Hercules took his bow, his quiver, and heavy club and started out in search of the beast.

When he had reached a little town which is in the neighborhood of Nemea he was kindly received by a good countryman, who promised to put him on the track of the lion if he would sacrifice the animal to Zeus.

Hercules promised, and the countryman went with him to show him the way. When they reached the place where traces of the lion were seen, Hercules said to his guide,

"Remain here thirty days. If I return safely from the lion-hunt you must sacrifice a sheep to Zeus, for he is the god who will have saved me. But if I am slain by the lion you must sacrifice the sheep to me, for after my death I shall be honored as a hero." Having said this, Hercules went his way.

He reached the wilderness of Nemea, where he spent several days in looking for the lion, but without success. Not a trace of him could be found, nor did he fall in with any human being, for there was no one bold enough to wander around in that wilderness. Finally he spied the lion as he was about to crawl into his den.

The lion was indeed worthy of his terrible fame. His size was prodigious, his eyes shot forth flames of fire, and his tongue licked his bloody chops. When he roared, the whole desert resounded.

But Hercules stood fearlessly near a grove from whence he might approach the lion, and suddenly shot at him with his bow and arrow, hitting him squarely in the breast. The arrow glanced aside, and slipping around the lion's neck, fell on a rock behind him. When Hercules saw this he knew that the lion was proof against arrows and must be killed in some other way, and seizing his club, he gave chase to him.

The lion made for a cave which had two mouths. Hercules closed up one of the entrances with heavy rocks and entered the other. He seized the lion by the throat and then came a terrible struggle, but Hercules squeezed him in his mighty arms until he gasped for breath, and at last lay dead.

Then Hercules took up the huge body and, throwing it easily over his shoulder, returned to the place where he had left the countryman. It was on the last of the thirty appointed days, and the rustic, supposing that Hercules had come to his death through the lion, was about to offer up a sheep as a sacrifice in his honor.

He rejoiced greatly when he saw Hercules alive and victorious, and the sheep was offered up to Zeus. Hercules left the little town and went to Mykenas to the house of his uncle and showed him the dead body of the terrible lion. Eurystheus was so greatly frightened at the sight that he hid himself within a tower whose walls were built of solid brass. And he ordered Hercules not to enter the city again, but to stay outside of its gates until he had performed the other labors.

Hercules stripped the skin from the lion with his fingers, although it was so tough, and knowing it to be arrow-proof, took it for a cloak and wore it as long as he lived.

The Second Labor: The Killing of the Hydra

Not far from Mykenas is a small lake called Lerna. It is formed from a large spring at the foot of a hill. In this lake there lived a water-snake called the Hydra. It was a snake of uncommon size, with nine heads. Eight of the heads were mortal, but the one in the middle was immortal.

The Hydra frequently came out of the water and swallowed up herds of cattle, laying waste the surrounding country. Eurystheus ordered Hercules to kill the snake, so he put on his lion's skin, and taking his club, started out. He mounted his chariot and took his faithful friend Lolaos, who acted as charioteer.

Every warrior had to have a charioteer to drive the horses, leaving him free to use both of his hands. But driving was by no means the charioteer's only duty; he had also to look out for danger and protect the warrior with his shield as well as to supply him with arrows from the quiver suspended at the side of every chariot, and with reserve spears when his own was broken in the fray.

It is clear, therefore, that the warrior's life was entirely in the hands of his charioteer, so it is no wonder that only the hero's dearest and most trusted friends were allowed to serve him in this way.

After driving along for a while through groves of olive-trees and past pleasant vineyards, they came to wild places and saw Lake Lerna gleaming through the trees. Having reached the lake, Hercules descended from the chariot, left the horses in care of Lolaos, and went to hunt for the snake.

He found it in a swampy place where it was hiding. Hercules shot some burning arrows at the Hydra and forced

it to come out. It darted
furiously at him, but
he met it fearlessly,
put his foot upon its
tail, and with his club
began to strike off its
heads. He could not accomplish
anything in this way, for as fast as
he knocked off one head two others
grew in its place.

The snake coiled itself so firmly around one of
Hercules' legs that he was no longer able to stir from the
place. Added to all this there came a huge crab to the
assistance of the snake. It crept up to Hercules' foot, and
seizing it with its sharp claws, inflicted painful wounds.
Hercules killed the crab with his club and called Lolaos to
help him.

Under Hercules' directions Lolaos produced a fire-brand
which he applied to the neck as fast as Hercules cut off one
of the snake's heads, in this way preventing them from
growing again. Finally it came the turn of the head which
could not die. Cutting it off Hercules buried it in the
ground, placing a heavy stone over it.

Then he dipped some arrows into the Hydra's blood,
which was poisonous, so that whoever was wounded by one

of them could not be healed. The least scratch inflicted by such an arrow was incurable.

Eurystheus, of course, had no word of praise for his great bondsman, but the people, knowing that the place was now safe, flocked to the land in great numbers and drained the lake, which was really not much more than a big marshy pond, and in their new homes they blessed the hero's name forever. That was the prize for which Hercules cared the most.

If you should go today to that old battlefield of Hercules you would still find the spring flowing from the rocks, but Lake Lerna exists only in story.

The Third Labor: The Golden Hind

The lower part of Greece is a most peculiar-looking bit of country. You would think it had been torn off from the bulk of the land but kept hanging on to it by a small narrow strip. Then, too, its shape is so queer that it has been compared to all sorts of things; sometimes to a mulberry leaf, sometimes to an open hand.

If we keep to the latter comparison, we will find that the part which answers to the palm of the hand is a large and intricate knot of high wooded mountains which shoot out spurs in all directions. These spurs with the land attached to them stretch out into the sea as so many small peninsulas and not badly represent the fingers of the hand. The central knot of mountains is even now different from the country all around.

The people there are wilder, very much given to robbery and violence and very slow to accept new ways of life or improvements of any kind. In the old heroic times of several thousand years ago that country was simply an impassable wilderness.

It was overcrowded with wild beasts, among which the bear must have been the most plentiful since the land was named after him, Arcadia the land of Bears. Wolves were known also to abound.

The men who had their villages in the narrow valleys by the mountain streams were fierce and lawless. There was nothing for them to do but to keep goats and hunt all day long. Arcadia was truly the paradise of hunters and therefore held as specially sacred to the beautiful huntress, the goddess, Artemis the Lady of the Chase. She roamed over hills and valleys and through woods and groves by moonlight to protect the herds and flocks, this beautiful daughter of Zeus.

In these same mountains of Arcadia there roamed a lovely Hind sacred to Queen Artemis, who gave her golden horns so that she might be known from other deer by the

huntsmen. Thus they might
be saved from the crime
of slaying what was
sacred to the gods.
Eurystheus
ordered Hercules
to bring him the
Hind alive, for he did not dare to have
her killed.

Hercules spent a whole year seeking her
from the mountaintops down to the valleys,
through tangles of brush, over streams, and in forests, but he
was not able to catch her. After a long chase he forced her at
last to take refuge on the side of a mountain and from that
place to go down to a river to drink.

In order that he might prevent the deer from crossing the
water, Hercules was obliged slightly to wound one of her
legs. Not till then was he able to secure his game and carry it
to Eurystheus.

On his way to Mykenae Hercules was met by Artemis,
who upbraided him for having captured the Hind belonging
to her. Hercules made answer,

"Great Goddess, if I have chased and caught thy deer, I
did it out of necessity, not impiety; for thou well knowest
that the gods ordered me to be a servant to Eurystheus and

he commanded me to catch the Hind."

With these words he soothed the anger of the goddess and brought the golden-horned Hind to Mykenae.

The Fourth Labor: The Erymanthian Boar

Elis is a beautiful plain lying to the north and west of Arcadia. Here, once in five years, there was a great festival in honor of Zeus, when all the men and boys ran races, wrestled, boxed, and played all sorts of games. Between Arcadia and Elis there is a high mountain range, called Erymanthos. There a terrible Boar had its lair.

The Boar frequently left its den and came down into the plains and killed cattle, destroyed fields of grain, and attacked people. Eurystheus, having heard of this Boar, made up his mind that he wanted the beast alive, and so ordered Hercules to bring it to him.

The hero put on his lion skin once more and started for the mountain. On his way he stopped at a little town where the Centaurs had their home. These strange people were half-man and half-horse. We have heard that they were really men, but such good riders that they seemed to be one with their mountain ponies.

Their home was just on the edge of a high plain, covered with oak trees and looking down across a wild valley, through which flowed the Erymanthos River. There were many forests and little streams and dreadful gorges in the valley, where these horsemen used to hunt and fish.

The Centaur Chief, Pholos, received Hercules as a guest and gave him cooked meat to eat, while he ate it raw himself, after the Centaurs' custom.

When Hercules had eaten his fill, he said to Pholos,

"Thy food is indeed good and tasteful. But I should enjoy it still more if I could have a sip of wine, for I am very thirsty." To which Pholos replied,

"My dear guest, we have very fine and fragrant wine in this mountain, and I should like nothing better than to give thee some of it. But I am afraid to do so, because it has a strong aroma, and the other Centaurs, if they smelt it, might come to my cave and want some. They are very fierce and lawless, and might do thee great harm."

"Let not that trouble thee," said Hercules. "I am not afraid of the Centaurs." So the wine was placed before him and he drank of it. In a little while a great noise was heard outside of the cave, a shouting of many wild voices, and a stamping of many horses' feet. What Pholos feared had come to pass. The Centaurs had smelt the fragrance of the wine and in full armor had made for the cave of Pholos. Then began a terrible fight. The Centaurs fell upon Hercules with pine branches, rocks, axes, and fire-brands, and the clouds, their mothers, poured a flood of water on him. But Hercules was too clever for them. He put two to flight, prevented others from entering the cave, and shot the rest down with his arrows.

Pholos was a kind-hearted chief, and hearing one of the Centaurs crying for help outside of his cave, went out to him and tried to pull the arrow from his wound, wondering at the same time that so slight a weapon could cause his death. But the arrow slipped out of his hand and struck his own foot. It made only a scratch, but it could not be healed, for the arrow was one of those which Hercules had dipped in the blood of the Hydra, and poor Pholos breathed his last.

The death of his kind host was a great sorrow to Hercules, for in those times, when there was so little safety in traveling, the bond of kindness and gratitude between host and guest was one of the closest and most sacred, often more so than that between members of the same family. In all their later lives, host and guest could never meet as enemies, and if the chances of war brought them face to face as foes, they were not expected to fight. They exchanged greetings and gifts and drove off in different directions.

Hercules therefore sincerely mourned his friend,

performed over him the proper funeral rites, and buried him with all due honors in the side of the mountain. There he left him, sore at heart, but comforted by knowing that he had done all he could do to reconcile the shade of Pholos, and that his soul would bear him no grudge in Spirit Land.

Then Hercules went on his way in search of the Boar. He soon spied him in a dense thicket and chased him to the very top of the mountain. The mountaintop was covered with deep snow, which prevented the Boar from running fast enough to escape. So Hercules ran up to him, caught him in a net, threw him over his shoulder, and carried him off alive to Mykenas.

It is said that Eurystheus hid himself in a large brazen bowl when he heard Hercules approaching the city, and that Hercules threw the Boar into the same brazen bowl as the safest place in which to keep him. How astonished Eurystheus must have been to find himself in such terrible company! And we can fancy that he scrambled out with all possible haste.

The Fifth Labor: The Augeian Stables

We have already read about Elis, a plain in the southwestern part of Greece, where all the people used to worship Zeus and where they built a wonderful temple in his honor. They built a temple to Hera, his wife, also, and many other temples which were filled with statues. What a fine time you would have if you could only go and see this beautiful land. Perhaps you will some time.

The temples are in ruins now, and they cover enough ground for a small town. The huge blocks of marble lie on the ground just as they fell, and there are the marble floors as people used to see them two thousand years ago. There is a high hill close to the ruins. It is called the mountain of Kronos, 'Old Father Time'. Kronos is said to have been one of the early kings of Elis and he was the father of Zeus. He swallowed up his children when they were babes, if we care to believe what is said of him, and the story could easily be true, for Time swallows everything if he is only long enough about it.

The strong men and the boys used to come to Elis to have athletic games in honor of Zeus. They ran races, they boxed, they shot arrows, and did all sorts of things to show how strong they were. There are two rivers at the foot of Mount Kronos, and beyond the rivers are many low hills where people used to sit and watch the games.

There was at one time a king of Elis, Augeias, who was so rich in cattle that he hardly knew what to do with them and consequently he built a stable miles long and drove his cows into it. He did this year after year and the herds kept growing larger. He could not get men enough to take care of his stables and the cows could hardly get into them on account of the filth, or if they did get in they were never sure of getting out again because the dirt was piled so high.

Eurystheus thought he had found a disagreeable and impossible task for Hercules, and so he ordered him to clean out the stables in one day. Hercules told Augeias that he must clean the barns and promised to do it in one day if he would give him one tenth of all his cows. The king thought Hercules would never be able to do it in one day and readily promised him in the presence of his son one tenth of the cows.

The king's stables were close to the two rivers, near Mount Kronos. Hercules cut channels and sent the rivers running into the stables. They rushed along and carried the dirt out so quickly that the king was astonished. He did not intend to pay the promised reward and pretended that he never made any such promise.

And he said he would have the matter come before a court and the judges should decide it. Then Hercules called the little prince as a witness before the judges, and the boy told the truth about it, which caused the king to fall into such a rage that he sent both his son and Hercules out of the country. Hercules left the land of Elis and went back to

Mykenae. But his heart was filled with contempt for the faithless king.

The Sixth Labor: The Birds of Stymphalos

On the northern limit of Arcadia is a huge cliff, over which pours a black ribbon of water. At the bottom of the cliff it is lost among piles of rocks. The water itself is not black, but it appears so because the rock is covered with black moss, and so the stream is called the Styx or Black Water.

The Styx is icy cold and it runs along under the ground so that it seems to belong to the dead, and is called the River of Death. When the gods used to make a promise which they did not dare to break they said, "I promise by the Styx." This promise was called "the Great Oath of the Gods."

Farther on in the land of Arcadia there is a vale called Stymphalos. It lies among the mountains and is open to the storms of winter and the floods of spring. And there are a lake and a city both called Stymphalos. The people of Athens hope to carry the water of this lake to Athens by means of an underground channel. All about the lake are hills covered with firs and plane trees.

Lake Stymphalos was the home of a countless number of birds which held noisy meetings in the woods. They had iron claws and their feathers were sharper than arrows. They were so strong and fierce that they dared attack men, and would tear them to pieces that they might feast upon human flesh. They bore a striking resemblance to the Harpies, and were the terror of all the people who lived near Stymphalos.

Eurystheus ordered Hercules to drive the birds away. So Hercules took his bow and quiver and went to the lake. But the forests were so dense that he could not see the birds, and he sat down to think of the best way to drive them out. Suddenly the goddess of wisdom came to him to help him.

The goddess gave him a huge rattle and told him how to use it. Hercules went up on to the highest mountain that lies near the lake and shook the rattle with a will. The birds were so frightened by the noise that they came out of the thick wood where their nests were and flew high up into the air.

Their heavy feathers fell like flakes in a driving

snowstorm. Hercules shot at the birds with his arrows. He killed a great many of them and the rest were so scared that they flew away and were never seen again at Stym phalos.

The Seventh Labor: The Mad Bull of Crete

There is an island south of Greece which is so large that it would take you from early morning until late at night to sail past it. There are high mountains all along the shore and they look as if they were covered with snow. There is a cave in one of the mountains where Zeus was hidden when he was a babe so that his father, Kronos, should not swallow him. The nymphs fed him on honey and a famous goat gave him milk.

The name of this island was Crete, and Minos ruled there as king. It was his duty to sacrifice to Poseidon, the God of the Sea, whatever came up out of the water.

Minos was rich and greedy. He loved his cattle better than the will of the gods. It came to pass that a wonderful Bull rose from the sea while Minos was king. When Minos saw him he admired the beauty of the animal so much that he resolved to keep him. He drove the Bull into his barn and sacrificed another to the God of the Sea.

Poseidon grew angry with him and caused the Bull to become mad so that no one dared to approach him.

Eurystheus ordered Hercules to catch him and bring him to Mykenae.

So Hercules went to Crete and begged Minos to give him the Bull. The king told him that he was entirely welcome to the Bull if he could catch him. Hercules seized him by the horns and bound his feet together and carried him off to Mykenae.

There he showed the mad animal to Eurystheus and then set him free. The Bull wandered off to Sparta and over the hills of Arcadia, and crossing the Isthmus, he reached Marathon, where he left the land and swam off into the sea.

The Eighth Labor: The Horses of Diomedes

Greece was bounded on the north by a wild and mountainous land, called Thrace. The natives were not of Greek stock and remained fierce, lawless, and cruel for a long time after Greece had become the most civilized of countries. They were so quarrelsome and such desperate fighters that their country was supposed to be the favorite residence of the war god, Ares.

The king who reigned in Thrace at the time of Hercules was so much worse than the rest of the people that he was said to be Ares' own son, and he was called the storm king. He was very fond of horses and kept a breed of them after his own heart. They were man-eating horses, which he fed on the flesh of any strangers who came to that country or that were wrecked on the shore, thus breaking the most sacred laws and making himself hated by men and gods. The horses were bloodthirsty and so furious that they had to be chained to their stalls.

Eurystheus commanded Hercules to bring these horses to his stables in Mykenae. This time Hercules took several friends with him, who helped him catch the horses and lead them to the shore. Diomedes, having heard of the robbery, started in pursuit with many armed men.

Hercules and his friends went by sea. They attacked the guards and led the horses down to the ship. A terrible battle followed, in which the wicked king was slain by Hercules, who threw him as food to the horses. The warriors who helped Diomedes were put to flight and some of Hercules' best men were also killed. With the rest he drove the horses into his ship and brought them safely to Mykenae.

Eurystheus, of course, had no intention of keeping them in his stables and had them set loose. They ran off into the forests of Arcadia and were never seen again. It was thought that they were devoured by the mountain wolves.

The Ninth Labor: The Girdle of Hippolyte

Eurystheus, as we have seen, sent Hercules a little farther every time in hopes of never seeing him again. It would take you a whole day going on the best steamer to get to Crete from Athens, and in those days, when steamers had not been thought of, the sailing must have been slow indeed. Eurystheus now sent the hero yet farther off to the Black Sea, on the southern shore of which there lived the Amazons, a nation of warlike women.

The Amazons were brought up like men. Their main occupation was war, and they were excellent horsewomen. They were sharp-shooters with the bow and arrow. Hippolyte, the queen of the Amazons, was a brave and handsome woman. She wore a celebrated girdle, the gift of Ares, as a sign of her queenly rank.

Eurystheus had a daughter who had heard of the beauty of the famous girdle which was worn by the Amazon queen. She begged her father to send Hercules to bring it to her.

Then Eurystheus ordered Hercules to fetch the girdle, and he manned a ship and sailed away, taking several companions with him.

After many wanderings they reached the Black Sea and sailed to the Amazon country. Queen Hippolyte was at once informed that some strangers had arrived from a far-off land, and she came down to the shore to learn why they had come. Hercules told her that a princess had sent him to get the girdle given her by Ares. Hippolyte admired the bold hero for his frankness and promised that she would give it to him.

But Hera changed herself into an Amazon and rushing into the midst of an army of them cried out,

"The strangers are carrying off our queen!" Then all the Amazons snatched up their arms and rushed on horseback to the ship. When Hercules saw them coming armed to attack his men, he thought Hippolyte had betrayed him and he slew her and took her girdle.

Then he attacked the rest of the Amazons and put them to flight. When the battle was over, Hercules and his companions went on board the ship and sailed for home.

Soon after they had started on their way to Mykenas they found Hesione, the daughter of Laomedon, on the shore chained to a rock. Laomedon was at that time king of Troy, and Hercules and his companions stopped to find out why the daughter of a great king had to suffer such a terrible punishment. She told Hercules that Apollo, the sun god, and Poseidon, the God of the Sea, once took on the form of man and began to build walls around the city of Troy. Her father promised to aid them but neglected to keep his promise. This conduct made the gods indignant and Apollo sent a pestilence to rage in the city while Poseidon sent a sea-monster which came up out of the ocean and devoured the people.

Laomedon asked the priest of Apollo how he might appease the wrath of the gods. The priest answered that the city would be freed from the double plague if Laomedon would chain his daughter to the rock on the shore where the monster might devour her.

Laomedon obeyed the oracle and had her chained to the cliff near the sea. Just then Hercules arrived and stopped near the shore, when Laomedon with hot tears entreated him to save his daughter. Hercules promised to do it under the condition that Laomedon should give him as a reward a famous horse in his possession.

Hercules killed the sea-monster, but Laomedon again did not keep his promise and Hercules left Troy, his heart filled with scorn for the faithless king. On his return to Mykense he gave the girdle of the Amazon queen to his cousin, the daughter of Eurystheus.

The Tenth Labor: The Cattle of Geryon

Iberia, now called Spain, lies at the farthest end of Europe, and beyond it, in the Atlantic, is an island which was once the home of Geryon, a famous giant. His body was as large around as three other men's bodies put together. He had three heads and three pairs of legs and six arms. He had huge wings also and carried dangerous weapons.

Geryon was the lord of many herds of cattle. He had one herd of red oxen, as red as the sky at the setting of the sun, and they were guarded by a trusty herdsman and a fierce two-headed dog. Eurystheus ordered Hercules to bring the cattle to Mykenae.

Hercules, having overcome numberless difficulties wandering through wild deserts and unknown lands, finally reached the open ocean, the end of all. There he erected as a monument two pillars opposite each other, one on the African shore, and one in Europe. These were called the Pillars of Hercules in those days, but now they are known as the Rocks of Ceuta and Gibraltar.

Helios, the Sun, admiring the bravery of Hercules, lent him his golden skiff, shaped like a cup. Helios always sailed round the world every night from west to east in this cup, and Hercules, although he feared a storm, took his place in the strange boat and started for the island where Geryon tended his red cattle. The world, as the Greeks saw it, was in the form of a great plate, and the ocean was a river surrounding it as the rim surrounds the plate.

When the two-headed dog saw Hercules he rushed at him with fury, and the herdsman also attacked him at the same time. Hercules slew them both with his club, took the cattle, and fled toward the boat. Then Geryon sprang upon him and forced him to fight for his life. They had a dreadful battle, in which Hercules drew his bow and shot at the giant with one of his deadly arrows and Geryon died.

Hercules at once drove the oxen down to the boat, and after a safe voyage landed them in Iberia. Then he started for home on foot, driving his cattle northward over the Pyrenees into Gaul or France. Here he was attacked by hundreds of people who wanted to rob him of his cattle.

Hercules shot at them with his arrows and killed great numbers, and they stoned him in return with large stones. Hercules would have lost the battle but Zeus sent down a shower of rocks of vast size, and Hercules hurled them at his foes, driving them away like frightened sheep. These enormous rocks are still to be seen in the south of France.

After this adventure Hercules drove his cattle over the Alps and down into Italy across the Tiber, and they came to the Seven Hills of Rome. In one of these hills there was a cave, the home of a lawless giant named Cacus. He was a creature of iron strength, and was hideously ugly. He breathed out fire and smoke, often killing people in this way, and everybody in all the country about feared him. Cacus saw Hercules coming with his cattle over the river and among the hills, and he determined to steal the cattle and hide them in his den.

So when Hercules was asleep and the cattle were grazing quietly, Cacus slipped out of his cave and, seizing great numbers of them by the tails, dragged them backward into the cavern that their tracks might point away from the cave and not toward it. When Hercules awoke he missed his cattle and began to look for them. He found their tracks and went in the direction they seemed to point out, getting farther and farther from their place of hiding. The oxen bellowed, and their noises were muffled by the rocks of the cavern, but Hercules heard them and returned to the Seven Hills. Listening intently he traced them to the right hill, but Cacus had braced a stone slab against the opening and it could not be moved from the outside.

Hercules went around to the other side of the hill and, tearing the stones away, forced a new entrance. He sprang into the cave and seized the terrible monster by the throat. Cacus blew flames into the hero's face and tried to burn him to death, but Hercules held on and strangled the giant to death. A volume of black smoke came from his mouth and a stream of melted lead as he fell back dead. Hercules tore the slab from the door of the cave and threw the body of Cacus out on the hill, and all the people came to see it and rejoice that their foe was slain. And they built an altar to Hercules and instituted games to be held every year in his honor.

Hercules left the Seven Hills and drove his cattle southward. Being tired, he lay down to rest on a mountain near Locri, and the grasshoppers came around him singing in such shrill tones that he could not sleep. He prayed to the gods to drive them away, and the gods swept them out of that region so that they never came back.

One of the wild oxen ran away to the southwest and escaped to an island. Hercules followed, driving the whole herd over to the island. The cattle swam across, and Hercules, sitting on the back of one of the oxen and holding on by its horns, was safely taken over. He captured the runaway and wandered for a long time through the island, enjoying the fresh water of the springs and the kindness of the people. Then he drove his cattle back to Italy and passed up the shores of the Ionian Sea.

But Hera sent gadflies to make the cattle wilder than they were before, and they scattered over the mountain heights as clouds are scattered by a hot wind. They fled far to the east, until they came to Thrace. There Hercules gathered together as many as he could and brought them to Mykenae, where Eurystheus sacrificed them to Hera.

The Eleventh Labor:
The Golden Apples of Hesperides

When the wedding between Zeus and Hera was celebrated all the gods brought presents. Mother Earth brought some apple trees as her gift. These trees bore precious golden apples, and Zeus and Hera were so pleased with their wonderful wedding present that they appointed four maidens, called the Daughters of the West, to guard the apples, and also they placed a dragon there with a hundred heads, who never slept.

The fruit was so inviting that even the maidens would have been tempted to eat it if the terrible dragon had not kept close to the tree. A roar like thunder came out of each of his hundred mouths and frightened everything away that dared approach the trees, and lightning darted from his eyes to strike down intruders.

The trees grew more and more beautiful from year to

year, and the apples were so heavy that the boughs bent beneath the golden load. They grew in the Garden of the Hesperides, in islands way off to the west, and were watered by springs of nectar which had their rise near the throne of Zeus.

Eurystheus had heard of the apples and he ordered Hercules to bring them to him. For a long time Hercules wandered about in various lands until he came to the river Rhone, where the water-goddesses or nymphs advised him to ask counsel from the ancient lord of the deep sea, who knew all the secrets of the ocean depths and whose wisdom was beyond that of the gods. He is called by many names, but his gentlest name is Nereus, and he does not like to be questioned unless he can take any shape he pleases.

He usually escapes intruders, but to those who are not afraid and who manage to grasp and to hold him, he freely opens the store of his wisdom. This was what Hercules did. Nereus took on the form of a lion, a serpent, a fish, a stream of water, and at last, of an old man, but Hercules held him close and learned from him the road to the Garden of the Hesperides.

Leaving Nereus, Hercules traveled south into Africa, where he met Antseos, a huge giant who lived in the desert. Antseos was a son of Earth and Ocean, and he was as strong as the terrible sandstorms. He was cruel to all travelers who crossed his domains and slew them, but he loved and protected the tiny Pygmies that lived all around him. No one had ever been able to vanquish him in battle, for Mother Earth gave him new strength and vigor every time he lay down or touched the ground.

Hercules wrestled with him and threw him down many times, but Antseos sprang up stronger than ever. At last Hercules caught him up with one hand, and holding him high in the air where he could not receive help from Mother Earth, squeezed him to death.

Hercules was tired out with this tremendous exertion and lay down in the desert to rest. But he did not sleep long, for a whole army of the little people, seeing their beloved giant lying dead, came with their weapons to attack Hercules. He found himself covered with them from head to foot. He sprang up, and quickly gathering up his lion's skin, crushed a multitude of the Pygmies and killed them.

Then he hurried away toward the east, going through many countries, until he came to India, and finding himself traveling in the wrong direction, turned to the north and west and came to the Caucasus Mountains.
Here he found Prometheus chained to the rocks of a high mountain-peak. Prometheus had taught mankind the use of fire and how to build houses and had otherwise interfered with the work of the gods, thereby bringing this

punishment upon himself. Hercules took pity on him and set him free. In return for this kindly act Prometheus told him the most direct way to the Garden of the Hesperides, which was through Scythia and the region of the Hyperboreans at the back of the North Wind.

On his way Hercules stopped to visit Atlas, who as a punishment for once having rebelled against the gods was obliged to carry the heavens on his shoulders.

"Let me relieve thee for awhile, friend Atlas," said Hercules, after greeting him in a most cordial manner.

"Let me take the heavens on my shoulders and I will let thee do me a great service in return. I must have the Golden Apples that grow in the Garden of the Hesperides to take to Eurystheus, and thou canst bring them to me."

Atlas gladly placed the heavy firmament on Hercules' shoulders and took his way to the Garden. There he contrived to put the many-headed dragon to sleep and then slay him. Taking possession of the Golden Apples, he returned with them to Hercules.

"I thank thee very much, friend Atlas," said Hercules. "Take thy place again and give me the apples."

"Nay, I have borne the weight of the heavens for a long time," answered Atlas. "Thou hadst better keep my place and I will carry the Golden Apples to Eurystheus."

Hercules was taken aback at this reply and began to

consider how he might escape from this unexpected dilemma. At last he spoke.

"Very well, I will willingly remain in thy place, friend Atlas," he said. "One thing only I must first ask of thee. Take the heavens back just for a moment while I get a pad to put on my head so that the weight may not hurt it. Otherwise the heavens will fall and crush us both."

Poor, simple old Atlas agreed to this, and putting the Golden Apples on the ground he again took the firmament on his shoulders. Hercules picked up the apples and went off saying,

"We must not bear malice toward each other, friend Atlas. Good-bye."

With this he departed and hastened back to Mykenae.

The Twelfth Labor: Hercules fetches Cerberus out of Hades

According to the terms of the doom that was laid upon Hercules, the performance of the last task was to free him from Eurystheus. Eleven were now fulfilled and the tyrant's heart failed him when he thought of what he might expect at the hands of the hero he had used so ill when once he was free from his power.

Cowards always fear those whom they have ill-treated,

so he determined to send Hercules on an errand from which he thought he could not possibly return. He had come back unharmed from every known and unknown country on the face of the earth, but who was ever known to return alive from the land of the dead? So Eurystheus as a last task ordered him to go down to Hades and bring out alive Cerberus, the three-headed dog that guards the entrance to the lower world, feeling sure that Hercules would remain forever in Hades.

Cerberus was a terrible monster. Besides having three heads, he had a tail which ended in a serpent's head, and all along his spine he had serpents' heads instead of hair. His duty was to see that no dead should escape from Hades after once entering its gates.

There was a long, dark cave leading down to Hades and the river Styx flowed across it. A white-haired old ferryman, Charon by name, waited with his boat on the shore to carry the spirits of all who died. There they were met by Minos, the great judge, who told them whether they could go into the fields of the Blessed or whether they were doomed to the region of the Unhappy. Charon's boat was but a delicate skiff and adapted only to carrying souls without bodies, so Hercules was not a welcome passenger.

Hercules found his way into Hades in spite of all the difficulties, and presenting himself to Pluto, the King of the

Dead, begged him to give him the Dog.

Pluto replied:

"Take him and lead him out into the world and thou shalt have him. But thou must not use any weapon."

Hercules answered,

"I will use no weapon but my hands, and with them alone I will conquer him."

Wearing his breastplate and clad in the lion's skin he approached Cerberus, who stood on guard at the gates. He threw his arms around the Dog's three heads and pressed them with all his might. The Dog fought with great fury, and bit him with the snake's mouth which he had at the end of his tail. Hercules threw his lion's skin over the head of the Dog and dragged him out by another gate into the daylight. Cerberus had never seen the light of the sun and was frightened beyond measure. He foamed at the mouth, and wherever the foam fell upon the ground it caused a poisonous plant to grow.

Hercules took Cerberus to Eurystheus, who was not pleased to see the Dog or the hero. Then he carried him back to Hades and restored him to Pluto, and so were the twelve great labors ended.

The Horse and the Olive

By James Baldwin

ON a steep stony hill in Greece there lived in early times a few very poor people who had not yet learned to build houses. They made their homes in little caves, which they dug in the earth or hollowed out among the rocks; and their food was the flesh of wild animals, which they hunted in the woods, with now and then a few berries or nuts. They did not even know how to make bows and arrows, but used slings and clubs and sharp sticks for weapons; and the little clothing they had was made of skins.

They lived on the top of the hill, because they were safe there from the savage beasts of the great forest around them, and safe also from the wild men who sometimes roamed through the land. The hill was so steep on every side that there was no way of climbing it save by a single narrow footpath which was always guarded by someone at the top.

One day when the men were hunting in the woods, they found a strange youth whose face was so fair and who was dressed so beautifully that they could hardly believe him to be a man like themselves. His body was so slender and lithe, and he moved so nimbly among the trees, that they fancied him to be a serpent in the guise of a human being; and they stood still in wonder and alarm. The young man spoke to them, but they could not understand a word that he said; then he made signs to them that he was hungry, and they gave him something to eat, and were no longer afraid. Had they been like the wild men of the woods, they might have killed him at once.

But they wanted their women and children to see the serpent man, as they called him, and hear him talk; and so they took him home with them to the top of the hill. They thought that after they had made a show of him for a few days, they would kill him and offer his body as a sacrifice to the unknown being whom they dimly fancied to have some sort of control over their lives.

But the young man was so fair and gentle that, after they had all taken a look at him, they began to think it would be a great pity to harm him. So they gave him food and treated him kindly; and he sang songs to them and played with their children, and made them happier than they had been for many a day. In a short time he learned to talk in their language; and he told them that his name was Cecrops, and that he had been shipwrecked on the seacoast not far away; and then he told them many strange things about the land from which he had come and to which he would never be able to return. The poor people listened and wondered; and it was not long until they began to love him and to look up to him as one wiser than themselves. Then they came to ask him about everything that was to be done, and there was not one of them who refused to do his bidding.

So Cecrops—the serpent man, as they still called him—became the king of the poor people on the hill. He taught them how to make bows and arrows, and how to set nets for birds, and how to take fish with hooks. He led them against the savage wild men of the woods, and helped them kill the fierce beasts that had been so great a terror to them. He showed them how to build houses of wood and to thatch them with the reeds which grew in the marshes. He taught them how to live in families instead of herding together like senseless beasts as they had always done before. And he told them about great Jupiter and the Mighty Folk who lived amid the clouds on the mountaintop.

By and by, instead of the wretched caves among the rocks, there was a little town on the top of the hill, with neat houses and a market place; and around it was a strong wall with a single narrow gate just where the footpath began to descend to the plain. But as yet the place had no name.

One morning while the king and his wise men were sitting together in the market place and planning how to make the town become a rich, strong city, two strangers were seen in the street. Nobody could tell how they came there. The guard at the gate had not seen them; and no man had ever dared to climb the narrow footway without his leave. But there the two strangers stood. One was a man, the other a woman; and they were so tall, and their faces were so grand and noble, that those who saw them stood still and wondered and said not a word.

The man had a robe of purple and green wrapped round his body, and he bore in one hand a strong staff with three sharp spear points at one end. The woman was not beautiful, but she had wonderful gray eyes; and in one hand she carried a spear and in the other a shield of curious workmanship.

"What is the name of this town?" asked the man.

The people stared at him in wonder, and hardly understood his meaning. Then an old man answered and said, "It has no name. We who live on this hill used to be called Cranæ; but since King Cecrops came, we have been so busy that we have had no time to think of names."

"Where is this King Cecrops?" asked the woman.

"He is in the market place with the wise men," was the answer.

"Lead us to him at once," said the man.

When Cecrops saw the two strangers coming into the market place, he stood up and waited for them to speak. The man spoke first: "I am Neptune," said he, "and I rule the sea."

"And I am Athena," said the woman, "and I give wisdom to men."

"I hear that you are planning to make your town become a great city," said Neptune, "and I have come to help you. Give my name to the place, and let me be your protector and patron, and the wealth of the whole world shall be yours. Ships from every land shall bring you merchandise and gold and silver; and you shall be the masters of the sea."

"My uncle makes you fair promises," said Athena; "but listen to me. Give my name to your city, and let me be your patron, and I will give you that which gold cannot buy: I will teach you how to do a thousand things of which you now know nothing. I will make your city my favorite home, and I will give you wisdom that shall sway the minds and hearts of all men until the end of time."

The king bowed, and turned to the people, who had all crowded into the market place.

"Which of these mighty ones shall we elect to be the protector and patron of our city?" he asked. "Neptune offers us wealth; Athena promises us wisdom. Which shall we choose?"

"Neptune and wealth!" cried many.

"Athena and wisdom!" cried as many others.

At last when it was plain that the people could not agree, an old man whose advice was always heeded stood up and said: "These mighty ones have only given us promises, and they have promised things of which we are ignorant. For who among us knows what wealth is or what wisdom is? Now, if they would only give us some real gift, right now and right here, which we can see and handle, we should know better how to choose."

"That is true! That is true!" cried the people.

"Very well, then," said the strangers, "we will each give you a gift, right now and right here, and then you may choose between us."

Neptune gave the first gift. He stood on the highest point of the hill where the rock was bare, and bade the people see his power. He raised his three-pointed spear high in the air, and then brought it down with great force. Lightning flashed, the earth shook, and the rock was split halfway down to the bottom of the hill. Then out of the yawning crevice there sprang a wonderful creature, white as milk, with long slender legs, an arching neck, and a mane and tail of silk.

The people had never seen anything like it before, and they thought it a new kind of bear or wolf or wild boar that had come out of the rock to devour them.

Some of them ran and hid in their houses, while others climbed upon the wall, and still others grasped their weapons in alarm. But when they saw the creature stand quietly by the side of Neptune, they lost their fear and came closer to see and admire its beauty.

"This is my gift," said Neptune. "This animal will carry your burdens for you; he will draw your chariots; he will pull your wagons and your plows; he will let you sit on his back and will run with you faster than the wind."

"What is his name?" asked the king.

"His name is Horse," answered Neptune.

Then Athena came forward. She stood a moment on a green grassy plot where the children of the town liked to play in the evening. Then she drove the point of her spear deep down in the soil. At once the air was filled with music, and out of the earth there sprang a tree with slender branches and dark green leaves and white flowers and violet green fruit.

"This is my gift," said Athena. "This tree will give you food when you are hungry; it will shelter you from the sun when you are faint; it will beautify your city; and the oil from its fruit will be sought by all the world."

"What is it called?" asked the king.

"It is called Olive," answered Athena.

Then the king and his wise men began to talk about the two gifts.

"I do not see that Horse will be of much use to us," said the old man who had spoken before. "For, as to the chariots and wagons and plows, we have none of them, and indeed do not know what they are; and who among us will ever want to sit on this creature's back and be borne faster than the wind? But Olive will be a thing of beauty and a joy for us and our children forever."

"Which shall we choose?" asked the king, turning to the people.

"Athena has given us the best gift," they all cried, "and we choose Athena and wisdom!"

"Be it so," said the king, "and the name of our city shall be Athens."

From that day the town grew and spread, and soon there was not room on the hilltop for all the people. Then houses were built in the plain around the foot of the hill, and a great road was built to the sea, three miles away; and in all the world there was no city more fair than Athens.

In the old market place on the top of the hill the people built a temple to Athena, the ruins of which may still be seen. The olive tree grew and flourished; and, when you visit Athens, people will show you the very spot where it stood. Many other trees sprang from it, and in time became a blessing both to Greece and to all the other countries round the great sea. As for the horse, he wandered away across the plains toward the north and found a home at last in distant Thessaly beyond the River Peneus. And I have heard it said that all the horses in the world have descended from that one which Neptune brought out of the rock; but of the truth of this story there may be some doubts.

The Story of Arachne

By James Baldwin

THERE was a young girl in Greece whose name was Arachne. Her face was pale but fair, and her eyes were big and blue, and her hair was long and like gold. All that she cared to do from morn till noon was to sit in the sun and spin; and all that she cared to do from noon till night was to sit in the shade and weave.

And oh, how fine and fair were the things which she wove in her loom! Flax, wool, silk—she worked with them all; and when they came from her hands, the cloth which she had made of them was so thin and soft and bright that men came from all parts of the world to see it. And they said that cloth so rare could not be made of flax, or wool, or silk, but that the warp was of rays of sunlight and the woof was of threads of gold.

Then as, day by day, the girl sat in the sun and span, or sat in the shade and wove, she said: "In all the world there is no yarn so fine as mine, and in all the world there is no cloth so soft and smooth, nor silk so bright and rare."

"Who taught you to spin and weave so well?" someone asked.

"No one taught me," she said. "I learned how to do it as I sat in the sun and the shade; but no one showed me."

"But it may be that Athena, the queen of the air, taught you, and you did not know it."

"Athena, the queen of the air? Bah!" said Arachne. "How could she teach me? Can she spin such skeins of yarn as these? Can she weave goods like mine? I should like to see her try. I can teach her a thing or two."

She looked up and saw in the doorway a tall woman wrapped in a long cloak. Her face was fair to see, but stern, oh, so stern! And her gray eyes were so sharp and bright that Arachne could not meet her gaze.

"Arachne," said the woman, "I am Athena, the queen of the air, and I have heard your boast. Do you still mean to say that I have not taught you how to spin and weave?"

"No one has taught me," said Arachne; "and I thank no one for what I know;" and she stood up, straight and proud, by the side of her loom.

"And do you still think that you can spin and weave as well as I?" said Athena.

Arachne's cheeks grew pale, but she said: "Yes. I can weave as well as you."

"Then let me tell you what we will do," said Athena. "Three days from now we will both weave; you on your loom, and I on mine. We will ask all the world to come and see us; and great Jupiter, who sits in the clouds, shall be the judge. And if your work is best, then I will weave no more so long as the world shall last; but if my work is best, then you shall never use loom or spindle or distaff again. Do you agree to this?"

"I agree," said Arachne.

"It is well," said Athena. And she was gone.

When the time came for the contest in weaving, all the world was there to see it, and great Jupiter sat among the clouds and looked on.

Arachne had set up her loom in the shade of a mulberry tree, where butterflies were flitting and grasshoppers chirping all through the livelong day. But Athena had set up her loom in the sky, where the breezes were blowing and the summer sun was shining; for she was the queen of the air.

Then Arachne took her skeins of finest silk and began to weave. And she wove a web of marvelous beauty, so thin and light that it would float in the air, and yet so strong that

it could hold a lion in its meshes;
and the threads of warp and
woof were of many colors, so
beautifully arranged and
mingled one with another that all
who saw were filled with delight.

"No wonder that the maiden
boasted of her skill," said the people.

And Jupiter himself nodded.

Then Athena began to weave. And
she took of the sunbeams that gilded the
mountaintop, and of the snowy fleece of
the summer clouds, and of the blue ether
of the summer sky, and of the bright green
of the summer fields, and of the royal purple
of the fall woods—and what do you suppose
she wove?

The web which she wove in the sky
was full of enchanting pictures
of flowers and gardens, and of castles
and towers, and of mountain heights,
and of men and beasts, and of giants
and dwarfs, and of the mighty beings who
dwell in the clouds with Jupiter. And those who looked
upon it were so filled with wonder and delight, that they

forgot all about the beautiful web which Arachne had woven. And Arachne herself was ashamed and afraid when she saw it; and she hid her face in her hands and wept.

"Oh, how can I live," she cried, "now that I must never again use loom or spindle or distaff?"

And she kept on, weeping and weeping and weeping, and saying, "How can I live?"

Then, when Athena saw that the poor maiden would never have any joy unless she were allowed to spin and weave, she took pity on her and said:

"I would free you from your bargain if I could, but that is a thing which no one can do. You must hold to your agreement never to touch loom or spindle again. And yet, since you will never be happy unless you can spin and weave, I will give you a new form so that you can carry on your work with neither spindle nor loom."

Then she touched Arachne with the tip of the spear which she sometimes carried; and the maiden was changed at once into a nimble spider, which ran into a shady place in the grass and began merrily to spin and weave a beautiful web.

I have heard it said that all the spiders which have been in the world since then are the children of Arachne; but I doubt whether this be true. Yet, for aught I know, Arachne still lives and spins and weaves; and the very next spider that you see may be she herself.

Bellerophon and Pegasus

By James Baldwin

PEOPLE said that the gods sent him to the earth. Of course it was very desirable to account in some way for the appearance of so wonderful a creature, and there was no easier way to do it. But to this day nobody knows anything about his origin. When first seen he was simply a beautiful horse with wings like a great bird's, and he could travel with equal ease in the air and on the ground.

A good many years ago—so many that we shall not bother about the date—this wonderful animal, after a long and wearisome flight above the clouds, alighted at a pleasant spot near the foot of Mount Helicon, in Boeotia. He was hot and thirsty, and having seen some reeds growing at that spot, he hoped that he would find there a stream of water, or at least a small pool, from which he could drink. But to his disappointment there wasn't a drop of water to be seen—nothing but a little patch of boggy ground where the tall grass grew rank and thick. In his anger he spread his wings and gave the earth a tremendous kick with both of his hind feet together. The ground was soft, and the force of the blow was such that a long, deep trench was opened in the boggy soil. Instantly a stream of water, cool and sweet and clear, poured out and filled the trench and ran as a swift brook across the plain toward the distant river. The horse drank his fill from the pleasant fountain which he himself had thus hollowed out; and then, greatly refreshed, unfolded his wings again and rose high in the air, ready for a flight across the sea to the distant land of Lycia.

Men were not long in finding out that the waters of the new spring at the foot of Mount Helicon had some strange properties, filling their hearts with a wonderful sense of whatever is beautiful and true and good, and putting music into their souls, and new songs into their mouths. And so they called the spring Hippocrene, or the Fountain of the Horse, and poets from all parts of the world went there to drink. But in later times the place fell into neglect, for, somehow, people were so busy with other things that they forgot the difference between poetry and doggerel, and nobody cared to drink from Hippocrene. And so the fountain was allowed to become choked with the stones and dirt that rolled down from the mountain; and soon wild grass and tall reeds hid the spot from view, and nobody from that day to this has been able to point out just where it is. But the horse?

We left him poised high in the air, with his head turned toward the sea and the distant land of Lycia. I do not know how long it took him to fly across, nor does it matter; but one day, full of vigor and strength, and beautiful as a poet's dream, he alighted on the great road that runs eastward a little way from the capital city of Lycia. So softly had he descended, and so quietly had he folded his great wings and set his feet upon the ground, that a young man who was walking thoughtfully along the way did not know of his presence until he had cantered up quite close to him.

The young man stopped and turned to admire the beautiful animal, and when he came quite near reached out his hand to stroke his nose. But the horse wheeled about and was away again as quick as an arrow sent speeding from a bow. The young man walked on again, and the horse soon returned and gamboled playfully around him, sometimes trotting swiftly back and forth along the roadway, sometimes rising in the

air and sailing in circles round and round him. At last, after much whistling and the offer of a handful of sweetmeats, the young man coaxed the horse so near to him that by a sudden leap he was able to throw himself astride of his back just in front of his great
gray wings.

"Now, my handsome
fellow," he cried, "carry me straight
forward to the country that lies beyond the
great northern mountains. I would not be afraid of
all the wild beasts in Asia if I could be sure of your help."
But the horse did not seem to understand him. He
flew first to the north, then to the south, then to the

north again, and sailed hither and thither gaily among the white clouds. At the end of an hour he alighted at the very spot from which he had risen, and his rider, despairing of making any progress with him, leaped to the ground and renewed his journey on foot. But the horse, who seemed to have taken a great liking to the young man, followed him, frisking hither and thither like a frolicsome dog, not afraid of him in the least, but very timid of all other travelers on the road. Late in the afternoon, when they had left the pleasant farmlands of Lycia behind them and had come to the border of a wild, deserted region, an old man, with a long white beard and bright glittering eyes, met them and stopped, as many others had already done, to admire the beautiful animal.

"Who are you, young man," he inquired, "and what are you doing with so handsome a steed here in this lonely place?"

"My name is Bellerophon," answered the young man, "and I am going by order of King Iobates to the country beyond the northern mountains, where I expect to slay the Chimaera, which lives there. But as for this horse, all I know is that he has followed me since early morning. Whose he is and from whence he came I cannot tell."

The old man was silent for a few moments as if in deep thought, while Bellerophon, very weary with his long walk, sat down on a stone to rest, and the horse strolled along by the roadside nipping the short grass.

"Do you see the white roof over there among the trees?" finally asked the old man. "Well, under it there is a shrine to the goddess Athena, of which I am the keeper. A few steps beyond it is my own humble cottage, where I spend my days in study and meditation. If you will go in and lodge with me for the night, I may be able to tell you something about the task that you have undertaken."

Bellerophon was very glad to accept the old man's invitation, for the sun had already begun to dip below the western hills. The hut contained only two rooms, but everything about it was very clean and cozy, and the kind host spared no pains to make his guest comfortable and happy. After they had eaten supper and were still reclining on couches at the side of the table, the old man looked Bellerophon sharply in the face and said: "Now tell me all about yourself and your kindred, and why you are going thus alone and on foot into the country of the Chimaera."

"My father," answered Bellerophon, "is Glaucus, the king of far-off Corinth, where he has great wealth in horses and in ships; and my grandfather was Sisyphus, of whom you have doubtless heard, for he was famed all over the world for his craftiness and his fine business qualities, that made him the richest of men. I was brought up in my father's house, and it was intended that I should succeed him as king of Corinth; but three years ago a sad misfortune happened to me. My younger brother and I were hunting among the wooded hills of Argos, and we were having fine sport, for we had taken much game. We had started home with our booty, and I, who was the faster walker, was some distance ahead of my brother, when, suddenly, a deer sprang up between me and the sun. Half-blinded by the light, I turned and let fly an arrow quickly. The creature bounded swiftly away, unhurt, but a cry of anguish from the low underbrush told me that I had slain my brother.

"Vainly did I try to stanch the flow of blood; vainly did I call upon the gods to save him and me. He raised his eyes to mine, smiled feebly, pressed my hand as in forgiveness, and was no more.

"I knew that I dared not return home, for the laws of our country are very severe against anyone who, though by accident, causes the death of another. Indeed, until I could be purified from my brother's blood, I dared not, as you know, look any man in the face. For a long time I wandered hither and thither, like a hunted beast, shunning the sight of every human being, and living upon nuts and fruits and such small game as I could bring down with my arrows. At length I bethought me that perhaps old King Proteus of Tiryns, in whose land I then was, might purify me; or if not, he might at least slay me at the altar, which would be better than living longer as a fugitive; and so, under the cover of night, I went down into Tiryns, and entering the temple with my cloak thrown over my head, knelt down at the shrine where penitent men are wont to seek purification.

"I need not tell you how the king found me and purified me and took me into his own house and treated me for a long time as his own son; it would make my story too long … But a few weeks ago I noticed that a great change had come over him, for he no longer showed me the kind attention which I had learned to expect of him. The queen, too, seemed to have become my enemy, and treated me with the haughtiest disdain. Indeed, I began to suspect that she was urging her husband to put me out of the way, and I should not have been surprised if he had banished me from his court. I was, of course, uncomfortable, and was trying to think of some excuse for leaving Tiryns, when the king, very early one morning, called me into his private chamber. He held in his hand a wooden tablet, sealed with his own signet, and he seemed to be greatly excited about something. 'Bellerophon,' he said, 'I have written on this tablet a letter of very great importance, which I wish to send to my father-in-law, King Iobates, of Lycia, beyond the sea. You are the only man whom I can trust to carry this letter, and so I beg that you will get ready to go at once. A ship is in the harbor already manned for the voyage, and the wind is fair. Before the sun rises you may be well out at sea.'

"I took the tablet and embarked, as he wished, without so much as bidding good-bye to any of his household. A good ship and fresh breezes carried me over the sea to Lycia, where I was welcomed most kindly by your good king Iobates. For he had known both my father and my grandfather, and he said that he owed me honor for their sakes. Nine days he held a great feast in his palace, and all the most famous philosophers, merchants, and warriors were invited to his table, in order that I might meet them and hear them talk.

"I had not forgotten the tablet that King Proteus had given me, and several times I had made a start to give it to Iobates; but I knew that it would be bad taste to speak of business at such a time. On the tenth day, however, after all the guests had gone home, he said to me: 'Now tell me what message you have brought from my son-in-law Proteus and my dear daughter Anteia. For I know that they have sent me some word.'

"Then I gave him the tablet. He untied the ribbon which bound the two blocks of wood together, and when he had broken the seal he lifted them apart and read that which was engraved on the wax between them. I do not know what this message was, but it must have been something of great importance, for the king's face grew very pale, and he staggered as if he would fall. Then he left the room very quickly, and I did not see him again until this morning, when he called me into his council-chamber. I was surprised to notice how haggard and worn he was, and how very old he seemed to have become within the past three days.

"'Young man,' he said, speaking rather sharply, I thought, 'Young man, they tell me that you are brave and fond of hunting wild beasts, and that you are anxious to win fame by doing some daring deed. I have word, only this morning, that the people who live on the other side of the northern mountains are in great dread of a strange animal that comes out of the caves and destroys their flocks, and sometimes carries their children off to its lair. Some say it is a lion, some a dragon, and some laugh at the whole affair and call it a goat. I think myself that it must be the very same beast that infested the mountain valleys some years ago, and was called by our wise men a Chimaera; and for the sake of the good people whom it annoys, I should like to have it killed. Everyone to whom I have spoken about it, however, is afraid to venture into its haunts.'

"'I am not afraid,' said I. 'I will start to the mountains this very hour, and if I don't bring you the head of the Chimaera to hang up in your halls, you may brand me as a coward.'

"'You are a brave young man,' said the king, 'and I will take you at your word, but I would advise you to lose no time in starting.'

"I was surprised at the way in which the king dismissed me, and the longer I thought about the matter the stranger it all seemed. But there was only one thing to do. I walked out of the king's palace, found the shortest road to Mount Climax, and—here I am!"

"Do you have any idea what it was that King Proteus wrote to King Iobates?" asked the old man.

"Why should I?"

"Then I will tell you. He wrote to say that you had been accused of treasonable crimes in Tiryns, and that, not wishing to harm you himself, he had sent you to Lycia to be put to death. King Iobates was loath to have this done, and so he has sent you out against the Chimaera, knowing that no man ever fought with that monster and lived. For she is a more terrible beast than you would believe. All the region beyond the mountains has been laid waste by her, hundreds of people have been slain by her fiery breath alone, and a whole army that was lately sent out against her was routed and put to flight. The king knows very well that she will kill you."

"But what kind of a beast is this Chimaera?" asked Bellerophon.

"She is a strange kind of monster," was the answer. "Her head and shoulders are those of a lion, her body is that of a goat, and her hinder parts are those of a dragon. She fights with her hot breath and her long tail, and she stays on the mountains by night, and goes down into the valleys by day."

"If I had only a shield, and my bow and arrows, and could ride the good winged horse whithersoever I wished him to go, I would not be afraid of all the Chimaeras in the world," said Bellerophon.

"Let me tell you something," said the old man. "Go out to the little temple in the grove before us and lie down to sleep at the foot of the shrine. Everybody knows that to people who are in need of help Athena often comes in dreams to give good advice. Perhaps she will favor you with her counsel and aid, if you only show that you have faith in her."

Bellerophon went at once to the little temple and stretched himself out on the floor close to the shrine of the goddess. The winged horse, who had been feeding on the grass, followed him to the door, and then lay down on the ground outside.

It was nearly morning when Bellerophon dreamed that a tall and stately lady, with large round eyes, and long hair that fell in ringlets upon her shoulders, came into the temple and stood beside him.

"Do you know who the winged steed is that waits outside the door for you?" she asked.

"Truly, I do not," answered Bellerophon. "But if I had some means of making him understand me, he might be my best friend and helper."

"His name is Pegasus," said the lady, "and he was born near the shore of the great western ocean. He has come to help you in your fight with the Chimaera, and you can guide him anywhere you wish if you will only put this ribbon into his mouth, holding on to the ends yourself."

With these words, she placed a beautiful bridle in Bellerophon's hands, and, turning about, walked silently away.

When the sun had risen and Bellerophon awoke, the bridle was lying on the floor beside him, and near it were a long bow with arrows and a shield. It was the first bridle that he had ever seen—some people say that it was the first that was ever made—and the young man examined it with great curiosity. Then he went out and quickly slipped the ribbon bit into the mouth of Pegasus, and leaped upon his back. To his great joy, he saw that now the horse understood all his wishes.

"Here are your bow and arrows and your shield," cried the old man, handing them to him. "Take them, and may Athena be with you in your fight with the Chimaera!"

At a word from Bellerophon, Pegasus rose high in the air, and then, turning, made straight northward toward the great mountains. It was evening when they reached Mount Climax, and quite dark when they at last hovered over the spot which the Chimaera was said to visit at night. Bellerophon would have passed on without seeing her, had not a burning mountain sent out a great sheet of flame that lighted up the valleys and gave him a plain view of the monster crouching in the shadow of a cliff. He fitted an arrow quickly in his bow and, as Pegasus paused above the edge of the cliff, he let fly directly at her fearful head. The arrow missed the mark, however, and struck the beast in the throat, giving her an ugly wound. Then you should have seen the fury of the Chimaera, how she reared herself on her hind feet; how she leaped into the air; how she beat the rocks with her long dragon's tail; how she puffed and fumed and roared and blew her fiery breath toward Pegasus, hoping to scorch his wings or smother both horse and rider with its poisonous fumes. Bellerophon, when he saw her in her mad rage, could no longer wonder that the whole country had been in terror of her.

"Now, my good Pegasus," he said, stroking the horse's mane, "steady yourself just out of her reach, and let me send her another keepsake!"

This time the arrow struck the beast in the back, and instead of killing her, only made her more furious than ever. She attacked everything that was in her reach, clawed the rocks, knocked trees down with her tail, and filled all the mountain-valleys with the noise of her mad roarings. The third arrow, however, was sent with a better aim, and the horrid creature, pierced to the heart, fell backward lifeless, and rolled over and over down the steep mountain side, and far out into the valley below.

Bellerophon slept on the mountain that night, while his steed kept watch by his side. In the morning he went down and found the Chimaera lying stiff and dead in the spot where she had rolled, while a score of gaping countrymen stood around at a safe distance, rejoicing that the monster which had laid waste their fields

and desolated their homes had at last
been slain. Bellerophon cut off the
creature's head, and remounting
Pegasus, set out on his
return to King Iobates.
Of course old
Iobates was astonished to see
Bellerophon come back with
the monster's head in his
arms. All that he did was
to thank the young hero
for the great service which he had
done for his country; and then he
began to study up some other means of
putting him out of the way.

At length, Bellerophon bethought him that,
since this world was beset with so many distressing
things, worse even than Chimaeras, he would leave it and
ride on the back of Pegasus to Heaven. There is no knowing
what he might have done, had not Zeus, just in the nick of
time, sent a gadfly to sting the horse. Pegasus made a wild
plunge to escape the fly, and Bellerophon, taken by surprise,
was tumbled to the earth. Strange to say, the hero was not
killed, but only blinded by his fall; and he never heard of
Pegasus again.

The Elephant's Child

From *Just So Stories*
By Rudyard Kipling

IN the high and far-off times, the Elephant, Oh Best Beloved, had no trunk. He had only a blackish, bulgy nose, as big as a boot, that he could wriggle about from side to side; but he couldn't pick up things with it. But there was one Elephant—a new Elephant—an Elephant's Child— who was full of 'satiable curtiosity, and that means he asked ever so many questions. And he lived in Africa, and he filled all Africa with his 'satiable curtiosities. He asked his tall aunt, the Ostrich, why her tail feathers grew just so, and his tall aunt the Ostrich spanked him with her hard, hard claw.

He asked his broad aunt, the Hippopotamus, why her eyes were red, and his broad aunt, the Hippopotamus, spanked him with her broad, broad hoof; and he asked his hairy uncle, the Baboon, why melons tasted just so, and his hairy uncle, the Baboon, spanked him with his hairy, hairy paw. And still he was full of 'satiable curtiosity! He asked questions about everything that he saw, or heard, or felt, or smelt, or touched, and all his uncles and his aunts spanked him. And still he was full of 'satiable curtiosity!

One fine morning in the middle of the Precession of the Equinoxes this 'satiable Elephant's Child asked a new fine question that he had never asked before. He asked, "What does the Crocodile have for dinner?"

Then everybody said, "Hush!" in a loud and dreadful tone, and they spanked him immediately and directly, without stopping, for a long time.

By and by, when that was finished, he came upon Kolokolo Bird sitting in the middle of a wait-a-bit thorn-bush, and he said, "My father has spanked me, and my mother has spanked me; all my aunts and uncles have spanked me for my 'satiable curtiosity; and still I want to know what the Crocodile has for dinner!"

Then Kolokolo Bird said, with a mournful cry, "Go to the banks of the great gray-green, greasy Limpopo River, all set about with fever-trees, and find out."

That very next morning, when there was nothing left of the Equinoxes, because the Precession had preceded according to precedent, this 'satiable Elephant's Child took a hundred pounds of bananas (the little short red kind), and a hundred pounds of sugar-cane (the long purple kind), and seventeen melons (the greeny-crackly kind), and said to all his dear families, "Goodbye. I am going to the great gray-green, greasy Limpopo River, all set about with fever-trees, to find out what the Crocodile has for dinner." And they all spanked him once more for luck, though he asked them most politely to stop.

Then he went away, a little warm, but not at all astonished, eating melons, and throwing the rind about, because he could not pick it up.

He went from Graham's Town to Kimberley, and from Kimberley to Khama's Country, and from Khama's Country he went east by north, eating melons all the time, till at last he came to the banks of the great gray-green, greasy Limpopo River, all set about with fever-trees, precisely as Kolokolo Bird had said.

Now you must know and understand, Oh Best Beloved, that till that very week, and day, and hour, and minute, this 'satiable Elephant's Child had never seen a Crocodile, and did not know what one was like. It was all his 'satiable curtiosity.

The first thing that he found was a Bi-Colored-Python-Rock-Snake curled round a rock.

"'Scuse me," said the Elephant's Child most politely, "but have you seen such a thing as a Crocodile in these promiscuous parts?"

"Have I seen a Crocodile?" said the Bi-Colored-Python-Rock-Snake, in a voice of dreadful scorn. "What will you ask me next?"

"'Scuse me," said the Elephant's Child, "but could you kindly tell me what he has for dinner?"

Then the Bi-Colored-Python-Rock-Snake uncoiled himself very quickly from the rock, and spanked the Elephant's Child with his scalesome, flailsome tail.

"That is odd," said the Elephant's Child, "because my father and my mother, and my uncle and my aunt, not to mention my other aunt, the Hippopotamus, and my other uncle, the Baboon, have all spanked me for my 'satiable curiosity—and I suppose this is the same thing.

So he said goodbye very politely to the Bi-Colored-Python-Rock-Snake, and helped to coil him up on the rock again, and went on, a little warm, but not at all astonished, eating melons, and throwing the rind about, because he could not pick it up, till he trod on what he thought was a log of wood at the very edge of the great gray-green, greasy Limpopo River, all set about with fever-trees.

But it was really the Crocodile, Oh Best Beloved, and the Crocodile winked one eye—like this!

"'Scuse me," said the Elephant's Child most politely, "but do you happen to have seen a Crocodile in these promiscuous parts?"

Then the Crocodile winked the other eye, and lifted half his tail out of the mud; and the Elephant's Child stepped back most politely, because he did not wish to be spanked again.

"Come hither, Little One," said the Crocodile. "Why do you ask such things?"

"'Scuse me," said the Elephant's Child most politely, "but my father has spanked me, my mother has spanked me, not to mention my tall aunt, the Ostrich, and my tall uncle, the Giraffe, who can kick ever so hard, as well as my broad aunt, the Hippopotamus, and my hairy uncle, the Baboon, and including the Bi-Colored-Python-Rock-Snake, with the scalesome, flailsome tail, just up the bank, who spanks harder than any of them; and so, if it's quite all the same to you, I don't want to be spanked any more."

"Come hither, Little One," said the Crocodile, "for I am

the Crocodile," and he wept crocodile-tears to show it was quite true.

Then the Elephant's Child grew all breathless, and panted, and kneeled down on the bank and said, "You are the very person I have been looking for all these long days. Will you please tell me what you have for dinner?"

"Come hither, Little One," said the Crocodile, "and I'll whisper."

Then the Elephant's Child put his head down close to the Crocodile's musky, tusky mouth, and the Crocodile caught him by his little nose, which up to that very week, day, hour, and minute, had been no bigger than a boot, though much more useful.

"I think," said the Crocodile—and he said it between his teeth, like this—"I think today I will begin with Elephant's Child!"

At this, Oh Best Beloved, the Elephant's Child was much annoyed, and he said, speaking through his nose, like this, "Led go! You are hurtig be!"

Then the Bi-Colored-Python-Rock-Snake scuffled down from the bank and said, "My young friend, if you do not now, immediately and instantly, pull as hard as ever you can, it is my opinion that your acquaintance in the large-pattern leather ulster" (and by this he meant the Crocodile) "will jerk you into yonder limpid stream before you can say Jack

Robinson." (This is the way Bi-Colored-Python-Rock-Snakes always talk).

Then the Elephant's Child sat back on his little haunches, and pulled, and pulled, and pulled, and his nose began to stretch. And the Crocodile floundered into the water, making it all creamy with great sweeps of his tail, and he pulled, and pulled, and pulled.

And the Elephant's Child's nose kept on stretching; and the Elephant's Child spread all his little four legs and pulled, and pulled, and pulled, and his nose kept on stretching; and the Crocodile threshed his tail like an oar, and he pulled, and pulled, and pulled, and at each pull the Elephant's Child's nose grew longer and longer—and it hurt him terribly!

Then the Elephant's Child felt his legs slipping, and he said through his nose, which was now nearly five feet long, "This is too butch for be!"

Then the Bi-Colored-Python-Rock-Snake came down from the bank, and knotted himself in a double-clove-hitch round the Elephant's Child's hind legs, and said, "Rash and inexperienced traveler, we will now seriously devote ourselves to a little high tension, because if we do not, it is my impression that yonder self-propelling man-of-war with the armor-plated upper deck" (and by this, Oh Best Beloved, he meant the Crocodile), "will permanently vitiate your future career." (That is the way all Bi-Colored-Python-Rock-Snakes always talk).

So he pulled, and the Elephant's Child pulled, and the Crocodile pulled; but the Elephant's Child and the Bi-Colored-Python-Rock-Snake pulled hardest; and at last the Crocodile let go of the Elephant's Child's nose with a plop that you could hear all up and down the Limpopo.

Then the Elephant's Child sat down most hard and sudden; but first he was careful to say "Thank you" to the Bi-Colored-Python-Rock-Snake; and next he was kind to his poor pulled nose, and wrapped it all up in cool banana leaves, and hung it in the great gray-green, greasy Limpopo to cool.

"What are you doing that for?" said the Bi-Colored-Python-Rock-Snake.

"'Scuse me," said the Elephant's Child, "but my nose is badly out of shape, and I am waiting for it to shrink.

"Then you will have to wait a long time, said the Bi-Colored-Python-Rock-Snake. "Some people do not know what is good for them."

The Elephant's Child sat there for three days waiting for his nose to shrink. But it never grew any shorter, and, besides, it made him squint. For, Oh Best Beloved, you will see and understand that the Crocodile had pulled it out into a really truly trunk, same as all Elephants have today.

At the end of the third day a fly came and stung him on the shoulder, and before he knew what he was doing he lifted up his trunk and hit that fly dead with the end of it.

"'Vantage number one!" said the Bi-Colored-Python-Rock-Snake. "You couldn't have done that with a mere-smear nose. Try and eat a little now."

Before he thought what he was doing the Elephant's Child put out his trunk and plucked a large bundle of grass, dusted it clean against his fore-legs, and stuffed it into his own mouth.

"Vantage number two!" said the Bi-Colored-Python-Rock-Snake. "You couldn't have done that with a mear-smear nose. Don't you think the sun is very hot here?"

"It is," said the Elephant's Child, and before he thought what he was doing he schlooped up a schloop of mud from the banks of the great gray-green, greasy Limpopo, and slapped it on his head, where it made a cool schloopy-sloshy mud-cap all trickly behind his ears.

"Vantage number three!" said the Bi-Colored-Python-Rock-Snake. "You couldn't have done that with a mere-smear nose. Now how do you feel about being spanked again?"

"'Scuse me," said the Elephant's Child, "but I should not like it at all."

"How would you like to spank somebody?" said the Bi-Colored-Python-Rock-Snake.

"I should like it very much indeed," said the Elephant's Child.

"Well," said the Bi-Colored-Python-Rock-Snake, "you will find that new nose of yours very useful to spank people with."

"Thank you," said the Elephant's Child, "I'll remember that; and now I think I'll go home to all my dear families and try."

So the Elephant's Child went home across Africa frisking and whisking his trunk. When he wanted fruit to eat he pulled fruit down from a tree, instead of waiting for it to fall as he used to do. When he wanted grass he plucked grass up from the ground, instead of going on his knees as he used to do. When the flies bit him he broke off the branch of a tree and used it as fly-whisk; and he made himself a new, cool, slushy-squishy mud-cap whenever the sun was hot. When he felt lonely walking through Africa he sang to himself down his trunk, and the noise was louder than several brass bands. He went especially out of his way to find a broad Hippopotamus (she was no relation of his), and he spanked her very hard, to make sure that the Bi-Colored-Python-Rock-Snake had spoken the truth about his new trunk. The rest of the time he picked up the melon rinds that he had dropped on his way to the Limpopo—for he was a Tidy Pachyderm.

One dark evening he came back to all his dear families, and he coiled up his trunk and said, "How do you do?" They were very glad to see him, and immediately said, "Come here and be spanked for your 'satiable curtiosity."

"Pooh," said the Elephant's Child. "I don't think you peoples know anything about spanking; but I do, and I'll show you." Then he uncurled his trunk and knocked two of his dear brothers head over heels.

"Oh Bananas!" said they, "where did you learn that trick, and what have you done to your nose?"

"I got a new one from the Crocodile on the banks of the great gray-green, greasy Limpopo River," said the Elephant's Child. "I asked him what he had for dinner, and he gave me this to keep."

"It looks very ugly," said his hairy uncle, the Baboon.

"It does," said the Elephant's Child. "But it's very useful," and he picked up his hairy uncle, the Baboon, by one hairy leg, and hove him into a hornet's nest.

Then that bad Elephant's Child spanked all his dear families for a long time, till they were very warm and greatly astonished. He pulled out his tall Ostrich aunt's tail feathers; and he caught his tall uncle, the Giraffe, by the hind-leg, and dragged him through a thorn-bush; and he shouted at his broad aunt, the Hippopotamus, and blew bubbles into her ear when she was sleeping in the water after meals; but he never let any one touch Kolokolo Bird.

At last things grew so exciting that his dear families went off one by one in a hurry to the banks of the great gray-green, greasy Limpopo River, all set about with fever-trees, to borrow new noses from the Crocodile. When they came back nobody spanked anybody any more; and ever since that day, Oh Best Beloved, all the Elephants you will ever see, besides all those that you won't, have trunks precisely like the trunk of the 'satiable Elephant's Child.

Mole lives with his good friend Ratty by the edge of the River. They have other friends, especially Toad, Badger, and the Otter, who has a large family.

The Piper at the Gates of Dawn

From *The Wind in the Willows*
By Kenneth Grahame

THE Willow-Wren was twittering his thin little song, hidden himself in the dark selvedge of the river bank. Though it was past ten o'clock at night, the sky still clung to and retained some lingering skirts of light from the departed day; and the sullen heats of the torrid afternoon broke up and rolled away at the dispersing touch of the cool fingers of the short midsummer night. Mole lay stretched on the bank, still panting from the stress of the fierce day that had been cloudless from dawn to late sunset, and waited for his friend to return. He had been on the river with some companions, leaving the Water Rat free to keep an engagement of long standing with Otter; and he had come back to find the house dark and deserted, and no sign of Rat, who was doubtless keeping it up late with his old comrade. It was still too hot to think of staying indoors, so he lay on some cool dock leaves, and thought over the past day and its doings, and how very good they all had been.

The Rat's light footfall was presently heard approaching over the parched grass. "Oh, the blessed coolness!" he said, and sat down, gazing thoughtfully into the river, silent and preoccupied.

"You stayed to supper, of course?" said the Mole presently.

"Simply had to," said the Rat. "They wouldn't hear of my going before. You know how kind they always are. And they made things as jolly for me as ever they could, right up to the moment I left. But I felt a brute all the time, as it was clear to me they were very unhappy, though they tried to hide it. Mole, I'm afraid they're in trouble. Little Portly is missing again; and you know what a lot his father thinks of him, though he never says much about it."

"What, that child?" said the Mole lightly. "Well, suppose he is; why worry about it? He's always straying off and getting lost, and turning up again; he's so adventurous. But no harm ever happens to him. Everybody hereabouts knows him and likes him, just as they do old Otter, and you may be sure some animal or other will come across him and bring him back again all right. Why, we've found him ourselves, miles from home, and quite self-possessed and cheerful!"

"Yes; but this time it's more serious," said the Rat gravely. "He's been missing for some days now, and the Otters have hunted everywhere, high and low, without finding the slightest trace. And they've asked every animal, too, for miles around, and no one knows anything about him. Otter's evidently more anxious than he'll admit. I got out of him that young Portly hasn't learnt to swim very well yet, and I can see he's thinking of the weir. There's a lot of water coming down still, considering the time of the year, and the place always had a fascination for the child. And then there are—well, traps and things—*you* know. Otter's not the fellow to be nervous about any son of his before it's time. And now he *is* nervous. When I left, he came out with me— said he wanted some air, and talked about stretching his legs. But I could see it wasn't that, so I drew him out and pumped him, and got it all from him at last. He was going to spend the night watching by the ford. You know the place where the old ford used to be, in bygone days before they built the bridge?"

"I know it well," said the Mole. "But why should Otter choose to watch there?"

"Well, it seems that it was there he gave Portly his first

swimming lesson," continued the Rat. "From that shallow, gravelly spit near the bank. And it was there he used to teach him fishing, and there young Portly caught his first fish, of which he was so very proud. The child loved the spot, and Otter thinks that if he came wandering back from wherever he is—if he *is* anywhere by this time, poor little chap—he might make for the ford he was so fond of; or if he came across it he'd remember it well, and stop there and play, perhaps. So Otter goes there every night and watches—on the chance, you know, just on the chance!"

They were silent for a time, both thinking of the same thing—the lonely, heart-sore animal, crouched by the ford, watching and waiting, the long night through—on the chance.

"Well, well," said the Rat presently, "I suppose we ought to be thinking about turning in." But he never offered to move.

"Rat," said the Mole, "I simply can't go and turn in, and go to sleep, and *do* nothing, even though there doesn't seem to be anything to be done. We'll get the boat out, and paddle up stream. The moon will be up in an hour or so, and then we will search as well as we can—anyhow, it will be better than going to bed and doing *nothing*."

"Just what I was thinking myself," said the Rat. "It's not the sort of night for bed anyhow; and daybreak is not so very far off, and then we may pick up some news of him from early risers as we go along."

They got the boat out, and the Rat took the sculls, paddling with caution. Out in midstream, there was a clear, narrow track that faintly reflected the sky; but wherever shadows fell on the water from bank, bush, or tree, they were as solid to all appearance as the banks themselves, and the Mole had to steer with judgment accordingly. Dark and deserted as it was, the night was full of small noises, song and chatter, and rustling, telling of the busy little population who were up and about, plying their trades and vocations through the night till sunshine should fall on them at last and send them off to their well-earned repose. The water's own noises, too, were more apparent than by day, its gurglings and "cloops" more unexpected and near at hand; and constantly they started at what seemed a sudden clear call from an actual articulate voice.

The line of the horizon was clear and hard against the sky, and in one particular quarter it showed black against a silvery climbing phosphorescence that grew and grew. At last, over the rim of the waiting earth the moon lifted with slow majesty till it swung clear of the horizon and rode off,

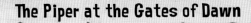

free of moorings; and once more they began to see surfaces—meadows widespread, and quiet gardens, and the river itself from bank to bank, all softly disclosed, all washed clean of mystery and terror, all radiant again as by day, but with a difference that was tremendous. Their old haunts greeted them again in other raiment, as if they had slipped away and put on this pure new apparel and come quietly back, smiling as they shyly waited to see if they would be recognized again under it.

Fastening their boat to a willow, the friends landed in this silent, silver kingdom, and patiently explored the hedges, the hollow trees, the runnels and their little culverts, the ditches, and dry waterways. Embarking again and crossing over, they worked their way up the stream in this manner, while the moon, serene and detached in a cloudless sky, did what she could, though so far off, to help them in their quest; till her hour came and she sank earthward reluctantly, and left them, and mystery once more held field and river.

Then a change began slowly to declare itself. The horizon became clearer, field and tree came more into sight, and somehow with a different look; the mystery began to drop away from them. A bird piped suddenly, and was still; and a light breeze sprang up and set the reeds and bulrushes rustling. Rat, who was in the stern of the boat, while Mole sculled, sat up suddenly and listened with a passionate intentness. Mole, who with gentle strokes was just keeping the boat moving while he scanned the banks with care, looked at him with curiosity.

"It's gone!" sighed the Rat, sinking back in his seat again. "So beautiful and strange and new. Since it was to end so soon, I almost wish I had never heard it. For it has roused a longing in me that is pain, and nothing seems worthwhile but just to hear that sound once more and go on listening to it forever. No! There it is again!" he cried, alert once more. Entranced, he was silent for a long space, spellbound.

"Now it passes on and I begin to lose it," he said presently. "Oh Mole! the beauty of it! The merry bubble and joy, the thin, clear, happy call of the distant piping! Such music I never dreamed of, and the call in it is stronger even than the music is sweet! Row on, Mole, row! For the music and the call must be for us."

The Mole, greatly wondering, obeyed. "I hear nothing myself," he said, "but the wind playing in the reeds and rushes and osiers."

The Rat never answered, if indeed he heard. Rapt, transported, trembling, he was possessed in all his senses by this new divine thing that caught up his helpless soul and swung and dandled it, a powerless but happy infant in a strong sustaining grasp.

In silence Mole rowed steadily, and soon they came to a point where the river divided, a long backwater branching off to one side. With a slight movement of his head Rat, who had long dropped the rudder lines, directed the rower to take the backwater. The creeping tide of light gained and gained, and now they could see the color of the flowers that gemmed the water's edge.

"Clearer and nearer still," cried the Rat joyously. "Now you must surely hear it! Ah—at last—I see you do!"

Breathless and transfixed the Mole stopped rowing as the liquid run of that glad piping broke on him like a wave, caught him up, and possessed him utterly. He saw the tears on his comrade's cheeks, and bowed his head, and understood. For a space they hung there, brushed by the purple loosestrife that fringed the bank; then the clear imperious summons that marched hand-in-hand with the intoxicating melody imposed its will on Mole, and mechanically he bent to his oars again. And the light grew steadily stronger, but no birds sang as they were wont to do at the approach of dawn; and but for the heavenly music all was marvelously still.

On either side of them, as they glided onward, the rich meadow-grass seemed that morning of a freshness and a greenness unsurpassable. Never had they noticed the roses so vivid, the willowherb so riotous, the meadowsweet so odorous and pervading. Then the murmur of the approaching weir began to hold the air, and they felt a consciousness that they were nearing the end, whatever it might be, that surely awaited their expedition.

A wide half-circle of foam and glinting lights and shining shoulders of green water, the great weir closed the backwater from bank to bank, troubled all the quiet surface with twirling eddies and floating foam streaks, and deadened all other sounds with its solemn and soothing rumble. In midmost of the stream, embraced in the weir's shimmering arm-spread, a small island lay anchored, fringed close with willow and silver birch and alder. Reserved, shy, but full of significance, it hid whatever it might hold behind a veil, keeping it till the hour should come, and, with the hour, those who were called and chosen.

Slowly, but with no doubt or hesitation whatever, and in something of a solemn expectancy, the two animals passed through the broken tumultuous water and moored their boat at the flowery margin of the island. In silence they landed, and pushed through the blossom and scented herbage and undergrowth that led up to the level ground, till they stood on a little lawn of a marvelous green, set round with Nature's own orchard trees—crab apple, wild cherry, and sloe.

"This is the place of my song-dream, the place the music played to me," whispered the Rat, as if in a trance. "Here, in this holy place, here if anywhere, surely we shall find Him!"

Then suddenly the Mole felt a great awe fall upon him, an awe that turned his muscles to water, bowed his head, and rooted his feet to the ground. It was no panic terror— indeed he felt wonderfully at peace and happy—but it was an awe that smote and held him and, without seeing, he knew it could only mean that some august presence was very, very near. With difficulty he turned to look for his friend and saw him at his side, cowed, stricken, and trembling violently. And still there was utter silence in the populous bird-haunted branches around them; and still the light grew and grew.

Perhaps he would never have dared to raise his eyes, but that, though the piping was now hushed, the call and the summons seemed still dominant and imperious. He might not refuse, were Death himself waiting to strike him instantly, once he had looked with mortal eye on things rightly kept hidden. Trembling he obeyed, and raised his humble head; and then, in that utter clearness of the imminent dawn, while Nature, flushed with fullness of incredible color, seemed to hold her breath for the event, he looked in the very eyes of the Friend and Helper; saw the backward sweep of the curved horns, gleaming in the growing daylight; saw the stern, hooked nose between the kindly eyes that were looking down on them humorously, while the bearded mouth broke into a half-smile at the corners; saw the rippling muscles on the arm that lay across the broad chest, the long supple hand still holding the pan-pipes only just fallen away from the parted lips; saw the splendid curves of the shaggy limbs disposed in majestic ease on the sward; saw, last of all, nestling between his very hooves, sleeping soundly in entire peace and contentment, the little, round, podgy, childish form of the baby otter. All this he saw, for one moment breathless and intense, vivid on the morning sky; and still, as he looked, he lived; and still, as he lived, he wondered.

"Rat!" he found breath to whisper, shaking. "Are you afraid?"

"Afraid?" murmured the Rat, his eyes shining with unutterable love. "Afraid! Of *him*? Oh, never, never! And yet—and yet—Oh, Mole, I am afraid!"

Then the two animals, crouching to the earth, bowed their heads and did worship.

Sudden and magnificent, the sun's broad golden disk showed itself over the horizon facing them; and the first rays, shooting across the level water-meadows, took the animals full in the eyes and dazzled them. When they were able to look once more, the vision had vanished, and the air was full of the carol of birds that hailed the dawn.

As they stared blankly in dumb misery deepening as they slowly realized all they had seen and all they had lost, a capricious little breeze, dancing up from the surface of the water, tossed the aspens, shook the dewy roses, and blew lightly and caressingly in their faces; and with its soft touch came instant oblivion. For this is the last, best gift that the kindly demigod is careful to bestow on those to whom he has revealed himself in their helping: the gift of forgetfulness. Lest the awful remembrance should remain and grow, and overshadow mirth and pleasure, and the great haunting memory should spoil all the afterlives of little animals helped out of difficulties, in order that they should be happy and lighthearted as before.

Mole rubbed his eyes and stared at Rat, who was looking about him in a puzzled sort of way.

"I beg your pardon; what did you say, Rat?" he asked.

"I think I was only remarking," said Rat slowly, "that this was the right sort of place, and that here, if anywhere, we should find him. And look! Why, there he is, the little fellow!" And with a cry of delight he ran toward the slumbering Portly.

But Mole stood still a moment, held in thought. As one wakened suddenly from a beautiful dream, who struggles to recall it, and can recapture nothing but a dim sense of the beauty of it, the beauty! Till that, too, fades away in its turn, and the dreamer bitterly accepts the hard, cold waking and all its penalties; so Mole, after struggling with his memory for a brief space, shook his head sadly and followed the Rat.

Portly woke up with a joyous squeak, and wriggled with pleasure at the sight of his father's friends, who had played with him so often in past days. In a moment, however, his face grew blank, and he fell to hunting round in a circle with pleading whine. As a child that has fallen happily asleep in its nurse's arms, and wakes to find itself alone and laid in a strange place, and searches corners and cupboards, and runs from room to room, despair growing silently in its heart, even so Portly searched the island and searched, dogged and unwearying, till at last the black moment came for giving it up, and sitting down and crying bitterly.

The Mole ran quickly to comfort the little animal; but Rat, lingering, looked long and doubtfully at certain hoof marks deep in the sward.

"Some great animal has been here," he murmured slowly and thoughtfully; and stood musing, musing; his mind strangely stirred.

"Come along, Rat!" called the Mole. "Think of poor Otter, waiting up there by the ford!"

Portly had soon been comforted by the promise of a treat—a jaunt on the river in Mr Rat's real boat; and the two animals conducted him to the water's side, placed him securely between them in the bottom of the boat, and paddled off down the backwater. The sun was fully up by now, and hot on them, birds sang lustily and without restraint, and flowers smiled and nodded from either bank, but somehow—so thought the animals—with less of richness and blaze of color than they seemed to remember seeing quite recently somewhere—they wondered where.

The main river reached again, they turned the boat's head upstream, toward the point where they knew their friend was keeping his lonely vigil..As they drew near the familiar ford, the Mole took the boat in to the bank, and they lifted Portly out and set him on his legs on the towpath, gave him his marching orders and a friendly farewell pat on the back, and shoved out into midstream. They watched the little animal as he waddled along the path contentedly and with importance; watched him till they saw his muzzle suddenly lift and his waddle break into a clumsy amble as he quickened his pace with shrill whines and wriggles of recognition. Looking up the river, they could see Otter start up, tense and rigid, from out of the shallows where he crouched in dumb patience, and could hear his amazed and joyous bark as he bounded up through the osiers onto the path. Then the Mole, with a strong pull on one oar, swung the boat round and let the full stream bear them down again whither it would, their quest now happily ended.

"I feel strangely tired, Rat," said the Mole, leaning wearily over his oars as the boat drifted. "It's being up all night, you'll say, perhaps; but that's nothing. We do as much half the nights of the week, at this time of the year. No; I feel as if I had been through something very exciting and rather terrible, and it was just over; and yet nothing particular has happened."

"Or something very surprising and splendid and beautiful," murmured the Rat, leaning back and closing his eyes. "I feel just as you do, Mole; simply dead tired, though not body tired. It's lucky we've got the stream with us, to take us home. Isn't it jolly to feel the sun again, soaking into one's bones! And hark to the wind playing in the reeds!"

"It's like music—far away music," said the Mole nodding drowsily.

"So I was thinking," murmured the Rat, dreamful and languid. "Dance music—the lilting sort that runs on without a stop—but with words in it, too—it passes into words and out of them again—I catch them at intervals— then it is dance music once more, and then nothing but the reeds' soft thin whispering."

"You hear better than I," said the Mole sadly. "I cannot catch the words."

"Let me try and give you them," said the Rat softly, his eyes still closed. "Now it is turning into words again—faint but clear:

> *'Lest the awe should dwell*
> *And turn your frolic to fret*
> *You shall look on my power at the helping hour*
> *But then you shall forget!'*

"Now the reeds take it up—'*forget, forget,*' they sigh, and it dies away in a rustle and a whisper. Then the voice returns:

> *'Lest limbs be reddened and rent*
> *I spring the trap that is set*
> *As I loose the snare you may glimpse me there*
> *For surely you shall forget!'*

"Row nearer, Mole, nearer to the reeds! It is hard to

catch, and grows each minute fainter:

> "*Helper and healer, I cheer*
> *Small waifs in the woodland wet*
> *Strays I find in it, wounds I bind in it*
> *Bidding them all forget!*"

"Nearer, Mole, nearer! No, it is no good; the song has died away into reed-talk."

"But what do the words mean?" asked the wondering Mole.

"That I do not know," said the Rat simply. "I passed them on to you as they reached me. Ah! Now they return again, and this time full and clear! This time, at last, it is the real, the unmistakable thing, simple—passionate—perfect—"

"Well, let's have it, then," said the Mole, after he had waited patiently for a few minutes, half-dozing in the hot sun.

But no answer came. He looked, and understood the silence. With a smile of much happiness on his face, and something of a listening look still lingering there, the weary Rat was fast asleep.

Tricks, Traps, and Mischief

*Tom lives in a small town in the southern
United States with his Aunt Polly, sister Mary,
and brother Sid. He is always having adventures
and getting into trouble.*

Tom Sawyer in Church

From *The Adventures of Tom Sawyer*
By Mark Twain

ABOUT half-past ten the cracked bell of the small
church began to ring, and presently the people began to
gather for the morning sermon. The Sunday school children
distributed themselves about the house and occupied pews
with their parents, so as to be under supervision. Aunt Polly
came, and Tom and Sid and Mary sat with her—Tom being
placed next to the aisle, in order that he might be as far away
from the open window and the seductive outside summer
scenes as possible.

The crowd filed up the aisles: the aged and needy
postmaster, who had seen better days; the mayor and his
wife—for they had a mayor there, among other

unnecessaries; the justice of the peace; the widow Douglass,
fair, smart, and forty, a generous, good-hearted soul and
well-to-do, her hill mansion the only palace in the town,
and the most hospitable and much the most lavish in the
matter of festivities that St. Petersburg could boast; the bent
and venerable Major and Mrs Ward; lawyer Riverson, the
new notable from a distance; next the belle of the village,
followed by a troop of lawn-clad and ribbon-decked young
heart-breakers; then all the young clerks in town in a
body—for they had stood in the vestibule sucking their
cane-heads, a circling wall of oiled and simpering admirers,
till the last girl had run their gauntlet; and last of all came
the Model Boy, Willie Mufferson, taking as heedful care of
his mother as if she were cut glass. He always brought his
mother to church, and was the pride of all the matrons. The
boys all hated him, he was so good. And besides, he had
been "thrown up to them" so much. His white handkerchief
was hanging out of his pocket behind, as usual on
Sundays—accidentally. Tom had no handkerchief, and he
looked upon boys who had as snobs.

The congregation being fully assembled, the bell rang
once more, to warn laggards and stragglers, and then a
solemn hush fell upon the church which was only broken by
the tittering and whispering of the choir in the gallery. The
choir always tittered and whispered all through the service.

There was once a church choir that was not ill-bred, but I have forgotten where it was, now. It was a great many years ago, and I can scarcely remember anything about it, but I think it was in some foreign country.

The minister gave out the hymn, and read it through with a relish, in a peculiar style which was much admired in that part of the country. His voice began on a medium key and climbed steadily up till it reached a certain point, where it bore with strong emphasis upon the topmost word and then plunged down as if from a spring-board:

> "Shall I be car-ri-ed toe the skies,
> On flow'ry *beds* of ease,
> Whilst others fight to win the prize,
> And sail thro' *bloody* seas?"

He was regarded as a wonderful reader. At church "sociables" he was always called upon to read poetry; and when he was through, the ladies would lift up their hands and let them fall helplessly in their laps, and "wall" their eyes, and shake their heads, as much as to say, "Words cannot express it; it is too beautiful, *too* beautiful for this mortal earth."

After the hymn had been sung, the Rev. Mr Sprague turned himself into a bulletin-board, and read off "notices" of meetings and societies and things till it seemed that the list would stretch out to the crack of doom—a queer custom which is still kept up in America, even in cities, away here in this age of abundant newspapers. Often, the less there is to justify a traditional custom, the harder it is to get rid of it.

And now the minister prayed. A good, generous prayer it was, and went into details: it pleaded for the church, and the little children of the church; for the other churches of the village; for the village itself; for the county; for the State; for the State officers; for the United States; for the churches of the United States; for Congress; for the President; for the officers of the Government; for poor sailors, tossed by stormy seas; for the oppressed millions groaning under the heel of European monarchies and Oriental despotisms; for such as have the light and the good tidings, and yet have not eyes to see nor ears to hear withal; for the heathen in the far islands of the sea; and closed with a supplication that the words he was about to speak might find grace and favor, and be as seed sown in fertile ground, yielding in time a grateful harvest of good. Amen.

There was a rustling of dresses, and the standing congregation sat down. The boy whose history this book relates did not enjoy the prayer, he only endured it—if he even did that much. He was restive all through it; he kept tally of the details of the prayer, unconsciously—for he was not listening, but he knew the ground of old, and the clergyman's regular route over it—and when a little trifle of new matter was interlarded, his ear detected it and his whole nature resented it; he considered additions unfair, and scoundrelly. In the midst of the prayer a fly had lit on the back of the pew in front of him and tortured his spirit by calmly rubbing its hands together, embracing its head with its arms, and polishing it so vigorously that it seemed to almost part company with the body, and the slender thread of a neck was exposed to view; scraping its wings with its hind legs and smoothing them to its body as if they had been coat-tails; going through its whole toilet as tranquilly as if it knew it was perfectly safe. As indeed it was; for as sorely as Tom's hands itched to grab for it they did not dare—he believed his soul would be instantly destroyed if he did such a thing while the prayer was going on. But with the closing sentence his hand began to curve and steal forward; and the instant the "Amen" was out the fly was a prisoner of war. His aunt detected the act and made him let it go.

The minister gave out his text and droned along monotonously through an argument that was so prosy that many a head by and by began to nod—and yet it was an argument that dealt in limitless fire and brimstone and thinned the predestined elect down to a company so small as to be hardly worth the saving. Tom counted the pages of the sermon; after church he always knew how many pages there had been, but he seldom knew anything else about the discourse. However, this time he was really interested for a little while. The minister made a grand and moving picture of the assembling together of the world's hosts at the millennium when the lion and the lamb should lie down together and a little child should lead them. But the pathos, the lesson, the moral of the great spectacle were lost upon the boy; he only thought of the conspicuousness of the principal character before the on-looking nations; his face lit with the thought, and he said to himself that he wished he could be that child, if it was a tame lion.

Now he lapsed into suffering again, as the dry argument was resumed. Presently he bethought him of a treasure he had and got it out. It was a large black beetle with formidable jaws—a "pinchbug," he called it. It was in a percussion-cap box. The first thing the beetle did was to take him by the finger. A natural fillip followed, the beetle went floundering into the aisle and lit on its back, and the hurt finger went into the boy's mouth. The beetle lay there working its helpless legs, unable to turn over. Tom eyed it, and longed for it; but it was safe out of

his reach. Other people uninterested in the sermon found relief in the beetle, and they eyed it too. Presently a vagrant poodle dog came idling along, sad at heart, lazy with the summer softness and the quiet, weary of captivity, sighing for change. He spied the beetle; the drooping tail lifted and wagged. He surveyed the prize; walked round it; smelt at it from a safe distance; walked round it again; grew bolder, and took a closer smell; then lifted his lip and made a gingerly snatch at it, just missing it; made another, and another; began to enjoy the diversion; subsided to his stomach with the beetle between his paws, and continued his experiments; grew weary at last, and then indifferent and absent-minded. His head nodded, and little by little his chin descended and touched the enemy, who seized it. There was a sharp yelp, a flirt of the poodle's head, and the beetle fell a couple of yards away, and lit on its back once more. The neighboring spectators shook with a gentle inward joy, several faces went behind fans and handkerchiefs, and Tom was entirely happy. The dog looked foolish, and probably felt so; but there was resentment in his heart, too, and a craving for revenge. So he went to the beetle and began a wary attack on it again; jumping at it from every point of a circle, lighting with his fore-paws within an inch of the creature, making even closer snatches at it with his teeth, and jerking his head till his ears flapped again. But he grew tired once more, after a while; tried to amuse himself with a fly but found no relief; followed an ant around, with his nose close to the floor, and quickly wearied of that; yawned, sighed, forgot the beetle entirely, and sat down on it. Then there was a wild yelp of agony and the poodle went sailing up the aisle; the yelps continued, and so did the dog; he crossed the house in front of the altar; he flew down the other aisle; he crossed before the doors; he clamored up the home stretch; his anguish grew with his progress, till presently he was but a woolly comet moving in its orbit with the gleam and the speed of light. At last the frantic sufferer sheered from its course, and sprang into its master's lap; he flung it out of the window, and the voice of distress quickly thinned away and died in the distance.

By this time the whole church was red-faced and suffocating with suppressed laughter, and the sermon had come to a dead standstill. The discourse was resumed presently, but it went lame and halting, all possibility of impressiveness being at an end; for even the gravest sentiments were constantly being received with a smothered burst of unholy mirth, under cover of some remote pew-back, as if the poor parson had said a rarely facetious thing. It was a genuine relief to the whole congregation when the ordeal was over and the benediction pronounced.

Tom Sawyer went home quite cheerful, thinking to himself that there was some satisfaction about divine service when there was a bit of variety in it. He had but one marring thought; he was willing that the dog should play with his pinchbug, but he did not think it was upright in him to carry it off.

Pinocchio is a wooden puppet carved by a poor man called Geppetto. Pinocchio comes to life, and loves Geppetto as a father. Pinocchio has many adventures after running away from school. A fairy, who assumes the form of a beautiful child, often comes to his rescue.

Pinocchio is Swallowed by the Dogfish

From *Pinocchio*

By Carlo Collodi

Whilst Pinocchio was swimming, he knew not whither, he saw in the midst of the sea a rock that seemed to be made of white marble, and on the summit there stood a beautiful little goat who bleated lovingly and made signs to him to approach.

But the most singular thing was this. The little goat's hair, instead of being white or black, or a mixture of two colors as is usual with other goats, was blue, and a very vivid blue, greatly resembling the hair of the beautiful Child.

I leave you to imagine how rapidly poor Pinocchio's heart

began to beat. He swam with redoubled strength and energy toward the white rock; and he was already half-way there when he saw, rising up out of the water and coming to meet him, the horrible head of a sea-monster. His wide-open, cavernous mouth and his three rows of enormous teeth would have been terrifying to look at even in a picture. And do you know what this sea-monster was?

This sea-monster was neither more nor less than that gigantic Dogfish, who, for his slaughter and for his insatiable voracity, had been named the "Attila of Fish and Fishermen."

Only to think of poor Pinocchio's terror at the sight of the monster. He tried to avoid it, to change his direction; he tried to escape, but that immense, wide-open mouth came toward him with the velocity of an arrow.

"Be quick, Pinocchio, for pity's sake!" cried the beautiful little goat, bleating.

And Pinocchio swam desperately with his arms, his chest, his legs, and his feet.

"Quick, Pinocchio, the monster is close upon you!"

And Pinocchio swam quicker than ever, and flew on with the rapidity of a ball from a gun. He had nearly reached the rock, and the little goat, leaning over toward the sea, had stretched out her fore-legs to help him out of the water!

But it was too late! The monster had overtaken him and,

drawing in his breath, he sucked in the poor puppet as he would have sucked a hen's egg; and he swallowed him with such violence and avidity that Pinocchio, in falling into the Dogfish's stomach, received such a blow that he remained unconscious for a quarter of an hour afterward.

When he came to himself again after the shock he could not in the least imagine in what world he was. All around him it was quite dark, and the darkness was so black and so profound that it seemed to him that he had fallen head downward into an inkstand full of ink. He listened, but he could hear no noise; only from time to time great gusts of wind blew in his face.

At first he could not understand where the wind came from, but at last he discovered that it came out of the monster's lungs. For you must know that the Dogfish suffered very much from asthma, and when he breathed it was exactly as if a north wind was blowing.

Pinocchio at first tried to keep up his courage, but when he had one proof after another that he was really shut up in the body of this sea-monster he began to cry and scream, and to sob out: "Help! help! Oh, how unfortunate I am! Will nobody come to save me?"

"Who do you think could save you, unhappy wretch?" said a voice in the dark that sounded like a guitar out of tune.

"Who is speaking?" asked Pinocchio, frozen with terror.

"It is I! I am a poor Tunny who was swallowed by the Dogfish at the same time that you were. And what fish are you?"

"I have nothing in common with fish. I am a puppet."

"Then, if you are not a fish, why did you let yourself be swallowed by the monster?"

"I didn't let myself be swallowed; it was the monster swallowed me! And now, what are we to do here in the dark?"

"Resign ourselves and wait until the Dogfish has digested us both."

"But I do not want to be digested!" howled Pinocchio, beginning to cry again.

"Neither do I want to be digested," added the Tunny; "but I am enough of a philosopher to console myself by thinking that when one is born a Tunny it is more dignified to die in the water than in oil."

"That is all nonsense!" cried Pinocchio.

"It is my opinion," replied the Tunny, "and opinions, so say the political Tunnies, ought to be respected."

"To sum it all up, I want to get away from here. I want to escape."

"Escape, if you are able!"

"Is this Dogfish who has swallowed us very big?" asked the puppet.

"Big! Why, only imagine, his body is two miles long without counting his tail."

Whilst they were holding this conversation in the dark, Pinocchio thought that he saw a light a long way off.

"What is that little light I see in the distance?" he asked.

"It is most likely some companion in misfortune who is waiting, like us, to be digested."

"I will go and find him. Do you not think that it may by chance be some old fish who perhaps could show us how to escape?"

"I hope it may be so, with all my heart, dear puppet."

"Goodbye, Tunny."

"Goodbye, puppet, and good fortune attend you."

"Where shall we meet again?"

"Who can say? It is better not even to think of it!"

Pinocchio, having taken leave of his friend the Tunny, began to grope his way in the dark through the body of the Dogfish, taking a step at a time in the direction of the light that he saw shining dimly at a great distance.

The farther he advanced the brighter became the light; and he walked and walked until at last he reached it; and when he reached it—what did he find? I will give you a thousand guesses. He found a little table spread out and on it a lighted candle stuck into a green glass bottle, and, seated at the table, was a little old man. He was eating some live fish, and they were so very much alive that whilst he was eating them they sometimes even jumped out of his mouth.

At this sight Pinocchio was filled with such great and unexpected joy that he became almost delirious. He wanted to laugh, he wanted to cry, he wanted to say a thousand things, and instead he could only stammer out a few confused and broken words. At last he succeeded in uttering a cry of joy, and, opening his arms, he threw them round the little old man's neck, and began to shout:

"Oh, my dear papa! I have found you at last! I will never leave you more, never more, never more!"

"Then my eyes tell me true?" said the little old man, rubbing his eyes; "then you are really my dear Pinocchio?"

"Yes, yes, I am Pinocchio, really Pinocchio! And you have quite forgiven me, have you not? Oh, my dear papa, how good you are! And to think that I, on the contrary—Oh! but if you only knew what misfortunes have been poured on my head, and all that has befallen me! Only imagine, the day that you, poor, dear papa, sold your coat to buy me a spelling-book, that I might go to school, I escaped to see the puppet show, and the showman wanted to put me on the fire, that I might roast his mutton, and he was the same that afterward gave me five gold pieces to take them to you, but I met the Fox and the Cat, who took me to the inn of The Red Craw-Fish, where they ate like wolves, and I left by myself in the middle of the night, and I encountered assassins who ran after me, and I ran away, and they followed, and I ran, and they always followed me, and I ran, until they hung me to a branch of a Big Oak, and the beautiful Child with blue hair sent a little carriage to fetch me, and the doctors when they saw me said immediately, 'If he is not dead, it is a proof that he is still alive,' and then by chance I told a lie, and my nose began to grow until I could no longer get through the door of the room, for which

reason I went with the Fox and the Cat to bury the four
gold pieces, for one I had spent at the inn, and the Parrot
began to laugh, and instead of two thousand gold pieces I
found none left, for which reason the judge when he heard
that I had been robbed had me immediately put in prison to
content the robbers, and then when I was coming away I
saw a beautiful bunch of grapes in a field, and I was caught
in a trap, and the peasant, who was quite right, put a dog
collar round my neck that I might guard the poultry yard,
and acknowledging my innocence let me go, and the
Serpent with the smoking tail began to laugh and broke a
blood-vessel in his chest, and so I returned to the house of
the beautiful Child, who was dead, and the Pigeon, seeing
that I was crying, said to me, 'I have seen your father who
was building a little boat to go in search of you,' and I said
to him, 'Oh! if I also had wings,' and he said to me, 'Do you
want to go to your father?' and I said, 'Without doubt! but
who will take me to him?' and he said to me, 'I will take
you,' and I said to him, 'How?' and he said to me, 'Get on
my back,' and so we flew all night, and then in the morning
all the fishermen who were looking out to sea said to me,
'There is a poor man in a boat who is on the point of being
drowned,' and I recognized you at once, even at that
distance, for my heart told me, and I made signs to you to
return to land."

"I also recognized you," said Geppetto, "and I would willingly have returned to the shore, but what was I to do! The sea was tremendous and a great wave upset my boat. Then a horrible Dogfish, who was near, as soon as he saw me in the water, came toward me, and, putting out his tongue, took hold of me and swallowed me as if I had been a little apple tart."

"And how long have you been shut up here?" asked Pinocchio.

"Since that day—it must be nearly two years ago; two years, my dear Pinocchio, that have seemed like two centuries!"

"And how have you managed to live? And where did you get the candle? And the matches to light it? Who gave them to you?"

"Stop, and I will tell you everything. You must know, then, that in the same storm in which my boat was upset a merchant vessel foundered. The sailors were all saved, but the vessel went to the bottom, and the Dogfish, who had that day an excellent appetite, after he had swallowed me, swallowed also the vessel."

"How?"

"He swallowed it in one mouthful, and the only thing that he spat out was the mainmast, that had stuck between his teeth like a fish bone. Fortunately for me, the vessel was laden with preserved meat in tins, biscuit, bottles of wine, dried raisins, cheese, coffee, sugar, candles, and boxes of wax matches. With this providential supply I have been able to live for two years. But I have arrived at the end of my resources; there is nothing left in the larder, and this candle that you see burning is the last that remains."

"And after that?"

"After that, dear boy, we shall both remain in the dark."

"Then, dear little papa," said Pinocchio, "there is no time to lose. We must think of escaping."

"Of escaping? How?"

"We must escape through the mouth of the Dogfish, throw ourselves into the sea and swim away."

"You talk well; but, dear Pinocchio, I don't know how to swim."

"What does that matter? I am a good swimmer, and you can get on my shoulders and I will carry you safely to shore."

"All illusions, my boy!" replied Geppetto, shaking his head with a melancholy smile. "Do you suppose it possible that a puppet like you, scarcely a yard high, could have the strength to swim with me on his shoulders!"

"Try it and you will see!"

Without another word Pinocchio took the candle in his hand, and, going in front to light the way, he said to his father: "Follow me, and don't be afraid."

And they walked for some time and traversed the body and the stomach of the Dogfish. But when they had arrived at the point where the monster's big throat began, they thought it better to stop to give a good look around and to choose the best moment for escaping.

Now, I must tell you that the Dogfish, being very old, and suffering from asthma and palpitation of the heart, was obliged to sleep with his mouth open. Pinocchio, therefore, having approached the entrance to his throat, and, looking up, could see beyond the enormous gaping mouth a large piece of starry sky and beautiful moonlight.

"This is the moment to escape," he whispered, turning to his father; "the Dogfish is sleeping like a dormouse, the sea is calm, and it is as light as day. Follow me, dear papa, and in a short time we shall be in safety."

They immediately climbed up the throat of the sea-monster, and, having reached his immense mouth, they began to walk on tiptoe down his tongue.

Before taking the final leap the puppet said to his father: "Get on my shoulders and put your arms tightly around my neck. I will take care of the rest."

As soon as Geppetto was firmly settled on his son's shoulders, Pinocchio, feeling sure of himself, threw himself into the water and began to swim. The sea was as smooth as oil, the moon shone brilliantly, and the Dogfish was sleeping so profoundly that even a cannonade would have failed to wake him.

Whilst Pinocchio was swimming quickly toward the shore he discovered that his father, who was on his shoulders with his legs in the water, was trembling as violently as if the poor man had an attack of ague fever.

Was he trembling from cold or from fear? Perhaps a little from both the one and the other. But Pinocchio, thinking it was from fear, said, to comfort him: "Courage, papa! In a few minutes we shall be safely on shore."

"But where is this blessed shore?" asked the little old man, becoming still more frightened, and screwing up his eyes as tailors do when they wish to thread a needle. "I have been looking in every direction and I see nothing but the sky and the sea."

"But I see the shore as well," said the puppet. "You must know that I am like a cat: I see better by night than by day."

Poor Pinocchio was making a pretense of being in good spirits, but in reality he was beginning to feel discouraged; his strength was failing, he was gasping and panting for breath. He could do no more, and the shore was still far off.

He swam until he had no breath left; then he turned his head to Geppetto and said in broken words: "Papa, help me, I am dying!"

The father and son were on the point of drowning when they heard a voice like a guitar out of tune saying: "Who is it that is dying?"

"It is I, and my poor father!"

"I know that voice! You are Pinocchio!"

"Precisely; and you?"

"I am the Tunny, your prison companion in the body of the Dogfish."

"And how did you manage to escape?"

"I followed your example. You showed me the road, and I escaped after you."

"Tunny, you have arrived at the right moment! I implore you to help us or we are lost."

"Willingly and with all my heart. You must, both of you, take hold of my tail and leave it to me to guide you. I will take you on shore in four minutes."

Geppetto and Pinocchio, as I need not tell you, accepted the offer at once; but, instead of holding on by his tail, they thought it would be more comfortable to get on the Tunny's back.

Having reached the shore, Pinocchio sprang first on land that he might help his father to do the same. He then turned to the Tunny and said to him in a voice full of emotion: "My friend, you have saved my papa's life. I can find no words with which to thank you properly. Permit me at least to give you a kiss as a sign of my eternal gratitude!"

The Tunny put his head out of the water and Pinocchio, kneeling on the ground, kissed him tenderly on the mouth. At this spontaneous proof of warm affection, the poor Tunny, who was not accustomed to it, felt extremely touched, and, ashamed to let himself be seen crying like a child, he plunged under the water and disappeared.

Rikki-tikki-tavi

From *The Jungle Book*
By Rudyard Kipling

THIS is the story of the great war that Rikki-tikki-tavi fought single-handed, through the bathrooms of the big bungalow in Segowlee cantonment. Darzee, the Tailorbird, helped him, and Chuchundra, the muskrat, who never comes out into the middle of the floor, but always creeps round by the wall, gave him advice, but Rikki-tikki did the real fighting.

He was a mongoose, rather like a little cat in his fur and his tail, but quite like a weasel in his head and his habits. His eyes and the end of his restless nose were pink. He could scratch himself anywhere he pleased with any leg, front or back, that he chose to use. He could fluff up his tail 'til it looked like a bottle brush, and his war cry as he scuttled through the long grass was: "Rikk-tikk-tikki-tikki-tchk!"

One day, a high summer flood washed him out of the burrow where he lived with his father and mother, and carried him, kicking and clucking, down a roadside ditch. He found a little wisp of grass floating there, and clung to it till he lost his senses. When he revived, he was lying in the hot sun on the middle of a path through a yard, very 'draggled indeed, and a small boy was saying, "Here's a dead mongoose. Let's have a funeral."

"No," said his mother, "let's take him in and dry him. Perhaps he isn't really dead."

They took him into the house, and a big man picked him up between his finger and thumb and said he was not dead but half choked. So they wrapped him in cotton wool, and warmed him over a little fire, and he opened his eyes and sneezed.

"Now," said the big man (he was an Englishman who had just moved into the bungalow), "don't frighten him, and we'll see what he'll do."

It is the hardest thing in the world to frighten a mongoose, because he is eaten up from nose to tail with curiosity. The motto of all the mongoose family is "Run and find out," and Rikki-tikki was a true mongoose. He looked at the cotton wool, decided that it was not good to eat, ran all round the table, sat up and put his fur in order, scratched himself, and jumped on the small boy's shoulder.

"Don't be frightened, Teddy," said his father. "That's his way of making friends."

"Ouch! He's tickling under my chin," said Teddy.

Rikki-tikki looked down between the boy's collar and neck, snuffed at his ear, and climbed down to the floor, where he sat rubbing his nose.

"Good gracious," said Teddy's mother, "and that's a wild creature! I suppose he's so tame because we've been kind to him."

"All mongooses are like that," said her husband. "If Teddy doesn't pick him up by the tail, or try to put him in a cage, he'll run in and out of the house all day long. Let's give him something to eat."

They gave him a little piece of raw meat. Rikki-tikki liked it immensely, and when it was finished he went out into the veranda and sat in the sunshine and fluffed up his fur to make it dry to the roots. Then he felt better.

"There are more things to find out about in this house," he said to himself, "than all my family could find out in all their lives. I shall certainly stay and find out."

He spent all that day roaming over the house. He nearly drowned himself in the bathtubs, put his nose into the ink on a writing table, and burned it on the end of the big man's cigar, for he climbed up in the big man's lap to see how writing was done. At nightfall he ran into Teddy's nursery to watch how kerosene lamps were lighted, and when Teddy went to bed Rikki-tikki climbed up too. But he was a restless companion, because he had to get up and attend to every noise all through the night, and find out what made it. Teddy's mother and father came in, the last thing, to look at their boy, and Rikki-tikki was awake on the pillow.

"I don't like that," said Teddy's mother. "He may bite the child."

"He'll do no such thing," said the father. "Teddy's safer with that little beast than if he had a bloodhound to watch him. If a snake came into the nursery now—" But Teddy's mother wouldn't think of anything so awful.

Early in the morning Rikki-tikki came to early breakfast in the veranda riding on Teddy's shoulder, and they gave him banana and some boiled egg. He sat on all their laps one after the other, because every well-brought-up mongoose always hopes to be a house mongoose some day and have rooms to run about in; and Rikki-tikki's mother (she used to live in the general's house at Segowlee) had carefully told Rikki what to do if ever he came across white men.

Then Rikki-tikki went out into the garden to see what

was to be seen. It was a large garden, only half-cultivated, with bushes, as big as summerhouses, of Marshal Niel roses, lime and orange trees, clumps of bamboos, and thickets of high grass. Rikki-tikki licked his lips. "This is a splendid hunting-ground," he said, and his tail grew bottle-brushy at the thought of it, and he scuttled up and down the garden, snuffing here and there till he heard very sorrowful voices in a thorn-bush.

It was Darzee, the Tailorbird, and his wife. They had made a beautiful nest by pulling two big leaves together and stitching them up the edges with fibers, and had filled the hollow with cotton and downy fluff. The nest swayed to and fro, as they sat on the rim and cried.

"What is the matter?" asked Rikki-tikki.

"We are very miserable," said Darzee. "One of our babies fell out of the nest yesterday and Nag ate him."

"H'm!" said Rikki-tikki, "that is very sad—but I am a stranger here. Who is Nag?"

Darzee and his wife only cowered down in the nest without answering, for from the thick grass at the foot of the bush there came a low hiss—a horrid cold sound that made Rikki-tikki jump back two clear feet. Then inch by inch out of the grass rose up the head and spread hood of Nag, the big black cobra, and he was five feet long from tongue to tail. When he had lifted one-third of himself clear of the ground, he stayed balancing to and fro exactly as a dandelion tuft balances in the wind, and he looked at Rikki-tikki with the wicked snake's eyes that never change their expression, whatever the snake may be thinking of.

"Who is Nag?" said he. "I am Nag. The great God Brahm put his mark upon all our people, when the first cobra spread his hood to keep the sun off Brahm as he slept. Look, and be afraid!"

He spread out his hood more than ever, and Rikki-tikki saw the spectacle-mark on the back of it that looks exactly like the eye part of a hook-and-eye fastening. He was afraid for the minute, but it is impossible for a mongoose to stay frightened for any length of time, and though Rikki-tikki had never met a live cobra before, his mother had fed him on dead ones, and he knew that all a grown mongoose's business in life was to fight and eat snakes. Nag knew that too and, at the bottom of his cold heart, he was afraid.

"Well," said Rikki-tikki, and his tail began to fluff up

again, "marks or no marks, do you think it is right for you to eat fledglings out of a nest?"

Nag was thinking to himself, and watching the least little movement in the grass behind Rikki-tikki. He knew that mongooses in the garden meant death sooner or later for him and his family, but he wanted to get Rikki-tikki off his guard. So he dropped his head a little, and put it on one side.

"Let us talk," he said. "You eat eggs. Why should not I eat birds?"

"Behind you! Look behind you!" sang Darzee.

Rikki-tikki knew better than to waste time in staring. He jumped up in the air as high as he could go, and just under him whizzed by the head of Nagaina, Nag's wicked wife. She had crept up behind him as he was talking, to make an end of him. He heard her savage hiss as the stroke missed. He came down almost across her back, and if he had been an old mongoose he would have known that then was the time to break her back with one bite; but he was afraid of the terrible lashing return stroke of the cobra. He bit, indeed, but did not bite long enough, and he jumped clear of the whisking tail, leaving Nagaina torn and angry.

"Wicked, wicked Darzee!" said Nag, lashing up as high as he could reach toward the nest in the thorn-bush. But Darzee had built it out of reach of snakes, and it only swayed to and fro.

Rikki-tikki felt his eyes growing red and hot (when a mongoose's eyes grow red, he is angry), and he sat back on his tail and hind legs like a little kangaroo, and looked all round him, and chattered with rage. But Nag and Nagaina had disappeared into the grass. When a snake misses its stroke, it never says anything or gives any sign of what it means to do next. Rikki-tikki did not care to follow them, for he did not feel sure that he could manage two snakes at once. So he trotted off to the gravel path near the house, and sat down to think. It was a serious matter for him.

If you read the old books of natural history, you will find they say that when the mongoose fights the snake and happens to get bitten, he runs off and eats some herb that cures him. That is not true. The victory is only a matter of quickness of eye and quickness of foot—snake's blow against mongoose's jump—and as no eye can follow the motion of a snake's head when it strikes, this makes things much more wonderful than any magic herb. Rikki-tikki knew he was a young mongoose, and it made him all the more pleased to think that he had managed to escape a blow from behind. It gave him confidence in himself, and when Teddy came running down the path, Rikki-tikki was ready to be petted.

But just as Teddy was stooping, something wriggled a little in the dust, and a tiny voice said: "Be careful. I am Death!" It was Karait, the dusty brown snakeling that lies for choice on the dusty earth; and his bite is as dangerous as the cobra's. But he is so small that nobody thinks of him, and so he does the more harm to people.

Rikki-tikki's eyes grew red again, and he danced up to Karait with the peculiar rocking, swaying motion that he had inherited from his family. It looks very funny, but it is so perfectly balanced a gait that you can fly off from it at any angle you please, and in dealing with snakes this is an advantage. If Rikki-tikki had only known, he was doing a much more dangerous thing than fighting Nag, for Karait is so small, and can turn so quickly, that unless Rikki bit him close to the back of the head, he would get the return stroke in his eye or his lip. But Rikki did not know. His eyes were all red, and he rocked back and forth, looking for a good place to hold. Karait struck out. Rikki jumped sideways and tried to run in, but the wicked little dusty gray head lashed within a fraction of his shoulder, and he had to jump over the body, and the head followed his heels close.

Teddy shouted to the house: "Oh, look here! Our mongoose is killing a snake." And Rikki-tikki heard a scream from Teddy's mother. His father ran out with a stick, but by the time he came up, Karait had lunged out once too far, and Rikki-tikki had sprung, jumped on the snake's back, dropped his head far between his forelegs, bitten as high up the back as he could get hold, and rolled away. That bite paralyzed Karait, and Rikki-tikki was just going to eat him up from the tail, after the custom of his family at dinner, when he remembered that a full meal makes a slow mongoose, and if he wanted all his strength and quickness ready, he must keep himself thin.

He went away for a dust bath under the castor-oil bushes, while Teddy's father beat the dead Karait. 'What is the use of that?' thought Rikki-tikki. 'I have settled it all'; and then Teddy's mother picked him up from the dust and hugged him, crying that he had saved Teddy from death, and Teddy's father said that he was a providence, and Teddy looked on with big scared eyes. Rikki-tikki was rather amused at all the fuss, which, of course, he did not understand. Teddy's mother might just as well have petted Teddy for playing in the dust. Rikki was thoroughly enjoying himself.

That night at dinner, walking to and fro among the wine-glasses on the table, he might have stuffed himself three times over with nice things. But he remembered Nag and Nagaina, and though it was very pleasant to be patted and petted by Teddy's mother, and to sit on Teddy's shoulder, his eyes would get red from time to time, and he would go off into his long war cry of "Rikk-tikk-tikki-tikki-tchk!"

Teddy carried him off to bed, and insisted on Rikki-tikki

sleeping under his chin. Rikki-tikki was too well bred to bite or scratch, but as soon as Teddy was asleep he went off for his nightly walk round the house, and in the dark he ran up against Chuchundra, the muskrat, creeping around by the wall. Chuchundra is a broken-hearted little beast. He whimpers and cheeps all the night, trying to make up his mind to run into the middle of the room. But he never gets there.

"Don't kill me," said Chuchundra, almost weeping. "Rikki-tikki, don't kill me!"

"Do you think a snake-killer kills muskrats?" said Rikki-tikki scornfully.

"Those who kill snakes get killed by snakes," said Chuchundra, more sorrowfully than ever. "And how am I to be sure that Nag won't mistake me for you some dark night?"

"There's not the least danger," said Rikki-tikki. "But Nag is in the garden, and I know you don't go there."

"My cousin Chua, the rat, told me—" said Chuchundra, and then he stopped.

"Told you what?"

"H'sh! Nag is everywhere, Rikki-tikki. You should have talked to Chua in the garden."

"I didn't—so you must tell me. Quick, Chuchundra, or I'll bite you!"

Chuchundra sat down and cried till the tears rolled off his

whiskers. "I am a very poor man," he sobbed. "I never had spirit enough to run out into the middle of the room. H'sh! I mustn't tell you anything. Can't you hear, Rikki-tikki?"

Rikki-tikki listened. The house was as still as still, but he thought he could just catch the faintest *scratch-scratch* in the world—a noise as faint as that of a wasp walking on a window-pane—the dry scratch of a snake's scales on brick-work. "That's Nag or Nagaina," he said to himself, "and he is crawling into the bathroom sluice. You're right, Chuchundra; I should have talked to Chua."

He stole off to Teddy's bathroom, but there was nothing there, and then to Teddy's mother's bathroom. At the bottom of the smooth plaster wall there was a brick pulled out to make a sluice for the bath water, and as Rikki-tikki stole in by the masonry curb where the bath is put, he heard Nag and Nagaina whispering together outside in the moonlight.

"When the house is emptied of people," said Nagaina to her husband, "he will have to go away, and then the garden will be our own again. Go in quietly, and remember that the big man who killed Karait is the first one to bite. Then come out and tell me, and we will hunt for Rikki-tikki together."

"But are you sure that there is anything to be gained by killing the people?" said Nag.

"Everything. When there were no people in the bungalow, did we have any mongoose in the garden? So long as the bungalow is empty, we are king and queen of the garden; and remember that as soon as our eggs in the melon bed hatch (as they may tomorrow), our children will need room and quiet."

"I had not thought of that," said Nag. "I will go, but there is no need that we should hunt for Rikki-tikki afterward. I will kill the big man and his wife, and the child if I can, and come away quietly. Then the bungalow will be empty, and Rikki-tikki will go."

Rikki-tikki tingled all over with rage and hatred at this, and then Nag's head came through the sluice, and his five feet of cold body followed it. Angry as he was, Rikki-tikki was very frightened as he saw the size of the big cobra. Nag coiled himself up, raised his head, and looked into the bathroom in the dark, and Rikki could see his eyes glitter.

"Now, if I kill him here, Nagaina will know; and if I fight him on the open floor, the odds are in his favour. What am I to do?" said Rikki-tikki-tavi.

Nag waved to and fro, and then

Rikki-tikki heard him drinking from the biggest water jar that was used to fill the bath.

"That is good," said the snake. "Now, when Karait was killed, the big man had a stick. He may have that stick still, but when he comes in to bathe in the morning he will not have a stick. I shall wait here till he comes. Nagaina—do you hear me? I shall wait here in the cool till daytime."

There was no answer from outside, so Rikki-tikki knew Nagaina had gone away. Nag coiled himself down, coil by coil, round the bulge at the bottom of the water jar, and Rikki-tikki stayed still as death. After an hour he began to move, muscle by muscle, toward the jar. Nag was asleep, and Rikki-tikki looked at his big back, wondering which would be the best place for a good hold.

"If I don't break his back at the first jump," said Rikki, "he can still fight. And if he fights—oh Rikki!" He looked at the thickness of the neck below the hood, but that was too much for him; and a bite near the tail would only make Nag savage.

"It must be the head," he said at last; "the head above the hood. And, when I am once there, I must not let go."

Then he jumped. The head was lying a little clear of the water jar, under the curve of it; and, as his teeth met, Rikki braced his back against the bulge of the red earthenware to hold down the head. This gave him just one second's purchase, and he made the most of it. Then he was battered to and fro as a rat is shaken by a dog—to and fro on the floor, up and down, and around in great circles, but his eyes were red and he held on as the body cart-whipped over the floor, upsetting the tin dipper and the soap dish and the flesh brush, and banged against the tin side of the bath. As he held he closed his jaws tighter and tighter, for he made sure he would be banged to death, and, for the honor of his family, he preferred to be found with his teeth locked. He was dizzy, aching, and felt shaken to pieces when something went off like a thunderclap just behind him. A hot wind knocked him senseless and red fire singed his fur. The big man had been wakened by the noise, and had fired both barrels of a shotgun into Nag just behind the hood.

Rikki-tikki held on with his eyes shut, for now he was quite sure he was dead. But the head did not move, and the big man picked him up and said, "It's the mongoose again, Alice. The little chap has saved our lives now."

Then Teddy's mother came in with a very white face, and saw what was left of Nag, and Rikki-tikki dragged himself to Teddy's bedroom and spent half the rest of the night shaking himself tenderly to find out whether he really was broken into forty pieces, as he fancied.

When morning came he was very stiff, but well pleased with his doings. "Now I have Nagaina to settle with, and she will be worse than five Nags, and there's no knowing when the eggs she spoke of will hatch. Goodness! I must go and see Darzee," he said.

Without waiting for breakfast, Rikki-tikki ran to the thorn-bush where Darzee was singing a song of triumph at the top of his voice. The news of Nag's death was all over the yard, for the sweeper had thrown the body on the garbage heap.

"Oh, you stupid tuft of feathers!" said Rikki-tikki angrily. "Is this the time to sing?"

"*Nag is dead—is dead—is dead!*" sang Darzee. "The valiant Rikki-tikki caught him by the head and held fast. The big man brought the bang-stick, and Nag fell in two pieces! He will never eat my babies again."

"All that's true enough. But where's Nagaina?" said Rikki-tikki, looking carefully round him.

"Nagaina came to the bathroom sluice and called for Nag," Darzee went on, "and Nag came out on the end of a stick—the sweeper picked him up on the end of a stick and threw him upon the garbage heap. Let us sing about the great, the red-eyed Rikki-tikki!" And Darzee filled his throat and sang.

"If I could get up to your nest, I'd roll your babies out!" said Rikki-tikki. "You don't know when to do the right thing at the right time. You're safe enough in your nest there, but it's war for me down here. Stop singing a minute, Darzee."

"For the great, the beautiful Rikki-tikki's sake I will stop," said Darzee. "What is it, oh killer of the terrible Nag?"

"Where is Nagaina, for the third time?"

"On the garbage heap by the stables, mourning for Nag. Great is Rikki-tikki with the white teeth."

"Bother my white teeth! Have you ever heard where she keeps her eggs?"

"In the melon bed, on the end nearest the wall, where the sun strikes nearly all day. She hid them there weeks ago."

"And you never thought it worth while to tell me? The end nearest the wall, you said?"

"Rikki-tikki, you are not going to eat her eggs?"

"Not eat exactly; no. Darzee, if you have a grain of sense you will fly off to the stables and pretend that your wing is broken, and let Nagaina chase you away to this bush. I must get to the melon-bed, and if I went there now she'd see me."

Darzee was a feather-brained little fellow who could never hold more than one idea at a time in his head. And just because he knew that Nagaina's children were born in eggs like his own, he didn't think at first that it was fair to kill them. But his wife was a sensible bird, and she knew that cobra's eggs meant young cobras later on. So she flew off from the nest, and left Darzee to keep the babies warm, and continue his song about the death of Nag. Darzee was very like a man in some ways.

She fluttered in front of Nagaina by the rubbish heap and cried out, "Oh, my wing is broken! The boy in the house threw a stone at me and broke it." Then she fluttered more desperately than ever.

Nagaina lifted up her head and hissed, "You warned Rikki-tikki when I would have killed him. Indeed and truly, you've chosen a bad place to be lame in." And she moved toward Darzee's wife, slipping along over the dust.

"The boy broke it with a stone!" shrieked Darzee's wife.

"Well! It may be some consolation to you when you're dead to know that I shall settle accounts with the boy. My husband lies on the garbage heap this morning, but before night the boy in the house will lie very still. What is the use of running away? I am sure to catch you. Little fool, look at me!"

Darzee's wife knew better than to do that, for a bird who looks at a snake's eyes gets so frightened that she cannot move. Darzee's wife fluttered on, piping sorrowfully, and never leaving the ground, and Nagaina quickened her pace.

Rikki-tikki heard them going up the path from the stables, and he raced for the end of the melon patch near the wall. There, in the warm litter above the melons, very cunningly hidden, he found twenty-five eggs, about the size of a bantam's eggs, but with whitish skin instead of shell.

"I was not a day too soon," he said, for he could see the baby cobras curled up inside the skin, and he knew that the minute they were hatched they could each kill a man or a mongoose. He bit off the tops of the eggs as fast as he could, taking care to crush the young cobras, and turned over the litter from time to time to see whether he had missed any. At last there were only three eggs left, and Rikki-tikki began to chuckle to himself, when he heard Darzee's wife screaming: "Rikki-tikki, I led Nagaina toward the house, and she has gone into the veranda, and—oh, come quickly—she means killing!"

Rikki-tikki smashed two eggs, and tumbled backward down the melon-bed with the third egg in his mouth, and scuttled to the veranda as hard as he could put foot to the ground. Teddy and his mother and father were there at early breakfast, but Rikki-tikki saw that they were not eating anything. They sat stone-still, and their faces were white. Nagaina was coiled up on the matting by Teddy's chair, within easy striking distance of Teddy's bare leg, and she was swaying to and fro, singing a song of triumph.

"Son of the big man that killed Nag," she hissed, "stay still. I am not ready yet. Wait a little. Keep very still, all you three! If you move I strike, and if you do not move I strike. Oh, foolish people, who killed my Nag!"

Teddy's eyes were fixed on his father, and all his father could do was to whisper, "Sit still, Teddy. You mustn't move. Teddy, keep still."

Then Rikki-tikki came up and cried, "Turn round, Nagaina. Turn and fight!"

"All in good time," said she, without moving her eyes. "I will settle my account with you presently. Look at your friends, Rikki-tikki. They are still and white. They are afraid. They dare not move, and if you come a step nearer I strike."

"Look at your eggs," said Rikki-tikki, "in the melon bed near the wall. Go and look, Nagaina!"

The big snake turned half around, and saw the egg on the veranda. "Ah-h! Give it to me," she said.

Rikki-tikki put his paws one on each side of the egg, and his eyes were blood-red. "What price for a snake's egg? For a young cobra? For a young king cobra? For the last—the very last of the brood? The ants are eating all the others down by the melon bed."

Nagaina spun clear round, forgetting everything for the sake of the one egg. Rikki-tikki saw Teddy's father shoot out a big hand, catch Teddy by the shoulder, and drag him across the little table with the teacups, safe and out of reach of Nagaina.

"Tricked! Tricked! Tricked! Rikk-tck-tck!" chuckled Rikki-tikki. "The boy is safe, and it was I—I—I that caught Nag by the hood last night in the bathroom." Then he began to jump up and down, all four feet together, his head close to the floor. "He threw me to and fro, but he could not shake me off. He was dead before the big man blew him in two. I did it! Rikki-tikki-tck-tck! Come then, Nagaina. Come and fight with me. You shall not be a widow long."

Nagaina saw that she had lost her chance of killing Teddy, and the egg lay between Rikki-tikki's paws. "Give me the egg, Rikki-tikki. Give me the last of my eggs, and I will go away and never come back," she said, lowering her hood.

"Yes, you will go away, and you will never come back. For you will go to the garbage heap with Nag. Fight, widow! The big man has gone for his gun! Fight!"

Rikki-tikki was bounding all round Nagaina, keeping just out of reach of her stroke, his little eyes like hot coals. Nagaina gathered herself together and flung out at him. Rikki-tikki jumped up and backward. Again and again and again she struck, and each time her head came with a whack on the matting of the veranda and she gathered herself together like a watch spring. Then Rikki-tikki danced in a circle to get behind her, and Nagaina spun round to keep her head to his head, so that the rustle of her tail on the matting sounded like dry leaves blown along by the wind.

He had forgotten the egg. It still lay on the veranda, and Nagaina came nearer and nearer to it, till at last, while Rikki-tikki was drawing breath, she caught it in her mouth, turned to the veranda steps, and flew like an arrow down the path, with Rikki-tikki behind her. When the cobra runs for her life, she goes like a whip-lash flicked across a horse's neck.

Rikki-tikki knew that he must catch her, or all the trouble would begin again. She headed straight for the long grass by the thorn-bush, and as he was running Rikki-tikki heard Darzee still singing his foolish little song of triumph. But Darzee's wife was wiser. She flew off her nest as Nagaina came along, and flapped her wings about Nagaina's head. If Darzee had helped they might have turned her, but Nagaina only lowered her hood and went on. Still, the instant's delay brought Rikki-tikki up to her, and as she plunged into the rat-hole where she and Nag used to live, his little white teeth were clenched on her tail, and he went down with her—and very few mongooses, however wise and old they may be, care to follow a cobra into its hole. It was dark in the hole; and Rikki-tikki never knew when it might open out and give Nagaina room to turn and strike at him. He held on savagely, and stuck out his feet to act as brakes on the dark slope of the hot, moist earth.

Then the grass by the mouth of the hole stopped waving, and Darzee said, "It is all over with Rikki-tikki! We must sing his death song. Valiant Rikki-tikki is dead! For Nagaina will surely kill him underground."

So he sang a very mournful song that he made up on the spur of the minute, and just as he got to the most touching part, the grass quivered again, and Rikki-tikki, covered with dirt, dragged himself out of the hole leg by leg, licking his whiskers. Darzee stopped with a little shout. Rikki-tikki shook some of the dust out of his fur and sneezed.

"It is all over," he said. "The widow will never come out again." And the red ants that live between the grass stems heard him, and began to troop down one after another to see if he had spoken the truth.

Rikki-tikki curled himself up in the grass and slept where he was—slept and slept till it was late in the afternoon, for he had done a hard day's work.

"Now," he said, when he awoke, "I will go back to the house. Tell the Coppersmith, Darzee, and he will tell the garden that Nagaina is dead."

The Coppersmith is a bird who makes a

noise exactly like the beating of a little hammer on a copper pot; and the reason he is always making it is because he is the town crier to every Indian garden, and tells all the news to everybody who cares to listen. As Rikki-tikki went up the path, he heard his "attention" notes like a tiny dinner gong, and then the steady "Ding-dong-tock! Nag is dead—dong! Nagaina is dead! Ding-dong-tock!" That set all the birds in the garden singing, and the frogs croaking, for Nag and Nagaina used to eat frogs as well as little birds.

When Rikki got to the house, Teddy and Teddy's mother (she looked very white still, for she had been fainting) and Teddy's father came out and almost cried over him; and that night he ate all that was given him till he could eat no more, and went to bed on Teddy's shoulder, where Teddy's mother saw him when she came to look late at night.

"He saved our lives and Teddy's life," she said to her husband. "Just think, he saved all our lives."

Rikki-tikki woke up with a jump, for the mongooses are light sleepers.

"Oh, it's you," said he. "What are you bothering for? All the cobras are dead. And if they weren't, I'm here."

Rikki-tikki had a right to be proud of himself. But he did not grow too proud, and he kept that garden as a mongoose should keep it, with tooth and jump and spring and bite, till never a cobra dared show its head inside the walls.

The Awful Fate of Mr Wolf

By Joel Chandler Harris

BRER Rabbit never saw no peace whatsoever. He couldn't leave home without Brer Wolf making a raid and toting off some of his family. Brer Rabbit, he built him a straw house, and it was torn down. Then he made a house out of pine boughs, and that went the same way. So then he made himself a bark house, and that was raided on. And every time he lost one of his houses, he lost one of his children.

At last Brer Rabbit got good and mad, he did, and cussed and then he went off, he did, got some carpenters and they built him a plank house with a rock foundation. After that he could have some peace and quiet. He went out and visited with his neighbors, and he came home and sat by the fire and smoked his pipe and read the newspapers, same like any man what's got a family. He made a hole, he did, in the cellar where the little rabbits could hide out when there was much of a racket in the neighborhood, and the latch of the front door catch on the inside.

Brer Wolf, he saw how the land lay, he did, and he laid low. The little rabbits were mighty skittish, but it got so that no cold chills ran up Brer Rabbit's back any more when he heard Brer Wolf go galloping by.

By and by, one day when Brer Rabbit was fixing for to call on Miss Coon, he heard a monstrous fuss and clatter up the big road, and almost before he could fix his ears for to listen, Brer Wolf ran in the door. The little rabbits, they went into the hole in the cellar, they did, like blowing out a candle. Brer Wolf was fairly covered with mud, and mighty well nigh out of wind.

"Oh, do pray save me, Brer Rabbit!" said Brer Wolf, said he. "Do please, Brer Rabbit! The dogs are after me, and they'll tear me up. Don't you hear them coming? Oh, do please save me, Brer Rabbit! Hide me somewhere where the dogs won't get me."

No quicker said than done.

"Jump in that chest there,
Brer Wolf", said Brer Rabbit, said
he. "Jump in there and make
yourself at home."

In jumped Brer Wolf, down came the lid, and into the hasp went the hook, and there Mr Wolf was. Then Brer Rabbit went to the looking-glass, he did, and winked at himself. And then he pulled the rocking chair in front of the fire, he did, and took a big chew of tobacco. Then Brer Rabbit sat there a long time, he did, turning his mind over and working his thinking machine. By and by he got up and sort of stirred around. Then Brer Wolf opened up,

"Are the dogs all gone, Brer Rabbit?"

"Seems like I hear one of
them smelling around the
chimney corner just now."

Then Brer Rabbit got the
kettle and filled it full of
water and put it on the fire.

"What are you doing now, Brer Rabbit?"

"I'm fixing for to make you a nice cup of tea, Brer Wolf."

Then Brer Rabbit went to the cupboard and got the gimlet, and commenced to bore little holes in the chest lid.

"What are you doing now, Brer Rabbit?"

"I'm boring little holes so you can get breath, Brer Wolf."

Then Brer Rabbit went out and got some more wood, and flung it on the fire.

"What are you doing now, Brer Rabbit?"

"I'm chunking up the fire so you won't get cold, Brer Wolf."

Then Brer Rabbit went down into the cellar and fetched out all his children.

"What are you doing now, Brer Rabbit?"

"I'm telling my children what a nice man you are, Brer Wolf."

And the children, they had to put their hands on their mouth for to keep from laughing. Then Brer Rabbit, he got the kettle and commenced to pour the hot water onto the chest lid.

"What's that I hear, Brer Rabbit?"

"You hear the wind a-blowing, Brer Wolf."

Then the water began to sift through.

"What's that I feel, Brer Rabbit?"

"You feel the fleas a-biting, Brer Wolf."

"They are biting might hard, Brer Rabbit."

"Turn over on the other side, Brer Wolf."

"What's that I feel now, Brer Rabbit?"

"You still feel the fleas, Brer Wolf."

"They are eating me up, Brer Rabbit."

And those were the last words of Brer Wolf, because the scalding water did the business.

Then Brer Rabbit called in his neighbors, he did, and they held a regular jubilee. And if you go to Brer Rabbit's house right now, I don't know but what you'll find Brer Wolf's hide hanging in the back porch, and all because he was so busy with other folks' doings.

*Bevis is a child growing up in Victorian England.
He loves to play for hours in his yard and the fields
surrounding it, watching the animals
and learning about their lives.*

The Spider and the Toad

From *Wood Magic*
By Richard Jeffries

ONE morning as little "Sir" Bevis (such was his pet
name) was digging in the farmhouse yard, he saw a
daisy, and throwing aside his spade, he sat down on the grass
to pick the flower to pieces. He pulled the pink-tipped
petals off one by one, and as they dropped they were lost.
Next he gathered a bright dandelion, and squeezed the white
juice from the hollow stem, which drying presently, left his
fingers stained with brown spots. Then he drew forth a
bennet from its sheath, and bit and sucked it till his teeth
were green from the sap. Lying at full length, he drummed
the earth with his toes, while the tall grass blades tickled his
cheeks.

Presently, rolling on his back, he drummed again with his heels. He looked up at the blue sky, but only for a moment, because the glare of light was too strong in his eyes. After a minute, he turned on his side, thrust out one arm, placed his head on it, and drew up one knee, as if going to sleep. His little brown wrist, bared by the sleeve shortening as he extended his arm, bent down the grass, and his still browner fingers played with the blades, and every now and then tore one off.

A flutter of wings sounded among the blossom on an apple tree close by, and instantly Bevis sat up, knowing it must be a goldfinch thinking of building a nest in the branches. If the trunk of the tree had not been so big, he would have tried to climb it at once, but he knew he could not do it, nor could he see the bird for the leaves and bloom. A puff of wind came and showered the petals down upon him; they fell like snowflakes on his face and dotted the grass.

Buzz! A great humble-bee, with a band of gold across his

back, flew up, and hovered near, wavering to and fro in the air as he stayed to look at a flower.

Buzz! Bevis listened, and knew very well what he was saying. It was, "This is a sweet little yard, my darling; a very pleasant yard; all grass and daisies, and apple trees, and narrow patches with flowers and fruit trees one side, and a wall and currant bushes another side, and a low box-hedge and a haha, where you can see the high mowing grass quite underneath you; and a round summerhouse in the corner, painted as blue inside as a hedge-sparrow's egg is outside; and then another haha with iron railings, which you are always climbing up, Bevis, on the fourth side, with stone steps leading down to a meadow, where the cows are feeding, and where they have left all the buttercups standing as tall as your waist, sir. The gate in the iron railings is not fastened, and besides, there is a gap in the box-hedge, and it is easy to drop down the haha wall, but that is mowing grass there. You know very well you could not come to any harm in the meadow; they said you were not to go outside the garden, but that's all nonsense, and very stupid. I am going outside the garden, Bevis. Good morning, dear. *Buzz!*" And the great humble-bee flew slowly between the iron railings, out among the buttercups, and away up the field.

Bevis went to the railings, and stood on the lowest bar; then he opened the gate a little way, but it squeaked so loud upon its rusty hinges that he let it shut again. He walked round the yard along beside the box-hedge to the patch by the lilac trees; they were single lilacs, which are much more beautiful than the double, and all bowed down with a mass of bloom. Some rhubarb grew there, and to bring it up the faster, they had put a round wooden box on it, hollowed out from the sawn butt of an elm, which was rotten within and easily scooped. The top was covered with an old board, and every time that Bevis passed he lifted up the corner of the board and peeped in, to see if the large red, swelling knobs were yet bursting.

One of these round wooden boxes had been split and spoilt, and half of it was left lying on the ground. Under this shelter a Toad had his house. Bevis peered in at him, and touched him with a twig to make him move an inch or two, for he was so lazy, and sat there all day long, except when it rained. Sometimes the Toad told him a story, but not very often, for he was a silent old philosopher, and not very fond of anybody. He had a nephew, quite a lively young fellow, in the cucumber frame on the other side of the lilac bushes, at whom Bevis also peered nearly every day after they had lifted the frame and propped it up with wedges.

The gooseberries were no bigger than beads, but he tasted two, and then a thrush began to sing on an ash tree in the hedge of the meadow. "Bevis! Bevis!" said the thrush, and he turned round to listen: "My dearest Bevis, have you forgotten the meadow, and the buttercups, and the sorrel? You know the sorrel, don't you, that tastes so pleasant if you nibble the leaf? And I have a nest in the bushes, not very far up the hedge, and you may take just one egg; there are only two yet. But don't tell any more boys about it, or we shall not have one left. That is a very sweet yard, but it is very small. I like all these fields to fly about in, and the swallows fly ever so much farther than I can; so far away and so high, that I cannot tell you how they find their way home to the chimney. But they will tell you, if you ask them. Good morning! I am going over the brook."

Bevis went to the iron railings and got up two bars, and looked over; but he could not yet make up his mind, so he went inside the summerhouse, which had one small round window. All the lower part of the blue walls was scribbled and marked with pencil, where he had written and drawn, and put down his ideas and notes. The lines were somewhat intermingled, and crossed each other, and some stretched out long distances, and came back in sharp angles. But Bevis knew very well what he meant when he wrote it all. Taking a stump of cedar pencil from his pocket, one end of it much gnawn, he added a few scrawls to the inscriptions, and then stood on the seat to look out of the round window, which was darkened by an old cobweb.

Once upon a time there was a very cunning Spider, a very cunning spider indeed. The old Toad by the rhubarb told Bevis there had not been such a cunning spider for many summers; he knew almost as much about flies as the old Toad, and caught such a great number that the Toad began to think there would be none left for him. Now the Toad was extremely fond of flies, and he watched the spider with envy, and grew more angry about it every day.

As he sat blinking and winking by the rhubarb in his house all day long, the Toad never left off thinking, thinking, thinking about this spider. And as he kept thinking, thinking, thinking, so he told Bevis, he recollected that he knew a great deal about a good many other things besides flies. So one day, after several weeks of thinking, he crawled out of his house in the sunshine, which he did not like at all, and went across the grass to the iron railings, where the spider had then got his web. The spider saw him coming, and being very proud of his cleverness, began to taunt and tease him.

"Your back is all over warts, and you are an old toad," he said. "You are so old, that I heard the swallows saying their great, great, great grandmothers, when they built in the chimney, did not know when you were born. And you have got foolish, and past doing anything, and so stupid that you hardly know when it is going to rain. Why, the sun is shining bright, you stupid old toad, and there isn't a chance of a single drop falling. You look very ugly down there in the grass. Now, don't you wish that you were me, and could catch more flies than you could eat?
Why, I can catch wasps and bees, and tie them up so tight with my threads that they cannot sting nor even move their wings, nor so much as wriggle their bodies. I am the very cleverest and most cunning spider that ever lived."

"Indeed, you are!" replied the Toad. "I have been thinking so all the summer;

and so much do I admire you, that I have come all this way, across in the hot sun, to tell you something."

"Tell me something!" said the spider, much offended. "I know everything."

"Oh, yes, honored sir," said the Toad; "you have such wonderful eyes, and such a sharp mind, it is true that you know everything about the sun, and the moon, and the earth, and flies. But, as you have studied all these great and important things, you could hardly see all the very little trifles like a poor old toad."

"Oh yes, I can. I know everything—everything!"

"But, sir," went on the Toad so humbly, "this is such a very little thing, and a spider like you in such a high position of life, could not mind me telling you such a mere nothing."

"Well, I don't mind," said the spider, "you may go on, and tell me, if you like."

"The fact is," said the Toad, "while I have been sitting in my hole, I have noticed that such a lot of the flies that come into this garden presently go into the summerhouse there, and when they are in the summerhouse, they always go to that little round window, which is sometimes quite black with them; for it is the nature of flies to buzz over glass."

"I do not know so much about that," said the spider; "for I have never lived in houses, being an independent insect;

but it is possible you may be right. At any rate, it is not of much consequence. You had better go up into the window, old toad." Now this was a sneer on the part of the spider.

"But I can't climb up into the window," said the Toad; "all I can do is to crawl about the ground, but you can run up a wall quickly. How I do wish I was a spider, like you. Oh, dear!" And then the Toad turned round, after bowing to the clever spider, and went back to his hole.

Now the spider was secretly very much mortified and angry with himself, because he had not noticed this about the flies going to the window in the summerhouse. At first he said to himself that it was not true; but he could not help looking that way now and then, and every time he looked, there was the window crowded with flies. They had all the yard to buzz about in, and all the fields, but instead of wandering under the trees, and over the flowers, they preferred to go into the summerhouse and crawl over the glass of the little window, though it was very dirty from so many feet. For a long time, the spider was too proud to go there too; but one day such a splendid bluebottle fly got in the window and made such a tremendous buzzing, that he could not resist it any more.

So he left his web by the railings, and climbed up the blue-painted wall, over Bevis' writings and marks, and spun such a web in the window as had never before been seen. It was the largest and the finest, and the most beautiful web that had ever been made, and it caught such a number of flies that the spider grew fatter every day. In a week's time he was so big that he could no longer hide in the crack he had chosen, he was quite a giant, and the Toad came across the grass one night and looked at him, but the spider was now so bloated he would not recognize the Toad.

But one morning a robin came to the iron railings, and perched on the top, and put his head a little on one side, to show his black eye the better. Then he flew inside the summerhouse, alighted in the window, and gobbled up the spider in an instant. The old Toad shut his eye and opened it again, and went on thinking, for that was just what he knew would happen. Ever so many times in his very long life he had seen spiders go up there, but no sooner had they got fat than a robin or a wren came in and ate them. Some of the clever spider's web was there still when Bevis looked out of the window, all dusty and draggled, with the skins and wings of some gnats and a dead leaf entangled in it.

The Bastables—Oswald, Dora, Dicky, Alice, Noel, and H.O. (Horace Octavius)—are staying at the house of a writer they call "Albert's uncle." A brother and sister, Daisy and Denny, are also staying. The children have formed a society to help them behave, which they call "The Wouldbegoods."

The Circus

From *The Wouldbegoods*
By E. Nesbit

THE ones of us who had started the Society of the Wouldbegoods began, at about this time, to bother. They said we had not done anything really noble—not worth speaking of, that is—for over a week, and that it was high time to begin again "with earnest endeavor," Daisy said. So then Oswald said, "All right; but there ought to be an end to everything. Let's each of us think of one really noble and unselfish act, and the others shall help to work it out. Then when everybody's had their go we'll write every single thing down in the Golden Deed book, and we'll draw two lines in red ink at the bottom, like Father does at the end of an account. And after that, if anyone wants to be good they can jolly well be good on our own, if at all."

The ones who had made the Society did not welcome this wise idea, but Dicky and Oswald were firm. So they had to agree. When Oswald is really firm, opposingness and obstinacy have to give way.

Dora said, "It would be a noble action to have all the school children from the village and give them tea and games in the paddock. They would think it so nice and good of us."

But Dicky showed her that this would not be *our* good act, but Father's, because he would have to pay for the tea, and he had already stood us the keepsakes for the soldiers, as well as having to stump up heavily over the coal barge. And it is in vain being noble and generous when someone else is paying for it all the time, even if it happens to be your father. Then three others had ideas at the same time and began to explain what they were.

We were all in the dining-room, and perhaps we were making a bit of a row. Anyhow, Oswald for one, does not blame Albert's uncle for opening his door and saying, "I suppose I must not ask for complete silence. That would be too much. But if you could whistle, or stamp with your feet, or shriek or howl—anything to vary the monotony of your well-sustained conversation."

Oswald said kindly, "We're awfully sorry. Are you busy?"

"Busy?" said Albert's uncle. "My heroine is now hesitating on the verge of an act which, for good or ill, must influence her whole subsequent career. You wouldn't like her to decide in the middle of such a row that she can't hear herself think?"

We said, "No, we wouldn't."

Then he said, "If any outdoor amusement should commend itself to you this bright mid-summer day—" So we all went out.

Then Daisy whispered to Dora—they always hang together. Daisy is not nearly so white-micey as she was at first, but she still seems to fear the deadly ordeal of public speaking.

Dora said, "Daisy's idea is a game that'll take us all day. She thinks keeping out of the way when he's making his heroine decide right would be a noble act, and fit to write in the Golden Book; and we might as well be playing something at the same time."

We all said "Yes, but what?" There was a silent interval.

"Speak up, Daisy, my child." Oswald said; "fear not to lay bare the utmost thoughts of that faithful heart."

Daisy giggled. Our own girls never giggle—they laugh right out or hold their tongues. Their kind brothers have taught them this. Then Daisy said, "If we could have a sort of play to keep us out of the way. I once read a story about an animal race. Everybody had an animal, and they had to go how they liked, and the one that got in first got the prize. There was a tortoise in it, and a rabbit, and a peacock, and sheep, and dogs, and a kitten."

This proposal left us cold, as Albert's uncle says, because we knew there could not be any prize worth bothering about. And though you may be ever ready and willing to do anything for nothing, yet if there's going to be a prize there must *be* a prize and there's an end of it.

Thus the idea was not followed up. Dicky yawned and said, "Let's go into the barn and make a fort."

So we did, with straw. It does not hurt straw to be messed about with like it does hay.

The downstairs—I mean down-ladder—part of the barn was fun too, especially for Pincher. There was as good ratting there as you could wish to see. Martha tried it, but she could not help running kindly beside the rat, as if she was in double harness with it. This is the noble bull-dog's gentle and affectionate nature coming out. We all enjoyed the ratting that day, but it ended, as usual, in the girls crying because of the poor rats. Girls cannot help this; we must not be waxy with them on account of it, they have their nature, the same as bull-dogs have, and it is this that makes them so useful in smoothing the pillows of the sick-bed and tending wounded heroes.

However, the forts, and Pincher, and the girls crying, and having to be thumped on the back, passed the time very agreeably till dinner. There was roast mutton with onion sauce, and a roly-poly pudding.

Albert's uncle said we had certainly effaced ourselves effectually, which means we hadn't bothered. So we determined to do the same during the afternoon, for he told us his heroine was by no means out of the wood yet.

And at first it was easy. Jam roly gives you a peaceful feeling and you do not at first care if you never play any runabout game ever any more. But after a while the torpor begins to pass away. Oswald was the first to recover from his.

He had been lying on his front part in the orchard, but now he turned over on his back and kicked his legs up, and said, "I say, look here; let's do something."

Daisy looked thoughtful. She was chewing the soft yellow parts of grass, but I could see she was still thinking about that animal race. So I explained to her that it would be very poor fun without a tortoise and a peacock, and she saw this, though not willingly.

It was H.O. who said, "Doing anything with animals is prime, if they only will. Let's have a circus!"

At the word the last thought of the pudding faded from Oswald's memory, and he stretched himself, sat up, and said, "Bully for H.O. Let's!"

The others also threw off the heavy weight of memory, and sat up and said "Let's!" too.

Never, never in all our lives had we had such a gay galaxy of animals at our command. The rabbits and the guinea-pigs, and even all the bright, glass-eyed, stuffed denizens of our late-lamented jungle paled into insignificance before the number of live things on the farm.

(I hope you do not think that the words I use are getting too long. I know they are the right words. And Albert's uncle says your style is always altered a bit by what you read. And I have been reading *The Vicomte de Bragelonne*. Nearly all my new words come out of those.)

"The worst of a circus is," Dora said, "that you've got to teach the animals things. A circus where the performing creatures hadn't learned performing would be a bit silly. Let's give up a week to teaching them and then have the circus."

Some people have no idea of the value of time. And Dora

is one of those people who do not understand the fact that when you want to do something, you want to do it immediately, and not a week later.

Oswald said the first thing was to collect the performing animals. "Then perhaps," he said, "we may find that they have hidden talents hitherto unsuspected by their harsh masters."

So Denny took a pencil and wrote a list of the animals required. This is it:

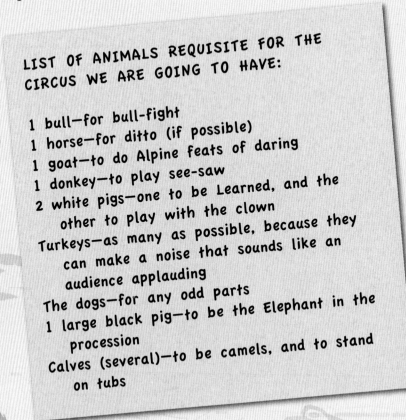

LIST OF ANIMALS REQUISITE FOR THE CIRCUS WE ARE GOING TO HAVE:

1 bull—for bull-fight
1 horse—for ditto (if possible)
1 goat—to do Alpine feats of daring
1 donkey—to play see-saw
2 white pigs—one to be Learned, and the
   other to play with the clown
Turkeys—as many as possible, because they
   can make a noise that sounds like an
   audience applauding
The dogs—for any odd parts
1 large black pig—to be the Elephant in the
   procession
Calves (several)—to be camels, and to stand
   on tubs

Daisy ought to have been captain because it was partly her idea, but she let Oswald be, because she is of a retiring character.

Oswald said, "The first thing is to get all the creatures together; the paddock at the side of the orchard is the place, because the hedge is good. When we've got the performers there we'll make a programme, and then dress for our parts. It's a pity there won't be any audience but the turkeys."

We took the animals in their right order, according to Denny's list. The bull was the first. He is black. He does not live in the cowhouse with the other horned people; he has a house all to himself two fields away. Oswald and Alice went to fetch him. They took a halter to lead the bull by, and a whip, not to hurt the bull with, but just to make him mind. The others were to try to get one of the horses while we were gone.

Oswald as usual was full of bright ideas. "I daresay," he said, "the bull will be shy at first, and he'll have to be goaded into the arena."

"But goads hurt," Alice said.

"They don't hurt the bull," Oswald said; "his powerful hide is too thick."

"Then why does he attend to it," Alice asked, "if it doesn't hurt?"

"Properly-brought-up bulls attend because they know

they ought," Oswald said. "I think I shall ride the bull," the brave boy went on. "A bull-fight, where an intrepid rider appears on the bull, sharing its joys and sorrows. It would be something quite new."

"You can't ride bulls," Alice said; "at least, not if their backs are sharp like cows."

But Oswald thought he could. The bull lives in a house made of wood and prickly furze bushes, and he has a yard to his house. You cannot climb on the roof of his house at all comfortably.

When we got there he was half in his house and half out in his yard, and he was swinging his tail because of the flies which bothered. It was a very hot day.

"You'll see," Alice said, "he won't want a goad. He'll be so glad to get out for a walk he'll drop his head in my hand like a tame fawn, and follow me lovingly all the way."

Oswald called to him. He said, "Bull! Bull! Bull! Bull!" because we did not know the animal's real name. The bull took no notice; then Oswald picked up a stone and threw it at the bull, not angrily, but just to make it pay attention. But the bull did not pay a farthing's worth of it. So then Oswald leaned over the iron gate of the bull's yard and just flicked the bull with the whiplash. And then the bull *did* pay attention. He started when the lash struck him, then suddenly he faced round, uttering a roar like that of the wounded King of Beasts, and putting his head down close to his feet he ran straight at the iron gate where we were standing.

Alice and Oswald mechanically turned away; they did not wish to annoy the bull any more, and they ran as fast as they could across the field so as not to keep the others waiting.

As they ran across the field Oswald had a dreamlike fancy that perhaps the bull had rooted up the gate with one paralysing blow, and was now tearing across the field after him and Alice, with the broken gate balanced on its horns. We climbed the stile quickly and looked back; the bull was still on the right side of the gate.

Oswald said, "I think we'll do without the bull. He did not seem to want to come. We must be kind to dumb animals."

Alice said, between laughing and crying, "Oh, Oswald, how can you!"

But we did do without the bull, and we did not tell the

others how we had hurried to get back. We just said, "The bull didn't seem to care about coming."

The others had not been idle. They had got old Clover, the cart-horse, but she would do nothing but graze, so we decided not to use her in the bull-fight, but to let her be the Elephant. The Elephant's is a nice quiet part, and she was quite big enough for a young one. Then the black pig could be Learned, and the other two could be something else. They had also got the goat; he was tethered to a young tree. The donkey was there. Denny was leading him in the halter. The dogs were there, of course—they always are. So now we only had to get the turkeys for the applause and the calves and pigs.

The calves were easy to get, because they were in their own house. There were five. And the pigs were in their houses too. We got them out after long and patient toil, and persuaded them that they wanted to go into the paddock, where the circus was to be. This is done by pretending to drive them the other way. A pig only knows two ways—the way you want him to go, and the other. But the turkeys knew thousands of different ways, and tried them all. They made such an awful row, we had to drop all ideas of ever hearing applause from their lips, so we came away and left them.

"Never mind," H.O. said, "they'll be sorry enough

afterward, nasty, unobliging things, because now they won't see the circus. I hope the other animals will tell them about it."

While the turkeys were engaged in baffling the rest of us, Dicky had found three sheep who seemed to wish to join the glad throng, so we let them.

Then we shut the gate of the paddock, and left the dumb circus performers to make friends with each other while we dressed.

Oswald and H.O. were to be clowns. It is quite easy with Albert's uncle's pyjamas, and flour on your hair and face, and the red they do the brick-floors with.

Alice had very short pink and white skirts, and roses in her hair and round her dress. Her dress was the pink calico and white muslin stuff off the dressing-table in the girls' room fastened with pins and tied round the waist with a small bath towel. She was to be the Dauntless Equestrienne, and to give an enchanting act of barebacked daring, riding either a pig or a sheep, whichever we found was freshest and most skittish. Dora was dressed for the Haute ecole, which means a riding-habit and a high hat. She took Dick's topper that he wears with his Etons, and a skirt of Mrs Pettigrew's. Daisy, dressed the same as Alice, taking the muslin from Mrs Pettigrew's dressing-table without saying anything beforehand. None of us would have advised this, and indeed

we were thinking of trying to put it back, when Denny and Noel, who were wishing to look like highwaymen, with brown-paper top-boots and slouch hats and Turkish towel cloaks, suddenly stopped dressing and gazed out of the window.

"Krikey!" said Dick, "come on, Oswald!" and he bounded like an antelope from the room.

Oswald and the rest followed, casting a hasty glance through the window. Noel had got brown-paper boots too, and a Turkish towel cloak. H.O. had been waiting for Dora to dress him up for the other clown. He had only his shirt and knickerbockers and his braces on. He came down as he was—as indeed we all did. And no wonder, for in the paddock, where the circus was to be, a blood-thrilling thing had transpired. The dogs were chasing the sheep. And we had now lived long enough in the country to know the fell nature of our dogs' improper conduct.

We all rushed into the paddock, calling to Pincher, and Martha, and Lady. Pincher came almost at once. He is a well-brought-up dog—Oswald trained him. Martha did not seem to hear. She is awfully deaf, but she did not matter so much, because the sheep could walk away from her easily. She has no pace and no wind. But Lady is a deer-hound. She is used to pursuing that fleet and antlered pride of the forest—the stag—and she can go like billyo. She was now far away in a distant region of the paddock, with a fat sheep just before her in full flight. I am sure if ever anybody's eyes did start out of their heads with horror, like in narratives of adventure, ours did then.

There was a moment's pause of speechless horror. We expected to see Lady pull down her quarry, and we know what a lot of money a sheep costs, to say nothing of its own personal feelings.

Then we started to run for all we were worth. It is hard to run swiftly as the arrow from the bow when you happen to be wearing pyjamas belonging to a grown-up person—as I was—but even so I beat Dicky. He said afterward it was because his brown-paper boots came undone and tripped him up. Alice came in third. She held on the dressing-table muslin and ran jolly well. But ere we reached the fatal spot all was very nearly up with the sheep. We heard a plop; Lady stopped and looked round. She must have heard us bellowing to her as we ran. Then she came toward us, prancing with happiness, but we said "Down!" and "Bad dog!" and ran sternly on.

When we came to the brook which forms the northern boundary of the paddock we saw the sheep struggling in the water. It is not very deep, and I believe the sheep could have stood up, and been well in its depth, if it had liked, but it would not try. It was a steepish bank. Alice and I got down and stuck our legs into the water, and then Dicky came down, and the three of us hauled that sheep up by its shoulders till it could rest on Alice and me as we sat on the bank. It kicked all the time we were hauling. It gave one extra kick at last, that raised it up, and I tell you that sopping wet, heavy, panting, silly donkey of a sheep sat there on our laps like a pet dog; and Dicky got his shoulder under it at the back and heaved to keep it from flumping off into the water again, while the others fetched the shepherd.

When the shepherd came he called us every name you can think of, and then he said, "Good thing master didn't come along. He would ha' called you some tidy names."

He got the sheep out, and took it and the others away. And the calves too. He did not seem to care about the other performing animals.

Alice, Oswald, and Dick had had almost enough circus for just then, so we sat in the sun and dried ourselves and wrote the programme of the circus. This was it:

PROGRAMME

1. Startling leap from the lofty precipice by the performing sheep. Real water, and real precipice. The gallant rescue. O. A. and D. Bastable. (We thought we might as well put that in though it was over and had happened accidentally.)
2. Graceful bare-backed equestrienne act on the trained pig, Eliza. A. Bastable.
3. Amusing clown interlude, introducing trained dog, Pincher, and the other white pig. H.O. and O. Bastable.
4. The See-Saw. Trained donkeys. (H.O. said we had only one donkey, so Dicky said H.O. could be the other. When peace was restored we went on to 5.)
5. Elegant equestrian act by D. Bastable. Haute ecole, on Clover, the incomparative trained elephant from the plains of Venezuela.
6. Alpine feat of daring. The climbing of the Andes, by Billy, the well-known acrobatic goat. (We thought we could make the Andes out of hurdles and things, and so we could have but for what always happens. (This is the unexpected. (This is a saying Father told me—but I see I am three deep in brackets so I will close them before I get into any more).).).
7. The Black but Learned Pig. ("I daresay he knows something," Alice said, "if we can only find out what." We did find out all too soon.)

We could not think of anything else, and our things were nearly dry—all except Dick's brown-paper top-boots, which were mingled with the gurgling waters of the brook.

We went back to the seat of action—which was the iron trough where the sheep have their salt put—and began to dress up the creatures.

We had just tied the Union Jack we made out of Daisy's flannel petticoat round the waist of the Black and Learned Pig, when we heard screams from the back part of the house, and suddenly we saw that Billy, the acrobatic goat, had got loose from the tree we had tied him to. (He had eaten all the parts of its bark that he could get at, but we did not notice it until next day, when led to the spot by a grown-up.)

The gate of the paddock was open. The gate leading to the bridge that goes over the moat to the back door was open too. We hastily proceeded in the direction of the screams, and, guided by the sound, threaded our way into the kitchen. As we went, Noel, ever fertile in melancholy ideas, said he wondered whether Mrs Pettigrew was being robbed, or only murdered.

In the kitchen we saw that Noel was wrong as usual. It was neither. Mrs Pettigrew, screaming like a steam-siren and waving a broom, occupied the foreground. In the distance the maid was shrieking in a hoarse and monotonous way, and trying to shut herself up inside a clothes-horse on which washing was being aired.

On the dresser—which he had ascended by a chair —was Billy, the acrobatic goat, doing his Alpine daring act. He had found out his Andes for himself, and even as we gazed he turned and tossed his head in a way that showed us some mysterious purpose was hidden beneath his calm exterior. The next moment he put his off-horn neatly behind the end plate of the next to the bottom row, and ran it along against the wall. The plates fell crashing on to the soup tureen and vegetable dishes which adorned the lower range of the Andes.

Mrs Pettigrew's screams were almost drowned in the discarding crash and crackle of the falling avalanche of crockery.

Oswald, though stricken with horror and polite regret, preserved the most dauntless coolness. Disregarding the mop which Mrs Pettigrew kept on poking at the goat in a timid yet cross way, he sprang forward, crying out to his trusty followers, "Stand by to catch him!"

But Dick had thought of the same thing, and ere Oswald could carry out his long-cherished and generallike design, Dicky had caught the goat's legs and tripped it up. The goat fell against another row of plates, righted itself hastily in the gloomy ruins of the soup tureen and the sauce-boats, and then fell again, this time toward Dicky. The two fell heavily on the ground together. The trusty followers had been so struck by the daring of Dicky and his lion-hearted brother, that they had not stood by to catch anything.

The goat was not hurt, but Dicky had a sprained thumb and a lump on his head like a black marble door-knob. He had to go to bed.

I will draw a veil and asterisks over what Mrs Pettigrew said. Also Albert's uncle, who was brought to the scene of ruin by her screams. Few words escaped our lips. There are times when it is not wise to argue; however, little what has occurred is really our fault.

When they had said what they deemed enough and we were let go, we all went out. Then Alice said distractedly, in a voice which she vainly strove to render firm, "Let's give up the circus. Let's put the toys back in the boxes—no, I don't mean that—the creatures in their places—and drop the whole thing. I want to go and read to Dicky."

Oswald has a spirit that no reverses can depreciate. He hates to be beaten. But he gave in to Alice, as the others said so too, and we went out to collect the performing troop and sort it out into its proper places.

Alas! We came too late. In the interest we had felt about whether Mrs Pettigrew was the abject victim of burglars or not, we had left both gates open again. The old horse—I mean the trained elephant from Venezuela—was there all right enough. The dogs we had beaten and tied up after the first act, when the intrepid sheep bounded, as it says in the programme. The two white pigs were there, but the donkey was gone. We heard his hoofs down the road, growing fainter and fainter, in the direction of the "Rose and Crown." And just round the gatepost we saw a flash of red and white and blue and black that told us, with dumb signification, that the pig was off in exactly the opposite direction. Why couldn't they have gone the same way? But no, one was a pig and the other was a donkey, as Denny said afterward.

Daisy and H.O. started after the donkey; the rest of us, with one accord, pursued the pig—I don't know why. It trotted quietly down the road; it looked very black against the white road, and the ends on the top, where the Union Jack was tied, bobbed brightly as it trotted. At first we thought it would be easy to catch up to it. This was an error.

When we ran faster it ran faster; when we stopped it stopped and looked round at us, and nodded. (I daresay you won't swallow this, but you may safely. It's as true as true, and so's all that about the goat. I give you my sacred word of honor.) I tell you the pig nodded as much as to say, 'Oh, yes. You think you will, but you won't!' and then as soon as we moved again off it went. That pig led us on and on, o'er miles and miles of strange country. One thing, it did keep to the roads. When we met people, which wasn't often, we called out to them to help us, but they only waved their arms and roared with laughter. One chap on a bicycle almost tumbled off his machine, and then he got off it and propped it against a gate and sat down in the hedge to laugh properly. You remember Alice was still dressed up as the gay equestrienne in the dressing-table pink and white, with rosy garlands, now very droopy, and she had no stockings on, only white sand-shoes, because she thought they would be easier than boots for balancing on the pig in the graceful bare-backed act.

Oswald was attired in red paint and flour and pyjamas, for a clown. It is really *impossible* to run speedfully in another man's pyjamas, so Oswald had taken them off, and wore his own brown knickerbockers belonging to his Norfolks. He had tied the pyjamas round his neck, to carry them easily. He was afraid to leave them in a ditch, as Alice suggested, because he did not know the roads, and for aught he recked they might have been infested with footpads. If it had been his own pyjamas it would have been different. (I'm going to ask for pyjamas next winter, they are so useful in many ways.)

Noel was a highwayman in brown-paper gaiters and bath towels and a cocked hat of newspaper. I don't know how he kept it on. And the pig was encircled by the dauntless banner of our country. All the same, I think if I had seen a band of youthful travelers in bitter distress about a pig I should have tried to lend a helping hand and not sat roaring in the hedge, no matter how the travelers and the pig might have been dressed.

It was hotter than anyone would believe who has never had occasion to hunt the pig when dressed for quite another part. The flour got out of Oswald's hair into his eyes and his mouth. His brow was wet with what the village blacksmith's was wet with, and not his fair brow alone. It ran down his face and washed the red off in streaks, and when he rubbed his eyes he only made it worse. Alice had to run holding the equestrienne skirts on with both hands, and I think the brown-paper boots bothered Noel from the first. Dora had her skirt over her arm and carried the topper in her hand. It was no use to tell ourselves it was a wild boar hunt—we were long past that.

At last we met a man who took pity on us. He was a kind-hearted man. I think, perhaps, he had a pig of his own —or, perhaps, children. Honor to his name!

He stood in the middle of the road and waved his arms. The pig right-wheeled through a gate into a private yard and cantered up the drive. We followed. What else were we to do, I should like to know?

The Learned Black Pig seemed to know its way. It turned first to the right and then to the left, and emerged on a lawn. "Now, all together!" cried Oswald, mustering his failing voice to give the word of command. "Surround him! Cut off his retreat!"

We almost surrounded him. He edged off toward the house.

"Now we've got him!" cried the crafty Oswald, as the pig got on to a bed of yellow pansies close against the red house wall.

All would even then have been well, but Denny, at the last, shrank from meeting the pig face to face in a manly way. He let the pig pass him, and the next moment, with a squeak that said "There now!" as plain as words, the pig bolted into a French window. The pursuers halted not. This was no time for trivial ceremony. In another moment the pig was a captive. Alice and Oswald had their arms round him under the ruins of a table that had had teacups on it, and around the hunters and their prey stood the startled members of a parish society for making clothes for the poor heathen, that the pig had led us into the very midst of. They were reading a missionary report or something when we ran our quarry to earth under their table. Even as he crossed the threshold I heard something about "black brothers being already white to the harvest." All the ladies had been sewing flannel things for the poor blacks while the curate read aloud to them. You think they screamed when they saw the pig and us? You are right.

On the whole, I cannot say that the missionary people behaved badly. Oswald explained that it was entirely the pig's doing, and asked pardon quite properly for any alarm the ladies had felt; and Alice said how sorry we were but really it was *not* our fault this time. The curate looked a bit nasty, but the presence of ladies made him keep his hot blood to himself.

When we had explained, we said, "Might we go?"

The curate said, "The sooner the better." But the Lady of the House asked for our names and addresses, and said she should write to our Father. (She did, and we heard of it too.)

They did not do anything to us, as Oswald at one time believed to be the curate's idea. They let us go.

And we went, after we had asked for a piece of rope to lead the pig by. "In case it should come back into your nice room," Alice said. "And that would be such a pity, wouldn't it?"

A little girl in a starched pinafore was sent for the rope. And as soon as the pig had agreed to let us tie it round his neck we came away. The scene in the drawing-room had not been long. The pig went slowly, "Like the meandering brook," Denny said. Just by the gate the shrubs rustled and opened, and the little girl came out. Her pinafore was full of cake.

"Here," she said. "You must be hungry if you've come all that way. I think they might have given you some tea after all the trouble you've had." We took the cake with correct thanks.

"I wish I could play at circuses," she said. "Tell me about it."

We told her while we ate the cake; and when we had done she said perhaps it was better to hear about than do, especially the goat's part and Dicky's.

"But I do wish auntie had given you tea," she said.

We told her not to be too hard on her aunt, because you have to make allowances for grown-up people. When we parted she said she would never forget us, and Oswald gave her his pocket button-hook and corkscrew combined for a keepsake.

Dicky's act with the goat (which is true, and no kid) was the only thing out of that day that was put in the Golden Deed book, and he put that in himself while we were hunting the pig.

Alice and me capturing the pig was never put in. We would scorn to write our own good actions, but I suppose Dicky was dull with us all away; and you must pity the dull, and not blame them.

I will not seek to unfold to you how we got the pig home, or how the donkey was caught (that was poor sport compared to the pig). Nor will I tell you a word of all that was said and done to the intrepid hunters of the Black and Learned. I have told you all the interesting part. Seek not to know the rest. It is better buried in obliquity.

The Hunters

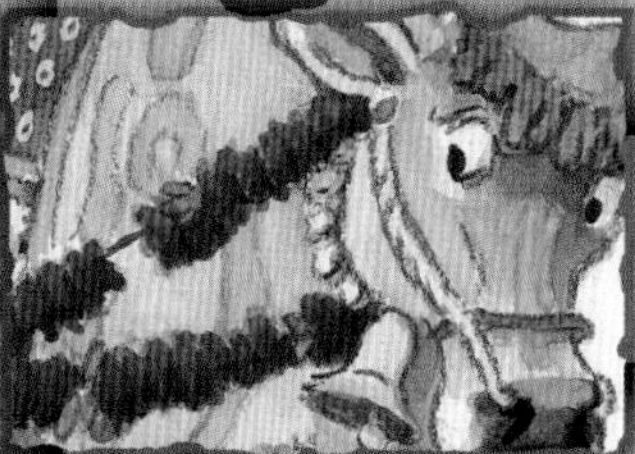

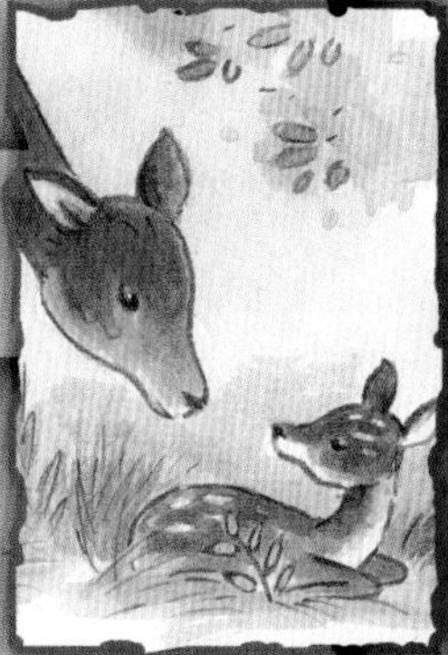

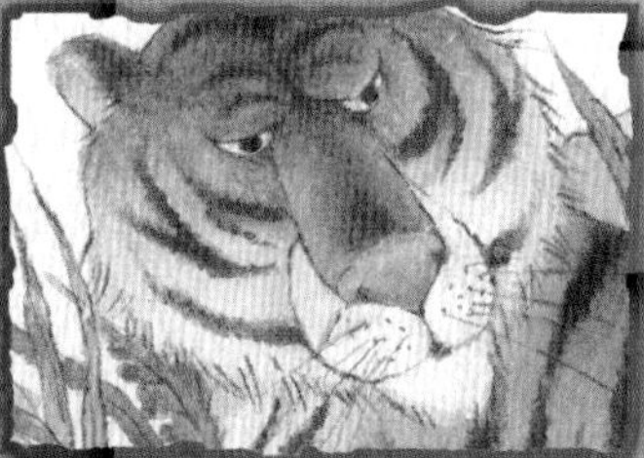

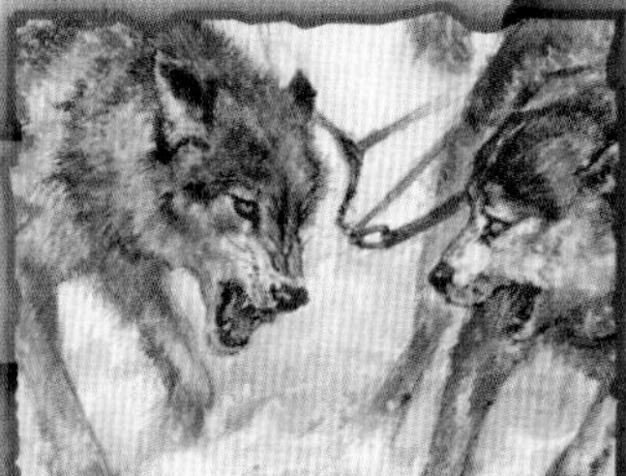

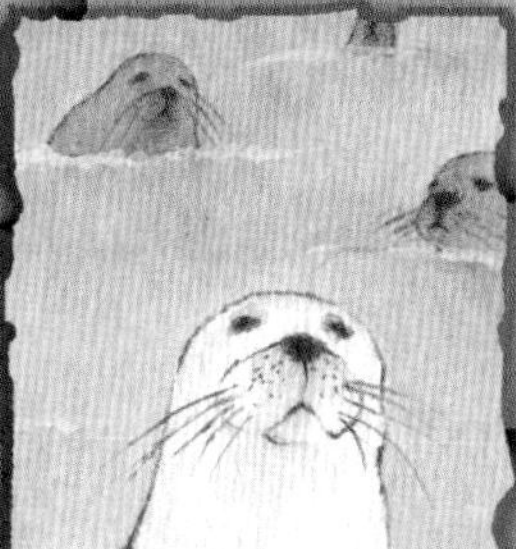

The Cow and the Python

By D. G. Mukerji

WHEN I was about eight years old, I began to notice things as a whole. Hitherto the events of the day, such as morning prayers and evening silence, had seemed islands of peace in a chaos of meaningless unrelated events, and people went to work, came home from the fields, went to bed, and each one of these actions appeared an invention of the moment. It never occurred to my child's mind that they formed the parts of a whole and were not mere unrelated incidents.

But a little before my eighth birthday a change was wrought in my perceptions when one of our cows gave birth to a heifer. I was entrusted with the task of looking after the calf when she was weaned from her mother six weeks later.

"The cowbell before the cow" is a proverb of the hills, and so my first care was to go to the smith for a brass bell. After that I had to call on the weaver for a cotton string which would be thick but soft enough for the tender young neck of Goma, which was the name I gave my little charge. Whenever she mooed it sounded "Go-Ma," meaning "O my mother, where art thou?" In the course of a fortnight I learned that the weaver, the blacksmith, the vendor of hay, were all related to me and my little cow.

One more experience revealed to my poor little mind the unity of life. It occurred during the Dipavali festival—the feast of lanterns—which as you know, is held after the fall rain is over, and is a kind of thanksgiving and harvest-home celebration. During that day in late October all the cows of our village were led in procession through its chief thoroughfare to the communal threshing floor, there to be let loose to wander home all by themselves.

My aunt and myself owned the third largest flock of cattle in the village, consisting of twenty cows, so ours had the third place in the procession. But no farmer displays all his cows; he generally selects half a dozen fine heads of cattle. I was charged with choosing our six finest beasts to walk in the procession. First of all I took Goma, then her mother, three more cows, and our bull Vrisa.

The selection was made in the morning. The rest of the

day I spent with one of our farm hands in washing and decorating the beasts. We took them to the river which ran at the south end of the village. The village ran from east to west and to our north bristled the Himalayas.

After their bath the animals were brought home to be decorated. First of all we painted each adult animal's horns in yellow. Then we strung garlands of red oleanders around their necks, and over their backs we flung purple, blue, orange, green, and silver shawls which were securely tied by strings around their glistening rumps. Next we painted their hoofs yellow. It took nearly the whole day before my flock was ready to march in the procession. Goma, who had not yet grown horns, nor a back ample enough to be covered with a gemshaming shawl, had to walk with nothing on but her brass bell. At the eleventh hour someone suggested that we should paint her hoofs yellow like the others, but I protested: "She shall wear no gold on her feet until she has horns to paint like shining banana skins. Not till then!"

My aunt, who agreed with me, ordered us to march along to the village temple whence the procession was to start. Our bull, Vrisa, garlanded in red oleander, his horns gleaming like spikes of gold, his back a shimmer of emerald, while his dewlap peeped out like shining steel in between clusters of flaming flowers, led our flock. Next to him marched our chief cowherd clad in spotless white and turbaned in tawny silk. He held a green bamboo stave in his left hand while his right rested on Vrisa's mountainous rump that swayed from side to side like the head of a sleepy child. I led the rear with Goma whose tinkling bell fretted the silence of the early evening.

Our house was the last one at the northern end of the village, and we were obliged to go far to the west to reach the temple compound, for the house of Heaven, as we called our village shrine, lay at the western end so that at dawn the rising sun's light fell on it in its purest splendor. It was a miracle of yellow sandstone about three stories high. In front of it spread a lawn large enough to accommodate more than five hundred people. Behind the shrine, out of sight, lay the low one-storied house of the priest. Slowly our Vrisa, throbbing with colors and fat, walked on to the green lawn, and stood facing the shrine. Soon from different directions came pouring flocks of cattle, their horns all yellow flame and their flanks dripping with stabbing colors.

In no time the place was filled with the noise of men and beasts.

Now the priest appeared on the top of the temple steps to give his benediction. He was robed in ocher. Slowly he lifted his hands and blessed us.

Just as the priest had finished, my little charge ran forward tinkling her bell. This was in good taste, I thought, for it marked the end of the ceremony at the temple. Now the procession formed itself, and we started for the communal threshing floor at the eastern extremity of our village. Shall I ever forget the wonder of that march?

We passed between houses, some of adobe with thatched roofs, some of brick and timber—but all filled that afternoon with faces of men and women not only of our village but from the neighboring city of Almora who had come to witness our festival. The hitherto dusty road that traversed our village had been swept and strewn with grains of rice, lotus leaves, and drawings and designs had been made by different families on their front walls and also in the dust of their thresholds. From every house rose a trumpeting sound of conch-shells blown by women, and over our heads were strewn flowers by young girls. One could hardly see the ruddy evening sky above our heads because of the Eel-leaves (cedar leaves) and little flowers that swarmed in the air ere they fell upon us.

At last we reached the communal threshing floor under the vast banyan tree where the village elders and my aunt Kuri received us. Here the elders blessed us before dismissing the cortege.

The oldest one said: "We are all brothers—man and beast. We are sharers in toil and suffering pain. We partake of one another's well-being: the life that is in the ox is the same life that beats in our blood: the milk that comes from the cow is the strength that is in our children's limbs. May you treat your animals well; may they in turn be moved by God to serve you abundantly."

With these words the gathering was dismissed. Just then Goma, that little mischief-maker, walked forward and began to devour the oleander garland from the neck of the bull at the head of the procession.

This was both terrible and humiliating in spite of the fact that she was hungry and only two months old. Had the owner of the bull been a good man he would have understood and forgiven, but instead he rushed forward in a rage and began to beat her back. Instantly she switched her tail, twisted her neck, and frisked off in the direction of the jungle and I followed after! It did not take us long to be out of the reach of the men and women at the threshing floor. I saw nothing but Goma's vanishing white body before me. I stumbled, fell, rose, and ran again after her. Before she had stopped running and before I knew where we were, it had grown quite dark.

Both of us suddenly realized that we had penetrated the outskirts of the jungle and were at the threshold of great danger. To ordinary observers the outer edges of a forest may seem safe at all times, but to those who know, evening and early morning are the two occasions when it is not safe to be there. At those times animals are going out to hunt or returning from their night's outing. Any man who lingers on the outskirts of a dense jungle may be killed by a tiger or leopard; a boy and a calf are in greater danger, because wild dogs, wolves, hyenas, and black panthers all seek to devour them.

So there we stood wondering about our fate in that Dipavali evening. In a moment there flashed through my mind the pictures of previous nights at Dipavali when the whole village was illuminated with lights, every house decorating its roof and walls with innumerable lamps. The village put on magic for a dress. But now behold, here I was lost in the jungle in the company of a cow hardly two months old!

Fortunately Goma had not yet learned to be afraid. Fear is taught by grown up men and beasts to their young. Once we learn to be afraid, we rarely shake off the habit, and I believe our fear frightens other beasts, causing them to attack us. While Goma stood there looking at me between eating mouthfuls of leaves from the surrounding dense saplings, I thought how hard it would be to find a way out in the surrounding dark, eloquent with a thousand noises of insects and animals. These sounds, however, betokened comparative safety, for were a tiger moving in our direction, all voices would have been hushed. "The more noise the safer the jungle" runs the proverb.

I put my hand on Goma's shoulder and started to lead her back. We kept steadily to the windward of the noises, but we had to do a good deal of tacking to avoid the less noisy places. After we had gone about half an hour, we were able to discern through the surrounding wall of foliage what I thought to be a haze of light in the sky betokening our nearness to the town of Mayavati. I felt happy, and Goma switched her tail in pleasure. But danger swoops down on you when you relax your vigilance. Something fell at our feet crushing under it all the insect and other noises that were running like water in the undergrowth. Goma groaned, then leaped. In a moment she was out of touch or hearing. I stood still, wondering at the heavy thing lying on the floor of the jungle. I kept on walking backward and peering into the midnight dark before me. Nothing could I see, but I heard *shush—sha—shush* near me. It kept on drawing nearer and nearer. I was convinced that it must be a python. If there had been a strong tree nearby I would have been lost, for the snake with its tail around the trunk for a lever could have held me so firmly in its coil that escape would have been impossible. But fortunately we were passing through grassy fields interspersed with saplings hardly ten feet high, too frail for the great snake to coil around. The moment I realized the nature of my enemy, I turned on my heels and ran, knowing that he could not catch me if I ran zigzagging away from him. I had not gone very far when I met a search party from the village out with lanterns and spikes looking for me. I was indeed very glad to see them. They had been searching for Goma and myself for nearly an hour. On my arrival home we found the calf already there. She had dashed from the jungle straight to the cowshed.

When I told the men who found me and my aunt about my having encountered a python they would hardly believe me, saying: "This is the tale of a frightened child." I was deeply chagrined but alas, they did not know that in another week's time they would pay for the folly of their scepticism.

I *must* give you some further description of our village before our story travels any further. How can I tell of the ways of parrots if I do not first describe the forest in which they live? As well as at the communal threshing floor and the temple grounds, people met and talked with one another by the river Avati, which was about the twentieth of a mile broad and too shallow for navigation, though during the spring when the snows melted in the Himalayas, or the rains swelled its waters in July, Avati attained the depth of nearly a dozen feet for a fortnight at a time. But the current was so swift at that season that swimming or floating on it meant utter disaster. The river ran between banks of ilex, deodar, and pine trees, and here and there its northern shore was pierced and secured by stone walls and yellow sandstone stairways commonly known as Ghauts. During the rainy season Avati would turn as tawny as the steps themselves but at other times she was as clear and bright as the eyes of a bird.

There on the Ghauts people met when they came to fetch water, about nine in the morning, an hour before bathing began. Since it was a one way current, without tides, whatever water was muddled after the drinking water was taken, became clear for the bathers downstream, and whatever they sullied, flowed out eastwards to the sea. The water was always clean. In the afternoon people bathed in it again before going to the temple for evening meditation, and about midday between the times when men made use of it, the animals bathed in Avati, and drank from it whenever they chose. We always took our cattle there at half past eleven and gave them their bath. It was wonderful to see their red, white, and gray sides drawn into the silver water, in whose depths the tall trees of the bank flung their reflections like torches of green.

One late November morning when women had come to fetch water from the river, they saw a python floating down stream. They came home and told their men-folk, but those of us who were in the fields did not hear of it, and punctually at eleven thirty we brought our herds of cattle to give them their bath. With the help of one of our hired men, I was busy scrubbing my beasts with straw as they came out of the water, usually one by one, but when two came out together the hired man took one and I the other. After they had been rubbed, they were sent down for a final dip. When they came out at last their sleek sides would drip with lambent water in the midday sun.

It was when Goma and her mother
had come up from the stream and the hired
man and I had begun to rub them—I of course
taking Goma—that suddenly a black rope swung
down from a tree above and gathered the cow, and
then my poor man, in its swift circling coil. In a trice,
where stood the two of them, groaned a dying man amid
the bellows of a dying beast. Goma and the rest of the
herd fled in panic leaving me face to face with the horrible
spectacle. I will never forget how the few feet of that
serpent's tail thinned itself almost to the size of a child's
wrist as it hung from the tree, tightening as its body
stretched and then letting go as the coils dropped upon its

victims. Ere he and the poor cow became crushed into pulp I fled from the spot.

It was not long before I met herds of cattle running pell-mell through the village streets. Apparently our stampeding herd had run into other people's cattle coming down to the river for their bath, and had communicated to them their panic. I shouted to the herdsmen the news of the calamity that I had witnessed on the river bank. Call after call was sounded by the priest at his temple on his conch shell.

Alas, by the time the village rallied to the river they found neither python nor victims. None knew where to search. But I told Kuri I was sure the monster could be found very near the place of the tragedy. So when in the evening we went to the temple to hear the priest read the scriptures and the epics, we drew him into a corner and I unburdened my mind to him.

The graybeard listened to me carefully, and said: "Take me tomorrow morning. I must now take my seat at the altar and read to you the story of Rama." Later on, I shall tell you of those readings that our priest gave in the temple every evening, and of the morality plays that were acted there at least once a month.

The following day after I had brought flowers to the temple and prayed there, the priest and I set out to find the murderer. I took him first to the outer jungle where I had encountered the enemy during the Dipavali evening. It proved an easy task in daylight. Lo, there lay long lines of grass and dry leaves crushed in a certain pattern. We followed it wherever it led. Those long sweeping lines thick as my waist could only have been made by a python. It did not take us long to reach the riverbank. No doubt he had gone there to take a drink. And while he was at it something from behind had frightened him and he fell into the swift current. The latter had borne him down past the Ghaut where human beings bathed. At last he reached the place where the river takes a sharp turn and where we always bathed the cattle. There the current is retarded by a kind of dam made by fallen boulders. We traced him as far as the soft ground on which he had crawled and the tree around which he had coiled his muddy body. After that we faced a perfect blank.

Purohit, the priest, and I tried hard to locate his present whereabouts but in vain. Dejected in spirit and baffled in mind, we sat down on the shore about midday just to rest our tired limbs. Slowly herdsmen brought their herds and bathed them. One by one the cows and oxen went home. At last came our own herd led by a new hired man named Gokul. He plunged into the water ahead of his charge. Then followed little Goma just to show that she too could share Gokul's fun. They played with each other in the water like children. It amused me so to see my little heifer so frisky and happy. I called her name. She obeyed instantly. She started toward the shore. Slowly, inch by inch, she struggled up. When she was ready to put her feet on dry ground, her eyes fell on something to her left. Then she stopped. As if she had seen death itself, her body quivered in terror. That was enough for the keen eye of the priest. He dashed forward into the water and stood waist deep looking at the spot where the calf's eyes were riveted. He shouted, "Mila, Mila!" (Found! Found!) That noise dug into Goma's being like a goad. She was driven up the shore by that "Mila, Mila," and ran home. The other cattle followed her example. The drumming of their hoofs on the ground frightened the python apparently, for the priest called to me to look before he also ran away.

The python could not creep away nor fight. He had eaten too much. It would take him at least a month to digest a youth of twenty and a medium-sized cow. I went into the water and stood near the priest. I looked and looked. At last under a tree from which the river, after eating half the ground, had receded, I saw something. Two eyes like dull crystals, and below them two protruding brown things like tusks. He looked like a most sinister image of Satan lying under the outer roots of a maple and

the thick shadows cast by its bough that overhung many feet
of water. A black mountain of half coiled python looking at
us with glassy eyes and out of the corner of its mouth
protruding the two horns of our cow. The uncanny sight
filled me with loathing and terror. It takes a serpent a long
time to dissolve the horns of its victim in its own saliva. As
you know, snakes large or small, cannot chew; they partly
crush their food in their
throats. The priest
said, "Let us
catch him
alive." We
went to the
village, which
had heard of the
python's presence
from our new herdsman, Gokul. The
able-bodied men asked advice of the serpent
charmers who said the snake was too large to
be caught by the flute, so the men set to work to erect a cage
of bamboo and cowhide thongs which took a day to finish.
When it was done it was lowered in front of the python. But
now the problem was to get him to move into it. Noises,
shouts, then men jumping over the roots of the tree, all
failed to make him move an inch.

There he lay, gripped by the act of digesting his food, a process more powerful than himself. The open cage was pushed close enough to the cavern mouth under the tree to allow just room enough for the front door, which was held up by a rope to the overhanging branch, to fall guillotine fashion, once he was inside.

But he did not budge from his place. So all the people left in disgust, saying, "What a stupid snake."

It was about the fourth day after our finding his hiding place that I went alone to carry out a plan of my own. When I reached the spot there was no adult about. I fetched pick, shovel, straw, and a lot of kindling wood. Next I dug a tunnel at the python's back, which was a slanting hole, descending deeper and deeper as it approached the beast. As I was half way through Purohit appeared. When he saw me he approved of my plan, and threw aside his priest's beads and cudgel, and took the pick from my already tired hands. He kept on digging harder and harder, and after we had worked another two hours, at about four in the afternoon he said: "I can hear him breathe. Go and get a crowbar."

When I fetched it he took it and jammed it right through the thin partition of loose soil and struck the serpent. He moved. We heard the roots of the tree tremble as his heavy body fell against them. But he did not move enough to please the priest. He jabbed a few times more, without getting a satisfactory result from the sleepy monster.

Then we laid the straw thick in the tunnel, almost next to the python's skin, then covered it with dry fall leaves. After placing the kindling wood on top, we set the tunnel on fire. I was ordered to go up the tree with a knife. I climbed away over and lay on the overhanging branch to which was tied the rope, that held up the door of the prison prepared for our enemy. My orders were to cut the rope as soon as the snake had entered the cage.

Slowly the smoke arose, and as luck would have it, lay in thick layers between me and everything below. In time it rose higher and began to hurt my eyes. I shouted to the priest a warning, "Call to me as loud as you can when the python enters the cage and you want the door to snap down, for I can see nothing. When I hear you I shall cut the rope."

Purohit shouted, "If he gets into the cage I will shout so that it will make you deaf. As soon as you hear me, cut that rope."

Whirl upon whirl of smoke arose, choking my nostrils and blinding my eyes. There I sat with my face over that all-powerful incense fume. I shut my eyes and concentrated all attention to catching the priest's warning cry. Of course the more I listened the more I heard the hiss and crackle of the fire and the noise of human voices. Apparently the whole village had returned there to witness the roasting of the python. They kept on talking to one another and sometimes shouting aloud. How on earth I could complete my task under those circumstances passed my comprehension.

It seemed as if hours passed. I was like one wrapped in midnight darkness of smoke and noise. Suddenly a dizzy spell seized me. I felt as if I should fall off the tree. I heard an awful uproar. In the midst of the thunderous racket I faintly heard someone say in a squeaking voice, "O thou grandsire of a monkey, cut the rope. Host thou not hear me, O half brother of a mule? Cut that rope."

But he who was abusing me did not know that I could see nothing in the smoke. All the same I blindly groped forward and slashed away under the bough with my knife, mostly cutting the air. But I persisted. Once I cut off a twig. Another time I thought I cut a branch. Then another branch—no, this was no branch! Ha, the rope! I went on sawing away at it. Harder and harder I worked. And by the increasing din and tumult I could make sure that I was cutting the rope. I redoubled my forces. Ultimately I put half my weight on the knife, then pulled. More noise from below. Then something snapped! That instant I lost my balance. But I had sense enough to throw away the knife as I fell from the tree. In a moment I was sinking in the river, down, down, down....

When I came to the surface of the water again, my face was almost against the thick and double bamboo bars of the cage in which writhed a huge gray-black mass of flesh. I looked more carefully. Yes, he had swallowed those two horns that had stuck out of his mouth when first we located him under the tree. That seemed to satisfy some strange curiosity in me. Another thing I noticed was the size of the brute. He must have been at least a foot in diameter. People around me said that they had never seen a python so large before. However, they were so glad that he was caged and ready to be sold to a museum that, except the priest and Kuri, no one interested himself in me, dripping, choking, and bruised.

This book is about the life of one of the beautiful deer that roam Exmoor, in the southwest of England. These deer used to be hunted, like foxes, by men riding horses with hounds. This extract comes from the beginning of the story.

The Calf's Childhood

From *The Story of a Red Deer*

By J. W. Fortescue

ONCE upon a time there was a little Red Deer Calf. You know what a Red Deer is, for you of all children have been brought up to know, though it may be that you have never seen a calf very close to you. A very pretty little fellow he was, downy-haired and white-spotted, though as yet his legs were rather long and his ears were rather large, for he was still only a very few weeks old. But he did not think himself a baby by any means, for he was an early calf and had been born in the second week in May; and a birthday in the second week in May is the greatest event that can occur in a Red Deer's family.

The first thing that he remembered was that he found

himself lying very snug and warm in a patch of fern, with the most beautiful pair of brown eyes that ever were seen gazing straight down upon him. And soon he was aware that they were the eyes of the Hind his mother, that they followed him wherever he went, and watched over him whatever he did, and that, whatever he might want, she was there to provide it for him. She always had a cosy bed ready for him in grass or fern; she washed him clean and brushed his little coat with her tongue every morning; and she taught him but two lessons: to lie as still as a mouse, and to do just as he was bid. For every morning before dawn she had to go afield to feed herself, farther than the little Calf could travel with her; and as she had no nurse to leave in charge of him, she just tucked him up as closely as she could, and told him to lie still till she came back. And like a good little fellow he obeyed her; which was well for him, for if he had taken it into his head to jump up and look about him, some evil man or beast might have seen him and made away with him; and then this story would never have been written.

Always just before the sun rose she came back, and every day she seemed to love him better, and every day he felt that she was more than the whole world to him. And morning after morning up rose the blessed sun, and drove the mist away, and sent a little ray forward through the fern to kiss him and bid him good morrow. And the mist left a drop on every blade and blossom, and said, "Goodbye, my little fellow; I shall come back again this evening"; and the drops nodded and sparkled and twinkled, and kept whispering, "Yes, coming back this evening," over and over again, till the sun said that he could stand it no longer and was obliged to dry them all up. Then rose a hum of many wings as the flies woke up, and went out for their day's work; but the breeze moved like a sentry over the bed of the little Calf and said to them, "Move on, move on; this little Calf must not be disturbed"; and they dared not disobey, for they knew that, if they did, he was certain sooner or later to send for his big brother, the Westerly Gale, who would blow them away with a vengeance. And all through the day the breeze kept singing through the graceful, yielding grass and the stubborn wiry heather; while mingled with it came snatches of a little song from the brown peat stream in the valley below him. He could not make out much of it except these words, which came over and over again: "Mother and child come here, come here, I am the friend of the wild Red Deer."

For some time they moved but little distance from the place where he was born, for his legs could not yet carry him very far; but as he grew stronger they wandered farther, till at last one day he found himself on high ground, and saw the world that he was to live in, his heritage of Exmoor. You know it, for you have seen it, fold upon fold of grass and heather, slashed by deep valleys and merry babbling streams, and bounded on the one hand by the blue sky and on the other by the blue sea. It was all his own, for he was a wild Red Deer. And he looked upon it with his great round eyes, and pricked his ears and tossed his little head; for the sun was shining warm above him, and the soft west wind blew fresh and untainted over the sea and flew across the moor, catching up all that was sweetest on its way from grass and gorse and heather, and bearing it straight to his nostrils. And he threw his little nose into the air and snuffed up the full, rich breeze; for no creature has a finer scent than a deer; and he felt that this was life indeed.

Then they went down, leaving the song of the wind ever fainter behind them; and in its stead rose the song of the peat stream bidding them come down to it. So they went; and there it was trickling down as clear as crystal, though as yellow as amber. There was but little water in it that fine midsummer, but it hastened on none the less over the stones in a desperate hurry, as are all Exmoor streams, to get to the sea. And it whispered its song as it went, but so low that they heard no words. They passed by a little shallow, and there the Calf saw dozens of little fry, scurrying about from stone to stone; and just below the shallow they came to a little brown, oily pool in a basin of rock. The Calf looked into it, and there he saw his own little form, and behind it his mother's sweet eyes watching over him. And then for the first time he noticed that his own coat was spotted while his mother's was red. But while he was staring at the water a fly suddenly came, and began to dance a reel over it to show what a fine fellow he was, when all of a sudden a neat little body, all brown and gold and red spots, leaped up out of the water, seized the fly in his mouth and fell back with a splash which broke the pretty picture all to pieces.

He shrank back, for he was rather startled, but his mother soon comforted him. "It was only a little Trout, my dear," she said, "only a greedy little Trout."

"But he was such a pretty little fellow," he said, for he had quite got over his fright; "I wish he would jump again."

But the Hind looked grave. "We are never unkind to the Trout," she said, "for they belong to the peat stream, but you must never become familiar with them. Fallow Deer, I believe, treat them as equals," and here she looked very proud, "but we do not. They are a lazy lot of fellows whose forefathers would not take the trouble to go down to the sea, whereby they might have grown into noble fish, with a coat as bright as the moon on the water. But they would not, and so they have remained small and ugly, and they never lose their spots. You must never be rude to them, for that would be unworthy of a Red Deer, but you must never make great friends with them. You may talk to little Salmon when we see them, for they lose their spots, but not to the Trout." For the Hind was a great lady, with much pride of race, which though it made her civil to everyone, taught her to be shy of idlers and low company.

"But, mother," said the poor little Calf, "I've got a spotted coat."

"But you will lose it, my darling," she said tenderly. "No, no, my child will be a true Red Deer."

So they left the water, and presently stopped while his mother plucked at a tuft of sweet grass among the heather; when to his astonishment a little gray ball of fur came bounding out of a hole in the ground, and another at his heels, and three more after them. And they ran around and around and played like mad things. And presently another, far bigger than they, came up slowly out of another hole, sat up on her hind legs, pricked her ears, and began to look about her.

Then catching sight of the Calf she crouched down, and

began in a very shrill voice, "Why, my dear tender heart" (for she was not only a Rabbit, but a Devonshire Rabbit, and of course spoke broad Devon), "if it isn't my little maister, and her ladyship too, begging your pardon, my lady. And sweetly pretty he is, my lady; and butiful you'm looking too, in your summer coat, so glossy as a chestnut, sure enough. And dear heart alive, how he groweth. Why, 'twas but a few days agone that my Bucky saith to me I don't rightly remember how many days agone, but I mind 'twas the very day when the old Grayhen up to Badg-worthy came to ask me if I had seen her poult for she's lost a poult, my lady, hath the poor soul, as your ladyship knoweth. Well, my Bucky saith to me, 'Bunny' saith he, 'you may depend that young maister will grow to be so fine a stag as ever was seen on Exmoor'."

Then without pausing an instant she called out at the top of her voice to one of the little rabbits: "Flossy-a! Come back, little bittlehead, come back, or the fox will catch 'ee!"

The Hind listened very graciously to this long speech, for she loved to hear good words of her Calf, and she was just a little pleased to hear of her own good looks. But she could not help looking beautiful, and she looked all the more so because she very seldom thought about it. So she returned the compliment by asking after Bunny and her family.

"Oh! Thank you, my lady," answered Bunny, "I reckon

we'm well. There han't been no man this way this long time,
thanks be; and there's plenty of meat, and not too much
rain. And the family's well, my lady; look to mun playing all
around, so gay; and my third family this spring, my lady
that I should say so! No, I reckon I can't complain; but oh,
my lady! They foxes, and they weasels! They do tell me that
the old vixen from Cornham Brake hath five cubs; and I
can't abide a vixen, never could. And they weasels they'm
small, but they'm worse than foxes. Now there's my Bucky.
He can't bide home, he saith, these fine days, but must go
and lie out. I says to mun, 'Bucky' I says, 'tis very well for
the likes of her ladyship to lie out every day, but you should
bide home to bury.' But no, he would go. 'Well then,
Bucky,' I says, 'I reckon that you'll grow a pair of horns like
his lordship, brow, bay, and trey, Bucky,' I says, 'and turn to
bay when the weasel's after 'ee. And with that he layeth back
his ears and away he goeth Flossy-a, come back, will 'ee, or
I'll give you what vor! Now there's that Flossy, my lady, so

like to her father as my two ears. She won't bide close to bury; and they do tell me that the vixen to Cornham has moved this way. It won't do, my lady, it won't do. Oh dear, dear, dear!" And she stopped for want of breath.

"Well, good evening, Bunny," said the Hind very kindly, "I must take my little son home. I shall see you again very soon."

"And good evening to your ladyship," answered Bunny, "and good evening to you, my pretty dear. Ah! you'm his lordship's son sure enough. I mind the time—"

But the Hind had moved on out of hearing, for when once an old Doe Rabbit begins to talk she never stops. Then presently the Calf said: "Mother, who is his lordship?"

And she answered, "He is your father, my darling. For the Red Deer are lords of this forest, and he is the lord of them all. And brow, bay, trey is the coronet that every good Stag wears, and which you too shall wear in due time, when you grow up." And he said no more, for to his mind there was nothing on earth half so beautiful as she was, and he asked no better than to grow up to be such another.

Now the very next day the Hind led her Calf away from the valley where they lay; and after traveling some little way, they met the most beautiful bird that the Calf had ever seen. His plumage was all of glossy black, which shone blue and green and purple in the sun, while to set it off he had a patch of pure white on each wing, and a spot of red above each eye; his tail was forked and bent outwards in two graceful curves, and his legs were feathered to the very heel. He flew toward them some little way, with an easy noiseless flight, and lighted just in front of them, as handsome a fellow as you will see in a summer's day.

"Well, good Master Blackcock," said the Hind, "has my lord not moved?"

"Not a step, my lady," said the bird; "he lieth so quiet as my wife when she's sitting, though the flies do worrit mun terrible."

"Then come along, son," she said. And she led him on and presently stopped and whispered, "Look." And there he saw such a sight as he had never dreamed of; a great Stag nearly twice the size of his mother, with horns half grown and velvet-black with flies, lying down motionless but for the constant twitching of his head.

The Calf could not see how big he was, till presently he rose on to his feet, and stretched himself, throwing his horns right back, with a mighty yawn. Then he stood for a minute or two blinking rather sleepily, but always shaking his head and wincing under the torment of the flies. His back was as broad as a bullock's and his coat shone with good living; and the little Calf looked with all his eyes, for he had made up his mind then and there to stand just like that and to stretch himself just like that, when he had grown to be such a fine stag as that.

But presently the Hind led him away and asked the Blackcock, "And where is my sister?" And the Blackcock led them on, and after a time, to the Calf's delight, they came in sight of two more Hinds and another little Calf. And all three caught the wind of them and came forward to meet them. One of the Hinds was very big and gray, and she had no Calf, but the other was smaller and bright red, and had at her foot as sweet a little Calf as ever you saw; and it was the smaller of the two Hinds that came to them first. Then both of the mothers laid their Calves down, and began to talk, but they had hardly exchanged a word, when the old gray Hind broke in.

"So it's you, Tawny, is it?" she said; "and you have brought a Calf with you, I see. I suppose I must ask, is it a stag or a hind?"

"A stag, Aunt Yeld," said the Lady Tawny (for that was the name of our Calf's mother); "do look at him for a minute. He does look so sweet in his bed."

"A stag, is it?" said Aunt Yeld with a little sniff. "Well, I suppose if people must have calves they had better have stags. Ruddy's here is a hind, but I never could see the attraction of any calf myself."

For Aunt Yeld, like some old maids (but by no means like

all) that have no children of their own, thought it the right thing to look down on Calves; and indeed she was rather a formidable old lady. She had two very big tushes in her upper jaw, which she was constantly showing, and she made a great point (when she was not flurried) of closing the claws of her hoofs very tight, and letting her hind feet fall exactly where her fore feet had fallen, which she knew to be the way of a stag.

Then Aunt Yeld turned around and said, "Now you two mustn't think of going. You are not fit to take care of yourselves, so you must stay with me, and I'll take care of you." You see she had quite forgotten what she said at first, for she had really a kind heart, though nothing could keep her from patronizing everyone.

So for many days they lived together, and Aunt Yeld always posted herself upwind of them to keep watch over them; and if our soldiers in their red coats were sentries half as good as she, they would be the best in the world. Now and again, though very seldom, the great Stag would join them and lie by them all day, chewing the cud and shaking his great head, which grew bigger every day. But he never uttered a word, unless it was to say, "Very good that growing wheat was this morning, to be sure," to which the Hind would answer, "I am so glad, dearest"; or it would be, "The turnips on Yarner farm are not coming on well in this dry weather, I am told; it's very annoying, for I was looking forward to my turnips," and then the Hind would say, "I am so sorry, dearest. How I hope it will rain soon!" For old stags are perhaps rather too fond of their dinners.

Once only he showed himself quite different, and that was when one day the Blackcock flew up to say that all the hills were coming down. Now the way the Blackcock got the idea into his head was this. He had been taking a bath in the dust at the foot of a great sheet of screes, the loose, flat stones on the hillside which you have often seen on the moor, and had enjoyed it greatly, fluffing out his feathers and flapping his great wings. But while he was in the middle of it a Jackdaw came flying overhead, and seeing this great ball of feathers rolling about, pitched down upon the screes to see what strange thing it might be. And as he came hopping down to look at it closer, he displaced one little stone, which displaced another little stone, and that another, until quite a number of stones were set moving, and came rushing down for twenty feet like a tiny cataract, close to the Blackcock's ear. Whereupon the Jackdaw flapped off cawing with fright, and the Blackcock flew away screaming to tell the deer that all the hills were coming down.

But when he came the old Stag stood up at once and said: "Lady Yeld, take the lead; Ruddy and Tawny, follow her. Steadily now, no hurrying!" Then they moved on a little way and stopped, the Stag always remaining behind them; for they could see that the hills were not coming down before them, and therefore they must have begun to fall behind them, if the Blackcock spoke truth. And that was why the Stag remained behind, to be nearest to the danger, as a gentleman should be.

The Deer stopped for a time, and at last the Stag said, "I can see nothing, hear nothing, and wind nothing. Are you quite sure the hills are all coming down, Blackcock? I think that you must have made some mistake." For the old Stag was a great gentleman, and always very civil and courteous.

But Aunt Yeld, who was quick of temper, stamped on the ground, and said almost out loud: "Bah! I believe the bird's as great an idiot as his wife."

The Blackcock looked very foolish, and was so much confused that he did not know what to answer; but the Lady Tawny said kindly: "Thank you, Blackcock, for coming. You mustn't let us keep you from your dinner." And though it was not his dinner-time, he was so glad of the excuse that he flew straight away to his wife, and told her all about it.

But except on this one occasion the Stag never bestirred himself; behaving very lazily, as I have told you, and never opening his mouth except to munch his food or talk of it. He never spoke a word to the Calf, for old stags are not very fond of calves; and you may be sure that the Calf never said a word to him, for he was terribly afraid of him; nor was he far wrong, for an old stag, while his head is growing, is almost as irritable as an old gentleman with a gouty toe. The only difference between the two is this: that the stag can eat and drink as much as he pleases, and do nothing but good to his head, while the more a gouty old gentleman eats and drinks, the worse for his toe. And it is just because they cannot eat and drink as much as they please that gouty old gentlemen are more irritable than stags; and I for one don't pity them, for a man is made to think of better things than his food and drink.

But if he could not talk to the Stag, he made great friends with Ruddy's Calf, who was the sweetest, gentlest little thing that you can imagine. And though she was a little smaller than he was, she could do nearly everything that he could. They ran races, and they tried which could jump the higher and which could spring the farther, and she was as fast and as active as he was. But one day he made her try to find out which could butt the other the harder. So they butted each other gently two or three times, and he liked it so much that he took a great run and butted her hard, and hurt her, though he had not meant it.

Then she cried, "Maa-a-a! You're very rude and rough. It's a shame to treat a little hind so; I sha'n't play any more." Of course they soon made it up again, but his mother told him to remember that she was only a little hind. And he remembered it, but he could not help thinking that it was far better to be a little stag.

One day they were lying out in the grass as usual, and our little Calf was having a great game of romps with the little Hind. The Stag was not with them, but Aunt Yeld was standing sentry, when all of a sudden she came back in a great fluster, not at all like a stag, as she was always trying to be.

"Quick, quick, quick!" she said. "I can wind them and I can see them. Call your Calves and let us go. Quick, quick!"

Then the two mothers rose up in a terrible fright. "Quick," said Aunt Yeld again. "Run away as fast as you can!"

"But our Calves can't keep up if we go fast," pleaded the two mothers.

"Bless the Calves, I never thought of that," said Aunt Yeld. "Wait a minute; look!"

Then they looked down across the rolling waves of grass

flecked by the shadows of the flying clouds, and a mile and a half away they saw a moving white mass, with a dark figure before it and another dark figure behind it. The mass stood in deep shadow, for a cloud hung over it; but the cloud passed away and then the sun flashed down upon it, and what the Deer saw (for they have far better eyes than you or I) was this. Twenty-five couples of great solemn hounds trotting soberly over the heather with a horseman in a white coat at their heads and another at their sterns, and the coats of hounds and horses shining as glossy as their own. A fresh puff of wind bore a wave of strange scent to the nostrils of the Deer, and our little Calf snuffed it and thought it the most unpleasant that he had ever tasted. "Remember it, my son," whispered his mother to him, "nasty though it be, and beware of it."

But Aunt Yeld stood always a little in advance, talking to herself. "I passed just in front of the place where they are now on my way back from breakfast this morning," she murmured. "I trust that scent has failed by this time. Ah!"

And as she spoke some of the hounds swung suddenly with one impulse toward them, but the horseman behind them galloped forward quick as thought, and turned them back; and there came on the wind the sound of a shrill yelp, which made all three of the Hinds quiver again. Then the mass began to move faster than before, and the Deer watched it go further and further away from them till at last it settled down to its first pace and vanished out of sight.

"Well, that is a mercy," said Aunt Yeld with a deep sigh. "I thought it was full early yet for those detestable creatures to begin their horrible work again. I think that we are safe now, but I'll just make sure in case of accidents."

And with that she began to trot about in the strangest fashion. For she made a great circle to the track by which she had come back from feeding in the early morning, and ran back along it for some way, and then she turned off it, and after a time made another circle which brought her to a little stream. Then she ran up the water and made another circle which brought her back again.

"There," she said, "if they do follow us, that will puzzle them." But the Lady Tawny had been looking at her Calf all the time, and now she spoke: "I am afraid to stay here any longer, Aunt Yeld. I will take my Calf far away to a quiet spot that I know of, and do you stop with sister and look after her." So they parted, and very sad they were at parting. She led her Calf away slowly, that he might not tire, but they had not gone very far when there ran past them a great Buck-Rabbit. He neither saw nor heard them, for his eyes were starting out of his head with fright; and he went on only for a little way and then lay down and squealed most miserably. Then they heard a faint sound rather like the yelp that they had heard from the hound, but much smaller; and presently there came five little bits of brown bodies, long, and lithe and slender, racing along on their tiny short legs far faster than you would have thought possible. They were following the line of the Rabbit, and the old mother Weasel led the way, speaking to the scent as loud as she could (and that was not very loud), "Forward, children, forward, forward," and the four little Weasels joined in chorus, "Forward, forward, forward"; then she cried, "Blood, children, blood," and they answered at the top of their pipes, "Blood, blood, blood, blood." And their fierce little eyes flashed, and their sharp little teeth gleamed as they dashed away through the grass; and I am afraid that the Buck-Rabbit had but a poor chance with them, though he was nearly as big as the whole five of them put together. For I suppose that, for its size, there is no creature on earth so fierce and blood-thirsty as a weasel; but remember, too, that he is also the pluckiest little beast that there is, and would fight you and me if we drove him too far.

The Calf was very much puzzled. "Why doesn't the Rabbit run on, mother, if he is afraid of the Weasels?" he said. "I should have run on as far as I could. Will they leave him alone because he lies down and squeals?"

But she answered sadly, "No, no! And, my son, if ever it should befall you that you must run for your life, as I fear may be only too likely, then keep up a brave heart and run on till you can run no more."

And he answered, "Yes, mother," and thought to himself that he would fight to the end too; for he hoped one day to grow into a good stag and have horns to fight with; and besides he was a brave little fellow. And, for my part, I think that the Calf was right; and if (as I hope may never be) after you are grown up, disappointment should lie in wait for you at every turn, and fate and your own fault should hunt you to despair, then run on bravely, and when you can run no more, face them and dare them to do their worst; but never, never, never lie down and squeal.

Early one morning, it must have been almost the last week in September, the peace of the oak coppice was disturbed by a terrible clamor. It began with a single deep *Ough, ough, ough!* then another voice chimed in with rather a shriller note, and then another and then another, and then a whole score more joined them in one thundering chorus.

And the Hind started to her feet in alarm, and led the Calf out of the wooded valley to the open moor above. There they stood listening; while the whole valley was filled with the tumult, as if a hundred demons had been let loose into it. Now and again it ceased for a moment, and all was still; then it began again with *Ough, ough, ough!* and it was hard to say exactly where the sound came from, for one side of the valley said it would hold it no longer, and tossed it over to the other, and the other said it wouldn't hold it either and tossed it back, so that the noise kept hovering between the two in the most bewildering way. But after a short time the clamor drew nearer to the Hind and Calf, and presently out came one of the Fox cubs, with his tongue lolling and his back crooked, looking desperately weary and woebegone. He went on for a little distance, as if to go away over the moor, but soon stopped and flung back with desperation into the covert. And the Hind trotted gently away, anxious but not alarmed. "They are not after us, my son, I think," she said.

Then the noise drew closer and closer, and out bounded a whole pack of hounds, with bristles erect and gleaming eyes, throwing their tongues furiously on the line of the Cub. They flashed over the scent for fifty yards, still yelling with all their might, and then they fell silent and spread out in all directions. Presently they recovered the line of the Cub, and turned back into the covert yelling louder than ever; but meanwhile two wild puppies had crossed the scent of the Hind and Calf and started after them as fast as they could run.

Then the Hind turned and fled and the Calf with her, as he had never fled before; but his poor little legs began speedily to tire, and he could not have held out for much longer, when suddenly he found himself poked down quick as though by his mother's nose into a tuft of fern.

"Lie still, my son, till I come back," she whispered; and so she left him. And there he lay panting, while the voices of the puppies came closer and closer to his hiding place; but he never moved, for his mother had bid him lie still. Then they rushed past him with a wild cry, for his mother had waited to lead them after herself; and their voices died away, and all was silent. Presently he heard a dull sound, coming, *drum, drum, drum*, louder and louder and louder; and then the earth began to shake, and a huge dark body seemed to be coming almost on to the top of him, but suddenly swerved aside just in time, and left him unharmed. Then the drumming died away, and after a time he heard a dismal yelping such as he had once heard before; but he did not know that it was a man and horse that had nearly galloped on to the top of him, and would have galloped quite on the top of him if the horse had not shied, nor that the man had given the puppies a thrashing for running a deer when they had been told to run a fox.

He was beginning to hope that his mother would soon come back, when he heard two voices quite unlike any that he had ever heard before, and saw riding toward him two people. One was a man with fair hair and blue eyes, and a face burned brown by the sun, and the other a girl, a year or there about younger than the man. She, too, had bright blue eyes, and very fair hair, and a very pretty face, at least the man seemed to think so, for he was always looking at it, though of course the Calf, having never seen such creatures before, could not judge if they were pretty or ugly. They came on till they were only at a little distance from him, and the man pulled up and, pointing to him, said very low, "Look."

And the girl whispered, "What a little duck! I wish I could take him home with me."

But the man said, "No, no, no. His mother will come and take him home presently, and the sooner we leave him alone the better she will be pleased." So they rode away, and he could hear them talking as they rode, for they seemed to have a great deal to say to each other. But what they talked about, and how they came to stay alone on the hill when the hounds were running down in the valley, is more than I can tell you.

Before very long his mother came back to him, and you may guess how glad he was to see her, and how she rejoiced to see him. After looking around to see that all was quiet, she led him away over the heather, and then down a very steep hillside among stunted gorse and loose stones, hot and burning from the sun.

"See, my son," she said, "this is the first time that you have been chased by hounds, but I fear that it may not be the last. Now, remember, no hound can run fast over this short gorse, for his feet are soft; while we do not mind it, for our feet are hard. And these loose stones are almost better for us than the gorse, for our scent hardly lies on them and they hurt a hound's feet almost as much as the gorse."

So they went to the bottom of the hill, and there was a peat stream singing its song; but all that the Calf could hear of it was this: "I carry no scent, come here, come here; I am the friend of the wild Red Deer."

The Hind led him up a shallow for a little way, and then she jumped out on to the opposite bank and followed it upward for a little way, and then she jumped into the water again and went down for a full hundred yards till they came to a comfortable shady spot, where they both left the water and lay down together. "Now, my son," she said, "here is another little lesson for you to learn. The song of the water is true; it carries no scent, and no hound can follow us in it unless he can see us. But a hound will always try the bank to find out where we have left the water; if we enter it up the stream he will try upward, and if we enter it down the stream he will try downward. So always, if you have time, try to make them work upward when you mean to go down, and downward when you mean to go up, as I have shown you today." And like a wise little fellow he took care to remember what she taught him.

They lay there together till the sun began to fall low, and then they rose and went down to the water to cross it. And there what should they see but a large shoal of little Fish with bright red spots, and bands, like the marks of a finger, striping their sides from gills to tail; for the stream was so clear that they could distinguish every mark upon them. The little Fish seemed to be very anxious about something, for they kept darting about, now spreading out and now all coming together again; and the Calf could hear them whispering, "Shall we ask her? Shall we, shall we?" And at last one little Fish rose, with a little splash, and said in a watery little voice:

"Oh! please can you tell us how far it is to the sea?"

"Why, my little fellow," said the Hind, "surely it isn't time for you to go to sea yet?"

"Oh, no," said the little Salmon, "for we haven't got our silver jackets yet. But we are so looking forward to it. Will our silver jackets come soon, do you think?"

"Not just yet, I expect," said the Hind kindly; "you must

have patience, you know, for a little time, only for a little time."

"Oh," said the little Salmon, in a sadly disappointed tone; and the whole shoal began to move away, but almost directly came back and began popping up to the surface of the water by dozens, saying, "Thank you," "thank you," "thank you." For little Salmon are not only very well-bred but very well-mannered besides, which all well-bred creatures ought to be, but unfortunately very often are not.

So they left the little Salmon, and went their way to the cliffs that overhang the sea, where they made their home in a great plantation of Scotch firs, so closely cropped by wind and salt that they cannot grow up into trees but run along the ground almost like ivy. And let me warn you, by the way, when you ride fast through these stunted plantations, as I hope you may many times, to grip your saddle tight with your legs and keep your toes turned in, or you may find yourself on the ground on the broad of your back; which will not hurt you in the least, but may lose you your start in a good run. Well, here they lay, and very much the Calf liked his new home; but they had not been there for three days when one morning they heard faint sounds of a great trampling of hoofs. It lasted for a long time, but they lay quite still, though the Hind was very uneasy. Then suddenly they heard the voice of hounds rise from the coverts on the cliff below them, and a man screaming at the top of his voice. The sounds came nearer, and then there was a great clatter of branches, and the great Stag, whom they had known on the moor, came bounding leisurely through the thicket. His head was thrown back, and very proud and very terrible he looked as he cantered straight up to them. He jerked his head impatiently at them, and said very sternly, "Off with you! quick!" And the Hind jumped up in terror and the Calf with her; and as they ran off they could see the old Stag lie down in their place with his great horns laid back on his shoulders, and his chin pressed tight to the ground.

But they had no time to lose, for the hounds were coming closer; so they bustled for a little way through the thicket, and then the Hind led the Calf into a path, because of course his little legs could not keep pace with hers in the tangle of the plantation. Thus they ran on for a little way, till they heard the sound of a horse coming toward them, when they turned into the thicket again and lay down. And presently a man in a red coat came trotting by with his eyes fixed on the ground, and meeting the hounds stopped them at once. Then he pulled out a horn, blew one single note, and trotted away with the hounds, just three couple of them, at his heels.

But the Hind and Calf lay still; and presently they heard two more horses coming gently along the path, and two human voices chattering very fast. And who should ride by but the pretty girl whom he had seen looking at him a few days before! A man was riding with her, but not the man that he had seen with her before, for this one was dark, and besides he was rather older; but as they passed they saw her smile at him, and open her pretty eyes at him, in a way that seemed to please him very well.

So they rode on till their chattering could be heard no more; and then another man came riding by on a gray horse, quite alone, whom the Calf recognized as the fair man that had been with the girl when first he saw her; and very doleful and miserable he seemed to be. For he stopped on the path opposite to them, looking down at the ground with a troubled face, and kept flicking savagely at the heather with his whip, till at last he flicked his poor horse on the nose by mistake, and was obliged to pat him and tell him how sorry he was. How long he might have stopped there no one knows; but all of a sudden the Hind and Calf heard a wild sound of men hallooing, and the horn sounding in quick, continuous notes. Then the man's face brightened up directly, and he caught hold of the gray horse by the head and galloped off as fast as he could go.

Directly after this, the Deer heard a mighty rush of hoofs all hastening to the same spot, the sound growing gradually fainter and fainter until all was still. But they lay fast till a white Seagull flew high over their heads chirping out, "They're gone, they're gone," in a doleful voice; not, you know, because he was sorry that all the men and horses were gone, but because Seagulls, for some reason, can never say anything cheerfully. And then the Hind arose and led the Calf cautiously out of the plantation to the open moor; and as they went they saw a long string of horses, reaching for two or three miles, toiling painfully one after the other; while far ahead the hounds, like white specks, kept creeping on and on and on, with a larger speck close to them which could be nothing else than a gray horse. So the Hind led the Calf on to a quiet valley, and there they lay down in peace.

And when the sun began to sink they saw, far away, the hounds and a very few horses with them, returning slowly and wearily home. But presently they were startled by voices much closer to them, and they saw the fair man on the gray horse and the pretty girl, riding side by side. The Hind was a little alarmed at first, but there was no occasion for it; for the pair were riding very close together, so close that his hand was on her horse's neck, and they seemed to be far too much occupied with each other to think of anything else. So they passed on; and after they were gone there came a loose horse, saddled and bridled, but covered all over with mire, and with a stirrup missing from the saddle.

And presently he lay down and rolled over and over till the girths parted with a crack and left the saddle on the ground; then he got up, hung up one hind leg in the reins, and kicked himself free; then he lay down again, and rubbed his cheeks against the heather until he had forced the bridle over his head; then he gave himself a great shake to make quite sure that he had got rid of everything, and at last he went down to the water and drank, and wandered off grazing as happy as could be.

Last of all came a man tramping wearily over the heather, with a stirrup in his hand; but the Calf hardly recognized him as the dark man whom he had seen in the morning, for his hat was crushed in, and his clothes caked with mire from head to foot. And he toiled on, looking around him on all sides, till he caught his foot in a tussock of grass, and fell on his nose; and what he said when he got up I don't know, though I might guess, for he looked very cross.

So he too passed out of sight, and the sun went down, and the mist stole over the face of the moor. The Hind and Calf were left alone. But they never saw that old Stag again.

The boy Mowgli was found in the jungle, and raised by a family of wolves. Shere Khan, the tiger, persuaded the rest of the pack to reject their leader, Akela, who defends Mowgli. Mowgli used fire ("the red flower") to frighten Shere Khan away, saving Akela's life. Then he decides to leave the jungle...

Tiger! Tiger!

From *The Jungle Book*

By Rudyard Kipling

What of the hunting, hunter bold?
Brother, the watch was long and cold.
What of the quarry ye went to kill?
Brother, he crops in the jungle still.
Where is the power that made your pride?
Brother, it ebbs from my flank and side.
Where is the haste that ye hurry by?
Brother, I go to my lair—to die.

WHEN Mowgli left the wolf's cave after the fight with the Pack at the Council Rock, he went down to the plowed lands where the villagers lived, but he would not stop there because it was too near to the jungle, and he knew that he had made at least one bad enemy at the Council. So he hurried on, keeping to the rough road that ran down the valley, and followed it at a steady jog-trot for nearly twenty miles, till he came to a country that he did not know. The valley opened out into a great plain dotted over with rocks and cut up by ravines. At one end stood a little village, and at the other the thick jungle came down in a sweep to the grazing grounds, and stopped there as though it had been cut off with a hoe. All over the plain, cattle and buffaloes were grazing, and when the little boys in charge of the herds saw Mowgli they shouted and ran away, and the yellow pariah dogs that hang about every Indian village barked. Mowgli walked on, for he was feeling hungry, and when he came to the village gate he saw the big thorn bush that was drawn up before the gate at twilight, pushed to one side.

"Umph!" he said, for he had come across more than one such barricade in his night rambles after things to eat. "So men are afraid of the People of the Jungle here also." He sat down by the gate, and when a man came out he stood up, opened his mouth, and pointed down it to show that he wanted food. The man stared, and ran back up the one street of the village shouting for the priest, who was a big, fat man dressed in white, with a red and yellow mark on his forehead. The priest came to the gate, and with him at least a hundred people, who stared and talked and shouted and pointed at Mowgli.

"They have no manners, these Men Folk," said Mowgli to himself. "Only the gray ape would behave as they do." So he threw back his long hair and frowned at the crowd.

"What is there to be afraid of?" said the priest. "Look at the marks on his arms and legs. They are the bites of wolves. He is but a wolf-child run away from the jungle."

Of course, in playing together, the cubs had often nipped Mowgli harder than they intended, and there were white scars all over his arms and legs. But he would have been the last person in the world to call these bites, for he knew what real biting meant.

"Arre! Arre!" said two or three women together. "To be bitten by wolves, poor child! He is a handsome boy. He has eyes like red fire. By my honor, Messua, he is not unlike thy boy that was taken by the tiger."

"Let me look," said a woman with heavy copper rings on her wrists and ankles, and she peered at Mowgli under the palm of her hand. "Indeed he is not. He is thinner, but he has the very look of my boy."

The priest was a clever man, and he knew that Messua was wife to the richest villager in the place. So he looked up at the sky for a minute and said solemnly: "What the jungle has taken the jungle has restored. Take the boy into thy house, my sister, and forget not to honor the priest who sees so far into the lives of men."

"By the Bull that bought me," said Mowgli to himself, "but all this talking is like another looking-over by the Pack! Well, if I am a man, a man I must become."

The crowd parted as the woman beckoned Mowgli to her hut, where there was a red lacquered bedstead, a great earthen grain chest with funny raised patterns on it, half a dozen copper cooking pots, an image of a Hindu god in a little alcove, and on the wall a real looking glass, such as they sell at the country fairs.

She gave him a long drink of milk and some bread, and then she laid her hand on his head and looked into his eyes; for she thought perhaps that he might be her real son come back from the jungle where the tiger had taken him. So she said, "Nathoo, O Nathoo!" Mowgli did not show that he knew the name. "Dost thou not remember the day when I gave thee thy new shoes?" She touched his foot, and it was almost as hard as horn. "No," she said sorrowfully, "those feet have never worn shoes, but thou art very like my Nathoo, and thou shalt be my son."

Mowgli was uneasy, because he had never been under a roof before. But as he looked at the thatch, he saw that he could tear it out any at time if he wanted to get away, and that the window had no fastenings.

"What is the good of a man," he said to himself at last, "if he does not understand man's talk? Now I am as silly and dumb as a man would be with us in the jungle. I must speak their talk."

It was not for fun that he had learned while he was with the wolves to imitate the challenge of bucks in the jungle and the grunt of the little wild pig. So, as soon as Messua pronounced a word, Mowgli would imitate it almost perfectly, and before dark he had learned the names of many things in the hut.

There was a difficulty at bedtime, because Mowgli would not sleep under anything that looked so like a panther trap as that hut, and when they shut the door he went through the window.

"Give him his will," said Messua's husband. "Remember he can never till now have slept on a bed. If he is indeed sent in the place of our son he will not run away."

So Mowgli stretched himself in some long, clean grass at the edge of the field, but before he had closed his eyes a soft gray nose poked him under the chin.

"Phew!" said Gray Brother (he was the eldest of Mother Wolf's cubs). "This is a poor reward for following thee twenty miles. Thou smellest of wood smoke and cattle— altogether like a man already. Wake, Little Brother; I bring news."

"Are all well in the jungle?" said Mowgli, hugging him. "All except the wolves that were burned with the Red Flower. Now, listen. Shere Khan has gone away to hunt far off till his coat grows again, for he is badly singed. When he returns he swears that he will lay thy bones in the Waingunga."

"There are two words to that. I also have made a little promise. But news is always good. I am tired tonight, very tired with new things, Gray Brother—but bring me the news always."

"Thou wilt not forget that thou art a wolf? Men will not make thee forget?" said Gray Brother anxiously.

"Never. I will always remember that I love thee and all in our cave. But also I will always remember that I have been cast out of the Pack."

"And that thou mayest be cast out of

another pack. Men are only men, Little Brother, and their talk is like the talk of frogs in a pond. When I come down here again, I will wait for thee in the bamboos at the edge of the grazing-ground."

For three months after that night Mowgli hardly ever left the village gate, he was so busy learning the ways and customs of men. First he had to wear a cloth around him, which annoyed him horribly; and then he had to learn about money, which he did not in the least understand, and about plowing, of which he did not see the use. Then the little children in the village made him very angry. Luckily, the Law of the Jungle had taught him to keep his temper, for in the jungle life and food depend on keeping your temper; but when they made fun of him because he would not play games or fly kites, or because he mispronounced some word, only the knowledge that it was unsportsmanlike to kill little naked cubs kept him from picking them up and breaking them in two.

He did not know his own strength in the least. In the jungle he knew he was weak compared with the beasts, but in the village people said that he was as strong as a bull.

And Mowgli had not the faintest idea of the difference that caste makes between man and man. When the potter's donkey slipped in the clay pit, Mowgli hauled it out by the tail, and helped to stack the pots for their journey to the market at Khanhiwara. That was very shocking, too, for the potter is a low-caste man, and his donkey is worse. When the priest scolded him, Mowgli threatened to put him on the donkey too, and the priest told Messua's husband that Mowgli had better be set to work as soon as possible; and the village head-man told Mowgli that he would have to go out with the buffaloes next day, and herd them while they grazed. No one was more pleased than Mowgli; and that night, because he had been appointed a servant of the village, as it were, he went off to a circle that met every evening on a masonry platform under a great fig-tree. It was the village club, and the head-man and the watchman and the barber, who knew all the gossip of the village, and old Buldeo, the village hunter, who had a Tower musket, met and smoked. The monkeys sat and talked in the upper branches, and there was a hole under the platform where a cobra lived, and he had his little platter of milk every night because he was sacred; and the old men sat around the tree and talked, and pulled at the big huqas (the water-pipes) till far into the night. They told wonderful tales of gods and men and ghosts; and Buldeo told even more wonderful ones of the ways of beasts in the jungle, till the eyes of the children sitting outside the circle bulged out of their heads. Most of the tales were about animals, for the jungle was always at their door. The deer and the wild pig grubbed up their crops, and now and again the tiger carried off a man at twilight, within sight of the village gates.

Mowgli, who naturally knew something about what they were talking of, had to cover his face not to show that he was laughing, while Buldeo, the Tower musket across his knees, climbed on from one wonderful story to another, and Mowgli's shoulders shook.

Buldeo was explaining how the tiger that had carried away Messua's son was a ghost-tiger, and his body was inhabited by the ghost of a wicked, old money-lender, who had died some years ago. "And I know that this is true," he said, "because Purun Dass always limped from the blow that he got in a riot when his account books were burned, and the tiger that I speak of limps, too, for the tracks of his pads are unequal."

"True, true, that must be the truth," said the graybeards, nodding together.

"Are all these tales such cobwebs and moon talk?" said Mowgli. "That tiger limps because he was born lame, as everyone knows. To talk of the soul of a money-lender in a beast that never had the courage of a jackal is child's talk."

Buldeo was speechless with surprise for a moment, and the head-man stared.

"Oho! It is the jungle brat, is it?" said Buldeo. "If thou art so wise, better bring his hide to Khanhiwara, for the Government has set a hundred rupees on his life. Better still, talk not when thy elders speak."

Mowgli rose to go. "All the evening I have lain here

listening," he called back over his shoulder, "and, except once or twice, Buldeo has not said one word of truth concerning the jungle, which is at his very doors. How, then, shall I believe the tales of ghosts and gods and goblins which he says he has seen?"

"It is full time that boy went to herding," said the head-man, while Buldeo puffed and snorted at Mowgli's impertinence.

The custom of most Indian villages is for a few boys to take the cattle and buffaloes out to graze in the early morning, and bring them back at night. The very cattle that would trample a white man to death allow themselves to be banged and bullied and shouted at by children that hardly come up to their noses. So long as the boys keep with the herds they are safe, for not even the tiger will charge a mob of cattle. But if they straggle to pick flowers or hunt lizards, they are sometimes carried off. Mowgli went through the village street in the dawn, sitting on the back of Rama, the great herd bull. The slaty-blue buffaloes, with their long, backward-sweeping horns and savage eyes, rose out their byres, one by one, and followed him, and Mowgli made it very clear to the children with him that he was the master. He beat the buffaloes with a long, polished bamboo, and told Kamya, one of the boys, to graze the cattle by themselves, while he went on with the buffaloes, and to be very careful not to stray away from the herd.

An Indian grazing ground is all rocks and scrub and tussocks and little ravines, among which the herds scatter and disappear. The buffaloes generally keep to the pools and muddy places, where they lie wallowing or basking in the warm mud for hours. Mowgli drove them on to the edge of the plain where the Waingunga came out of the jungle; then he dropped from Rama's neck, trotted off to a bamboo clump, and found Gray Brother.

"Ah," said Gray Brother, "I have waited here very many days. What is the meaning of this cattle-herding work?"

"It is an order," said Mowgli. "I am a village herd for a while. What news of Shere Khan?"

"He has come back to this country, and has waited here a long time for thee. Now he has gone off again, for the game is scarce. But he means to kill thee."

"Very good," said Mowgli. "So long as he is away do thou or one of the four brothers sit on that rock, so that I can see thee as I come out of the village. When he comes back wait for me in the ravine by the dhak tree in the center of the plain. We need not walk into Shere Khan's mouth."

Then Mowgli picked out a shady place, and lay down and slept while the buffaloes grazed around him. Herding in India is one of the laziest things in the world. The cattle move and crunch, and lie down, and move on again, and they do not even low. They only grunt, and the buffaloes very seldom say anything, but get down into the muddy pools one after another, and work their way into the mud till only their noses and staring china-blue eyes show above the surface, and then they lie like logs. The sun makes the rocks dance in the heat, and the herd children hear one kite (never any more) whistling almost out of sight overhead, and they know that if they died, or a cow died, that kite would sweep down, and the next kite miles away would see him drop and follow, and the next, and the next, and almost before they were dead there would be a score of hungry kites come out of nowhere. Then they sleep and wake and sleep again, and weave little baskets of dried grass and put grasshoppers in them; or catch two praying mantises and make them fight; or string a necklace of red and black jungle nuts; or watch a lizard basking on a rock, or a snake hunting a frog near the wallows. Then they sing long, long songs with odd native quavers at the end of them, and the day seems longer than most people's whole lives, and perhaps they make a mud castle with mud figures of men and horses and buffaloes, and put reeds into the men's hands, and pretend that they are kings and the figures are their armies, or that they are gods to be worshipped. Then evening comes and the children call, and the buffaloes lumber up out of the sticky mud with noises like gunshots going off one after the other, and they all string across the gray plain back to the twinkling village lights.

Day after day Mowgli would lead the buffaloes out to their wallows, and day after day he would see Gray Brother across the plain (so he knew that Shere Khan had not come back), and day after day he would lie on the grass listening to the noises around him, and dreaming of old days in the jungle. If Shere Khan had made a false step with his lame paw up in the jungles by the Waingunga, Mowgli would have heard him in those long, still mornings.

At last a day came when he did not see Gray Brother at the signal place, and he laughed and headed the buffaloes for the ravine by the dhak tree, which was all covered with golden-red flowers. There sat Gray Brother, every bristle on his back lifted.

"He has hidden for a month to throw thee off thy guard. He crossed the ranges last night with Tabaqui, hot-foot on thy trail," said the Wolf, panting.

Mowgli frowned. "I am not afraid of Shere Khan, but Tabaqui is very cunning."

"Have no fear," said Gray Brother, licking his lips a little. "I met Tabaqui in the dawn. Now he is telling all his wisdom to the kites, but he told me everything before I broke his back. Shere Khan's plan is to wait for thee at the village gate this evening—for thee and for no one else. He is lying up now, in the big dry ravine of the Waingunga."

"Has he eaten today, or does he hunt empty?" said Mowgli, for the answer meant life and death to him.

"He killed at dawn—a pig—and he has drunk too. Remember, Shere Khan could never fast, even for the sake of revenge."

"Oh! Fool, fool! What a cub's cub it is! Eaten and drunk too, and he thinks that I shall wait till he has slept! Now, where does he lie up? If there were but ten of us we might pull him down as he lies. These buffaloes will not charge unless they wind him, and I cannot speak their language. Can we get behind his track so that they may smell it?"

"He swam far down the Waingunga to cut that off," said Gray Brother.

"Tabaqui told him that, I know. He would never have thought of it alone." Mowgli stood with his finger in his mouth, thinking. "The big ravine of the Waingunga. That opens out on the plain not half a mile from here. I can take the herd around through the jungle to the head of the ravine and then sweep down—but he would slink out at the foot. We must block that end. Gray Brother, canst thou cut the herd in two for me?"

"Not I, perhaps—but I have brought a wise helper." Gray Brother trotted off and dropped into a hole. Then there lifted up a huge gray head that Mowgli knew well, and the hot air was filled with the most desolate cry of all the jungle—the hunting howl of a wolf at midday.

"Akela! Akela!" said Mowgli, clapping his hands. "I might have known that thou wouldst not forget me. We have a big work in hand. Cut the herd in two, Akela. Keep the cows and calves together, and the bulls and the plow buffaloes by themselves."

The two wolves ran in and out of the herd, which snorted and threw up its head, and separated into two clumps. In one, the cow-buffaloes stood with their calves in the center, and glared and pawed, ready, if a wolf would only stay still, to charge down and trample the life out of him. In the other, the bulls and the young bulls snorted and stamped, but though they looked more imposing they were much less dangerous, for they had no calves to protect. No six men could have divided the herd so neatly.

"What orders!" panted Akela. "They are trying to join again."

Mowgli slipped on to Rama's back. "Drive the bulls away to the left, Akela. Gray Brother, when we are gone, hold the cows together, and drive them into the foot of the ravine."

"How far?" said Gray Brother, panting and snapping.

"Till the sides are higher than Shere Khan can jump," shouted Mowgli. "Keep them there till we come down." The bulls swept off as Akela bayed, and Gray Brother stopped in front of the cows. They charged down on him, and he ran just before them to the foot of the ravine, as Akela drove the bulls far to the left.

"Well done! Another charge and they are fairly started. Careful, now—careful, Akela. A snap too much and the bulls will charge. Hujah! This is wilder work than driving black-buck. Didst thou think these creatures could move so swiftly?" Mowgli called.

"I have—have hunted these too in my time," gasped Akela in the dust. "Shall I turn them into the jungle?"

"Ay! Turn. Swiftly turn them! Rama is mad with rage. Oh, if I could only tell him what I need of him today."

The bulls were turned, to the right this time, and crashed into the standing thicket. The other herd children, watching with the cattle half a mile away, hurried to the village as fast as their legs could carry them, crying that the buffaloes had gone mad and run away.

But Mowgli's plan was simple enough. All he wanted to do

was to make a big circle uphill and get at the head of the
ravine, and then take the bulls down it and catch Shere
Khan between the bulls and the cows; for he knew that after
a meal and a full drink Shere Khan would not be in any
condition to fight or to clamber up the sides of the ravine.
He was soothing the buffaloes now by voice, and Akela had
dropped far to the rear, only whimpering once or twice to
hurry the rear-guard. It was a long, long circle, for they did
not wish to get too near the ravine and give Shere Khan
warning. At last Mowgli rounded up the bewildered herd at
the head of the ravine on a grassy patch that sloped steeply
down to the ravine itself. From that height you could see
across the tops of the trees down to the plain below;
but what Mowgli looked at was the sides of the
ravine, and he saw with a great deal of
satisfaction that they ran nearly

straight up and down, while the vines and creepers that
hung over them would give no foothold to a tiger who
wanted to get out.

"Let them breathe, Akela," he said, holding up his hand.
"They have not winded him yet. Let them breathe. I must
tell Shere Khan who comes. We have him in the trap."

He put his hands to his mouth and shouted down the
ravine—it was almost like shouting down a tunnel—and the
echoes jumped from rock to rock.

After a long time there came back the
drawling, sleepy snarl of a full-fed tiger
just wakened.

"Who calls?" said Shere Khan,
and a splendid peacock fluttered up
out of the ravine screeching.

"I, Mowgli. Cattle
thief, it is time to
come to the Council
Rock! Down—
hurry them down,
Akela! Down,
Rama, down!"

The herd paused for
an instant at the edge of
the slope, but Akela gave tongue

in the full hunting-yell, and they pitched over one after the other, just as steamers shoot rapids, the sand and stones spurting up around them. Once started, there was no chance of stopping, and before they were fairly in the bed of the ravine Rama winded Shere Khan and bellowed.

"Ha! Ha!" said Mowgli, on his back. "Now thou knowest!" and the torrent of black horns, foaming muzzles, and staring eyes whirled down the ravine just as boulders go down in floodtime; the weaker buffaloes being shouldered out to the sides of the ravine where they tore through the creepers. They knew what the business was before them— the terrible charge of the buffalo herd against which no tiger can hope to stand. Shere Khan heard the thunder of their hoofs, picked himself up, and lumbered down the ravine, looking from side to side for some way of escape, but the walls of the ravine were straight and he had to hold on, heavy with his dinner and his drink, willing to do anything rather than fight. The herd splashed through the pool he had just left, bellowing till the narrow cut rang. Mowgli heard an answering bellow from the foot of the ravine, saw Shere Khan turn (the tiger knew if the worst came to the worst it was better to meet the bulls than the cows with their calves), and then Rama tripped, stumbled, and went on again over something soft, and, with the bulls at his heels, crashed full into the other herd, while the weaker buffaloes were lifted clean off their feet by the shock of the meeting. That charge carried both herds out into the plain, goring and stamping and snorting. Mowgli watched his time, and slipped off Rama's neck, laying about him right and left with his stick.

"Quick, Akela! Break them up. Scatter them, or they will be fighting one another. Drive them away, Akela. Hai, Rama! Hai, hai, hai! My children. Softly now, softly! It is all over."

Akela and Gray Brother ran to and fro nipping the buffaloes' legs, and though the herd wheeled once to charge up the ravine again, Mowgli managed to turn Rama, and the others followed him to the wallows.

Shere Khan needed no more trampling. He was dead, and the kites were coming for him already.

"Brothers, that was a dog's death," said Mowgli, feeling for the knife he always carried in a sheath around his neck now that he lived with men. "But he would never have shown fight. His hide will look well on the Council Rock. We must get to work swiftly."

A boy trained among men would never have dreamed of skinning a ten-foot tiger alone, but Mowgli knew better than anyone else how an animal's skin is fitted on, and how it can be taken off. But it was hard work, and Mowgli slashed and tore and grunted for an hour, while the wolves lolled out their tongues, or came forward and tugged as he ordered them.

Presently a hand fell on his shoulder, and looking up he saw Buldeo with the Tower musket. The children had told the village about the buffalo stampede, and Buldeo went out angrily, only too anxious to correct Mowgli for not taking better care of the herd. The wolves dropped out of sight as soon as they saw the man coming.

"What is this folly?" said Buldeo angrily. "To think that thou canst skin a tiger! Where did the buffaloes kill him? It is the Lame Tiger too, and there is a hundred rupees on his head. Well, well, we will overlook thy letting the herd run off, and perhaps I will give thee one of the rupees of the reward when I have taken the skin to Khanhiwara." He fumbled in his waist cloth for flint and steel, and stooped down to singe Shere Khan's whiskers. Most native hunters always singe a tiger's whiskers to prevent his ghost from haunting them.

"Hum!" said Mowgli, half to himself as he ripped back the skin of a forepaw. "So thou wilt take the hide to Khanhiwara for the reward, and perhaps give me one rupee? Now it is in my mind that I need the skin for my own use. Heh! Old man, take away that fire!"

"What talk is this to the chief hunter of the village? Thy luck and the stupidity of thy buffaloes have helped thee to this kill. The tiger has just fed, or he would have gone twenty miles by this time. Thou canst not even skin him properly, little beggar brat, and forsooth I, Buldeo, must be told not to singe his whiskers. Mowgli, I will not give thee one anna of the reward, but only a very big beating. Leave the carcass!"

"By the Bull that bought me," said Mowgli, who was trying to get at the shoulder, "must I stay babbling to an old ape all noon? Here, Akela, this man plagues me."

Buldeo, who was still stooping over Shere Khan's head, found himself sprawling on the grass, with a gray wolf standing over him, while Mowgli went on skinning as though he were alone in all India.

"Ye-es," he said, between his teeth. "Thou art altogether right, Buldeo. Thou wilt never give me one anna of the reward. There is an old war between this lame tiger and myself—a very old war, and—I have won."

To do Buldeo justice, if he had been ten years younger he would have taken his chance with Akela had he met the wolf in the woods, but a wolf who obeyed the orders of this boy who had private wars with man-eating tigers was not a common animal. It was sorcery, magic of the worst kind, thought Buldeo, and he wondered whether the amulet around his neck would protect him. He lay as still as still, expecting every minute to see Mowgli turn into a tiger too.

"Maharaj! Great King," he said at last in a husky whisper.

"Yes," said Mowgli, without turning his head, chuckling a little.

"I am an old man. I did not know that thou wast anything

more than a herdsboy. May I rise up and go away, or will thy servant tear me to pieces?"

"Go, and peace go with thee. Only, another time do not meddle with my game. Let him go, Akela."

Buldeo hobbled away to the village as fast as he could, looking back over his shoulder in case Mowgli should change into something terrible. When he got to the village he told a tale of magic and enchantment and sorcery that made the priest look very grave.

Mowgli went on with his work, but it was nearly twilight before he and the wolves had drawn the great gay skin clear of the body.

"Now we must hide this and take the buffaloes home! Help me to herd them, Akela."

The herd rounded up in the misty twilight, and when they got near the village Mowgli saw lights, and heard the conches and bells in the temple blowing and banging. Half the village seemed to be waiting for him by the gate. "That is because I have killed Shere Khan," he said to himself. But a shower of stones whistled about his ears, and the villagers shouted: "Sorcerer! Wolf's brat! Jungle demon! Go away! Get hence quickly or the priest will turn thee into a wolf again. Shoot, Buldeo, shoot!"

The old Tower musket went off with a bang, and a young buffalo bellowed in pain.

"More sorcery!" shouted the villagers. "He can turn bullets. Buldeo, that was thy buffalo."

"Now what is this?" said Mowgli, bewildered, as the stones flew thicker.

"They are not unlike the Pack, these brothers of thine," said Akela, sitting down composedly. "It is in my head that, if bullets mean anything, they would cast thee out."

"Wolf! Wolf's cub! Go away!" shouted the priest, waving a sprig of the sacred tulsi plant.

"Again? Last time it was because I was a man. This time it is because I am a wolf. Let us go, Akela."

A woman—it was Messua—ran across to the herd, and cried: "Oh, my son, my son! They say thou art a sorcerer who can turn himself into a beast at will. I do not believe, but go away or they will kill thee. Buldeo says thou art a wizard, but I know thou hast avenged Nathoo's death."

"Come back, Messua!" shouted the crowd. "Come back, or we will stone thee."

Mowgli laughed a little short ugly laugh, for a stone had hit him in the mouth. "Run back, Messua. This is one of the foolish tales they tell under the big tree at dusk. I have at least paid for thy son's life. Farewell; and run quickly, for I shall send the herd in more swiftly than their brickbats. I am no wizard, Messua. Farewell!"

"Now, once more, Akela," he cried. "Bring the herd in."

The buffaloes were anxious enough to get to the village. They hardly needed Akela's yell, but charged through the gate like a whirlwind, scattering the crowd right and left.

"Keep count!" shouted Mowgli scornfully. "It may be that I have stolen one of them. Keep count, for I will do your herding no more. Fare you well, children of men, and thank Messua that I do not come in with my wolves and hunt you up and down your street."

He turned on his heel and walked away with the Lone Wolf, and as he looked up at the stars he felt happy. "No more sleeping in traps for me, Akela. Let us get Shere Khan's skin and go away. No, we will not hurt the village, for Messua was kind to me."

When the moon rose over the plain, making it look all milky, the horrified villagers saw Mowgli, with two wolves at his heels and a bundle on his head, trotting across at the steady wolf's trot that eats up the long miles like fire. Then they banged the temple bells and blew the conches louder than ever. And Messua cried, and Buldeo embroidered the story of his adventures in the jungle, till he ended by saying that Akela stood up on his hind legs and talked like a man.

The moon was just going down when Mowgli and the two wolves came to the hill of the Council Rock, and they stopped at Mother Wolf's cave.

"They have cast me out from the Man-Pack, Mother,"

shouted Mowgli, "but I come with the hide of Shere Khan to keep my word."

Mother Wolf walked stiffly from the cave with the cubs behind her, and her eyes glowed as she saw the skin.

"I told him on that day, when he crammed his head and shoulders into this cave, hunting for thy life, Little Frog—I told him that the hunter would be the hunted. It is well done."

"Little Brother, it is well done," said a deep voice in the thicket. "We were lonely in the jungle without thee," and Bagheera came running to Mowgli's bare feet.

They clambered up the Council Rock together, and Mowgli spread the skin out on the flat stone where Akela used to sit, and pegged it down with four slivers of bamboo, and Akela lay down upon it, and called the old call to the Council, "Look—look well, O Wolves," exactly as he had called when Mowgli was first brought there.

Ever since Akela had been deposed, the Pack had been without a leader, hunting and fighting at their own pleasure. But they answered the call from habit; and some of them were lame from the traps they had fallen into, and some limped from shot wounds, and some were mangy from eating bad food, and many were missing. But they came to the Council Rock, all that were left of them, and saw Shere Khan's striped hide on the rock, and the huge claws dangling at the end of the empty dangling feet. It was then that Mowgli made up a song that came up into his throat all by itself, and he shouted it aloud, leaping up and down on the rattling skin, and beating time with his heels till he had no more breath left, while Gray Brother and Akela howled between the verses.

"Look well, O Wolves. Have I kept my word?" said Mowgli. And the wolves bayed "Yes," and one tattered wolf howled: "Lead us again, O Akela. Lead us again, O Man-cub, for we be sick of this lawlessness, and we would be the Free People once more."

"Nay," purred Bagheera, "that may not be. When ye are full-fed, the madness may come upon you again. Not for nothing are ye called the Free People. Ye fought for freedom, and it is yours. Eat it, O Wolves."

"Man-Pack and Wolf-Pack have cast me out," said Mowgli. "Now I will hunt alone in the jungle."

"And we will hunt with thee," said the four cubs.

So Mowgli went away and hunted with the four cubs in the jungle from that day on. But he was not always alone, because, years afterward, he became a man and married.

But that is a story for grown-ups.

*The story of a ferocious animal, part-wolf
and part-dog, and its struggle for survival.
This is the chilling opening chapter.*

The Trail of the Meat

From *White Fang*

By Jack London

DARK spruce forest frowned on either side of the frozen waterway. The trees had been stripped by a recent wind of their white covering of frost, and they seemed to lean toward each other, black and ominous, in the fading light. A vast silence reigned over the land. The land itself was a desolation, lifeless, without movement, so lone and cold that the spirit of it was not even that of sadness. There was a hint in it of laughter, but of a laughter more terrible than any sadness—a laughter that was mirthless as the smile of the sphinx, a laughter cold as the frost and partaking of the grimness of infallibility. It was the masterful and incommunicable wisdom of eternity laughing at the futility of life and the effort of life. It was the Wild, the savage, frozen-hearted Northland Wild.

But there was life, abroad in the land and defiant. Down the frozen waterway toiled a string of wolfish dogs. Their bristly fur was rimed with frost. Their breath froze in the air as it left their mouths, spouting forth in spumes of vapor that settled upon the hair of their bodies and formed into crystals of frost. A leather harness was on the dogs, and leather traces attached them to a sled which dragged along behind. The sled was without runners. It was made of stout birch-bark, and its full surface rested on the snow. The front end of the sled was turned up, like a scroll, in order to force down and under the bore of soft snow that surged like a wave before it. On the sled, securely lashed, was a long and narrow oblong box. There were other things on the sled—blankets, an ax, and a coffee-pot and frying-pan; but prominent, occupying most of the space, was the long and narrow oblong box.

In advance of the dogs, on wide snowshoes, toiled a man. At the rear of the sled toiled a second man. On the sled, in the box, lay a third man whose toil was over, a man whom the Wild had conquered and beaten down until he would never move nor struggle again. It is not the way of the Wild to like movement. Life is an offense to it, for life is movement; and the Wild aims always to destroy movement.

It freezes the water to prevent it running to the sea; it drives the sap out of the trees till they are frozen to their mighty hearts; and most ferociously and terribly of all does the Wild harry and crush into submission man—man who is the most restless of life, ever in revolt against the dictum that all movement must in the end come to the cessation of movement.

But at front and rear, unawed and indomitable, toiled the two men who were not yet dead. Their bodies were covered with fur and soft-tanned leather. Eyelashes and cheeks and lips were so coated with the crystals from their frozen breath that their faces were not discernible. This gave them the seeming of ghostly masques, undertakers in a spectral world at the funeral of some ghost. But under it all they were men, penetrating the land of desolation and mockery and silence, puny adventurers bent on colossal adventure, pitting themselves against the might of a world as remote and alien and pulseless as the abysses of space.

They traveled on without speech, saving their breath for the work of their bodies. On every side was the silence, pressing upon them with a tangible presence. It affected their minds as the many atmospheres of deep water affect the body of the diver. It crushed them with the weight of unending vastness and unalterable decree. It crushed them into the remotest recesses of their own minds, pressing out of them, like juices from the grape, all the false ardors and exaltations and undue self-values of the human soul, until they perceived themselves finite and small, specks and motes, moving with weak cunning and little wisdom amid the play and inter-play of the great blind elements and forces.

An hour went by, and a second hour. The pale light of the short sunless day was beginning to fade, when a faint far cry arose on the still air. It soared upward with a swift rush, till it reached its topmost note, where it persisted, palpitant and tense, and then slowly died away. It might have been a lost soul wailing, had it not been invested with a certain sad fierceness and hungry eagerness. The front man turned his head until his eyes met the eyes of the man behind. And then, across the narrow oblong box, each nodded to the other.

A second cry arose, piercing the silence with needlelike shrillness. Both men located the sound. It was to the rear, somewhere in the snow expanse they had just traversed. A third and answering cry arose, also to the rear and to the left of the second cry.

"They're after us, Bill," said the man at the front.

His voice sounded hoarse and unreal, and he had spoken with apparent effort.

"Meat is scarce," answered his comrade. "I ain't seen a rabbit sign for days."

Thereafter they spoke no more, though their ears were keen for the hunting-cries that continued to rise behind them.

At the fall of darkness they swung the dogs into a cluster of spruce trees on the edge of the waterway and made a camp. The coffin, at the side of the fire, served for seat and table. The wolf-dogs, clustered on the far side of the fire, snarled and bickered among themselves, but evinced no inclination to stray off into the darkness.

"Seems to me, Henry, they're stayin' remarkable close to camp," Bill commented.

Henry, squatting over the fire and settling the pot of coffee with a piece of ice, nodded. Nor did he speak till he had taken his seat on the coffin and begun to eat.

"They know where their hides is safe," he said. "They'd sooner eat grub than be grub. They're pretty wise, them dogs."

Bill shook his head. "Oh, I don't know."

His comrade looked at him curiously. "First time I ever heard you say anything about their not bein' wise."

"Henry," said the other, munching with deliberation the beans he was eating, "did you happen to notice the way them dogs kicked up when I was a-feedin' 'em?"

"They did cut up more'n usual," Henry acknowledged.

"How many dogs 've we got, Henry?"

"Six."

"Well, Henry…" Bill stopped for a moment, in order that his words might gain greater significance. "As I was sayin', Henry, we've got six dogs. I took six fish out of the bag. I gave one fish to each dog, an', Henry, I was one fish short."

"You counted wrong."

"We've got six dogs," the other reiterated dispassionately. "I took out six fish. One Ear didn't get no fish. I came back to the bag afterward an' got 'm his fish."

"We've only got six dogs," Henry said.

"Henry," Bill went on. "I won't say they was all dogs, but there was seven of 'm that got fish."

Henry stopped eating to glance across the fire and count the dogs.

"There's only six now," he said.

"I saw the other one run off across the snow," Bill announced with cool positiveness. "I saw seven."

Henry looked at him commiseratingly, and said, "I'll be almighty glad when this trip's over."

"What d'ye mean by that?" Bill demanded.

"I mean that this load of ourn is gettin' on your nerves, an' that you're beginnin' to see things."

"I thought of that," Bill answered gravely. "An' so, when I saw it run off across the snow, I looked in the snow an' saw its tracks. Then I counted the dogs an' there was still six of 'em. The tracks is there in the snow now. D'ye want to look at 'em? I'll show 'em to you."

Henry did not reply, but munched on in silence, until, the meal finished, he topped it with a final cup of coffee. He wiped his mouth with the back of his hand and said: "Then you're thinkin' as it was—"

A long wailing cry, fiercely sad, from somewhere in the darkness, had interrupted him. He stopped to listen to it, then he finished his sentence with a wave of his hand toward the sound of the cry, "—one of them?"

Bill nodded. "I'd a blame sight sooner think that than anything else. You noticed yourself the row the dogs made."

Cry after cry, and answering cries, were turning the silence into a bedlam. From every side the cries arose, and the dogs betrayed their fear by huddling together and so close to the fire that their hair was scorched by the heat. Bill threw on more wood, before lighting his pipe.

"I'm thinking you're down in the mouth some," Henry said.

"Henry…" He sucked meditatively at his pipe for some time before he went on. "Henry, I was a-thinkin' what a blame sight luckier he is than you an' me'll ever be."

He indicated the third person by a downward thrust of the thumb to the box on which they sat.

"You an' me, Henry, when we die, we'll be lucky if we get enough stones over our carcasses to keep the dogs off of us."

"But we ain't got people an' money an' all the rest, like him," Henry rejoined. "Long-distance funerals is somethin' you an' me can't exactly afford."

"What gets me, Henry, is what a chap like this, that's a lord or something in his own country, and that's never had to bother about grub nor blankets; why he comes a-buttin' round the Godforsaken ends of the earth—that's what I can't exactly see."

"He might have lived to a ripe old age if he'd stayed at home," Henry agreed.

Bill opened his mouth to speak, but changed his mind. Instead, he pointed toward the wall of darkness that pressed about them from every side. There was no suggestion of form in the utter blackness; only could be seen a pair of eyes gleaming like live coals. Henry indicated with his head a second pair, and a third. A circle of the gleaming eyes had drawn about their camp. Now and again a pair of eyes moved, or disappeared to appear again a moment later.

The unrest of the dogs had been increasing, and they stampeded, in a surge of sudden fear, to the near side of the fire, cringing and crawling about the legs of the men. In the scramble one of the dogs had been overturned on the edge of the fire, and it had yelped with pain and fright as the smell of its singed coat possessed the air. The commotion caused the circle of eyes to shift restlessly for a moment and even to withdraw a bit, but it settled down again as the dogs became quiet.

"Henry, it's a blame misfortune to be out of ammunition."

Bill had finished his pipe and was helping his companion to spread the bed of fur and blanket upon the spruce boughs which he had laid over the snow before supper. Henry grunted, and began unlacing his mocassins.

"How many cartridges did you say you had left?" he asked.

"Three," came the answer. "An' I wisht 'twas three hundred. Then I'd show 'em what for, damn 'em!"

He shook his fist angrily at the gleaming eyes, and began securely to prop his moccasins before the fire.

"An' I wisht this cold snap'd break," he went on. "It's ben fifty below for two weeks now. An' I wisht I'd never started on this trip, Henry. I don't like the looks of it. I don't feel right, somehow. An' while I'm wishin', I wisht the trip was over an' done with, an' you an' me a-sittin' by the fire in Fort McGurry just about now an' playing cribbage—that's what I wisht."

Henry grunted and crawled into bed. As he dozed off he was aroused by his comrade's voice.

"Say, Henry, that other one that come in an' got a fish—why didn't the dogs pitch into it? That's what's botherin' me."

"You're botherin' too much, Bill," came the sleepy response. "You was never like this before. You jes' shut up now, an' go to sleep, an' you'll be all hunkydory in the mornin'. Your stomach's sour, that's what's botherin' you."

The men slept, breathing heavily, side by side, under the one covering. The fire died down, and the gleaming eyes drew closer. The dogs clustered together in fear, now and again snarling menacingly as a pair of eyes drew close. Once their uproar became so loud that Bill woke up. He got out of bed carefully, so as not to disturb the sleep of his comrade, and threw more wood on the fire. As it began to flame up, the circle of eyes drew farther back. He glanced casually at the huddling dogs. He rubbed his eyes and looked at them more sharply. Then he crawled back into the blankets.

"Henry," he said. "Oh, Henry."

Henry groaned as he passed from sleep to waking, and demanded, "What's wrong now?"

"Nothin'," came the answer; "only there's seven of 'em again. I just counted."

Henry acknowledged receipt of the information with a grunt that slid into a snore as he drifted back into sleep.

In the morning it was Henry who awoke first and routed his companion out of bed. Daylight was yet three hours away, though it was already six o'clock; and in the darkness Henry went about preparing breakfast, while Bill rolled the blankets and made the sled ready for lashing.

"Say, Henry," he asked suddenly, "how many dogs did you say we had?"

"Six."

"Wrong," Bill proclaimed triumphantly.

"Seven again?" Henry queried.

"No, five; one's gone."

"The hell!" Henry cried in wrath, leaving the cooking to come and count the dogs.

"You're right, Bill," he concluded. "Fatty's gone."

"An' he went like greased lightnin' once he got started. Couldn't 've seen 'm for smoke."

"No chance at all," Henry concluded. "They jes' swallowed 'm alive. I bet he was yelpin' as he went down their throats, damn 'em!"

"He always was a fool dog," said Bill.

"But no fool dog ought to be fool enough to go off an'

commit suicide that way." He looked over the remainder of the team with a speculative eye that summed up instantly the salient traits of each animal. "I bet none of the others would do it."

"Couldn't drive 'em away from the fire with a club," Bill agreed. "I always did think there was somethin' wrong with Fatty anyway."

And this was the epitaph of a dead dog on the Northland trail—less scant than the epitaph of many another dog, of many a man.

Breakfast eaten and the slim camp-outfit lashed to the sled, the men turned their backs on the cheery fire and launched out into the darkness. At once began to rise the cries that were fiercely sad—cries that called through the darkness and cold to one another and answered back. Conversation ceased. Daylight came at nine o'clock. At midday the sky to the south warmed to rose-color, and marked where the bulge of the earth intervened between the meridian sun and the northern world. But the rose-color swiftly faded. The gray light of day that remained lasted until three o'clock, when it, too, faded, and the pall of the Arctic night descended upon the lone and silent land.

As darkness came on, the hunting-cries to right and left and rear drew closer—so close that more than once they sent surges of fear through the toiling dogs, throwing them into short-lived panics.

At the conclusion of one such panic, when he and Henry had got the dogs back in the traces, Bill said: "I wisht they'd strike game somewheres, an' go away an' leave us alone."

"They do get on the nerves horrible," Henry sympathized.

They spoke no more until camp was made.

Henry was bending over and adding ice to the babbling pot of beans when he was startled by the sound of a blow, an exclamation from Bill, and a sharp snarling cry of pain from among the dogs. He straightened up in time to see a dim form disappearing across the snow into the shelter of the dark. Then he saw Bill, standing amid the dogs, half triumphant, half crestfallen, in one hand a stout club, in the other the tail and part of the body of a sun-cured salmon.

"It got half of it," he announced; "but I got a whack at it jes' the same. D'ye hear it squeal?"

"What'd it look like?" Henry asked.

"Couldn't see. But it had four legs an' a mouth an' hair an' looked like any dog."

"Must be a tame wolf, I reckon."

"It's damned tame, whatever it is, comin' in here at feedin' time an' gettin' its whack of fish."

That night, when supper was finished and they sat on the oblong box and pulled at their pipes, the circle of gleaming eyes drew in even closer than before.

"I wisht they'd spring up a bunch of moose or something, an' go away an' leave us alone," Bill said.

Henry grunted with an intonation that was not all sympathy, and for a quarter of an hour they sat on in silence, Henry staring at the fire, and Bill at the circle of eyes that burned in the darkness just beyond the firelight.

"I wisht we was pullin' into McGurry right now," he began again.

"Shut up your wishin' and your croakin'," Henry burst out angrily. "Your stomach's sour. That's what's ailin' you. Swallow a spoonful of sody, an' you'll sweeten up wonderful an' be more pleasant company."

In the morning Henry was aroused by fervid blasphemy that proceeded from the mouth of Bill. Henry propped himself up on an elbow and looked to see his comrade standing among the dogs beside the replenished fire, his arms raised in objurgation, his face distorted with passion.

"Hello!" Henry called. "What's up now?"

"Frog's gone," came the answer.

"No."

"I tell you yes."

Henry leaped out of the blankets and to the dogs. He counted them with care, and then joined his partner in cursing the power of the Wild that had robbed them of another dog.

"Frog was the strongest dog of the bunch," Bill pronounced finally.

"An' he was no fool dog neither," Henry added.

And so was recorded the second epitaph in two days.

A gloomy breakfast was eaten, and the four remaining dogs were harnessed to the sled. The day was a repetition of the days that had gone before. The men toiled without speech across the face of the frozen world. The silence was unbroken save by the cries of their pursuers, that, unseen, hung upon their rear. With the coming of night in the mid-afternoon, the cries sounded closer as the pursuers drew in according to their custom; and the dogs grew excited and frightened, and were guilty of panics that tangled the traces and further depressed the two men.

"There, that'll fix you fool critters," Bill said with satisfaction that night, standing erect at completion of his task.

Henry left the cooking to come and see. Not only had his partner tied the dogs up, but he had tied them, after the Indian fashion, with sticks. About the neck of each dog he had fastened a leather thong. To this, and so close to the neck that the dog could not get his teeth to it, he had tied a stout stick four or five feet in length. The other end of the stick, in turn, was made fast to a stake in the ground by means of a leather thong. The dog was unable to gnaw through the leather at his own end of the stick. The stick prevented him from getting at the leather that fastened the other end.

Henry nodded his head approvingly.

"It's the only contraption that'll ever hold One Ear," he said. "He can gnaw through leather as clean as a knife an' jes' about half as quick. They all'll be here in the mornin' hunkydory."

"You jes' bet they will," Bill affirmed. "If one of em' turns up missin', I'll go without my coffee."

"They jes' know we ain't loaded to kill," Henry remarked at bedtime, indicating the gleaming circle that hemmed them in. "If we could put a couple of shots into 'em, they'd be more respectful. They come closer every night. Get the firelight out of your eyes an' look hard—there! Did you see that one?"

For some time the two men amused themselves with

watching the movement of vague forms on the edge of the firelight. By looking closely and steadily at where a pair of eyes burned in the darkness, the form of the animal would slowly take shape. They could even see these forms move at times.

A sound among the dogs attracted the men's attention. One Ear was uttering quick, eager whines, lunging at the length of his stick toward the darkness, and desisting now and again in order to make frantic attacks on the stick with his teeth.

"Look at that, Bill," Henry whispered.

Full into the firelight, with a stealthy, sidelong movement, glided a doglike animal. It moved with commingled mistrust and daring, cautiously observing the men, its attention fixed on the dogs. One Ear strained the full length of the stick toward the intruder and whined with eagerness.

"That fool One Ear don't seem scairt much," Bill said in a low tone.

"It's a she-wolf," Henry whispered back, "an' that accounts for Fatty an' Frog. She's the decoy for the pack. She draws out the dog an' then all the rest pitches in an' eats 'm up."

The fire crackled. A log fell apart with a loud spluttering noise. At the sound of it the strange animal leaped back into the darkness.

"Henry, I'm a-thinkin'," Bill announced.

"Thinkin' what?"

"I'm a-thinkin' that was the one I lambasted with the club."

"Ain't the slightest doubt in the world," was Henry's response.

"An' right here I want to remark," Bill went on, "that that animal's familiarity with campfires is suspicious an' immoral."

"It knows for certain more'n a self-respectin' wolf ought to know," Henry agreed. "A wolf that knows enough to come in with the dogs at feedin' time has had experiences."

"Ol' Villan had a dog once that run away with the wolves," Bill cogitates aloud. "I ought to know. I shot it out of the pack in a moose pasture over on Little Stick. An' Ol' Villan cried like a baby. Hadn't seen it for three years, he said. Ben with the wolves all that time."

"I reckon you've called the turn, Bill. That wolf's a dog, an' it's eaten fish many's the time from the hand of man."

"An if I get a chance at it, that wolf that's a dog'll be jes' meat," Bill declared. "We can't afford to lose no more animals."

"But you've only got three cartridges," Henry objected.

"I'll wait for a dead sure shot," was the reply.

In the morning Henry renewed the fire and cooked breakfast to the accompaniment of his partner's snoring.

"You was sleepin' jes' too comfortable for anything," Henry told him, as he routed him out for breakfast. "I hadn't the heart to rouse you."

Bill began to eat sleepily. He noticed that his cup was empty and started to reach for the pot. But the pot was beyond arm's length and beside Henry.

"Say, Henry," he chided gently, "ain't you forgot somethin'?"

Henry looked about with great carefulness and shook his head. Bill held up the empty cup.

"You don't get no coffee," Henry announced.

"Ain't run out?" Bill asked anxiously.

"Nope."

"Ain't thinkin' it'll hurt my digestion?"

"Nope."

A flush of angry blood pervaded Bill's face. "Then it's jes' warm an' anxious I am to be hearin' you explain yourself," he said.

"Spanker's gone," Henry answered.

Without haste, with the air of one resigned to misfortune Bill turned his head, and from where he sat counted the dogs.

"How'd it happen?" he asked apathetically.

Henry shrugged his shoulders. "Don't know. Unless One Ear gnawed 'm loose. He couldn't a-done it himself, that's sure."

"The darned cuss." Bill spoke gravely and slowly, with no hint of the anger that was raging within. "Jes' because he couldn't chew himself loose, he chews Spanker loose."

"Well, Spanker's troubles is over anyway; I guess he's digested by this time an' cavortin' over the landscape in the bellies of twenty different wolves," was Henry's epitaph on this, the latest lost dog. "Have some coffee, Bill."

But Bill shook his head.

"Go on," Henry pleaded, elevating the pot.

Bill shoved his cup aside. "I'll be ding-dong-danged if I do. I said I wouldn't if ary dog turned up missin', an' I won't."

"It's darn good coffee," Henry said enticingly.

But Bill was stubborn, and he ate a dry breakfast washed

down with mumbled curses at One Ear for the trick he had played.

"I'll tie 'em up out of reach of each other tonight," Bill said, as they took the trail.

They had traveled little more than a hundred yards, when Henry, who was in front, bent down and picked up something with which his snowshoe had collided. It was dark, and he could not see it, but he recognized it by the touch. He flung it back, so that it struck the sled and bounced along until it fetched up on Bill's snowshoes.

"Mebbe you'll need that in your business," Henry said.

Bill uttered an exclamation. It was all that was left of Spanker—the stick with which he had been tied.

"They ate 'm hide an' all," Bill announced. "The stick's as clean as a whistle. They've ate the leather offen both ends. They're damn hungry, Henry, an' they'll have you an' me guessin' before this trip's over."

Henry laughed defiantly. "I ain't been trailed this way by wolves before, but I've gone through a whole lot worse an' kept my health. Takes more'n a handful of them pesky critters to do for yours truly, Bill, my son."

"I don't know, I don't know," Bill muttered ominously.

"Well, you'll know all right when we pull into McGurry."

"I ain't feelin' special enthusiastic," Bill persisted.

"You're off color, that's what's the matter with you,"

Henry dogmatized. "What you need is quinine, an' I'm goin' to dose you up stiff as soon as we make McGurry."

Bill grunted his disagreement with the diagnosis, and lapsed into silence. The day was like all the days. Light came at nine o'clock. At twelve o'clock the southern horizon was warmed by the unseen sun; and then began the cold gray of afternoon that would merge, three hours later, into night.

It was just after the sun's futile effort to appear, that Bill slipped the rifle from under the sled-lashings and said: "You keep right on, Henry, I'm goin' to see what I can see."

"You'd better stick by the sled," his partner protested. "You've only got three cartridges, an' there's no tellin' what might happen."

"Who's croaking now?" Bill demanded triumphantly.

Henry made no reply, and plodded on alone, though often he cast anxious glances back into the gray solitude where his partner had disappeared. An hour later, taking advantage of the cut-offs around which the sled had to go, Bill arrived.

"They're scattered an' rangin' along wide," he said, "keeping up with us an' lookin' for game at the same time. You see, they're sure of us, only they know they've got to wait to get us. In the meantime they're willin' to pick up anything eatable that comes handy."

"You mean they think they're sure of us," Henry objected.

But Bill ignored him. "I seen some of them. They're pretty thin. They ain't had a bite in weeks I reckon, outside of Fatty an' Frog an' Spanker; an' there's so many of 'em that that didn't go far. They're remarkable thin. Their ribs is like washboards, an' their stomachs is right up against their backbones. They're pretty desperate, I can tell you. They'll be goin' mad, yet, an' then watch out."

A few minutes later, Henry, who was now traveling behind the sled, emitted a low, warning whistle. Bill turned and looked, then quietly stopped the dogs. To the rear, from around the last bend and plainly into view, on the very trail they had just covered, trotted a furry, slinking form. Its nose was to the trail, and it trotted with a peculiar, sliding, effortless gait. When they halted, it halted, throwing up its head and regarding them steadily with nostrils that twitched as it caught and studied the scent of them.

"It's the she-wolf," Bill answered.

The dogs had lain down in the snow, and he walked past them to join his partner in the sled. Together they watched the strange animal that had pursued them for days and that had already accomplished the destruction of half their dog-team.

After a searching scrutiny, the animal trotted forward a few steps. This it repeated several times, till it was a short hundred yards away. It paused, head up, close by a clump of spruce trees, and with sight and scent studied the outfit of the watching men. It looked at them in a strangely wistful way, after the manner of a dog; but in its wistfulness there was none of the dog affection. It was a wistfulness bred of hunger, as cruel as its own fangs, as merciless as the frost itself.

It was large for a wolf, its gaunt frame advertising the lines of an animal that was among the largest of its kind.

"Stands pretty close to two feet an' a half at the shoulders," Henry commented. "An' I'll bet it ain't far from five feet long."

"Kind of strange color for a wolf," was Bill's criticism. "I never seen a red wolf before. Looks almost cinnamon to me."

The animal was certainly not cinnamon-colored. Its coat was the true wolf-coat. The dominant color was gray, and yet there was to it a faint reddish hue—a hue that was baffling, that appeared and disappeared, that was more like an illusion of the vision, now gray, distinctly gray, and again giving hints and glints of a vague redness of color not classifiable in terms of ordinary experience.

"Looks for all the world like a big husky sled-dog," Bill said. "I wouldn't be s'prised to see it wag its tail."

"Hello, you husky!" he called. "Come here, you whatever-your-name-is."

"Ain't a bit scairt of you," Henry laughed.

Bill waved his hand at it threateningly and shouted loudly; but the animal betrayed no fear. The only change in it that they could notice was an accession of alertness. It still regarded them with the merciless wistfulness of hunger. They were meat, and it was hungry; and it would like to go in and eat them if it dared.

"Look here, Henry," Bill said, unconsciously lowering his voice to a whisper because of what he imitated. "We've got three cartridges. But it's a dead shot. Couldn't miss it. It's got away with three of our dogs, an' we oughter put a stop to it.

What d'ye say?"

Henry nodded his consent. Bill cautiously slipped the gun from under the sled-lashing. The gun was on the way to his shoulder, but it never got there. For in that instant the she-wolf leaped sidewise from the trail into the clump of spruce trees and disappeared.

The two men looked at each other. Henry whistled long and comprehendingly.

"I might have knowed it," Bill chided himself aloud as he replaced the gun. "Of course a wolf that knows enough to come in with the dogs at feedin' time, 'd know all about shooting-irons. I tell you right now, Henry, that critter's the cause of all our trouble. We'd have six dogs at the present time, 'stead of three, if it wasn't for her. An' I tell you right now, Henry, I'm goin' to get her. She's too smart to be shot in the open. But I'm goin' to lay for her. I'll bushwhack her as sure as my name is Bill."

"You needn't stray off too far in doin' it," his partner admonished. "If that pack ever starts to jump you, them three cartridges'd be wuth no more'n three whoops in hell. Them animals is damn hungry, an' once they start in, they'll sure get you, Bill."

They camped early that night. Three dogs could not drag the sled so fast nor for so long hours as could six, and they were showing unmistakable signs of playing out. The men went early to bed, Bill first seeing to it that the dogs were tied out of gnawing-reach of one another.

But the wolves were growing bolder, and the men were aroused more than once from their sleep. So near did the wolves approach, that the dogs became frantic with terror, and it was necessary to replenish the fire from time to time in order to keep the adventurous marauders at safer distance.

"I've hearn sailors talk of sharks followin' a ship," Bill remarked, as he crawled back into the blankets after one such replenishing of the fire. "Well, them wolves is land sharks. They know their business better'n we do, an' they ain't a-holdin' our trail this way for their health. They're goin' to get us. They're sure goin' to get us, Henry."

"They've half got you a'ready, a-talkin' like that," Henry retorted sharply. "A man's half licked when he says he is. An' you're half eaten from the way you're goin' on about it."

"They've got away with better men than you an' me," Bill answered.

"Oh, shet up your croakin'. You make me all-fired tired."

Henry rolled over angrily on his side, but was surprised that Bill made no similar display of temper. This was not Bill's way, for he was easily angered by sharp words. Henry thought long over it before he went to sleep, and as his eyelids fluttered down and he dozed off, the thought in his mind was: "There's no mistakin' it, Bill's almighty blue. I'll have to cheer him up tomorrow."

The day began auspiciously. They had lost no dogs during the night, and they swung out upon the trail and into the silence, the darkness, and the cold with spirits that were fairly light. Bill seemed to have forgotten his forebodings of the previous night, and even waxed facetious with the dogs when, at midday, they overturned the sled on a bad piece of trail.

It was an awkward mix-up. The sled was upside down and jammed between a tree-trunk and a huge rock, and they were forced to unharness the dogs in order to straighten out the tangle. The two men were bent over the sled and trying to right it, when Henry observed One Ear sidling away.

"Here, you, One Ear!" he cried, straightening up and turning around on the dog.

But One Ear broke into a run across the snow, his traces trailing behind him. And there, out in the snow of their back track, was the she-wolf waiting for him. As he neared her, he became suddenly cautious. He slowed down to an alert and mincing walk and then stopped. He regarded her carefully and dubiously, yet desirefully. She seemed to smile at him, showing her teeth in an ingratiating rather than a menacing way. She moved toward him a few steps, playfully, and then halted. One Ear drew near to her, still alert and cautious, his tail and ears in the air, his head held high.

He tried to sniff noses with her, but she retreated playfully and coyly. Every advance on his part was accompanied by a corresponding retreat on her part. Step by step she was luring him away from the security of his human companionship. Once, as though a warning had in vague ways flitted through his intelligence, he turned his head and looked back at the overturned sled, at his team-mates, and at the two men who were calling to him.

But whatever idea was forming in his mind, was dissipated by the she-wolf, who advanced upon him, sniffed noses with him for a fleeting instant, and then resumed her coy retreat before his renewed advances.

In the meantime, Bill had bethought himself of the rifle. But it was jammed beneath the overturned sled, and by the time Henry had helped him to right the load, One Ear and the she-wolf were too close together and the distance too great to risk a shot.

Too late One Ear learned his mistake. Before they saw the cause, the two men saw him turn and start to run back toward them. Then, approaching at right angles to the trail and cutting off his retreat they saw a dozen wolves, lean and gray, bounding across the snow. On the instant, the she-wolf's coyness and playfulness disappeared. With a snarl she sprang upon One Ear. He thrust her off with his shoulder, and, his retreat cut off and still intent on regaining the sled, he altered his course in an attempt to circle around to it. More wolves were appearing every moment and joining in the chase. The she-wolf was one leap behind One Ear and holding her own.

"Where are you goin'?" Henry suddenly demanded, laying his hand on his partner's arm.

Bill shook it off. "I won't stand it," he said. "They ain't a-goin' to get any more of our dogs if I can help it."

Gun in hand, he plunged into the underbrush that lined the side of the trail. His intention was apparent enough. Taking the sled as the center of the circle that One Ear was making, Bill planned to tap that circle at a point in advance of the pursuit. With his rifle, in the broad daylight, it might be possible for him to awe the wolves and save the dog.

"Say, Bill!" Henry called after him. "Be careful! Don't take no chances!"

Henry sat down on the sled and watched. There was nothing else for him to do. Bill had already gone from sight; but now and again, appearing and disappearing among the underbrush and the scattered clumps of spruce, could be seen One Ear. Henry judged his case to be hopeless. The dog was thoroughly alive to its danger, but it was running on the outer circle while the wolf-pack was running on the inner and shorter circle. It was vain to think of One Ear so outdistancing his pursuers as to be able to cut across their circle in advance of them and to regain the sled.

The different lines were rapidly approaching a point. Somewhere out there in the snow, screened from his sight by trees and thickets, Henry knew that the wolf-pack, One Ear, and Bill were coming together. All too quickly, far more quickly than he had expected, it happened. He heard a shot, then two shots, in rapid succession, and he knew that Bill's ammunition was gone. Then he heard a great outcry of snarls and yelps. He recognized One Ear's yell of pain and terror, and he heard a wolf-cry that bespoke a stricken animal. And that was all. The snarls ceased. The yelping died away. Silence settled down again over the lonely land.

He sat for a long while upon the sled. There was no need for him to go and see what had happened. He knew it as though it had taken place before his eyes. Once, he roused with a start and hastily got the ax out from underneath the lashings. But for some time longer he sat and brooded, the two remaining dogs crouching and trembling at his feet.

At last he arose in a weary manner, as though all the resilience had gone out of his body, and proceeded to fasten the dogs to the sled. He passed a rope over his shoulder, a man-trace, and pulled with the dogs. He did not go far. At the first hint of darkness he hastened to make a camp, and he saw to it that he had a generous supply of firewood. He fed the dogs, cooked and ate his supper, and made his bed close to the fire.

But he was not destined to enjoy that bed. Before his eyes closed the wolves had drawn too near for safety. It no longer required an effort of the vision to see them. They were all about him and the fire, in a narrow circle, and he could see them plainly in the firelight lying down, sitting up, crawling forward on their bellies, or slinking back and forth. They even slept. Here and there he could see one curled up in the snow like a dog, taking the sleep that was now denied himself.

He kept the fire brightly blazing, for he knew that it alone intervened between the flesh of his body and their hungry fangs. His two dogs stayed close by him, one on either side, leaning against him for protection, crying and whimpering, and at times snarling desperately when a wolf approached a little closer than usual. At such moments, when his dogs snarled, the whole circle would be agitated, the wolves coming to their feet and pressing tentatively forward, a chorus of snarls and eager yelps rising about him. Then the circle would lie down again, and here and there a wolf would resume its broken nap.

But this circle had a continuous tendency to draw in upon him. Bit by bit, an inch at a time, with here a wolf bellying forward, and there a wolf bellying forward, the circle would narrow until the brutes were almost within springing distance. Then he would seize brands from the fire and hurl them into the pack. A hasty drawing back always resulted, accompanied by angry yelps and frightened snarls when a well-aimed brand struck and scorched a too daring animal.

Morning found the man haggard and worn, wide-eyed from want of sleep. He cooked breakfast in the darkness, and at nine o'clock, when, with the coming of daylight, the wolf pack drew back, he set about the task he had planned through the long hours of the night. Chopping down young saplings, he made them cross-bars of a scaffold by lashing them high up to the trunks of standing trees. Using the sled-lashing for a heaving rope, and with the aid of the dogs, he hoisted the coffin to the top of the scaffold.

"They got Bill, an' they may get me, but they'll sure never get you, young man," he said, addressing the dead body in its tree-sepulchre.

Then he took the trail, the lightened sled bounding along behind the willing dogs; for they, too, knew that safety lay in the gaining of Fort McGurry. The wolves were now more open in their pursuit, trotting sedately behind and ranging along on either side, their red tongues lolling out, their lean sides showing the undulating ribs with every movement. They were very lean, mere skin-bags stretched over bony frames, with strings for muscles—so lean that Henry found it in his mind to marvel that they still kept their feet and did not collapse forthright in the snow.

He did not dare travel until dark. At midday, not only did the sun warm the southern horizon, but it even thrust its upper rim, pale and golden, above the skyline. He received it as a sign. The days were growing longer. The sun was returning. But scarcely had the cheer of its light departed, than he went into camp. There were still several hours of gray daylight and somber twilight, and he utilised them in chopping an enormous supply of fire-wood.

With night came horror. Not only were the starving wolves growing bolder, but lack of sleep was telling upon Henry. He dozed despite himself, crouching by the fire, the blankets about his shoulders, the ax between his knees, and on either side a dog pressing close against him. He awoke once and saw in front of him, not a dozen feet away, a big gray wolf, one of the largest of the pack. And even as he looked, the brute deliberately stretched himself after the manner of a lazy dog, yawning full in his face and looking upon him with a possessive eye, as if, in truth, he were merely a delayed meal that was soon to be eaten.

This certitude was shown by the whole pack. Fully a score he could count, staring hungrily at him or calmly sleeping in the snow. They reminded him of children gathered about a spread table and awaiting permission to begin to eat. And he was the food they were to eat! He wondered how and when the meal would begin.

As he piled wood on the fire he discovered an appreciation of his own body which he had never felt before. He watched his moving muscles and was interested in the cunning mechanism of his fingers. By the light of the fire he crooked his fingers slowly and repeatedly now one at a time, now all together, spreading them wide or making quick gripping movements. He studied the nail-formation, and prodded the fingertips, now sharply, and again softly, gauging the while the nerve-sensations produced. It fascinated him, and he grew suddenly fond of this subtle flesh of his that worked so beautifully and smoothly and delicately. Then he would cast a glance of fear at the wolf-circle drawn expectantly about him, and like a blow the realization would strike him that this wonderful body of his, this living flesh, was no more than so much meat, a quest of ravenous animals, to be torn and slashed by their hungry fangs, to be sustenance to them as the moose and the rabbit had often been sustenance to him.

He came out of a doze that was half nightmare, to see the red-hued she-wolf before him. She was not more than half a dozen feet away sitting in the snow and wistfully regarding him. The two dogs were whimpering and snarling at his feet, but she took no notice of them. She was looking at the man, and for some time he returned her look. There was nothing threatening about her. She looked at him merely with a great wistfulness, but he knew it to be the wistfulness of an equally great hunger. He was the food, and the sight of him excited in her the gustatory sensations. Her mouth opened, the saliva drooled forth, and she licked her chops with the pleasure of anticipation.

A spasm of fear went through him. He reached hastily for a brand to throw at her. But even as he reached, and before his fingers had closed on the missile, she sprang back into safety; and he knew that she was used to having things thrown at her. She had snarled as she sprang away, baring her white fangs to their roots, all her wistfulness vanishing, being replaced by a carnivorous malignity that made him shudder. He glanced at the hand that held the brand, noticing the cunning delicacy of the fingers that gripped it, how they adjusted themselves to all the inequalities of the surface, curling over and under and about the rough wood, and one little finger, too close to the burning portion of the brand, sensitively and automatically writhing back from the hurtful heat to a cooler gripping-place; and in the same instant he seemed to see a vision of those same sensitive and delicate fingers being crushed and torn by the white teeth of the she-wolf. Never had he been so fond of this body of his as now when his tenure of it was so precarious.

All night, with burning brands, he fought off the hungry pack. When he dozed despite himself, the whimpering and snarling of the dogs aroused him. Morning came, but for the first time the light of day failed to scatter the wolves. The man waited in vain for them to go. They remained in a circle about him and his fire, displaying an arrogance of possession that shook his courage born of the morning light.

He made one desperate attempt to pull out on the trail. But the moment he left the protection of the fire, the boldest wolf leaped for him, but leaped short. He saved himself by springing back, the jaws snapping together a scant six inches from his thigh. The rest of the pack was now up and surging upon him, and a throwing of firebrands right and left was necessary to drive them back to a respectful distance.

Even in the daylight he did not dare leave the fire to chop fresh wood. Twenty feet away towered a huge dead spruce. He spent half the day extending his campfire to the tree, at any moment a half dozen burning faggots ready at hand to fling at his enemies. Once at the tree, he studied the surrounding forest in order to fell the tree in the direction of the most firewood.

The night was a repetition of the night before, save that the need for sleep was becoming overpowering. The snarling of his dogs was losing its efficacy. Besides, they were snarling all the time, and his benumbed and drowsy senses no longer took note of changing pitch and intensity. He awoke with a start. The she-wolf was less than a yard from him. Mechanically, at short range, without letting go of it, he thrust a brand full into her open and snarling mouth. She sprang away, yelling with pain, and while he took delight in the smell of burning flesh and hair, he watched her shaking her head and growling wrathfully a score of feet away.

But this time, before he dozed again, he tied a burning pine-knot to his right hand. His eyes were closed but few minutes when the burn of the flame on his flesh awakened him. For several hours he adhered to this program. Every time he was thus awakened he drove back the wolves with flying brands, replenished the fire, and rearranged the pine-knot on his hand. All worked well, but there came a time when he fastened the pine-knot insecurely. As his eyes closed it fell away from his hand.

He dreamed. It seemed to him that he was in Fort McGurry. It was warm and comfortable, and he was playing cribbage with the Factor. Also, it seemed to him that the fort was besieged by wolves. They were howling at the very gates, and sometimes he and the Factor paused from the game to listen and laugh at the futile efforts of the wolves to get in. And then, so strange was the dream, there was a crash. The door was burst open. He could see the wolves flooding into the big living room of the fort. They were leaping straight for him and the Factor. With the bursting open of the door, the noise of their howling had increased tremendously. This howling now bothered him. His dream was merging into something else—he knew not what; but through it all, following him, persisted the howling.

And then he awoke to find the howling real. There was a

great snarling and yelping. The wolves were rushing him. They were all about him and upon him. The teeth of one had closed upon his arm. Instinctively he leaped into the fire, and as he leaped, he felt the sharp slash of teeth that tore through the flesh of his leg. Then began a fire fight. His stout mittens temporarily protected his hands, and he scooped live coals into the air in all directions, until the campfire took on the semblance of a volcano.

But it could not last long. His face was blistering in the heat, his eyebrows and lashes were singed off, and the heat was becoming unbearable to his feet. With a flaming brand in each hand, he sprang to the edge of the fire. The wolves had been driven back. On every side, wherever the live coals had fallen, the snow was sizzling, and every little while a retiring wolf, with wild leap and snort and snarl, announced that one such live coal had been stepped upon.

Flinging his brands at the nearest of his enemies, the man thrust his smouldering mittens into the snow and stamped about to cool his feet. His two dogs were missing, and he well knew that they had served as a course in the protracted meal which had begun days before with Fatty, the last course of which would likely be himself in the days to follow.

"You ain't got me yet!" he cried, savagely shaking his fist at the hungry beasts; and at the sound of his voice the whole circle was agitated, there was a general snarl, and the she-wolf slid up close to him across the snow and watched him with hungry wistfulness.

He set to work to carry out a new idea that had come to him. He extended the fire into a large circle. Inside this circle he crouched, his sleeping outfit under him as a protection against the melting snow. When he had thus disappeared within his shelter of flame, the whole pack came curiously to the rim of the fire to see what had become of him. Hitherto they had been denied access to the fire, and they now settled down in a close-drawn circle, like so many dogs, blinking and yawning and stretching their lean bodies in the unaccustomed warmth. Then the she-wolf sat down, pointed her nose at a star, and began to howl. One by one the wolves joined her, till the whole pack, on haunches, with noses pointed skyward, was howling its hunger cry.

Dawn came, and daylight. The fire was burning low. The fuel had run out, and there was need to get more. The man attempted to step out of his circle of flame, but the wolves surged to meet him. Burning brands made them spring aside, but they no longer sprang back. In vain he strove to drive them back. As he gave up and stumbled inside his circle, a wolf leaped for him, missed, and landed with all four feet in the coals. It cried out with terror, at the same time snarling, and scrambled back to cool its paws in the snow.

The man sat down on his blankets in a crouching position. His body leaned forward from the hips. His shoulders, relaxed and drooping, and his head on his knees advertised that he had given up the struggle. Now and again he raised his head to note the dying down of the fire. The circle of flame and coals was breaking into segments with openings in between. These openings grew in size, the segments diminished.

"I guess you can come an' get me any time," he mumbled. "Anyway, I'm goin' to sleep."

Once he awakened, and in an opening in the circle, directly in front of him, he saw the she-wolf gazing at him.

Again he awakened, a little later, though it seemed hours to him. A mysterious change had taken place—so mysterious a change that he was shocked wider awake. Something had happened. He could not understand at first. Then he discovered it. The wolves were gone. Remained only the trampled snow to show how closely they had pressed him. Sleep was welling up and gripping him again, his head was sinking down upon his knees, when he roused with a sudden start.

There were cries of men, and churn of sleds, the creaking of harnesses, and the eager whimpering of straining dogs. Four sleds pulled in from the river bed to the camp among the trees. Half a dozen men were about the man who crouched in the center of the dying fire. They were shaking and prodding him into consciousness. He looked at them like a drunken man and maundered in strange, sleepy speech.

"Red she-wolf...Come in with the dogs at feedin' time...First she ate the dog-food...Then she ate the dogs...An' after that she ate Bill..."

"Where's Lord Alfred?" one of the men bellowed in his ear, shaking him roughly.

He shook his head slowly. "No, she didn't eat him…He's roostin' in a tree at the last camp."

"Dead?" the man shouted.

"An' in a box," Henry answered. He jerked his shoulder petulantly away from the grip of his questioner. "Say, you lemme alone…I'm jes' plump tuckered out…Goo' night, everybody."

His eyes fluttered and went shut. His chin fell forward on his chest. And even as they eased him down upon the blankets his snores were rising on the frosty air.

But there was another sound. Far and faint it was, in the remote distance, the cry of the hungry wolf-pack as it took the trail of other meat than the man it had just missed.

The White Seal

From *The Jungle Book*
By Rudyard Kipling

Oh! hush thee, my baby, the night is behind us,
And black are the waters that sparkled so green.
The moon, o'er the combers, looks downward to find us
At rest in the hollows that rustle between.
Where billow meets billow, then soft be thy pillow,
Ah, weary wee flipperling, curl at thy ease!
The storm shall not wake thee, nor shark overtake thee,
Asleep in the arms of the slow-swinging seas!

Seal Lullaby

ALL these things happened several years ago at a place
called Novastoshnah, or North East Point, on the Island

of St. Paul, away and away in the Bering Sea. Limmershin, the Winter Wren, told me the tale when he was blown onto the rigging of a steamer going to Japan, and I took him down into my cabin and warmed and fed him for a couple of days till he was fit to fly back to St. Paul's again. Limmershin is a very quaint little bird, but he knows how to tell the truth.

Nobody comes to Novastoshnah except on business, and the only people who have regular business there are the seals. They come in the summer months by hundreds and hundreds of thousands out of the cold gray sea. For Novastoshnah Beach has the finest accommodation for seals of any place in all the world.

Sea Catch knew that, and every spring would swim from whatever place he happened to be in—would swim like a torpedo-boat straight for Novastoshnah and spend a month fighting with his companions for a good place on the rocks, as close to the sea as possible. Sea Catch was fifteen years old, a huge gray fur seal with almost a mane on his shoulders, and long, wicked dog teeth. When he heaved himself up on his front flippers he stood more than four feet clear of the ground, and his weight, if anyone had been bold enough to weigh him, was nearly seven hundred pounds. He was scarred all over with the marks of savage fights, but he was always ready for just one fight more. He would put his head on one side, as though he were afraid to look his enemy in the face; then he would shoot it out like lightning, and when the big teeth were firmly fixed on the other seal's neck, the other seal might get away if he could, but Sea Catch would not help him.

Yet Sea Catch never chased a beaten seal, for that was against the Rules of the Beach. He only wanted room by the sea for his nursery. But as there were forty or fifty thousand other seals hunting for the same thing each spring, the whistling, bellowing, roaring, and blowing on the beach was something frightful.

From a little hill called Hutchinson's Hill, you could look over three-and-a-half miles of ground covered with fighting seals; and the surf was dotted all over with the heads of seals hurrying to land and begin their share of the fighting. They fought in the breakers, they fought in the sand, and they fought on the smooth-worn basalt rocks of the nurseries, for they were just as stupid and unaccommodating as men. Their wives never came to the island until late in May or early in June, for they did not care to be torn to pieces; and the young seals who had not begun housekeeping went inland about half a mile through the ranks of the fighters and played about on the sand dunes in droves and legions, and rubbed off every single green thing that grew. They were called the holluschickie—the bachelors—and there were perhaps two or three hundred thousand of them at Novastoshnah alone.

Sea Catch had just finished his forty-fifth fight one spring when Matkah, his soft, sleek, gentle-eyed wife, came up out of the sea, and he caught her by the scruff of the neck and dumped her down on his reservation, saying gruffly: "Late as usual. Where have you been?"

It was not the fashion for Sea Catch to eat anything during the four months he stayed on the beaches, and so his temper was generally bad. Matkah knew better than to answer back. She looked round and cooed: "How thoughtful of you. You've taken the old place again."

"I should think I had," said Sea Catch. "Look at me!"

He was scratched and bleeding in twenty places; one eye was almost out, and his sides were torn to ribbons.

"Oh, you men, you men!" Matkah said, fanning herself with her hind flipper. "Why can't you be sensible and settle your places quietly? You look as though you had been fighting with the Killer Whale."

"I haven't been doing anything but fighting since the middle of May. The beach is disgracefully crowded this season. I've met at least a hundred seals from Lukannon Beach, house hunting. Why can't people stay where they belong?"

"I've often thought we should be much happier if we hauled out at Otter Island instead of this crowded place," said Matkah.

"Bah! Only the holluschickie go to Otter Island. If we went there they would say we were afraid. We must preserve appearances, my dear."

Sea Catch sunk his head proudly between his fat shoulders and pretended to go to sleep for a few minutes, but all the time he was keeping a sharp lookout for a fight. Now that all the seals and their wives were on the land, you could hear their clamor miles out to sea above the loudest gales. At the lowest counting there were over a million seals on the beach—old seals, mother seals, tiny babies, and holluschickie, fighting, scuffling, bleating, crawling, and playing together— going down to the sea and coming up from it in gangs and regiments, lying over every foot of ground as far as the eye could reach, and skirmishing about in brigades through the fog. It is nearly always foggy at Novastoshnah, except when the sun comes out and makes everything look all pearly and rainbow-colored for a little while.

Kotick, Matkah's baby, was born in the middle of that confusion, and he was all head and shoulders, with pale, watery blue eyes, as tiny seals must be, but there was something about his coat that made his mother look at him very closely.

"Sea Catch," she said, at last, "our baby's going to be white!"

"Empty clam-shells and dry seaweed!" snorted Sea Catch. "There never has been such a thing in the world as a white seal."

"I can't help that," said Matkah; "there's going to be now." And she sang the low, crooning seal song that all the mother seals sing to their babies:

> *You mustn't swim till you're six weeks old,*
> *Or your head will be sunk by your heels;*
> *And summer gales and Killer Whales*
> *Are bad for baby seals.*

> *Are bad for baby seals, dear rat,*
> *As bad as bad can be;*
> *But splash and grow strong,*
> *And you can't be wrong.*
> *Child of the Open Sea!*

Of course the little fellow did not understand the words at first. He paddled and scrambled about by his mother's side, and learned to scuffle out of the way when his father was fighting with another seal, and the two rolled and roared up and down the slippery rocks. Matkah used to go to sea to get things to eat, and the baby was fed only once in two days, but then he ate all he could and throve upon it.

The first thing he did was to crawl inland, and there he met tens of thousands of babies of his own age, and they played together like puppies, went to sleep on the clean sand, and played again. The old people in the nurseries took no notice of them, and the holluschickie kept to their own grounds, and the babies had a beautiful playtime.

When Matkah came back from her deep-sea fishing she would go straight to their playground and call as a sheep calls for a lamb, and wait until she heard Kotick bleat. Then she would take the straightest of straight lines in his direction, striking out with her fore flippers and knocking the youngsters head over heels right and left. There were always a few hundred mothers hunting for their children through the playgrounds, and the babies were kept lively. But, as Matkah told Kotick, "So long as you don't lie in muddy water and get mange, or rub the hard sand into a cut or scratch, and so long as you never go swimming when there is a heavy sea, nothing will hurt you here."

Little seals can no more swim than little children, but they are unhappy till they learn. The first time that Kotick went down to the sea a wave carried him out beyond his depth, and his big head sank and his little hind flippers flew up exactly as his mother had told him in the song, and if the next wave had not thrown him back again he would have drowned.

After that, he learned to lie in a beach pool and let the wash of the waves just cover him and lift him up while he paddled, but he always kept his eye open for big waves that might hurt. He was two weeks learning to use his flippers; and all that while he floundered in and out of the water, and coughed and grunted and crawled up the beach and took catnaps on the sand, and went back again, until at last he found that he truly belonged to the water.

Then you can imagine the times that he had with his companions, ducking under the rollers; or coming in on top of a comber and landing with a swash and a splutter as the big wave went whirling far up the beach; or standing up on his tail and scratching his head as the old people did; or playing "I'm the King of the Castle" on slippery, weedy rocks that just stuck out of the wash. Now and then he would see a thin fin, like a big shark's fin, drifting along close to shore, and he knew that that was the Killer Whale, the Grampus, who eats young seals when he can get them; and Kotick would head for the beach like an arrow, and the fin would jig off slowly, as if it were looking for nothing at all.

Late in October the seals began to leave St. Paul's for the deep sea, by families and tribes, and there was no more fighting over the nurseries, and the holluschickie played anywhere they liked. "Next year," said Matkah to Kotick, "you will be a holluschickie; but this year you must learn how to catch fish."

They set out together across the Pacific, and Matkah showed Kotick how to sleep on his back with his flippers tucked down by his side and his little nose just out of the water. No cradle is so comfortable as the long, rocking swell of the Pacific. When Kotick felt his skin tingle all over, Matkah told him he was learning the "feel of the water," and that tingly, prickly feelings meant bad weather coming, and he must swim hard and get away.

"In a little time," she said, "you'll know where to swim to, but just now we'll follow Sea Pig, the Porpoise, for he is very wise." A school of porpoises were ducking and tearing through the water, and little Kotick followed them as fast as he could.

"How do you know where to go to?" he panted. The leader of the school rolled his white eye and ducked under. "My tail tingles, youngster," he said. "That means there's a gale behind me. Come along! When you're south of the Sticky Water (he meant the Equator) and your tail tingles, that means there's a gale in front of you and you must head north. Come along! The water feels bad here."

This was one of very many things that Kotick learned, and he was always learning. Matkah taught him to follow the cod and the halibut along the under-sea banks and wrench the rockling out of his hole among the weeds; how to skirt the wrecks lying a hundred fathoms below water and dart like a rifle bullet in at one porthole and out at another as the fishes ran; how to dance on the top of the waves when the lightning was racing all over the sky, and wave his flipper politely to the stumpy-tailed Albatross and the Man-of-war Hawk as they went down the wind; how to jump three or four feet clear of the water like a dolphin, flippers close to the side and tail curved; to leave the flying fish alone because they are all bony; to take the shoulder-piece out of a cod at full speed ten fathoms deep, and never to stop and look at a boat or a ship, but particularly a row-boat. At the end of six months what Kotick did not know about deep-sea fishing was not worth the knowing. And all that time he never set flipper on dry ground.

One day, however, as he was lying half-asleep in the warm water somewhere off the Island of Juan Fernandez, he felt faint and lazy all over, just as human people do when the spring is in their legs, and he remembered the good firm beaches of Novastoshnah seven thousand miles away, the games his companions played, the smell of the seaweed, the seal roar, and the fighting. That very minute he turned north, swimming steadily, and as he went on he met scores of his mates, all bound for the same place, and they said: "Greeting, Kotick! This year we are all holluschickie, and we can dance the Fire-dance in the breakers off Lukannon and play on the new grass. But where did you get that coat?"

Kotick's fur was almost pure white now, and though he felt very proud of it, he only said, "Swim quickly! My bones are aching for the land." And so they all came to the beaches where they had been born, and heard the old seals, their fathers, fighting in the rolling mist.

That night Kotick danced the Fire-dance with the yearling seals. The sea is full of fire on summer nights all the way down from Novastoshnah to Lukannon, and each seal leaves a wake like burning oil behind him and a flaming flash when he jumps, and the waves break in great phosphorescent streaks and swirls. Then they went inland to the holluschickie grounds and rolled up and down in the new wild wheat and told stories of what they had done while they had been at sea. They talked about the Pacific as boys would talk about a wood that they had been nutting in, and if anyone had understood them he could have gone away and made such a chart of that ocean as never was. The older holluschickie romped down from Hutchinson's Hill crying: "Out of the way, youngsters! The sea is deep and you don't know all that's in it yet. Wait till you've rounded the Horn. Hi, you yearling, where did you get that white coat?"

"I didn't get it," said Kotick. "It grew." And just as he was going to roll the speaker over, a couple of black-haired men with flat red faces came from behind a sand dune, and Kotick, who had never seen a man before, coughed and lowered his head. The holluschickie just bundled off a few yards and sat staring stupidly. The men were no less than Kerick Booterin, the chief of the seal-hunters on the island, and Patalamon, his son. They came from the little village not half a mile from the sea nurseries, and they were deciding what seals they would drive up to the killing pens—for the seals were driven just like sheep—to be turned into seal-skin jackets later on.

"Ho!" said Patalamon. "Look! There's a white seal!"

Kerick Booterin turned nearly white under his oil and smoke, for he was an Aleut, and Aleuts are not clean people. Then he began to mutter a prayer. "Don't touch him, Patalamon. There has never been a white seal since—since I was born. Perhaps it is old Zaharrof's ghost. He was lost last year in the big gale."

"I'm not going near him," said Patalamon. "He's unlucky. Do you really think he is old Zaharrof come back? I owe him for some gulls' eggs."

"Don't look at him," said Kerick. "Head off that drove of four-year-olds. The men ought to skin two hundred today, but it's the beginning of the season and they are new to the work. A hundred will do. Quick!"

Patalamon rattled a pair of seal's shoulder bones in front of a herd of holluschickie and they stopped dead, puffing and blowing. Then he stepped near and the seals began to move, and Kerick headed them inland, and they never tried to get back to their companions. Hundreds and hundreds of thousands of seals watched them being driven, but they went on playing just the same. Kotick was the only one who asked questions, and none of his companions could tell him anything, except that the men always drove seals in that way for six weeks or two months of every year.

"I am going to follow," he said, and his eyes nearly popped out of his head as he shuffled along in the wake of the herd.

"The white seal is coming after us," cried Patalamon. "That's the first time a seal has ever come to the killing-grounds alone."

"Hsh! Don't look behind you," said Kerick. "It is Zaharrof's ghost! I must speak to the priest about this."

The distance to the killing-grounds was only half a mile, but it took an hour to cover, because if the seals went too fast Kerick knew that they would get heated and then their fur would come off in patches when they were skinned. So they went on very slowly, past Sea Lion's Neck, past Webster House, till they came to the Salt House just beyond the sight of the seals on the beach. Kotick followed, panting and wondering. He thought that he was at the world's end, but the roar of the seal nurseries behind him sounded as loud as the roar of a train in a tunnel. Then Kerick sat down on the moss and pulled out a heavy pewter watch and let the drove cool off for thirty minutes, and Kotick could hear the fog-dew dripping off the brim of his cap. Then ten or twelve men, each with an iron-bound club three or four feet long, came up, and Kerick pointed out one or two of the drove that were bitten by their companions or too hot, and the men kicked those aside with their heavy boots made of the skin of a walrus' throat, and then Kerick said, "Let go!" and then the men clubbed the seals on the head as fast as they could.

Ten minutes later little Kotick did not recognize his friends any more, for their skins were ripped off from the nose to the hind flippers, whipped off and thrown down on the ground in a pile. That was enough for Kotick. He turned and galloped (a seal can gallop very swiftly for a short time) back to the sea; his little new mustache bristling with horror. At Sea Lion's Neck, where the great sea lions sit on the edge of the surf, he flung himself flipper-overhead into the cool water and rocked there, gasping miserably. "What's here?" said a sea lion gruffly, for as a rule the sea lions keep themselves to themselves.

"Scoochnie! Ochen scoochnie!" ("I'm lonesome, very lonesome!") said Kotick. "They're killing all the holluschickie on all the beaches!"

The Sea Lion turned his head inshore. "Nonsense!" he said. "Your friends are making as much noise as ever. You must have seen old Kerick polishing off a drove. He's done that for thirty years."

"It's horrible," said Kotick, backing water as a wave went over him, and steadying himself with a screw stroke of his flippers that brought him all standing within three inches of a jagged edge of rock.

"Well done for a yearling!" said the Sea Lion, who could appreciate good swimming. "I suppose it is rather awful from your way of looking at it, but if you seals will come here year after year, of course the men get to know of it, and unless you can find an island where no men ever come you will always be driven."

"Isn't there any such island?" began Kotick.

"I've followed the poltoos (the halibut) for twenty years, and I can't say I've found it yet. But look here—you seem to have a fondness for talking to your betters—suppose you go to Walrus Islet and talk to Sea Vitch. He may know something. Don't flounce off like that. It's a six-mile swim, and if I were you I should haul out and take a nap first, little one."

Kotick thought that that was good advice, so he swam round to his own beach, hauled out, and slept for half an hour, twitching all over, as seals will. Then he headed straight for Walrus Islet, a little low sheet of rocky island almost due northeast from Novastoshnah, all ledges and rock and gulls' nests, where the walrus herded by themselves.

He landed close to old Sea Vitch—the big, ugly, bloated, pimpled, fat-necked, long-tusked walrus of the North Pacific, who has no manners except when he is asleep—as he was then, with his hind flippers half in and half out of the surf.

"Wake up!" barked Kotick, for the gulls were making a great noise.

"Hah! Ho! Hmph! What's that?" said Sea Vitch, and he struck the next walrus a blow with his tusks and waked him up, and the next struck the next, and so on till they were all awake and staring in every direction but the right one.

"Hi! It's me," said Kotick, bobbing in the surf and looking like a little white slug.

"Well! May I be—skinned!" said Sea Vitch, and they all looked at Kotick as you can fancy a club full of drowsy old gentlemen would look at a little boy.

Kotick did not care to hear any more about skinning just then; he had seen enough of it. So he called out: "Isn't there any place for seals to go where men don't ever come?"

"Go and find out," said Sea Vitch, shutting his eyes. "Run away. We're busy here."

Kotick made his dolphin-jump in the air and shouted as loud as he could: "Clam-eater! Clam-eater!" He knew that Sea Vitch never caught a fish in his life but always rooted for clams and seaweed; though he pretended to be a very terrible person. Naturally the Chickies and the Gooverooskies and the Epatkas—the Burgomaster Gulls and the Kittiwakes and the

Puffins, who are always looking for a chance to be rude, took up the cry, and—so Limmershin told me—for nearly five minutes you could not have heard a gun fired on Walrus Islet. All the population was yelling and screaming "Clam-eater! Stareek (old man)!" while Sea Vitch rolled from side to side grunting and coughing.

"Now will you tell?" said Kotick, all out of breath.

"Go and ask Sea Cow," said Sea Vitch. "If he is living still, he'll be able to tell you."

"How shall I know Sea Cow when I meet him?" said Kotick, sheering off.

"He's the only thing in the sea uglier than Sea Vitch," screamed a Burgomaster gull, wheeling under Sea Vitch's nose. "Uglier, and with worse manners! Stareek!"

Kotick swam back to Novastoshnah, leaving the gulls to scream. There he found that no one sympathized with him in his little attempt to discover a quiet place for the seals. They told him that men had always driven the holluschickie—it was part of the day's work—and that if he did not like to see ugly things he should not have gone to the killing grounds. But none of the other seals had seen the killing, and that made the difference between him and his friends. Besides, Kotick was a white seal.

"What you must do," said old Sea Catch, after he had heard his son's adventures, "is to grow up and be a big seal like your father, and have a nursery on the beach, and then they will leave you alone. In another five years you ought to be able to fight for yourself."

Even gentle Matkah, his mother, said: "You will never be able to stop the killing. Go and play in the sea, Kotick." And Kotick went off and danced the Fire-dance with a very heavy little heart.

That autumn he left the beach as soon as he could, and set off alone because of a notion in his bullet-head. He was going to find Sea Cow, if there was such a person in the sea, and he was going to find a quiet island with good firm beaches for seals to live on, where men could not get at them. So he explored and explored by himself from the North to the South Pacific, swimming as much as three hundred miles in a day and a night. He met with more adventures than can be told, and narrowly escaped being caught by the Basking Shark, and the Spotted Shark, and the Hammerhead, and he met all the untrustworthy ruffians that loaf up and down the seas, and the heavy polite fish, and the scarlet spotted scallops that are moored in one place for hundreds of years, and grow very proud of it; but he never met Sea Cow, and he never found an island that he could fancy.

If the beach was good and hard, with a slope behind it for seals to play on, there was always the smoke of a whaler on the horizon, boiling down blubber, and Kotick knew what that meant. Or else he could see that seals had once visited the island and been killed off, and Kotick knew that where men had come once they would come again.

He picked up with an old stumpy-tailed albatross, who told him that Kerguelen Island was the very place for peace and quiet, and when Kotick went down there he was all but smashed to pieces against some wicked black cliffs in a heavy sleet-storm with lightning and thunder. Yet as he pulled out against the gale he could see that even there had once been a seal nursery. And it was so in all the other islands that he visited.

Limmershin gave a long list of them, for he said that Kotick spent five seasons exploring, with a four months' rest each year at Novastoshnah, when the holluschickie used to make fun of him and his imaginary islands. He went to the Galapagos, a horrid dry place on the Equator, where he was nearly baked to death; he went to the Georgia Islands, the Orkneys, Emerald Island, Little Nightingale Island, Gough's Island, Bouvet's Island, the Crossets, and even to a little speck of an island south of the Cape of Good Hope. But everywhere the People of the Sea told him the same things. Seals had come to those islands once upon a time, but men had killed them all off. Even when he swam thousands of miles out of the Pacific and got to a place called Cape

Corrientes (that was when he was coming back from Gough's Island), he found a few hundred mangy seals on a rock and they told him that men came there too.

That nearly broke his heart, and he headed round the Horn back to his own beaches; and on his way north he hauled out on an island full of green trees, where he found an old, old seal who was dying, and Kotick caught fish for him and told him all his sorrows. "Now," said Kotick, "I am going back to Novastoshnah, and if I am driven to the killing-pens with the holluschickie I shall not care."

The old seal said, "Try once more. I am the last of the Lost Rookery of Masafuera, and in the days when men killed us by the hundred thousand there was a story on the beaches that some day a white seal would come out of the North and lead the seal people to a quiet place. I am old, and I shall never live to see that day, but others will. Try once more."

And Kotick curled up his mustache (it was a beauty) and said, "I am the only white seal that has ever been born on the beaches, and I am the only seal, black or white, who ever thought of looking for new islands."

This cheered him immensely; and when he came back to Novastoshnah that summer, Matkah, his mother, begged him to marry and settle down, for he was no longer a holluschick but a full-grown sea-catch, with a curly white mane on his shoulders, as heavy, as big, and as fierce as his father. "Give me another season," he said. "Remember, Mother, it is always the seventh wave that goes farthest up the beach."

Curiously enough, there was another seal who thought that she would put off marrying till the next year, and Kotick danced the Fire-dance with her all down Lukannon Beach the night before he set off on his last exploration. This time he went westward, because he had fallen on the trail of a great shoal of halibut, and he needed at least one hundred pounds of fish a day to keep him in good condition. He chased them till he was tired, and then he curled himself up and went to sleep on the hollows of the ground swell that sets in to Copper Island. He knew the coast perfectly well, so about midnight, when he felt himself gently bumped on a weed-bed, he said, "Hm, tide's running strong tonight," and turning over under water opened his eyes slowly and stretched. Then he jumped like a cat, for he saw huge things nosing about in the shoal water and browsing on the heavy fringes of the weeds.

"By the Great Combers of Magellan!" he said, beneath his mustache. "Who in the Deep Sea are these people?"

They were like no walrus, sea lion, seal, bear, whale, shark, fish, squid, or scallop that Kotick had ever seen before. They were between twenty and thirty feet long, and they had no hind flippers, but a shovel-like tail that looked as if it had been whittled out of wet leather. Their heads were the most foolish-looking things you ever saw, and they balanced on the ends of their tails in deep water when they weren't grazing, bowing solemnly to each other and waving their front flippers as a fat man waves his arm.

"Ahem!" said Kotick. "Good sport, gentlemen?" The big things answered by bowing and waving their flippers like the Frog Footman. When they began feeding again Kotick saw that their upper lip was split into two pieces that they could twitch apart about a foot and bring together again with a whole bushel of seaweed between the splits. They tucked the stuff into their mouths and chumped solemnly.

"Messy style of feeding, that," said Kotick. They bowed again, and Kotick began to lose his temper. "Very good," he said. "If you do happen to have an extra joint in your front flipper you needn't show off so. I see you bow gracefully, but I should like to know your names." The split lips moved and twitched; and the glassy green eyes stared, but they did not speak.

"Well!" said Kotick. "You're the only people I've ever met uglier than Sea Vitch—and with worse manners."

Then he remembered in a flash what the Burgomaster gull had screamed to him when he was a little yearling at Walrus Islet, and he tumbled backward in the water, for he knew that he had found Sea Cow at last.

The sea cows went on schlooping and grazing and chumping in the weed, and Kotick asked them questions in every language that he had picked up in his travels; and the Sea People talk nearly as many languages as human beings. But the sea cows did not answer because Sea Cow cannot talk. He has only six bones in his neck where he ought to have seven, and they say under the sea that that prevents him from speaking even to his companions. But, as you know, he has an extra joint in his foreflipper, and by waving it up and down and about he makes what answers to a sort of clumsy telegraphic code.

By daylight Kotick's mane was standing on end and his temper was gone where the dead crabs go. Then the Sea Cow began to travel northward very slowly, stopping to hold absurd bowing councils from time to time, and Kotick followed them, saying to himself, "People who are such idiots as these are would have been killed long ago if they hadn't found out some safe island. And what is good enough for the Sea Cow is good enough for the Sea Catch. All the same, I wish they'd hurry."

It was weary work for Kotick. The herd never went more than forty or fifty miles a day, and stopped to feed at night, and kept close to the shore all the time; while Kotick swam round them, and over them, and under them, but he could not hurry them up one-half mile. As they went farther north they held a bowing council every few hours, and Kotick nearly bit off his mustache with impatience till he saw that they were following up a warm current of water, and then he respected them more.

One night they sank through the shiny water—sank like stones—and for the first time since he had known them began to swim quickly. Kotick followed, and the pace astonished him, for he never dreamed that Sea Cow was anything of a swimmer. They headed for a cliff by the shore—a cliff that ran down into deep water, and plunged into a dark hole at the foot of it, twenty fathoms under the sea. It was a long, long swim, and Kotick badly wanted fresh air before he was out of the dark tunnel they led him through.

"My wig!" he said, when he rose into open water at the farther end. "It was a long dive, but it was worth it."

The sea cows had separated and were browsing lazily along the edges of the finest beaches that Kotick had ever seen. There were long stretches of smooth-worn rock running for miles, exactly fitted to make seal-nurseries, and there were playgrounds of hard sand sloping inland behind them, and there were rollers for seals to dance in, and long grass to roll in, and sand dunes to climb up and down, and, best of all, Kotick knew by the feel of the water, which never deceives a true sea catch, that no men had ever come there.

The first thing he did was to assure himself that the fishing was good, and then he swam along the beaches and counted up the delightful low sandy islands half hidden in the beautiful rolling fog. Away to the northward, out to sea, ran a line of bars and shoals and rocks that would never let a ship come within six miles of the beach, and between the islands and the mainland was a stretch of deep water that ran up to the perpendicular cliffs, and somewhere below the cliffs was the mouth of the tunnel.

"It's Novastoshnah over again, but ten times better," said Kotick. "Sea Cow must be wiser than I thought. Men can't come down the cliffs, even if there were any men; and the shoals to seaward would knock a ship to splinters. If any place in the sea is safe, this is it."

He began to think of the seal he had left behind him, but though he was in a hurry to go back to Novastoshnah, he thoroughly explored the new country, so that he would be able to answer all questions.

Then he dived and made sure of the mouth of the tunnel, and raced through to the southward. No one but a sea cow or a seal would have dreamed of there being such a place, and when he looked back at the cliffs even Kotick could hardly believe that he had been under them.

He was six days going home, though he was not swimming slowly; and when he hauled out just above Sea Lion's Neck the first person he met was the seal who had been waiting for him, and she saw by the look in his eyes that he had found his island at last.

But the holluschickie and Sea Catch, his father, and all the other seals laughed at him when he told them what he had discovered, and a young seal about his own age said, "This is all very well, Kotick, but you can't come from no one knows where and order us off like this. Remember we've been fighting for our nurseries, and that's a thing you never did. You preferred prowling about in the sea."

The other seals laughed at this, and the young seal began twisting his head from side to side. He had just married that year, and was making a great fuss about it.

"I've no nursery to fight for," said Kotick. "I only want to show you all a place where you will be safe. What's the use of fighting?"

"Oh, if you're trying to back out, of course I've no more to say," said the young seal with an ugly chuckle.

"Will you come with me if I win?" said Kotick. And a green light came into his eye, for he was very angry at having to fight at all.

"Very good," said the young seal carelessly. "If you win, I'll come."

He had no time to change his mind, for Kotick's head was out and his teeth sunk in the blubber of the young seal's neck. Then he threw himself back on his haunches and hauled his enemy down the beach, shook him, and knocked him over. Then Kotick roared to the seals: "I've done my best for you these five seasons past. I've found you the island where you'll be safe, but unless your heads are dragged off your silly necks you won't believe. I'm going to teach you now. Look out for yourselves!"

Limmershin told me that never in his life—and Limmershin sees ten thousand big seals fighting every year—never in all his little life did he see anything like Kotick's charge into the nurseries. He flung himself at the biggest sea catch he could find, caught him by the throat, choked him and bumped him and banged him till he grunted for mercy, and then threw him aside and attacked the next. Kotick had never fasted for four months as the big seals did every year, and his deep-sea swimming trips kept him in perfect condition, and, best of all, he had never fought before. His curly white mane stood up with rage, and his eyes flamed, and his big dog teeth glistened, and he was splendid to look at. Old Sea Catch, his father, saw him tearing past, hauling the grizzled old seals about as though they had been halibut, and upsetting the young bachelors in all directions; and Sea Catch gave a roar and shouted: "He may be a fool, but he is the best fighter on the beaches! Don't tackle your father, my son! He's with you!"

Kotick roared in answer, and old Sea Catch waddled in with his mustache on end, blowing like a locomotive, while Matkah and the seal that was going to marry Kotick cowered down and admired their men-folk. It was a gorgeous fight, for the two fought as long as there was a seal that dared lift up his head, and when there were none they paraded grandly up and down the beach side by side, bellowing.

At night, just as the Northern Lights were winking and flashing through the fog, Kotick climbed a bare rock and looked down on the scattered nurseries and the torn and bleeding seals. "Now," he said, "I've taught you your lesson."

"My wig!" said old Sea Catch, boosting himself up stiffly, for he was fearfully mauled. "The Killer Whale himself could not have cut them up worse. Son, I'm proud of you, and what's more, I'll come with you to your island—if there is such a place."

"Hear you, fat pigs of the sea. Who comes with me to the Sea Cow's tunnel? Answer, or I shall teach you again," roared Kotick.

There was a murmur like the ripple of the tide all up and down the beaches. "We will come," said thousands of tired voices. "We will follow Kotick, the White Seal."

Then Kotick dropped his head between his shoulders and shut his eyes proudly. He was not a white seal any more, but red from head to tail. All the same he would have scorned to look at or touch one of his wounds.

A week later he and his army (nearly ten thousand holluschickie and old seals) went north to the Sea Cow's tunnel, Kotick leading them. The seals that stayed at Novastoshnah called them idiots. Next spring, when they all met off the fishing banks of the Pacific, Kotick's seals told tales of the new beaches beyond Sea Cow's tunnel and more and more seals left Novastoshnah. It was not all done at once, for the seals aren't very clever, and they need time to think things over, but each year more seals went away from Novastoshnah, and Lukannon, and the other nurseries, to the quiet, sheltered beaches where Kotick sits all summer, getting bigger, fatter, and stronger each year, while the holluschickie play around him, in that sea where no man comes.

Tall
Tales

The stories of Sinbad were based on the experiences of sailors from Iraq. Sinbad is a merchant who makes many voyages to trade his goods. In this extract he tells the story of one of his most amazing adventures.

The Giant Roc

From *The Second Voyage of Sinbad the Sailor*

I DESIGNED, after my first voyage, to spend the rest of my days at Bagdad, but it was not long ere I grew weary of an indolent life, and I put to sea a second time, with merchants of known probity. We embarked on board a good ship, and, after recommending ourselves to God, set sail. We traded from island to island, and exchanged commodities with great profit. One day we landed on an island covered with several sorts of fruit trees, but we could see neither man nor animal. We walked in the meadows, along the streams that watered them. While some diverted themselves with gathering flowers, and others fruits, I took my wine and provisions, and sat down near a stream betwixt two high trees, which formed a thick shade. I made a good meal, and afterward fell sleep. I cannot tell how long I slept, but when I awoke the ship was gone.

In this sad condition I was ready to die with grief. I cried out in agony, beat my head and breast, and threw myself upon the ground, where I lay some time in despair. I upbraided myself a hundred times for not being content with the produce of my first voyage, that might have sufficed me all my life. But all this was in vain, and my repentance came too late. At last I resigned myself to the will of God. Not knowing what to do, I climbed to the top of a lofty tree, from whence I looked about on all sides, to see if I could discover anything that could give me hope. When I gazed toward the sea I could see nothing but sky and water; but looking over the land, I beheld something white; and coming down, I took what provision I had left and went toward it, the distance being so great that I could not distinguish what it was.

As I approached, I thought it to be a white dome, of a prodigious height and extent; and when I came up to it, I touched it, and found it to be very smooth. I went round to see if it was open on any side, but saw it was not, and that there was no climbing up to the top, as it was so smooth. It was at least fifty paces round.

By this time the sun was about to set, and all of a sudden the sky became as dark as if it had been covered with a thick cloud. I was much astonished at this sudden darkness, but much more when I found it was occasioned by a bird of a monstrous size, that came flying toward me. I remembered that I had often heard mariners speak of a miraculous bird called the roc, and conceived that the great dome which I so much admired must be its egg. In short, the bird alighted, and sat over the egg. As I perceived her coming, I crept close to the egg, so that I had before me one of the legs of the bird, which was as big as the trunk of a tree. I tied myself strongly to it with my turban, in hopes that the roc next morning would carry me with her out of this desert island. After having passed the night in this condition, the bird flew away as soon as it was daylight, and carried me so high that I could not discern the earth; she afterward descended with so much rapidity that I lost my senses. But when I found myself on the ground, I speedily untied the knot, and had scarcely done so, when the roc, having taken up a serpent of a monstrous length in her bill, flew away.

The spot where it left me was encompassed on all sides by

mountains, that seemed to reach above the clouds, and so steep that there was no possibility of getting out of the valley. This was a new perplexity; so that when I compared this place with the desert island from which the roc had brought me, I found that I had gained nothing by the change.

As I walked through this valley, I perceived it was strewn with diamonds, some of which were of surprising bigness. I took pleasure in looking upon them; but shortly I saw at a distance such objects as greatly diminished my satisfaction, and which I could not view without terror, namely, a great number of serpents, so monstrous that the least of them was capable of swallowing an elephant. They retired in the daytime to their dens, where they hid themselves from the roc, their enemy, and came out only in the night.

I spent the day in walking about in the valley, resting myself at times in such places as I thought most convenient. When night came on I went into a cave, where I thought I might repose in safety. I secured the entrance, which was low and narrow, with a great stone, to preserve me from the serpents; but not so far as to exclude the light. I supped on part of my provisions, but the serpents, which began hissing round me, put me into such extreme fear that I did not sleep. When day appeared the serpents retired, and I came out of the cave, trembling. I can justly say that I walked upon diamonds without feeling any inclination to touch them. At last I sat down, and notwithstanding my apprehensions, not having closed my eyes during the night, fell asleep, after having eaten a little more of my provisions. But I had scarcely shut my eyes when something that fell by me with a great noise awakened me. This was a large piece of raw meat; and at the same time I saw several others fall down from the rocks in different places.

I had always regarded as fabulous what I had heard sailors and others relate of the valley of diamonds, and of the stratagems employed by merchants to obtain jewels from thence; but now I found that they had stated nothing but the truth. For the fact is, that the merchants come to the neighborhood of this valley, when the eagles have young ones, and throwing great joints of meat into the valley, the diamonds, upon whose points they fall, stick to them; the eagles, which are stronger in this country than anywhere else, pounce with great force upon those pieces of meat, and carry them to their nests on the precipices of the rocks to feed their young: the merchants at this time run to their nests, disturb, and drive off the eagles by their shouts, and take away the diamonds that stick to the meat.

I perceived in this device the means of my deliverance.

Having collected together the largest diamonds I could find, and put them into the leather bag in which I used to carry my provisions, I took the largest of the pieces of meat,

tied it close round me with the
cloth of my turban, and then
laid myself upon the ground,
with my face downward, the
bag of diamonds being made
fast to my girdle.

I had scarcely placed myself in this
posture when one of the eagles, having
taken me up with the piece of meat to which I was fastened,
carried me to his nest on the top of the mountain. The
merchants immediately began their shouting to frighten the
eagles; and when they had obliged them to quit their prey,
one of them came to the nest where I was. He was much
alarmed when he saw me; but recovering himself, instead of
inquiring how I came thither, began to quarrel with me, and
asked why I stole his goods.

"You will treat me," replied I, "with more civility when
you know me better. Do not be uneasy; I have diamonds
enough for you and myself, more than all the other
merchants together. Whatever they have they owe to chance;
but I selected for myself, in the bottom of the valley, those
which you see in this bag."

I had scarcely done speaking, when the other merchants
came crowding about us, much astonished to see me; but
they were much more surprised when I told them my story.

They conducted me to their encampment; and there, having opened my bag, they were surprised at the largeness of my diamonds, and confessed that they had never seen any of such size and perfection. I prayed the merchant who owned the nest to which I had been carried (for every merchant had his own) to take as many for his share as he pleased. He contented himself with one, and that, too, the least of them; and when I pressed him to take more, without fear of doing me any injury, "No," said he, "I am very well satisfied with this, which is valuable enough to save me the trouble of making any more voyages, and will raise as great a fortune as I desire."

I spent the night with the merchants, to whom I related my story a second time, for the satisfaction of those who had not heard it. I could not moderate my joy when I found myself delivered from the danger I have mentioned. I thought myself in a dream, and could scarcely believe myself out of danger.

The merchants had thrown their pieces of meat into the valley for several days; and each of them being satisfied with the diamonds that had fallen to his lot, we left the place the next morning, and travelled near high mountains, where there were serpents of a prodigious length, which we had the good fortune to escape. We took shipping at the first port we reached, and touched at the isle of Roha, where the trees grow that yield camphor. This tree is so large, and its branches so thick, that one hundred men may easily sit under its shade. The juice, of which the camphor is made, exudes from a hole bored in the upper part of the tree, and is received in a vessel, where it thickens to a consistency, and becomes what we call camphor. After the juice is thus drawn out, the tree withers and dies.

In this island is also found the rhinoceros, an animal less than the elephant but larger than the buffalo. It has a horn upon its nose, about a cubit in length; this horn is solid, and cleft through the middle. The rhinoceros fights with the elephant, runs his horn into his belly, and carries him off upon his head; but the blood and the fat of the elephant running into his eyes and making him blind, he falls to the ground; and then, strange to relate, the roc comes and carries them both away in her claws, for food for her young ones.

I pass over many other things peculiar to this island, lest I should weary you. Here I exchanged some of my diamonds for merchandise. From hence we went to other islands, and at last, having touched at several trading towns of the continent, we landed at Bussorah, from whence I proceeded to Bagdad. There I immediately gave large presents to the poor, and lived honorably upon the vast riches I had brought, and gained with so much fatigue.

Alice has fallen down a rabbit hole into a magical land where she encounters many strange creatures. In this extract, her companion is a gryphon, a creature with the body of a lion and the head and shoulders of an eagle.

The Mock Turtle's Story

From *Alice's Adventures in Wonderland*
By Lewis Carroll

T HEY had not gone far before they saw the Mock Turtle in the distance, sitting sad and lonely on a little ledge of rock, and, as they came nearer, Alice could hear him sighing as if his heart would break. She pitied him deeply. "What is his sorrow?" she asked the Gryphon, and the Gryphon answered, very nearly in the same words as before, "It's all his fancy, that: he hasn't got no sorrow, you know. Come on!"

So they went up to the Mock Turtle, who looked at them with large eyes full of tears, but said nothing.

"This here young lady," said the Gryphon, "she wants for to know your history, she do."

"I'll tell it her," said the Mock Turtle in a deep, hollow tone. "Sit down, both of you, and don't speak a word till I've finished."

So they sat down, and nobody spoke for some minutes. Alice thought to herself, "I don't see how he can *even* finish, if he doesn't begin." But she waited patiently.

"Once," said the Mock Turtle at last, with a deep sigh, "I was a real Turtle."

These words were followed by a very long silence, broken only by an occasional exclamation of "Hjckrrh!" from the Gryphon, and the constant heavy sobbing of the Mock Turtle. Alice was very nearly getting up and saying, "Thank you, sir, for your interesting story," but she could not help thinking there *must* be more to come, so she sat still and said nothing.

"When we were little," the Mock Turtle went on at last, more calmly, though still sobbing a little now and then, "we went to school in the sea. The master was an old Turtle—we used to call him Tortoise—"

"Why did you call him Tortoise, if he wasn't one?" Alice asked.

"We called him Tortoise because he taught us," said the Mock Turtle angrily: "really you are very dull!"

"You ought to be ashamed of yourself for asking such a simple question," added the Gryphon; and then they both sat silent and looked at poor Alice, who felt ready to sink into the earth.

At last the Gryphon said to the Mock Turtle, "Drive on, old fellow! Don't be all day about it!" and he went on in these words: "Yes, we went to school in the sea, though you mayn't believe it—"

"I never said I didn't!" interrupted Alice.

"You did," said the Mock Turtle.

"Hold your tongue!" added the Gryphon, before Alice could speak again. The Mock Turtle went on.

"We had the best of educations—in fact, we went to school every day—"

"*I've* been to a day-school, too," said Alice; "you needn't be so proud as all that."

"With extras?" asked the Mock Turtle a little anxiously.

"Yes," said Alice, "we learned French and music."

"And washing?" said the Mock Turtle.

"Certainly not!" said Alice indignantly.

"Ah! Then yours wasn't a really good school," said the Mock Turtle in a tone of great relief. "Now at *ours* they had at the end of the bill, 'French, music, *and washing*—extra'."

"You couldn't have wanted it much," said Alice; "living at the bottom of the sea."

"I couldn't afford to learn it." said the Mock Turtle with a sigh. "I only took the regular course."

"What was that?" inquired Alice.

"Reeling and Writing, of course, to begin with," the Mock Turtle replied; "and then the different branches of Arithmetic—Ambition, Distraction, Uglification, and Derision."

"I never heard of 'Uglification'," Alice ventured to say. "What is it?"

The Gryphon lifted up both its paws in surprise. "What! Never heard of uglifying!" it exclaimed. "You know what to beautify is, I suppose?"

"Yes," said Alice doubtfully: "it means… to… make… anything… prettier."

"Well, then," the Gryphon went on, "if you don't know what to uglify is, you *are* a simpleton."

Alice did not feel encouraged to ask any more questions about it, so she turned to the Mock Turtle, and said, "What else had you to learn?"

"Well, there was Mystery," the Mock Turtle replied, counting off the subjects on his flappers, "Mystery, ancient and modern, with Seaography: then Drawling—the Drawling-master was an old conger-eel, that used to come once a week: *he* taught us Drawling, Stretching, and Fainting in Coils."

"What was *that* like?" said Alice.

"Well, I can't show it you myself," the Mock Turtle said: "I'm too stiff. And the Gryphon never learnt it."

"Hadn't time," said the Gryphon: "I went to the Classics master, though. He was an old crab, *he* was."

"I never went to him," the Mock Turtle said with a sigh: "he taught Laughing and Grief, they used to say."

"So he did, so he did," said the Gryphon, sighing in his turn; and both creatures hid their faces in their paws.

"And how many hours a day did you do lessons?" said Alice, in a hurry to change the subject.

"Ten hours the first day," said the Mock Turtle: "nine the next, and so on."

"What a curious plan!" exclaimed Alice.

"That's the reason they're called lessons," the Gryphon remarked: "because they lessen from day to day."

This was quite a new idea to Alice, and she thought it over a little before she made her next remark. "Then the eleventh day must have been a holiday?"

"Of course it was," said the Mock Turtle.

"And how did you manage on the twelfth?" Alice went on eagerly.

"That's enough about lessons," the Gryphon interrupted in a very decided tone: "tell her something about the games now."

The Mock Turtle sighed deeply, and drew the back of one flapper across his eyes. He looked at Alice, and tried to speak, but for a minute or two sobs choked his voice. "Same as if he had a bone in his throat," said the Gryphon: and it set to work shaking him and punching him in the back. At last the Mock Turtle recovered his voice, and, with tears running down his cheeks, he went on again: "You may not have lived much under the sea," ("I haven't," said Alice) "and perhaps you were never even introduced to a lobster," (Alice began to say, "I once tasted—" but checked herself hastily, and said, "No, never") "—so you can have no idea what a delightful thing a Lobster Quadrille is!"

"No, indeed," said Alice. "What sort of a dance is it?"

"Why," said the Gryphon, "you first form into a line along the seashore—"

"Two lines!" cried the Mock Turtle. "Seals, turtles,

salmon, and so on; then, when you've cleared all the jellyfish out of the way—"

"*That* generally takes some time," interrupted the Gryphon.

"—you advance twice—"

"Each with a lobster as a partner!" cried the Gryphon.

"Of course," the Mock Turtle said: "advance twice, set to partners—"

"—change lobsters, and retire in the same order," continued the Gryphon.

"Then, you know," the Mock Turtle went on, "you throw the—"

"The lobsters!" shouted the Gryphon, with a bound into the air.

"—as far out to sea as you can—"

"Swim after them!" screamed the Gryphon.

"Turn a somersault in the sea!" cried the Mock Turtle, capering wildly about.

"Back to land again, and that's all the first figure," said the Mock Turtle, suddenly dropping his voice; and the two creatures, who had been jumping about like mad things all this time, sat down again very sadly and quietly, and looked at Alice.

"It must be a very pretty dance," said Alice timidly.

"Would you like to see a little of it?" said the Mock Turtle.

"Very much indeed," said Alice.

"Come, let's try the first figure!" said the Mock Turtle to the Gryphon. "We can do without lobsters, you know. Which shall sing?"

"Oh, *you* sing," said the Gryphon. "I've forgotten the words."

So they began solemnly dancing round and round Alice, every now and then treading on her toes when they passed too close, and waving their forepaws to mark the time, while the Mock Turtle sang this, very slowly and sadly:

"'Will you walk a little faster?' said a whiting to a snail.
'There's a porpoise close behind us, and he's treading on
my tail.'
See how eagerly the lobsters and the turtles all advance!
They are waiting on the shingle—will you come and
join the dance?
Will you, won't you, will you, won't you, will you join
the dance?
Will you, won't you, will you, won't you, won't you join
the dance?

"'You can really have no notion how delightful it will be
When they take us up and throw us, with the lobsters,
 out to sea!'
But the snail replied 'Too far, too far!' and gave a look
 askance
Said he thanked the whiting kindly, but he would not
 join the dance.
Would not, could not, would not, could not, would not
 join the dance.
Would not, could not, would not, could not, could not
 join the dance.

"'What matters it how far we go?' his scaly friend replied.
'There is another shore, you know, upon the other side.
The further off from England the nearer is to France
Then turn not pale, beloved snail, but come and join
 the dance
Will you, won't you, will you, won't you, will you join
 the dance?
Will you, won't you, will you, won't you, won't you join
 the dance?'"

"Thank you, it's a very interesting dance to watch," said
Alice, feeling very glad that it was over at last: "and I do so
like that curious song about the whiting!"

"Oh, as to the whiting," said the Mock Turtle, "they—you've seen them, of course?"

"Yes," said Alice, "I've often seen them at dinn—" she checked herself hastily.

"I don't know where Dinn may be," said the Mock Turtle, "but if you've seen them so often, of course you know what they're like."

"I believe so," Alice replied thoughtfully. "They have their tails in their mouths—and they're all over crumbs."

"You're wrong about the crumbs," said the Mock Turtle: "crumbs would all wash off in the sea. But they *have* their tails in their mouths; and the reason is—" here the Mock Turtle yawned and shut his eyes. "Tell her about the reason and all that," he said to the Gryphon.

"The reason is," said the Gryphon, "that they *would* go with the lobsters to the dance. So they got thrown out to sea. So they had to fall a long way. So they got their tails fast in their mouths. So they couldn't get them out again. That's all."

"Thank you," said Alice, "it's very interesting. I never knew so much about a whiting before."

"I can tell you more than that, if you like," said the Gryphon. "Do you know why it's called a whiting?"

"I never thought about it," said Alice. "Why?"

"*It does the boots and shoes,*" the Gryphon replied very solemnly.

Alice was thoroughly puzzled. "Does the boots and shoes!" she repeated in a wondering tone.

"Why, what are *your* shoes done with?" said the Gryphon. "I mean, what makes them so shiny?"

Alice looked down at them, and considered a little before she gave her answer. "They're done with blacking, I believe."

"Boots and shoes under the sea," the Gryphon went on in a deep voice, "are done with a whiting. Now you know."

"And what are they made of?" Alice asked in a tone of great curiosity.

"Soles and eels, of course," the Gryphon replied rather impatiently, "any shrimp could have told you that."

"If I'd been the whiting," said Alice, whose thoughts were still running on the song, "I'd have said to the porpoise, 'Keep back, please: we don't want *you* with us!'"

"They were obliged to have him with them," the Mock Turtle said: "no wise fish would go anywhere without a porpoise."

"Wouldn't it really?" said Alice in a tone of great surprise.

"Of course not," said the Mock Turtle: "why, if a fish came to *me*, and told me he was going a journey, I should say 'With what porpoise?'"

"Don't you mean 'purpose'?" said Alice.

"I mean what I say," the Mock Turtle replied in an offended tone. And the Gryphon added "Come, let's hear some of *your* adventures."

"I could tell you my adventures—beginning from this morning," said Alice a little timidly: "but it's no use going back to yesterday, because I was a different person then."

"Explain all that," said the Mock Turtle.

"No, no! The adventures first," said the Gryphon in an impatient tone: "explanations take such a dreadful time."

So Alice began telling them her adventures from the time when she first saw the White Rabbit. She was a little nervous about it just at first, the two creatures got so close to her, one on each side, and opened their eyes and mouths so *very* wide, but she gained courage as she went on. Her listeners were perfectly quiet till she got to the part about her repeating *You are old, Father William,* to the Caterpillar, and the words all coming different, and then the Mock Turtle drew a long breath, and said, "That's very curious."

"It's all about as curious as it can be," said the Gryphon.

"It all came different!" the Mock Turtle repeated thoughtfully. "I should like to hear her try and repeat something now. Tell her to begin." He looked at the Gryphon as if he thought it had some kind of authority over Alice.

"Stand up and repeat *Tis the Voice of the Sluggard,*" said the Gryphon.

"How the creatures order one about, and make one repeat lessons!" thought Alice; "I might as well be at school at once." However, she got up, and began to repeat it, but her head was so full of the Lobster Quadrille, that she hardly knew what she was saying, and the words came very queer indeed:

"Tis the voice of the Lobster; I heard him declare,
'You have baked me too brown, I must sugar my hair.'
As a duck with its eyelids, so he with his nose
Trims his belt and his buttons, and turns out his toes."

"That's different from what I used to say when I was a child," said the Gryphon.

"Well, I never heard it before," said the Mock Turtle; "but it sounds uncommon nonsense."

Alice said nothing; she had sat down with her face in her hands, wondering if anything would *ever* happen in a natural way again.

"I should like to have it explained," said the Mock Turtle.

"She can't explain it," said the Gryphon hastily. "Go on with the next verse."

"But about his toes?" the Mock Turtle persisted. "How *could* he turn them out with his nose, you know?"

"It's the first position in dancing." Alice said; but was dreadfully puzzled by the whole thing, and longed to change the subject.

"Go on with the next verse," the Gryphon repeated impatiently: "it begins 'I passed by his garden'."

Alice did not dare to disobey, though she felt sure it would all come wrong, and she went on in a trembling voice:

"I passed by his garden, and marked, with one eye,
How the Owl and the Panther were sharing a pie—"

"What *is* the use of repeating all that stuff," the Mock Turtle interrupted, "if you don't explain it as you go on? It's by far the most confusing thing I ever heard!"

"Yes, I think you'd better leave off," said the Gryphon, and Alice was only too glad to do so.

"Shall we try another figure of the Lobster Quadrille?" the Gryphon went on. "Or would you like the Mock Turtle to sing you a song?"

"Oh, a song, please, if the Mock Turtle would be so kind," Alice replied, so eagerly that the Gryphon said, in a rather offended tone, "Hm! No accounting for tastes! Sing her 'Turtle Soup', will you, old fellow?"

The Mock Turtle sighed deeply, and began, in a voice sometimes choked with sobs, to sing this:

"Beautiful Soup, so rich and green,
Waiting in a hot tureen!
Who for such dainties would not stoop?
Soup of the evening, beautiful Soup!
Soup of the evening, beautiful Soup!
Beau-ootiful Soo-oop! Beau-ootiful Soo-oop!
Soo-oop of the e-e-evening, Beautiful, beautiful Soup!

"Beautiful Soup! Who cares for fish,
Game, or any other dish?
Who would not give all else
for two pennyworth only of beautiful Soup?
Pennyworth only of beautiful Soup?
Beau-ootiful Soo-oop! Beau-ootiful Soo-oop!
Soo-oop of the e-e-evening, Beautiful, beautiful Soup!"

"Chorus again!" cried the Gryphon, and the Mock Turtle had just begun to repeat it, when a cry of "The trial's beginning!" was heard in the distance.

"Come on!" cried the Gryphon, and, taking Alice by the hand, it hurried off, without waiting for the end of the song.

"What trial is it?" Alice panted as she ran; but the Gryphon only answered, "Come on!" and ran the faster, while more and more faintly came, carried on the breeze that followed them, the melancholy words: *"Soo-oop of the e-e-evening, beautiful, beautiful Soup!"*

The Curly-haired Hen

By Auguste Vimar

"Oh Grandfather, tell us a story, do. You know, the one you began the other evening about Mother Etienne's big farm. You remember. The weather is so bad and we can't go out. Go on, Grandfather, please."

Coaxingly the three children clung round their grandfather, looking at him beseechingly. He, adoring the children as he did, loved to hear them plead. At last he began:

"Since you have been very good, and you want it so much, I will tell you the wonderful story of Mother Etienne's farm and the still more wonderful story of what happened to one of its occupants.

"Love animals, my children, be kind to them, care for them, and you will surely have your reward.

"Mother Etienne was a good stout woman with a very kind heart. While still young she was so unfortunate as to lose her husband and her son of whom she was very fond. This made her, as you can imagine, very, very sad. She wouldn't listen to any new offers of marriage, though she had plenty of them. Instead, she devoted her life, her whole existence, to the attentive, nay I ought to say, the maternal care, of the animals on her farm, making them as comfortable as could be.

"She had, as I said before, a most excellent heart, the good Mother Etienne. You shall see that presently.

"This good woman then lived on her big farm, very spacious and admirably situated. A slate roof covered the large house; the granaries, stables, and outhouses were sheltered by old thatching upon which grew moss and lichen.

"Let me tell you now, dear children, who were the chief occupants of the farm. First there was big Coco—a fine Normandy horse—bay-colored and very fat, whose silky coat had a purple sheen; he had a star on his forehead and a pink mark between his eyes. He was very gentle and answered to the voice of his mistress. If Mother Etienne passed by his stable he never failed to scent her and whinnied at once. That was his way of showing his friendliness and saying, 'Good morning.'

"His good mistress spoiled him with all sorts of dainties. Sometimes a crust of bread, sometimes a handful of carrots, but what he loved best of all was sugar. If you had given him a whole loaf he would soon have eaten it up.

"Coco had for stable companions three fine Swiss cows. Their names were La Blonde, Blanchotte, and Nera. You know what the colors were for the names, don't you?

"Petit-Jacques, the stable boy, took care of them. On fine days he led them to pasture into a bog paddock near the farm up against a pretty wood of silver beeches. A large pond of clear water covered one corner of the meadow and lost itself in the reeds and iris. There the fine big cows went to quench their thirst; quantities of frogs went there, too, to play leap-frog. It was a veritable earthly Paradise.

"From the farm Mother Etienne caught the sound of the large bronze bells each with its different low note, which hung round the necks of the cows; thus she could superintend their comings and goings without interrupting her various occupations. For the farm was very big, as I told you, and had many animals on it.

"After the stables and coachhouses came the piggery, the rabbit hutches, and finally an immense poultry-yard divided into a thousand compartments, and sheltering a whole horde of poultry of all sorts; fowls of all kinds and of all breeds, geese, guinea fowl, pigeons, ducks, and what all besides. What wasn't there in that prodigious poultry-yard?

"Mother Etienne spent most of her time there, for the smaller and more delicate the creatures the more interest and care she gave them. 'The weak need so much protection,' this excellent woman would say, and she was right.

"So for the baby ducks her tenderness was limitless. What dangers had to be avoided to raise successfully all these tiny folks! Did a pig escape? Immediately danger threatened the poultry-yard. For a pig has terrible teeth and he doesn't care what he eats—he would as soon crunch a little duckling as a carrot. So she had to watch every minute, every second even. For besides, in spite of the vigilance of Labrie, the faithful watchdog, sometimes rats would suck the blood of the young pigeons. Once even a whole litter of rabbits was destroyed that way.

"To dispose of the products of her farm, Mother Etienne drove twice a week to market in her market-cart drawn by Coco. She was famed for the best vegetables, the purest and creamiest milk; in short, the eggs she sold were the freshest, the poultry and rabbits the tenderest and most juicy to be had. As soon as she and Coco came trotting into the market there was a rush to get to her first. There, as everywhere, everyone loved Mother Etienne.

"Thus time passed peacefully at the big farm.

"One day, however, the quiet was disturbed by a little drama which convulsed the calm but busy spot.

"Mother Etienne had given to a Cochin-China hen, which she had christened Yollande, some white duck's eggs to sit on. The batch of fifteen eggs had all come out. It was really wonderful to see these fifteen baby ducks, yellow as canaries, beaks and webbed feet pink, swarming around the big patient sitting mother, ducking under her wings, to come out presently and clamber helter-skelter onto her broad back. As often happens with nurses, Yollande loved the ducklings as her own children, and without worrying about their shape or plumage, so different from her own, she showered upon them proofs of the tenderest affection. Did a fly pass within their reach, all these little ones jumped at it,

tumbling in their efforts to catch it. The little yellow balls with their wide-awake air never took a second's rest.

"Well cared for and well fed, they grew so rapidly that soon they had to have more space. Mother Etienne housed them then on the edge of the pond in a latticed coop opening onto a sloping board which led down to the water. It was, as it were, a big swimming bath, which grew gradually deeper and deeper. The ducks and geese loved to plunge in and hardly left the water except to take their meals.

"Yollande felt very out of place in this new dwelling. The ducklings on the contrary, urged on by their instinct, madly enjoyed it and rushed pell-mell into the water. This inexplicable impulse terrified their mama. She was, in fact, 'as mad as a wet hen'.

"She ran up and down, her feathers on end, her face swollen, her crest red, clucking away, trying to persuade her babies not to venture into the water. For hens, like cats, hate the water. It was unspeakable torture to her. The children would not listen; deaf to her prayers, her cries, these rascally babies ventured farther and farther out. They were at last and for the first time in their favorite element, lighter than little corks, they floated, dived, plunged, raced, fought, playing all sorts of tricks.

"Meanwhile, Yollande was eating her heart out. She

rushed to and fro, keeping her eyes glued on the disobedient ones. Suddenly she saw a mother-duck chasing her darlings. This was more than she could bear—driven by her maternal instinct she leapt like a fury to the aid of her family.

"A flap or two of her wings and she was above the water into which she fell at the deepest part.

"Splashing, struggling madly in the midst of her frightened brood, she was soon exhausted and succumbing to syncope, she sank to the bottom.

"The surface of the water closed above her. The little ones did not realize what had happened—very quickly recovering from their momentary fright, they went on with their games—splashing the water with their beaks and amusing themselves as though nothing were the matter.

"Mother Etienne, busy giving green apples to the pigs, bran to the rabbits, and corn to the pigeons, came back presently, and could not see the big Yollande beside the pond, only her children floating far, far away on the water. Surprised she drew nearer, called, but in vain. The mother-hen had disappeared. Then only did she understand the tragedy that had occurred. She called for help. Petit-Jacques immediately opened the big sluice and the water ran out, but much too slowly for their impatience. At last they began to see the bottom, and soon the body of poor Yollande was discovered stiff and motionless.

"There was general consternation at the farm. Petit-Jacques, by means of a long pole, seized her and drew her to land at Mother Etienne's feet. Labrie came up and sniffed sadly at the body of the unhappy hen. In vain they dried her and rubbed her—nothing did any good. 'She's quite dead, alas,' said Mother Etienne with tears in her eyes, 'but it was my own fault. I ought to have closed down the lattice and this misfortune would not have happened. It really is a great pity—such a fine hen. She weighs at least eight pounds. There, Germaine, take her and weigh her.'

"Germaine was the maid and also the cousin of Petit-Jacques, of whom she was very fond. She was a fine buxom girl of eighteen, strong and well-grown. She loved animals, too, but her feeling for them could not be compared to Mother Etienne's.

"'Germaine, take away poor Yollande, I am quite upset by this trouble. You will bury her this evening, in a corner of the kitchen-garden—deep enough to prevent any animal digging her up. I leave it to you—do it carefully.'

"The girl bore away the fine hen in her apron. 'How heavy she is—it is a shame,' and blowing apart the feathers, she saw the skin underneath as yellow and plump as you could wish. Mechanically she plucked a few feathers. 'After all,' she said, 'it isn't as though she had died—she was drowned, quite a clean death; she's firm and healthy, only an hour ago she was as strong and well as could be. Why shouldn't we eat her? We'll stew her because, though she is not old, she is not exactly in her first youth, but there's a lot on her—with a dressing of carrots and nutmeg, a bunch of herbs, and a tomato, with a calf's foot to make a good jelly, I believe she'd make a lovely dinner.'

"Saying this she went on plucking Yollande. All the feathers, large and small, gone, a little down was left, so to get rid of this she lit an old newspaper and held her over it. 'Madame won't know anything and will enjoy her as much as we shall. There's enough on her for two good meals.'

"Quite decided, instead of burying her, she wrapped the future stew carefully in a perfectly clean cloth and put it on a shelf in the kitchen out of the way of flies or accident.

"During this time Mother Etienne was busy making as warm a home as she could for the fifteen little orphans. Poor darlings. In a wicker-basket she covered a layer of straw with another of wadding and fine down. Upon this she put the ducklings one by one, and covered the whole with feathers; then closing the lid, she carried the basket to the stable where the air was always nice and warm. All this took time; it was about six o'clock in the evening, the sun was going down, throwing a last oblique smile into the kitchen, gleaming here and there on the shining copper which hung on the walls.

"As for Germaine, she, with Petit-Jacques to help her, had gone to milk the cows. Mother Etienne soon joined them, and the two women came back to the house together.

"Horror of horrors! What a terrible sight. Pale with fear they stood on the threshold of the kitchen not daring to move—to enter. Their hearts were in their mouths. A ghost stood there in front of them—Yollande—and Germaine fell at Mother Etienne's feet in utter consternation. Yollande? Yes, Yollande, but what a Yollande! Heavens! Yollande plucked, literally plucked! Yollande emerging from her shroud like Lazarus from his tomb! Yollande risen from the dead! A cry of anguish burst from the heart of kind Mother Etienne. 'Yollande, oh, Yollande!' The Cochin-China replied by a long shudder.

"This is what had happened. On falling into the water, Yollande after struggling fiercely succumbed to syncope, and her lungs ceasing to act she had ceased to breathe, so the water had not entered her lungs. That is why she was not drowned. Life was, so to speak, suspended. The syncope lasted some time. The considerable heat to which she was subjected when Germaine held her above the flaming newspaper had brought about a healthy reaction and in the solitude of the kitchen she had recovered consciousness.

"After the first moment of terror was over, Germaine confessed her plan to Mother Etienne, who, glad to find Yollande still alive, forgave Germaine the disobedience which had saved her.

"But the hen was still shivering, shaking in every limb, her skin all goose-flesh. Dragging after her travesty of a tail, she jumped onto the kitchen table which she shook with her shivering.

"'We can't leave her like that any longer,' said Mother Etienne, 'we must cover her up somehow,' and straight away she wrapped her up in all the cloths she could lay her hands on. Germaine prepared some hot wine with sugar in it, and the two women fed her with it in spoonfuls—then they took a good drink of it themselves. All three at once felt the better for it. Yollande spent the night in these hastily made swaddling clothes between two foot-warmers which threw out a gentle and continuous heat and kept away the catarrh with which the poor Cochin-China was threatened. The great question which arose now was how they were to protect her from the cold in future. Both of them cogitated over it.

"Several times during the night, Mother Etienne and the maid came to look at the hen, who, worn out by such a long day of fatigue and suffering, at last closed her eyes, relaxed, and slept till morning.

"Nevertheless she was the first in the house to wake up, and at dawn began to cackle vigorously. Germaine hastened to her, bringing a quantity of corn which the hen, doubtless owing to her fast of the day before, ate greedily.

"Now the important thing was to find her a practical costume. The weather was mild but there was great danger in allowing her to wander about in a garb as light as it was primitive. The mornings and evenings were cool and might bring on a cold, inflammation or congestion of the lungs, rheumatism, or what not.

"At all costs a new misfortune must be avoided. At last they dressed her in silk cunningly fashioned and lined with wadding. Thus garbed her entry into the poultry-yard was a subject of astonishment to some, fear to others, and excitement to most of the birds she met on her way.

"In vain Mother Etienne strove to tone down the colors of the stuffs, to modify the cut of the garments, but Yollande long remained an object of surprise and antipathy to the majority of the poultry.

"The scandal soon reached its climax. 'That hen must be mad,' said an old duck to his wife.

"'Just imagine dressing up like that; she'll come along one of these days in a bathing suit,' cried a young rooster who prided himself on his wit.

"A young turkey tugged at her clothes, trying to pull them off, and all the others looked on laughing and hurling insults. They vied with one another in sarcastic speeches. At last, after a time, as the saying goes, familiarity bred contempt. The fear which her companions had felt at first soon changed into a familiarity often too great for the unhappy Cochin-China. They tried to see who could play her the shabbiest trick. Hens are often as cruel as men, which is saying a great deal.

"Poor Yollande, in spite of her size, her solidity, and strength, nearly always emerged half-dressed. Her companions could not stand her dressed like that, the sight of her irritated them. Not content with tearing her clothes they often pecked at the poor creature as well.

"Mother Etienne did her best to improve these costumes in every way, but it was as impossible to find perfection as the philosopher's stone.

"They hoped at the farm that in time the feathers would grow again. Meanwhile it was hard on the hen.

"Nothing of the sort happened; one, two, three months passed and not the least vestige of down appeared on the hen, who had to be protected like a human being from the changes of climate and so forth. Like a well-to-do farmer's wife Yollande had her linen-chest and a complete outfit.

"It was, I assure you, my dear children, kept up most carefully. There was always a button to sew on, a buttonhole to remake, or a tear to be mended. Thus constantly in touch with the household Madame Hen soon thought she belonged to it. Indeed, worn out by the teasing of her companions, by the constant arguments she had with them, and touched on the other hand by the affectionate care of her mistresses, Yollande stayed more and more in the house. Coddled and swathed in her fantastic costumes, she sat in the chimney corner like a little Cinderella changed into a hen; from this corner she quietly watched; nothing escaped her notice.

"Meanwhile her reputation had grown, not only amongst her comrades, but among all the animals of the neighborhood, who, hearing her discussed, were anxious to see her.

"Woe to the cat or dog who dared venture too far into the room! Very annoyed at this impertinent curiosity, she would leap upon the importunate stranger and punish him terribly with her sharp beak. Of course he would run off howling and frightened to death. It was very funny to watch.

"Mother Etienne and Germaine were much amused at

these little comedies, and whenever visitors came to the farm they would try to provoke one. Everyone enjoyed them hugely.

"Germaine treated Yollande like a doll. She made her all sorts of fashionable clothes. The Cochin-China would be dressed sometimes like a man, sometimes like a woman. She had made her quite a collection of little trousers and vests, which had style, I can tell you. She had copied, too, from a circus she had seen, an English clown's costume which was most becoming. Nothing could be funnier than to watch this tiny dwarf, to see her strut, jump, dance, coming and going, skipping around suddenly—one moment skittish, the next very important.

"Petit-Jacques loved to tease her, but not roughly; he would push her with his foot, and make her jump at him impatiently, looking perfectly ridiculous in her quaint dress. You could have sworn she was a miniature clown. Add to all this, the queer inarticulate sounds she made when she was angry, and even then you can have no idea how very amusing these pantomimes were.

"Soon the fame of Yollande spread far and wide. She became celebrated throughout the district. Instead of asking Mother Etienne how she was, people asked, 'How's your hen today, Mother Etienne?'

"One day a peddler, such as often come round to villages,

laden like a mule, and leading by the bridle an ass still more laden, appeared at the farm. Both looked well but tired and dusty—they seemed to have had a long journey.

"Father Gusson, such was the good man's name, sold all sorts of things, from tooth-brushes to shoes, including hardware, glassware, notions, drugs, and even patent medicines.

"Mother Etienne received him kindly and after letting him show her the things in which she was interested, she offered him refreshment and suggested that he should take a little rest at the farm. This he accepted without needing any pressing.

"The donkey, relieved straightway from his load, was led into the paddock, where he wallowed in the tall grass, rolling on his back, his feet in the air. He enjoyed cleaning himself up like this after his dusty journey, then, rested, he took his luncheon, choosing here and there the daintiest morsels; after which he lay down and philosophized at length.

"All this time, Mother Etienne and Germaine were buying, tempted by one thing after another, silks, laces, stuffs for dresses, and a number of toilet articles, for both were, though you would not have suspected it, rather coquettish. Father Gusson—delighted with his visit to the farm and the business he had done there—was anxious to leave Mother Etienne a little remembrance.

"'Madame,' he said, holding out a small china jar carefully sealed with parchment, 'assuredly you do not need this just now, but if I should never come back, and if it should happen that one day your beautiful hair should grow thin, turn gray, or fall out, you have only to rub your head with this sweet-scented ointment and at once your hair will grow again thick and of its original color. I cannot—alas!— give you the recipe, it is a secret left me by my parents.'

"Then Father Gusson bade farewell to the two women and went on his way with Neddy, both much refreshed by their pleasant rest.

"Mother Etienne handed Germaine the precious pot of ointment to put with their other purchases into the big cupboard, and they thought no more about it.

"One day as she sat by the fire with Yollande, watching the dinner, a bright and whimsical idea occurred to the maid. 'Supposing I were to try the ointment on the hen? It might be good for feathers too. Anyhow, it could not do any harm.'

"Saying this she went, found the ointment, and delicately rubbed a little onto Yollande's head. Yollande did not appear to mind at all. Germaine did this three days running.

"Two weeks later Mother Etienne while dressing her hen, as she did each day, found a thick reddish down sprouting round her head like a little flat wig. She showed it to

Germaine, who paid no attention, having quite forgotten her childish trick.

"But during the next few days the wig prospered; the hair was two finger-breadths long, very thick, and curly. Mother Etienne could not understand it at all. Germaine could not, at first, make up her mind to confess to her mistress what she had done.

"At last one evening, Mother Etienne being in a particularly good humor, the young girl took courage and told her all about it. Far from scolding her, her mistress was delighted, and so pleased at the news that she there and then undressed Yollande and rubbed her from head to foot with Father Gusson's marvelous ointment. She did the thing thoroughly, rubbing it into every pore. Then they made a good fire so that the poor little model, thus exposed, should not take cold.

"After that they watched her every instant; they were for ever undressing her to see if the cure was working—they could hardly bear to wait. Just think, if it were to succeed, it would be the end and aim of all their care. Yollande could once again take her proper place in the world.

"At last what had happened to the head, happened to the body too. Before a week had gone by a thick down completely covered the big hen. The good women, much wondering, imagined that as it grew stronger the hair would

change into feathers. Anxiously they awaited the change. Nothing of the sort happened. The hair remained hair, red—Titian red—fine, and soft, curling round your fingers, admirable in quality and color.

"The hair on the head, older than that on the rest of the body, was much longer, which suggested to the mischievous Germaine the idea of making her an elaborate headdress. Nothing like it had ever been seen before.

"Soon Yollande was able to discard some of her clothes. Her breast and back required for a time yet a little covering, but this grew gradually less and less.

"Naturally the phenomenon was much discussed in the neighborhood, and it attracted many and delightful visitors to the farm, all of whom Mother Etienne welcomed cordially. Yollande was less pleased with this desire to inspect her. Generally some unbeliever would tug at her hair, a painful experience for her. So, except toward her mistress and Germaine, she had become exceedingly vindictive and watchful. Every time she had the chance she pecked with her short, stout beak at the person indiscreet enough to take such liberties. One little visitor, more daring than the rest, nearly lost his finger over it.

"The fame of the curly-haired hen was tremendous, it spread even beyond the limits of the district. It was really worth a journey to see her. They wrote of it in the newspapers. The *Daily Mirror*, I think it was, had a fine long article about her.

"But in certain quarters, the whole thing was looked upon as a 'fish story'."

The Cat-hood of Maurice

By E. Nesbit

TO have your hair cut is not painful, nor does it hurt to have your whiskers trimmed. But round wooden shoes, shaped like bowls, are not comfortable wear, however much it may amuse the onlooker to see you try to walk in them. If you have a nice fur coat like a company promoter's, it is most annoying to be made to swim in it. And if you had a tail, surely it would be solely your own affair; that any one should tie a tin can to it would strike you as an unwarrantable impertinence—to say the least.

Yet it is difficult for an outsider to see these things from the point of view of both the persons concerned. To Maurice, scissors in hand, alive and earnest to snip, it seemed the most natural thing in the world to shorten the stiff whiskers of Lord Hugh Cecil by a generous inch. He did not understand how useful those whiskers were to Lord Hugh, both in sport and in the more serious business of getting a living.

Also it amused Maurice to throw Lord Hugh into ponds, though Lord Hugh only once permitted this liberty. To put walnuts on Lord Hugh's feet and then to watch him walk on ice was, in Maurice's opinion, as good as a play. Lord Hugh was a very favorite cat, but Maurice was discreet, and Lord Hugh, except under violent suffering, was at that time anyhow, dumb.

But the empty sardine-tin attached to Lord Hugh's tail and hind legs—this had a voice, and, rattling against stairs, banisters, and the legs of stricken furniture, it cried aloud for vengeance. Lord Hugh, suffering violently, added his voice, and this time the family heard. There was a chase, a chorus of "Poor pussy!" and "Pussy, then!" and the tail and the tin and Lord Hugh were caught under Jane's bed. The tail and the tin acquiesced in their rescue. Lord Hugh did not. He fought, scratched, and bit. Jane carried the scars of that rescue for many a long week.

When all was calm Maurice was sought and, after some little natural delay, found—in the boot-cupboard.

"Oh, Maurice!" his mother almost sobbed, "how can you? What will your father say?"

Maurice thought he knew what his father would do.

"Don't you know," the mother went on, "how wrong it is to be cruel?"

"I didn't mean to be cruel," Maurice said. And, what is more, he spoke the truth. All the unwelcome attentions he had showered on Lord Hugh had not been exactly intended to hurt that stout veteran—only it was interesting to see what a cat would do if you threw it in the water, or cut its whiskers, or tied things to its tail.

"Oh, but you must have meant to be cruel," said mother, "and you will have to be punished."

"I wish I hadn't," said Maurice, from the heart.

"So do I," said his mother, with a sigh; "but it isn't the first time; you know you tied Lord Hugh up in a bag with the hedgehog only last Tuesday week. You'd better go to your room and think it over. I shall have to tell your father directly he comes home."

Maurice went to his room and thought it over. And the more he thought the more he hated Lord Hugh. Why couldn't the beastly cat have held his tongue and sat still? That, at the time would have been a disappointment, but now Maurice wished it had happened. He sat on the edge of his bed and savagely kicked the edge of the green Kidderminster carpet, and hated the cat.

He hadn't meant to be cruel; he was sure he hadn't; he

wouldn't have pinched the cat's feet or squeezed its tail in the door, or pulled its whiskers, or poured hot water on it. He felt himself ill-used, and knew that he would feel still more so after the inevitable interview with his father.

But that interview did not take the immediately painful form expected by Maurice. His father did not say, "Now I will show you what it feels like to be hurt." Maurice had braced himself for that, and was looking beyond it to the calm of forgiveness which should follow the storm in which he should so unwillingly take part. No; his father was already calm and reasonable—with a dreadful calm, a terrifying reason.

"Look here, my boy," he said. "This cruelty to dumb animals must be checked—severely checked."

"I didn't mean to be cruel," said Maurice.

"Evil," said Mr. Basingstoke, for such was Maurice's surname, "is wrought by want of thought as well as want of heart. What about your putting the hen in the oven?"

"You know," said Maurice, pale but determined, "you know I only wanted to help her to get her eggs hatched quickly. It says in 'Fowls for Food and Fancy' that heat hatches eggs."

"But she hadn't any eggs," said Mr. Basingstoke.

"But she soon would have," urged Maurice. "I thought a stitch in time—"

"That," said his father, "is the sort of thing that you must learn not to think."

"I'll try," said Maurice, miserably hoping for the best.

"I intend that you shall," said Mr. Basingstoke. "This afternoon you go to Dr. Strongitharm's for the remaining week of term. If I find any more cruelty taking place during the holidays you will go there permanently. You can go and get ready."

"Oh, father, please not," was all Maurice found to say.

"I'm sorry, my boy," said his father, much more kindly; "it's all for your own good, and it's as painful to me as it is to you—remember that. The cab will be here at four. Go and put your things together, and Jane shall pack for you."

So the box was packed. Mabel, Maurice's kiddy sister, cried over everything as it was put in. It was a very wet day.

"If it had been any school but old Strong's," she sobbed.

She and her brother knew that school well: its windows, dulled with wire blinds, its big alarm bell, the high walls of its grounds, bristling with spikes, the iron gates, always locked, through which gloomy boys, imprisoned, scowled on a free world. Dr. Strongitharm's was a school "for backward and difficult boys." Need I say more?

Well, there was no help for it. The box was packed, the cab was at the door. The farewells had been said. Maurice determined that he wouldn't cry and he didn't, which gave

him the one touch of pride and joy that such a scene could
yield. Then at the last moment, just as father had one leg in
the cab, the Taxes called. Father went back into the house to
write a check. Mother and Mabel had retired in tears.
Maurice used the reprieve to go back after his postage-stamp
album. Already he was planning how to impress the other
boys at old Strong's, and his was a very fair collection. He
ran up into the schoolroom, expecting to find it empty. But

someone was there: Lord Hugh, in
the very middle of the ink-stained
table-cloth.

"You brute," said Maurice; "you
know jolly well I'm going away, or
you wouldn't be here." And, indeed,
the room had never, somehow, been a
favorite of Lord Hugh's.

"Meaow," said Lord Hugh.

"Mew!" said Maurice, with scorn.
"That's what you always say. All that
fuss about a sardine-tin. Anyone would have thought you'd
be only too glad to have it to play with. I wonder how you'd
like being a boy? Lickings, and lessons, and impots, and sent
back from breakfast to wash your ears. You wash yours
anywhere—I wonder what they'd say to me if I washed my
ears on the drawing-room hearthrug?"

"Meaow," said Lord Hugh, and washed an ear.

"Mew," said Maurice again; "that's all you can say."

"Oh, no, it isn't," said Lord Hugh, and stopped his ear-washing.

"I say!" said Maurice in awestruck tones.

"If you think cats have such a jolly time," said Lord Hugh, "why not be a cat?"

"I would if I could," said Maurice, "and fight you—"

"Thank you," said Lord Hugh.

"But I can't," said Maurice.

"Oh, yes, you can," said Lord Hugh. "You've only got to say the word."

"What word?"

Lord Hugh told him the word; but I will not tell you, for fear you should say it by accident and then be sorry.

"And if I say that, I shall turn into a cat?"

"Of course," said the cat.

"Oh, yes, I see," said Maurice. "But I'm not taking any, thanks. I don't want to be a cat for always."

"You needn't," said Lord Hugh. "You've only got to get someone to say to you, 'Please leave off being a cat and be Maurice again', and there you are."

Maurice thought of Dr. Strongitharm's. He also thought of the horror of his father when he should find Maurice gone, vanished, not to be traced. 'He'll be sorry, then,'

Maurice told himself, and to the cat he said: "Right—I'll do it. What's the word, again?"

"—," said the cat.

"—," said Maurice; and suddenly the table shot up to the height of a house, the walls to the height of tenement buildings, the pattern on the carpet became enormous, and Maurice found himself on all fours. He tried to stand up on his feet, but his shoulders were oddly heavy. He could only rear himself upright for a moment, and then fell heavily on his hands. He looked down at them; they seemed to have grown shorter and fatter, and were encased in black fur gloves. He felt a desire to walk on all fours— tried it—did it. It was very odd—the movement of the arms straight from the shoulder, more like the movement of the piston of an engine than anything Maurice could think of at that moment.

"I am asleep," said Maurice. "I am dreaming this. I am dreaming I am a cat. I hope I dreamed that about the sardine-tin and Lord Hugh's tail, and Dr. Strong's."

"You didn't," said a voice he knew and yet didn't know, "and you aren't dreaming this."

"Yes, I am," said Maurice; "and now I'm going to dream that I fight that beastly black cat, and give him the best licking he ever had in his life. Come on, Lord Hugh."

A loud laugh answered him.

"Excuse my smiling," said the voice he knew and didn't know, "but don't you see—you are Lord Hugh!"

A great hand picked Maurice up from the floor and held him in the air. He felt the position to be not only undignified but unsafe, and gave himself a shake of mingled relief and resentment when the hand set him down on the inky table-cloth.

"You are Lord Hugh now, my dear Maurice," said the voice, and a huge face came quite close to his. It was his own face, as it would have seemed through a magnifying glass. And the voice—oh, horror!—the voice was his own voice— Maurice Basingstoke's voice. Maurice shrank from the voice, and he would have liked to claw the face, but he had had no practice.

"You are Lord Hugh," the voice repeated, "and I am Maurice. I like being Maurice. I am so large and strong. I could drown you in the water-butt, my poor cat—oh, so easily. No, don't spit and swear. It's bad manners—even in a cat."

"Maurice!" shouted Mr. Basingstoke from between the door and the cab.

Maurice, from habit, leaped toward the door.

"It's no use your going," said the thing that looked like a giant reflection of Maurice; "it's me he wants."

"But I didn't agree to your being me."

"That's poetry, even if it isn't grammar," said the thing that looked like Maurice. "Why, my good cat, don't you see that if you are I, I must be you? Otherwise we should interfere with time and space and as likely as not destroy the solar system. Oh, yes—I'm you, right enough, and shall be, till someone tells you to change from Lord Hugh into Maurice. And now you've got to find some one to do it."

("Maurice!" thundered the voice of Mr. Basingstoke).

"That'll be easy enough," said Maurice.

"Think so?" said the other.

"But I shan't try yet. I want to have some fun first. I shall catch heaps of mice!"

"Think so? You forget that your whiskers are cut off— Maurice cut them. Without whiskers, how can you judge of the width of the places you go through? Take care you don't get stuck in a hole that you can't get out of or go in through, my good cat."

"Don't call me a cat," said Maurice, and felt that his tail was growing thick and angry.

"You are a cat, you know—and that little bit of temper that I see in your tail reminds me—"

Maurice felt himself gripped round the middle, abruptly lifted, and carried swiftly through the air. The quickness of the movement made him giddy. He saw nothing, felt nothing, except a sort of long sea-sickness, and then suddenly he was not being moved. He could see now. He could feel. He was being held tight in a sort of vice—a vice covered with checkered cloth. It looked like the pattern, very much exaggerated, of his school knickerbockers. It was. He was being held between the hard, relentless knees of that creature that had once been Lord Hugh, and to whose tail he had tied a sardine-tin. Now he was Lord Hugh, and something was being tied to his tail. Something mysterious, terrible. Very well, he would show that he was not afraid of anything that could be attached to tails. The string rubbed his fur the wrong way—it was that that annoyed him, not the string itself; and as for what was at the end of the string, what could that matter to any sensible cat?

Maurice was quite decided that he was—and would keep on being—a sensible cat.

The string, however, and the uncomfortable, tight position between those checkered knees—something or other was getting on his nerves.

"Maurice!" shouted his father below, and the be-catted

Maurice bounded between the knees of the creature that wore his clothes and his looks.

"Coming, father," this thing called, and sped away, leaving Maurice on the servant's bed—under which Lord Hugh had taken refuge, with his tin-can, so short and yet so long a time ago. The stairs re-echoed to the loud boots which Maurice had never before thought loud; he had often, indeed, wondered that anyone could object to them. He wondered now no longer.

He heard the front door slam. That thing had gone to Dr. Strongitharm's. That was one comfort. Lord Hugh was a boy now; he would know what it was to be a boy. He, Maurice, was a cat, and he meant to taste fully all catty pleasures, from milk to mice. Meanwhile he was without mice or milk, and, unaccustomed as he was to a tail, he could not but feel that all was not right with his own. There was a feeling of weight, a feeling of discomfort, of positive terror. If he should move, what would that thing that was tied to his tail do? Rattle, of course. Oh, but he could not bear it if that thing rattled. Nonsense; it was only a sardine-tin. Yes, Maurice knew that. But all the same—if it did rattle! He moved his tail the least little soft inch. No sound. Perhaps really there wasn't anything tied to his tail. But he couldn't be sure unless he moved. But if he moved the thing would rattle, and if it rattled Maurice felt sure that he would expire or go mad. A mad cat. What a dreadful thing to be! Yet he couldn't sit on that bed for ever, waiting, waiting, waiting for the dreadful thing to happen.

"Oh, dear," sighed Maurice the cat. "I never knew what people meant by 'afraid' before."

His cat-heart was beating heavily against his furry side. His limbs were getting cramped—he must move. He did. And instantly the awful thing happened. The sardine-tin touched the iron of the bed-foot. It rattled.

"Oh, I can't bear it, I can't," cried poor Maurice, in a heartrending meaow that echoed through the house. He leaped from the bed and tore through the door and down the stairs, and behind him came the most terrible thing in the world. People might call it a sardine-tin, but he knew better. It was the soul of all the fear that ever had been or ever could be. It rattled.

Maurice who was a cat flew down the stairs; down, down—the rattling horror followed. Oh, horrible! Down, down! At the foot of the stairs the horror, caught by something—a banister, a stair-rod—stopped. The string on Maurice's tail tightened, his tail was jerked, he was stopped. But the noise had stopped too. Maurice lay only just alive at the foot of the stairs.

It was Mabel who untied the string and soothed his terrors with strokings and tender words. Maurice was surprised to find what a nice little girl his sister really was.

"I'll never tease you again," he tried to say, softly—but that was not what he said. What he said was "Purrrr."

"Dear pussy, nice poor pussy, then," said Mabel, and she hid away the sardine-tin and did not tell any one. This seemed unjust to Maurice until he remembered that, of course, Mabel thought that he was really Lord Hugh, and that the person who had tied the tin to his tail was her brother Maurice. Then he was half-grateful. She carried him down, in soft, safe arms, to the kitchen, and asked cook to give him some milk.

"Tell me to change back into Maurice," said Maurice who was quite worn out by his cattish experiences. But no one heard him. What they heard was, "Meaow-Meaow-Meeeaow!"

Then Maurice saw how he had been tricked. He could be changed back into a boy as soon as any one said to him, "Leave off being a cat and be Maurice again," but his tongue had no longer the power to ask any one to say it.

He did not sleep well that night. For one thing he was not accustomed to sleeping on the kitchen hearthrug, and the blackbeetles were too many and too cordial. He was glad when cook came down and turned him out into the garden, where the October frost still lay white on the yellowed stalks of sunflowers and nasturtiums. He took a walk, climbed a tree, failed to catch a bird, and felt better. He began also to feel hungry. A delicious scent came stealing out of the back kitchen door. Oh, joy, there were to be herrings for breakfast! Maurice hastened in and took his place on his usual chair.

His mother said, "Down, puss," and gently tilted the chair so that Maurice fell off it. Then the family had herrings. Maurice said, "You might give me some," and he said it so often that his father, who, of course, heard only mewings, said, "For goodness' sake put that cat out of the room."

Maurice breakfasted later, in the dustbin, on herring heads. But he kept himself up with a splendid idea. They would give him milk presently, and then they should see.

He spent the afternoon sitting on the sofa in the dining-room, listening to the conversation of his father and mother. It is said that listeners never hear any good of themselves. Maurice heard so much that he was surprised and humbled. He heard his father say that he was a fine, plucky little chap, but he needed a severe lesson, and Dr. Strongitharm was the man to give it to him. He heard his mother say things that made his heart throb in his throat and the tears prick behind those green cat-eyes of his. He had always thought his parents a little bit unjust. Now they did him so much more than justice that he felt quite small and mean inside his cat-skin.

"He's a dear, good, affectionate boy," said mother. "It's only his high spirits. Don't you think, darling, perhaps you were a little hard on him?"

"It was for his own good," said father.

"Of course," said mother; "but I can't bear to think of him at that dreadful school."

"Well—," father was beginning, when Jane came in with the tea-things on a clattering tray, whose sound made Maurice tremble in every leg. Father and mother began to talk about the weather.

Maurice felt very affectionately to both his parents. The natural way of showing this was to jump on to the sideboard and thence on to his father's shoulders. He landed there on his padded feet, light as a feather, but father was not pleased.

"Bother the cat!" he cried. "Jane, put it out of the room."

Maurice was put out. His great idea, which was to be carried out with milk, would certainly not be carried out in the dining-room. He sought the kitchen, and, seeing a milk-can on the window-ledge, jumped up beside the can and patted it as he had seen Lord Hugh do.

"My!" said a friend of Jane's who happened to be there, "Ain't that cat clever—a perfect moral, I call her."

"He's nothing to boast of this time," said cook. "I will say for Lord Hugh he's not often taken in with an empty can."

This was naturally mortifying for Maurice, but he pretended not to hear, and jumped from the window to the tea-table and patted the milk jug.

"Come," said the cook, "that's more like it," and she poured him out a full saucer and set it on the floor.

Now was the chance Maurice had longed for. Now he could carry out that idea of his. He was very thirsty, for he had had nothing since that delicious breakfast in the dustbin. But not for worlds would he have drunk the milk. No. He carefully dipped his right paw in it, for his idea was to make letters with it on the kitchen oil-cloth. He meant to write "Please tell me to leave off being a cat and be Maurice again," but he found his paw a very clumsy pen, and he had to rub out the first "P" because it only looked like an accident. Then he tried again and actually did make a "P" that any fair-minded person could have read quite easily.

"I wish they'd notice," he said, and before he got the "L" written they did.

"Drat the cat," said cook; "look how he's messing

the floor up." And she took away the milk.

Maurice put pride aside and mewed to have the milk put down again. But he did not get it.

Very weary, very thirsty, and very tired of being Lord Hugh, he presently found his way to the schoolroom, where Mabel with patient toil was doing her home-lessons. She took him on her lap and stroked him while she learned her French verb. He felt that he was growing very fond of her. People were quite right to be kind to dumb animals. Presently she had to stop stroking him and do a map. And after that she kissed him and put him down and went away. All the time she had been doing the map, Maurice had had but one thought: Ink.

The moment the door had closed behind her—how sensible people were who closed doors gently—he stood up in her chair with one paw on the map and the other on the ink. Unfortunately, the inkstand top was made to dip pens in, and not to dip paws. But Maurice was desperate. He deliberately upset the ink—most of it rolled over the table-cloth—and fell pattering on the carpet, but with what was left he wrote quite plainly, across the map:

PLEASE TELL LORD HUGH
TO STOP BEING A CAT
AND BE MAURICE AGAIN

"There!" he said; "they can't make any mistake about that." They didn't. But they made a mistake about who had done it, and Mabel was deprived of jam with her supper bread.

Her assurance that some naughty boy must have come through the window and done it while she was not there convinced nobody, and, indeed, the window was shut and bolted.

Maurice, wild with indignation, did not mend matters by seizing the opportunity of a few minutes' solitude to write:

IT WAS NOT MABEL
IT WAS MAURICE,
I MEAN LORD HUGH

because when that was seen Mabel was instantly sent to bed.

"It's not fair!" cried Maurice.

"My dear," said Maurice's father, "if that cat goes on mewing to this extent you'll have to get rid of it."

Maurice said not another word. It was bad enough to be a cat, but to be a cat that was "got rid of!" He knew how people got rid of cats. In a stricken silence he left the room and slunk up the stairs—he dared not mew again, even at the door of Mabel's room. But when Jane went in to put Mabel's light out Maurice crept in too, and in the dark tried with stifled mews and purrs to explain to Mabel how sorry he was. Mabel stroked him and he went to sleep, his last waking thought amazement at the blindness that had once made him call her a silly little kid.

If you have ever been a cat you will understand something of what Maurice endured during the dreadful days that followed. If you have not, I can never make you understand fully. There was the affair of the fishmonger's tray balanced on the wall by the back door—the delicious curled-up whiting; Maurice knew as well as you do that one mustn't steal fish out of other people's trays, but the cat that he was didn't know. There was an inward struggle—and Maurice was beaten by the cat-nature. Later he was beaten by the cook.

Then there was that very painful incident with the butcher's dog, the flight across gardens, the safety of the plum tree gained only just in time.

And, worst of all, despair took hold of him, for he saw that nothing he could do would make any one say those simple words that would release him. He had hoped that Mabel might at last be made to understand, but the ink had failed him; she did not understand his subdued mewings, and when he got the cardboard letters and made the same sentence with them Mabel only thought it was that naughty boy who came through locked windows. Somehow he could not spell before any one—his nerves were not what they had been. His brain now gave him no new ideas. He felt that he was really growing like a cat in his mind. His interest in his meals grew beyond even what it had been when they were a schoolboy's meals. He hunted mice with growing enthusiasm, though the loss of his whiskers to measure narrow places with made hunting difficult.

He grew expert in bird-stalking, and often got quite near to a bird before it flew away, laughing at him. But all the time, in his heart, he was very, very miserable. And so the week went by.

Maurice in his cat shape dreaded more and more the time when Lord Hugh in the boy shape should come backfrom Dr. Strongitharm's. He knew—who better?— exactly the kind of things boys do to cats, and he trembled to the end of his handsome half-Persian tail.

And then the boy came home from Dr. Strongitharm's, and at the first sound of his boots in the hall Maurice in the cat's body fled with silent haste to hide in the boot-cupboard.

Here, ten minutes later, the boy that had come back from Dr. Strongitharm's found him.

Maurice fluffed up his tail and unsheathed his claws. Whatever this boy was going to do to him Maurice meant to resist, and his resistance should hurt the boy as much as possible. I am sorry to say Maurice swore softly among the boots, but cat-swearing is not really wrong.

"Come out, you old duffer," said Lord Hugh in the boy shape of Maurice. "I'm not going to hurt you."

"I'll see to that," said Maurice, backing into the corner, all teeth and claws.

"Oh, I've had such a time!" said Lord Hugh. "It's no use, you know, old chap; I can see where you are by your green eyes. My word, they do shine. I've been caned and shut up in a dark room and given thousands of lines to write out."

"I've been beaten, too, if you come to that," mewed Maurice. "Besides the butcher's dog."

It was an intense relief to speak to some one who could understand his mews.

"Well, I suppose it's Pax for the future," said Lord Hugh; "if you won't come out, you won't. Please leave off being a cat and be Maurice again."

And instantly Maurice, amid a heap of goloshes and old tennis bats, felt with a swelling heart that he was no longer a cat. No more of those undignified four legs, those tiresome pointed ears, so difficult to wash, that furry coat, that contemptible tail, and that terrible inability to express all one's feelings in two words: "mew" and "purr."

He scrambled out of the cupboard, and the boots and galoshes fell off him like spray off a bather.

He stood upright in those very checkered knickerbockers that were so terrible when their knees held one vicelike, while things were tied to one's tail. He was face to face with another boy, exactly like himself.

"You haven't changed, then—but there can't be two Maurices."

"There shan't be; not if I know it," said the other boy; "a boy's life is a dog's life. Quick, before anyone comes."

"Quick what?" asked Maurice.

"Why tell me to leave off being a boy, and to be Lord Hugh Cecil again."

Maurice told him at once. And at once the boy was gone, and there was Lord Hugh in his own shape, purring politely, yet with a watchful eye on Maurice's movements.

"Oh, you needn't be afraid, old chap. It's Pax right enough," Maurice murmured in the ear of Lord Hugh. And Lord Hugh, arching his back under Maurice's stroking hand, replied with a *purrrr-meaow* that spoke volumes.

"Oh, Maurice, here you are. It is nice of you to be nice to Lord Hugh, when it was because of him you—"

"He's a good old chap," said Maurice, carelessly. "And you're not half a bad old girl. See?"

Mabel almost wept for joy at this magnificent compliment, and Lord Hugh himself took on a more happy and confident air.

Please dismiss any fears which you may entertain that after this Maurice became a model boy. He didn't. But he was much nicer than before. The conversation which he overheard when he was a cat makes him more patient with his father and mother. And he is almost always nice to Mabel, for he cannot forget all that she was to him when he wore the shape of Lord Hugh. His father attributes all the improvement in his son's character to that week at Dr. Strongitharm's—which, as you know, Maurice never had. Lord Hugh's character is unchanged. Cats learn slowly and with difficulty.

Only Maurice and Lord Hugh know the truth—Maurice has never told it to any one except me, and Lord Hugh is a very reserved cat. He never at any time had that free flow of mew which distinguished and endangered the cat-hood of Maurice.

Author Biographies

James Baldwin 1841–1925

Bucephalus (p.56); *The Horse and the Olive* (p.128);
The Story of Arachne (p.138); *Bellerophon and Pegasus* (p.144)

Baldwin was born in Indiana, and was largely self-educated. He spent the first part of his life as a teacher, but spent the last 30 years of his career working in publishing. At the age of 41 he published his first book, *The Story of Siegfried*, and he went on to write or edit more than fifty others, some on teaching, but mostly stories for children on themes of mythology, biography, fable, legend, and literature.

Mary E. Burt 1850–1918

The Labors of Hercules (p.90)

An American editor and writer, Burt compiled many collections of stories and poems for children. She believed it was important to study the lives of great heroes, saying they were role models to which children might aspire. Of the stories of Hercules she wrote: "It is not elegant literature alone that boys need, but inspiring ideals that will impel them to stand fearlessly to their guns, to do the hard thing with untiring perseverance, to reach the result with unerring insight."

Lewis Carroll 1832–98

Alice's Adventures in Wonderland (p.446)

Carroll's real name was Charles Lutwidge Dodgson. He spent his entire adult life as an academic at Oxford University, teaching and studying mathematics and logic. Childless himself, Carroll made great efforts to entertain other people's children, and it was while out on a boat trip with the three daughters of a friend (Lorina, Alice and Edith Liddell) that he invented the story that would later evolve into *Alice's Adventures in Wonderland*. A second book, *Through the Looking-Glass and What Alice Found There* was published in 1872.

Carlo Collodi 1826–90

Pinocchio (p.202)

Collodi's real name was Carlo Lorenzini. He was born in Italy, the son of a cook and a servant, and worked as a journalist during Italy's struggle for independence before turning to the translation of fairy stories. His own fairy story, *Pinocchio*, was first serialized in a children's newspaper in 1881. The story of the puppet whose nose grew when he told a lie was an immediate success, but Collodi died before the work achieved the worldwide fame it has today.

P. H. Emerson 1856–1936

The Death of Gelert (p.84)

Peter Emerson was born in Cuba and moved to England in 1869. He trained as a doctor and became a successful surgeon, but abandoned medicine to become a photographer. Emerson was a great naturalist and some of his most successful photographs were of nature studies. His great many other interests and talents included writing detective stories, playing champion-level billiards, and studying meteorology.

J. W. Fortescue 1859–1933

The Story of a Red Deer (p.304)

Primarily a military historian, the Honorable John Fortescue was the son of an Earl and grew up in a stately home in Devon, England. He spent his childhood exploring the moors, hunting and studying the animals that lived there. Fortescue was famous for his 20-volume work, *A History of the British Army*, which he wrote between 1899 and 1930, while working as librarian of Windsor Castle.

Kenneth Grahame 1859–1932

The Wind in the Willows (pp.30 and 172)

Born in Edinburgh, Scotland, Grahame had an unsettled childhood. His mother died when he was five, and the Grahame children were looked after by their grandmother. Unable to afford a university education, Grahame took a clerkship in the Bank of England. He began to write about the characters that would go on to appear in *The Wind in the Willows* in letters to his son. His epitaph reads: "To the beautiful memory of Kenneth Grahame, husband of Elspeth and father of Alastair, who passed the River on the 6 July 1932, leaving childhood and literature through him the more blest for all time."

Joel Chandler Harris 1845–1908

The Awful Fate of Mr. Wolf (p.240)

Harris grew up in Georgia, and went to work on a plantation, where he listened to the songs and folk stories of the recently freed black slaves. It was from these that he constructed his tales of Bre'r Rabbit, the trickster who always finds a way out of trouble. They were innovative in their use of dialect, and had a huge success across the United States and overseas.

Richard Jeffries 1848–95

Wood Magic (p.246)

Jeffries grew up on a small farm in Wiltshire, England where he spent much of his time roaming the countryside. He became a journalist, and wrote travel books, essays, and children's novels, all characterized by a love of nature and close observations of its smallest details. The critic, Walter Besant, on reading Jeffries said: "Why, we must have been blind all our lives; here were the most wonderful things possible going on under our very noses, but we saw them not!"

Rudyard Kipling 1865–1936

Just So Stories (pp.12 and 160); *The Jungle Book* (pp.216, 334, and 406)

Kipling was born in India, and his early childhood was very happily spent there. At the age of seven he was sent to live in England, a miserable experience that he never forgot. At school he was encouraged to write by his headmaster, and on returning to India he became a journalist, writing poems and stories in his spare time that were published alongside his other work. He was the youngest-ever recipient of the Nobel Prize for literature.

Jack London 1876–1916

White Fang (p.362)

London was born in California, into a working class family. During his early life he was a sailor, a gold prospector, and a tramp. He served time in prison for vagrancy, but always longed to write. In 1903 *The Call of the Wild* received worldwide acclaim, but London was also a master of the short story, often drawing on his own life experiences to tell tales of rough outdoor life.

D. G. Mukerji 1890–1936

The Cow and the Python (p.284)

Dhan Gopal Mukerji was born in a northern Indian village and emigrated to the United States when he was 20. There he worked as a lecturer, and wrote stories, winning the Newberry Medal in 1928. A champion of conservation, his first book *Kari, the Elephant* promoted the idea that people should live in harmony with nature. In 1929 he wrote: "You cannot destroy one species of animal without upsetting the whole balance of life. Life is a whole, there is no escape from this."

E. Nesbit 1858–1924

The Wouldbegoods (p.256); *The Cat-hood of Maurice* (p.482)

Edith Nesbit led an unconventional life, smoking heavily at a time when few women did and preferring to wear loose flowing dresses rather than the stiff, corseted style of the age. She wrote over forty books of fiction for children, and has been called the first modern children's writer. She created the idea of combining realistic characters and settings with magical elements, and her books include *The Railway Children, The Five Children and It,* and *The Treasure Seekers.*

Zenaide A. Ragozin 1825–1934

The Labors of Hercules (p.90)

Russian-born Ragozin had no formal education but was a keen scholar. She specialized in studying ancient history, especially the Middle Eastern civilizations. She traveled widely in Europe before emigrating to the United States in 1874 and taking US citizenship. Her work consists of both extremely scholarly works for adults, as well as retellings and translations for children.

Anna Sewell 1820–1978

Black Beauty (p.62)

Born into a devout Quaker family, Anna Sewell lived a quiet, religious life. Lamed in an accident at the age of fourteen, she often traveled by carriage, and hated the cruel treatment of the carriage horses. She wrote *Black Beauty* in response to this, saying its special aim was "to induce sympathy, kindness, and an understanding treatment of horses." Its sales broke publishing records and *Black Beauty* is said to be the sixth bestselling book in the English language.

Mark Twain 1835–1910

The Adventures of Tom Sawyer (p.192)

Twain's real name was Samuel Langhorne Clements. He was born in Missouri, two weeks before the appearance of Halley's Comet. He trained as a river pilot, then worked as a journalist and began writing travel books and novels. These included *The Adventures of Tom Sawyer* and *The Adventures of Huckleberry Finn*, which were largely based on his own childhood experiences. In 1910, he said: "I came in with Halley's Comet... it is coming again next year and I expect to go out with it. It will be the greatest disappointment of my life if I don't." He died within one day of the comet's arrival.

Auguste Vimar 1851–1916

The Curly-Haired Hen (p.462)

Nicholas Stanislaus Auguste Vimar was a French painter, sculptor, designer, illustrator, and watercolor artist, who also wrote his own books. His particular skill was in illustrating animals and his lively, colorful pictures were used in magazines and many children's books.

ACKNOWLEDGMENTS

The publishers would like to thank the following artists who have contributed to this book:

Beehive Illustration

Neil Chapman: *The Elephant's Child, The Cow and the Python, The Curly-haired Hen*

John Dillow: *Dulce Domum, The Piper at the Gates of Dawn, The Circus*

Frank Endersby: *Black Beauty's Final Home, The Calf's Childhood*

Elena Selivanova: *Tiger! Tiger!, The White Seal*

Rupert Van Wyk: *Bucephalus, The Horse and the Olive, Bellerophon and Pegasus, The Spider and the Toad, The Mock Turtle's Story, The Cat-hood of Maurice*

Linden Artists

Richard Hook: *The Death of Gellert*

Patricia Ludlow: *The Trail of the Meat*

Jo Empson: *Tom Sawyer in Church, Pinnochio is Swallowed by the Dogfish, Rikki-tikki-tavi*